...dulthood. She's the proud au...
...ooks with Arabesque, Kimani Roman...
...s & Boon Desire as well as her own indie works.

...en she's not at home crafting one of her spicy ...mances with compelling heroes and feisty heroines ...h a dash of family drama, she is gourmet cooking or ...velling the globe seeking out her next adventure. ...r more info, visit yahrahstjohn.com or find her on ...ebook, Instagram, Twitter, BookBub or Goodreads.

...arlene Sands** is a *USA TODAY* bestselling author of ...ntemporary romance and stories set in the American ...st. She's been honoured with the *National Readers' ...hoice* Award, the CataRomance Reviewers' Choice ...ward and is a double recipient of the Booksellers' Best ...ward. Her 2014 Mills & Boon Desire title was named ...e Best Desire of the Year.

...harlene knows a little something about romance—she ...arried her high school sweetheart! And her perfect day ...ncludes reading, drinking mocha cappuccinos, watching ...allmark movies and riding bikes with her hubby. She has ...wo adult children and four sweet young princesses, who make her smile every day. Visit her at charlenesands.com to ke... ...Find her o... ...ook. com/... ...nds

Also by Yahrah St. John

The Stewart Heirs
At the CEO's Pleasure
His Marriage Demand
Red Carpet Redemption

Locketts of Tuxedo Park
Consequences of Passion

Also by Charlene Sands

Craving a Real Texan
Sunset Surrender
Sunset Seduction
The Secret Heir of Sunset Ranch
Redeeming the CEO Cowboy

BLIND DATE WITH THE SPARE HEIR

YAHRAH ST. JOHN

THE FAKE ENGAGEMENT FAVOUR

CHARLENE SANDS

MILLS & BOON

First Published in Great Britain 2021
by Mills & Boon, an imprint of HarperCollins*Publishers* Ltd
1 London Bridge Street, London, SE1 9GF

www.harpercollins.co.uk

HarperCollins*Publishers*
1st Floor, Watermarque Building,
Ringsend Road, Dublin 4, Ireland

ISBN: 978-0-263-28302-0

0821

MIX
Paper from responsible sources
FSC™ C007454

This book is produced from independently certified FSC™ paper to ensure responsible forest management.

For more information visit: www.harpercollins.co.uk/green

Printed and bound in Spain
by CPI, Barcelona

BLIND DATE WITH THE SPARE HEIR

YAHRAH ST. JOHN

To my dad for encouraging me to succeed.

One

"Yet another article, Julian." Angelique Lockett sighed in frustration. "Must you continue to live up to your repute as Atlanta's most eligible bachelor?"

Julian shrugged as he glanced at his mother with her elegantly coiffed, black shoulder-length hair and her A-line 1950s-style dress. It wasn't like he was trying to be notorious for his playboy ways. He just happened to like the fairer sex.

He'd thought about not attending this Sunday's family dinner at the Locketts' ten-bedroom estate in Atlanta's Tuxedo Park, but he hated to disappoint her. So Julian had prepared himself for her wrath over yet another article about his exploits, this time at a fall fashion show for one of Atlanta's up-and-coming designers. *Was it his fault he'd managed to snag both the designer and the model who'd been her muse?*

Julian wasn't as tall as his father, his older brother, Roman, or his younger brother, Xavier, who once again had skipped the family dinner. They were each well over six feet. But what he lacked in height, he more than made up for in charm and snappy dress. Something about his light brown eyes, handsome face and perpetual five-o'clock shadow made the women of Atlanta powerless to resist him. It had earned him the reputation of incorrigible flirt and ladies' man.

"Aren't you ready to settle down, like Roman?" She glanced over at his brother, who sat across the table with his wife, Shantel, who also happened to be Julian's best friend.

His Shantel.

Or, at least, she had been until Roman had managed to steal her, taking away his safety net. Julian and Shantel had met at a college party when he'd attended Morehouse and Shantel, Spelman. Their platonic friendship had endured for over a decade, through his many love affairs, Shantel's breakup with her high-school sweetheart and her mother's suicide.

He'd always looked at Shantel as a little sister, but somewhere in the back of his mind, he'd wondered if they might give it a go when he was ready to settle down. *Maybe, unconsciously, she'd been his backup plan.* But Roman had ended that dream and now the two lovebirds were sitting there making goo-goo eyes at one another.

Julian wanted to barf. He couldn't ever see himself falling in love, but he also didn't like continually upsetting his mother. Besides, seeing how deeply Roman and Shantel loved one another, he couldn't help but wonder if, perhaps, there might be something to all this love stuff. *Was he missing out by not having found his soul mate?*

He finally answered his mother's question. "Perhaps."

Everyone stopped talking and turned to look at him—as if he'd lost his marbles.

"What?" He shrugged.

"You're serious?" Giana asked. Born less than a year

apart, he and his baby sister were quite close. Other than Shantel, Giana was his go-to person if he needed advice. And he certainly hadn't discussed *this* with her.

"Why not? If Mother wants to set me up with someone, where's the harm?"

Angelique raised a brow. "If I set you up, and that's a big *if*—" she fixed her light brown eyes on him "—do I have your word that you'll behave with the utmost respect and that I won't hear of any shenanigans?"

"Scout's honor." Julian raised three fingers.

"You were a terrible Boy Scout." Roman laughed, sipping his single malt scotch. "You hated the outdoors, much less getting your hands dirty."

"While you were always a high achiever," Julian scoffed, even though he knew everything Roman said was true. "Always trying to get as many merit badges as possible."

"There's nothing wrong with wanting to be the best," Josiah responded from the head of the table. "You could learn a thing or two from your brother about responsibility."

And there it was. The ever-present competition egged on by their father. Julian wasn't surprised. Roman was the favorite, constantly being pushed by their father to succeed because he was the eldest son and would eventually take over the Atlanta Cougars football franchise. Josiah had rarely taken an interest in Julian, which was why he was closer to his mother.

"Well, *I*, for one, am happy to hear that you're open to the idea of settling down, Julian." Angelique spoke up as she always did when her husband tried to pit the two brothers against one another. "I'll set something up soon."

"Thanks, Mom." Julian wiped his mouth and tossed his napkin on the table as he stood. "Dinner was great, as always." He walked toward his mother. "We'll talk soon," he whispered, kissing her cheek.

"Run away like you always do," Josiah chided.

"Josiah!"

Julian detected rebuke in his mother's tone, but didn't care. You would think an MD behind his name would garner his father's respect, but Julian knew otherwise. Even though Josiah had demanded he pursue sports medicine, the man had never been fully happy with his son's chosen profession. It totally irked his father that Julian wasn't playing or managing the team, just doing what he could to ensure the old man's players stayed off the injury list.

His father preferred discussing franchise business with Roman or playing football with Xavier. Or at least he had until Xavier's accident had ended his career as a quarterback.

Ignoring his father's blustering from the other end of the table, Julian quickly hugged Giana and Shantel and shook Roman's hand before leaving the room.

He knew he wasn't the favorite son, but living with the fact never got any easier.

He'd nearly made his escape when he heard the distinctive click of high heels behind him.

"Julian, wait up!" Giana called out as he made his way across the marble foyer to the front door.

He turned to find his beautiful chocolate sister walking briskly toward him. As always, looking chic and polished, she wore her hair in a loose chignon and wispy bangs. Her red handkerchief dress, its one shoulder strap braided to match the belt around her slender waist, complemented her ever-on-the-mark sophistication.

She caught up with him at the door and spun him around. "Were you just going to ignore me?"

"That was the plan."

"You know Daddy didn't mean any harm."

"'It's just how he is…'" Julian responded. "I know the spiel, Giana. You've said it a thousand times. Why do you always defend his bad behavior?"

"Why do you always think the worst of him?"

"Because I'm quite certain that if our father could have picked another infant in the maternity ward, he would have. I'm nothing like Roman or Xavier. Both are macho tough guys who live and breathe ambition. They have that drive Josiah looks for. I don't. Sometimes I wonder if they swapped babies and I belong to another family."

"Don't say that," Giana said, glancing behind her as if she expected Josiah to appear out of thin air.

Bless her heart, his sister was the apple of their father's eye, a real daddy's girl. Thus she could never believe he didn't feel that way about all his children.

"I speak the truth, Giana. You just don't want to admit it, and that's fine. You can continue to put your head in the sand, but I'm going to live in the real world where nothing I do will ever please him."

"You sound like Roman."

Julian snorted. "Is it any wonder? From the day I was born, he's always tried to pit me and Roman against each other. We're nothing alike." His voice rose. "And I don't want to be. I'm comfortable in my own skin and I could care less if Josiah likes it or not."

"Now *that*," Giana replied, "is a lie."

Did his little sister know something he didn't?

She moved forward, right into his personal space. "You may fool everyone else with this I-don't-care attitude, but you don't fool me for a second. You would give your left arm for *half* the adoration Daddy piles on Roman and Xavier."

"I'm leaving."

Giana chuckled as Julian rushed out the door. He hated that his baby sister knew him so well. Because...maybe, deep down, in places he didn't like to look too hard, Julian secretly wished his father would love him as much as he did the rest of his children.

* * *

Elyse Harper attempted to lift all 170 pounds of her father, Frank Robinson, off the floor of the local bar where he'd passed out yet again. "C'mon, Daddy, it's time to go."

"I'll help you, Elyse," Matt said as he eyed her from his place behind the bar. The hunky blond bartender with a dozen tattoos was dressed in his customary muscle shirt and faded jeans.

Elyse knew Matt fancied her. She tried to ignore him, but whenever he called about her father, she had no choice. She usually didn't fuss with her appearance when she came running to the bar, but today Matt had caught her right after work.

As soon as she'd received Matt's call, she'd rushed from her one-bedroom apartment in Midtown, still dressed in work attire and in full makeup. She'd seen Matt practically salivate as he'd eyed her belted shirt dress and high-heeled sandals.

"Thanks, Matt."

Together, Elyse and Matt lifted her father from the floor and carried him to her Toyota Camry idling by the curb.

Once they had her father safely in the back seat, Elyse closed the door. "Thank you so much for calling me."

"Of course. But, Elyse, you need to convince Frank to go to rehab. His drinking is only getting worse."

"I know. Trust me, I've tried to talk some sense into him, but he refuses to listen."

"Well, you get home safe, okay?"

Elyse nodded as she slid into the driver's seat.

She drove the couple of miles to Frank's place—a modest, affordable one-bedroom apartment—in the Old Fourth Ward. When they arrived, it took everything she had to rouse him from his drunken slumber and get him inside. Luckily, he lived on the first floor and she was able to maneuver him inside the apartment without much fuss. Once there, she settled him on the bed, pulled off his shoes, and covered him with the worn blanket.

When she finally left his building half an hour later, Elyse let out a long heavy sigh. She didn't know how much longer she could continue to clean up the mess that was her father's life.

Feeling downtrodden, she walked the few steps to her car and got inside, but she didn't immediately drive off. Instead, she let the tears she'd been holding flow freely. She couldn't believe how far her father had fallen from grace. Once upon a time, he'd been a man of big dreams, with a wife and daughter who'd worshipped the ground he'd walked on.

How had it all gone wrong?

Elyse knew how. There was only one person to blame.

Josiah Lockett.

The football tycoon had learned of her father's gambling habit. Rather than get him in rehab, Josiah swindled her father out of his rightful share of the Atlanta Cougars during a game of poker, leaving them to a life of poverty, living from paycheck to paycheck. Things had only gotten worse when Elyse's mother, Nadine Harper Robinson, had gotten sick with breast cancer and passed away when Elyse was in her early teens. The medical bills had steadily piled up, overwhelming her father, who'd already been broken from having given up the Cougars and he'd started drinking. Instead of helping his best friend get control of his addictions, Josiah had used their friendship to get control of the franchise so he could have it all for himself and get rich.

And now here they were. On an endless merry-go-round with Frank headfirst in a bottle of whiskey, his solace of choice. It shouldn't be like this. Her father should have his due. It was time Josiah Lockett got his just deserts.

But how—?

Her phone pinged. She had set alerts for whenever the

Lockett name appeared on social media, and the tone cued the latest mention.

This one was interesting.

> Julian Lockett spotted on a date with a mystery woman. Could this femme fatale be the key to winning Atlanta's most eligible playboy?

Elyse closed the app.

From what she knew of the second oldest of the Lockett children, Julian was the love 'em and leave 'em type. Anytime the word *commitment* was whispered, he ran in the opposition direction. So who could the lucky woman be and how could Elyse use the information to her advantage?

Two

As one of the sports doctors for the Atlanta Cougars, Julian had a weekly Monday meeting with the other physicians, medical trainers and strength and conditioning staff. He knew some of the other medical team thought he'd only gotten the job due to nepotism, but Julian was okay with that.

He let them think what they wanted because, at the end of the day, Julian knew he'd earned his place at the table and he had the credentials to back it up. He'd gone to Morehouse, then to Johns Hopkins for medical school. His residency in physical medicine and rehabilitation had ended with a two-year fellowship in primary care sports medicine.

Sure, he would have liked to have gone into orthopedic surgery, but with competition being so stiff, the residency programs had only taken about 10 percent of medical students. While his grades had been good, they'd not been good enough, no matter how hard he'd worked.

Josiah hadn't let him forget it, either.

Regardless, Julian had known, without an element of doubt, that he could still be an asset as a primary care physician with a specialty in sports medicine. Josiah had agreed he could be one of the Atlanta Cougars' full-time physicians—though not as the team's lead.

In his day-to-day work, Julian now treated any medical issue a Cougars' athlete may face, including the evaluation and treatment of musculoskeletal injuries.

And that was exactly what he was going to do this morning. After the weekly meeting, he'd changed clothes and was prepping to assist with the rehabilitation of an athlete's syndesmotic injury. Julian could have let one of the trainers handle him, but this was his specialty and a part of the job he liked.

On his way to the therapy and recovery rooms, Julian ran into Xavier, who was in a tank top and gym shorts. "Hey, where were you last night?" Julian inquired.

"I was…uh, busy," Xavier responded.

"Busy with a woman?" Julian picked up on what Xavier wasn't saying. At six foot two and 230 pounds, his younger brother had once been quite the quarterback. With his physique, cropped hair and coffee-colored good looks, Xavier had made many a lady swoon.

Xavier glared at him, which told Julian he wasn't about to elaborate.

"You didn't miss much," Julian continued. "Father was on his soapbox, reminding me I'll never be as good as Roman, and Mother wants to set me up."

"Yeah, I think Roman getting hitched and Shantel's pregnancy has Mama visualizing lots of grandbabies running around. You need to curb her."

Julian rolled his eyes. "As if that's possible."

"So what are you going to do?"

"I'm going to give her what she wants," Julian responded evenly. "I've agreed to allow her to set me up on a few dates. After which, she'll see the error of her ways and leave me in peace."

Xavier laughed. "Do you know our mother? She never gives up. When I was in rehab after my injury, Roman may have flown with me to Denver, but it was Mama who kept visiting."

"She had to ensure her baby boy was okay."

"When Mama gets something in her head, you're not going to be able to convince her otherwise. So mark my words, Julian, you've just dug your own grave. Because Mama won't give up until you're headed down the aisle."

Julian frowned. Although he was open to the idea of committing himself to one woman, he wasn't sure he was ready to jump on the marriage bandwagon. He would go through the motions to appease his mother, but he doubted there was any woman out there with the power to change his mind.

Julian was bored to tears.

Cassandra Harris was the second date his mother had arranged in the last two weeks. The first had been an unmitigated disaster. Julian had arrived late thanks to overtime work on one of the defensive back's legs.

When he'd realized the time, he'd rushed home, showered and sped to the upscale restaurant to no avail. His date had been livid. His usual charms had failed on the uptight attorney and she'd eventually cut the evening short, stating she had a case to prepare for the court the following day. Julian hadn't been sad about it, silently admitting he'd much rather spend the evening watching paint dry.

And now here he was with yet another of Angelique's finds. On paper, Cassandra had all the right qualifications in his mother's book. She was educated, from a good family, beautiful, and talented in her own right as a junior college professor of literature. But she and Julian didn't have a thing in common.

For starters, Cassandra was an academic. She enjoyed scholarly activities, like reading, writing and the opera. Although he didn't mind attending the odd opera, he was by no means an enthusiast; he much preferred theater. When Julian asked if she liked to go to events like fashion shows or football games, she'd looked at him as though he'd lost his marbles.

Didn't she realize his family owned a football empire? Football games were a *must.* Quite frankly, Julian needed more stimulation than this woman could offer. He was thankful when she opted to forgo dessert, making the excuse of an early morning and the need to get home.

After dinner, Julian did the polite thing. He walked Cassandra to her car and bid her adieu. As soon as he made it to his Bugatti Veyron, Julian turned on his favorite Sirius station and loudly played some old R & B. He had to jam the vision of the evening from his mind. If this was his mother's idea of his ideal woman, she was sorely mistaken.

A half hour later, he was pulling into the parking space at his penthouse when the display on the dash read Mom. Julian rolled his eyes and prayed for inner peace. Turning off the ignition, he plopped his earbud into his ear as he exited the vehicle. "Hey, Mom. What's going on?"

"Hello, darling. I was just checking in to see how your evening went with Cassandra?"

Julian sighed.

"Oh dear." He heard the disappointment in his mother's voice. "Don't tell me—you and Cassandra were not a match?"

"C'mon, Mom, you had to know that someone as introverted as Cassandra wouldn't be interested in a flamboyant extrovert like me."

"I suppose," she responded. "I thought perhaps she might ground you. Make you more settled."

"I appreciate your help, Mom. Really, I do." Julian pressed the button for the elevator. "But until you bring me someone with a more vivacious personality, your matchmaking is designed to fail."

"All right, I'll give it some further thought. Until then, you'll keep your promise to not go out of your way to stir up any bad press?"

"I gave you my word and I meant it." Julian stepped inside the elevator. "I'm being a real Scout." *Much to my chagrin.*

He ended the call several minutes later, thankful for a reprieve. It would take his mother a while to find a more suitable candidate. In the interim, he needed some fun.

The elevator chimed and he exited.

Opening the door to his penthouse condo, Julian instantly relaxed. The two-bedroom unit was his haven. The complex itself—the Charles—located in the center of Buckhead Village, offered plenty of amenities.

Kicking off his shoes, he walked across the two-thousand-square-foot condo to the corner living room. Plopping down onto the plush sectional that fronted the folding glass doors leading to the terrace, he pulled out his phone. He knew exactly what would get him out of this funk. Some time with the boys.

"Xavier, you up for a game of poker?"

"This is great, Elyse," her boss, Pierre King, said at Friday's morning meeting when Elyse presented him with options to help an embattled rock star try to clean up his public image. "You really have a knack for figuring your way out of tight spots."

"Thank you." Elyse beamed with pride. She'd been working at King Public Relations for three years and, although relatively new, was ambitious and one day wanted to partner in the firm. Elyse envisioned herself as a gladiator in training. The woman who would one day bring down Josiah Lockett and restore to her father all he was rightfully due.

"Keep it up," Pierre said. "If you do, there's no stopping how far you can go."

Elyse left his office feeling on top of the world. It helped that she'd worn her best outfit; a tailored burnt-orange skirt suit with her Manolo jewel-buckled pumps. She walked with confidence to her cubicle, but was stopped along the way by her coworker Andrea Stevens.

The tall, freckle-faced brunette was wearing her favorite wraparound dress and high-heeled sandals. "Way to go!" Andrea high-fived her.

"Thank you, ma'am."

"I think a celebration is in order. How about lunch?" Andrea added quickly, "On me."

"Sounds fabulous."

Twenty minutes later, Elyse and Andrea were seated in an upscale eatery sipping Perrier while they waited for their respective orders of salmon and chicken Waldorf salad.

"I can't believe how well today went," Elyse said, sitting back in her chair.

"C'mon, Elyse." Andrea regarded her. "You're one of the most ambitious people I know. You're not going to stop until you're on top."

"Is that such a bad thing?" she asked. "You know more than anyone how difficult it's been for me."

"How is your father doing?"

"Same. Wallowing in self-pity. I don't understand it, Andrea. I got him settled in this new place, made sure he got a job, and still he falls off the wagon. It's disheartening."

"You can't keep doing this, Elyse. You have to let him

know, in no uncertain terms, that unless he sobers up, you're done with him."

"That's easier said than done, Drea. He's the only family I have in life."

Andrea frowned. "You have me, Elyse."

Elyse had known Andrea since college, and she was one of her oldest and dearest friends. She'd even helped Elyse get the job at King PR.

"I know. I know," Elyse responded. Uncomfortable with the direction the conversation was heading, she made up an excuse to bail. "Pardon me for a moment. I've gotta go to the ladies' room."

Elyse rushed to her feet and walked quickly to the restroom. Once inside, she moved into the accessible stall, which contained its own sink and mirror, and looked at her reflection. She knew Andrea was right. She should let her father sink or swim on his own, but how could she? If she gave up on him now, he'd have nothing left and then where would he end up? No, no, it was up to her to right the wrongs.

Elyse was touching up her makeup when she heard the door swish open.

"Girl, I'm so excited about my date tonight," a woman said from the other side of the stall door.

"Oh yeah? Anyone I know?" her friend asked.

"You wouldn't believe it if I told you, Janis."

"Try me."

"Julian Lockett."

"No way."

"Yes, way. Julian's mom and my mom are sorors, and Mrs. Lockett is upset that Julian's tomfoolery with the ladies always lands him in the gossip blogs. She wants him to clean up his act and settle down."

"With you? Omigod, that's incredible, Tiffany. He's such a stud. I heard he really knows his way around the bedroom."

"Janis!"

Elyse could hear the water running, so the woman must have turned on the taps.

"I'm not going out with him to get him into bed. At least, not yet. No, my goal is to end up with his ring on my finger." She spoke the last several words in singsong.

"Julian Lockett has never been the settle-down kind."

"He hasn't met me yet," Tiffany replied.

"So when do you see him?"

The taps were turned off. "We're meeting tonight at Bacchanalia for dinner."

"Oh, I've been dying to go there," Janis gushed.

Elyse heard paper towels being ripped from a dispenser. "So have I."

"I'm so envious," Janis responded, and Elyse could make out the sound of the door opening and closing as the women left.

Now alone in the restroom, Elyse listened as the women's footsteps receded in the hallway. Damn, Tiffany had left without ever revealing the time for their dinner reservation. But that wasn't a problem for Elyse. She could talk her way around anyone.

This was kismet. She happened to be in the right place at the right time to overhear that Mrs. Lockett was playing matchmaker for Julian. It was *the* most interesting development to fall into Elyse's lap in a long time. Her window of opportunity into the Lockett inner circle had finally opened.

After Elyse and Andrea had returned to the office, while Andrea went back to work, Elyse set upon a secret mission. During lunch, while Andrea had rattled on about her live-in boyfriend not helping out with chores, Elyse had been concocting a plan to meet the illustrious Julian Lockett.

Not only had she called Bacchanalia to learn the time

for Julian's dinner reservation, she'd contacted his c
to change the time to half an hour earlier. It would give h
a chance to go in Tiffany's stead. By the time Tiffany arrived, she'd already have Julian's attention.

When she wanted to be, Elyse could be very convincing, and Julian was a man, after all. A ladies' man, from what she'd read. There wasn't a skirt out there he couldn't talk a woman out of, one article had said. Elyse was certain Julian would be eager to please, to show how charming he was, but he needn't bother when it came to her. Elyse wasn't remotely interested.

Julian was the weakest link in the Lockett family, a Lothario without much substance. She'd done her research. Roman, the eldest, was a commanding executive with a new wife and a baby on the way. Then there was Xavier, the former Atlanta Cougars' quarterback phenom. Though, since breaking his knee, word had it he wasn't the same man he'd once been. That he was broken and therefore of no use. Xavier had no role with the Cougars so he wouldn't be useful to her plan.

And then there was Giana Lockett.

Elyse had researched ways to make contact, but it turned out Giana was just as ambitious as her eldest brother. She was all business and was rumored to be a workaholic. She rarely dated and didn't have any close friends, there had been no avenue forward with her.

That left Julian. Dating him would offer her the chance to get close to him. And maybe, eventually, to the family—so she could wreak havoc on Josiah.

Oh yes. With a little luck and the sexiest dress she could find, Julian Lockett was going to be putty in her hands.

Julian wasn't looking forward to tonight's dinner. If he could have found a way to get out of yet another blind date, he would have. When his assistant had told him Tiffany

Mayes had called, he'd hoped it was to cancel. Instead, she'd asked if they could meet a half hour earlier because she had some important business to attend to in the morning. That was fine with him. Perhaps that meant she'd call it an early night and he would be home before nine?

Anyway, his mother hadn't told him much about Tiffany other than that she was a debutante and charity fundraiser. Given how bad the other two blind dates had gone, Julian hadn't bothered to look her up on social media. She'd be just as boring as the previous two dates, so why make the effort? He'd done this to humor his mother on the off chance that maybe, just maybe, he'd meet someone worth settling down with. So far, they'd all been clunkers.

As he pulled his Bugatti to the curb in front of Bacchanalia, and handed his keys to the valet, Julian couldn't help but think, How pretentious this restaurant was. He knew his mother loved it because of its Michelin rating. But he would rather have gone to Manuel's—the new restaurant owned by an up-and-coming Jamaican chef. Julian loved the food so much, he raved about it on social media. The place had become so busy thanks to Julian's tweets, the chef had given him his own table. If the choice had been his tonight, it's where he would have gone. He could take off his suit jacket and they could kick up their heels and really get to know each other.

Instead, he walked through the double doors, and was immediately greeted by a maître d' wearing a suit and tie. "Good evening, Mr. Lockett. Welcome to Bacchanalia."

"Thank you."

"Allow me to show you to your seat," Julian was glad he was early. It would allow him to order a stiff drink to prepare him for dinner.

The maître d' led him to a private candlelit table for two in a secluded corner. It was all "romance" and had his mother's hand all over it. Justin sat in the proffered seat and accepted the menu and wine selection. "Thank you and bring me a bourbon, please."

"Of course, I'll get Elliott, your server, on it right away, sir."

Julian glanced around the room and noticed several pairs of eyes on him. It wasn't unusual for his father and Roman to come to places like this, but Julian favored a more laid-back vibe. In any event, he'd be on his best behavior—for his mother.

Thankfully, the server quickly came with a tray holding a tumbler of brown liquid. "Your bourbon, Mr. Lockett. Would you like to wait till your guest arrives to order wine?"

"I'm here."

Julian turned to see a goddess walking toward him.

Three

Julian's brain registered that the woman had to be Tiffany Mayes, but his lungs were being starved of oxygen. He had to blink a few times to remind himself to pick his jaw up from the floor, take a breath, and stop staring. She wasn't just beautiful, she was striking, with almond-shaped brown eyes, incredibly thick lashes and lush, pouting lips.

Her hair was short and chic with wispy bangs coming forward to reveal a round face. She had a slender figure, curves in the right places, and her strapless gold dress and gold strappy sandals did her justice. She looked like a Greek goddess.

"Tiffany?" he questioned.

She shook her head. "I'm afraid Tiffany isn't coming."

"No?" He raised an insouciant brow.

She shook her head. "I gave her a different time to meet you and commandeered her place instead."

An old-fashioned switcheroo. Julian, impressed, couldn't suppress a laugh. "Really?"

She came toward Julian and he caught a whiff of her floral scent, which made him eager to lean forward when she offered her hand. "The name's Elyse Harper." Her hand was small, but Julian noticed it was elegant and perfectly manicured.

"Julian."

"Pleasure." She gave him a soft, enchanting smile and a hot tsunami of lust swept through him at the sight. He wanted more. "May I sit down?" Her eyes went to the empty seat beside his.

"Of course. I admit, I'm at a loss as to why anyone would go through so much trouble to meet me." Julian was glad for the interruption. The dates his mother set him up with had been miserable and he was in no mood for a repeat, but this beautiful interloper intrigued him.

"Oh c'mon, Julian. You reputation is legendary," Elyse stated. "Any woman would be eager to make your acquaintance."

"And you're among the eager masses?" His forehead creased with his doubt that that was true. A woman this beautiful had to have men lined up at her door. And if he was lucky, he would be one of them.

Elyse cocked her head to one side and offered a self-mocking smile. "Yes, I suppose I am."

"Well, then, you should know the first thing about me." Julian downed the remaining swallow of his bourbon. "This place isn't my speed. So how about we get out of here and go someplace else?"

"Sounds great." She rose and Julian was right there helping to move her chair aside. He offered her his arm and she accepted. After paying for his drink, they left the restaurant.

Once outside, Julian handed the valet his ticket, but Elyse tried to slip out of his grasp. "I should get my car and follow you."

He shook his head. "Since you wanted to meet me so badly, then you must know I may have a reputation, but I'm no serial killer. My family is a staple in this community and I wouldn't do anything to damage our name. I'll bring you back here when the evening is over."

Her eyes grew round and amusement flashed across them. "All right."

The valet eased Julian's Bugatti Veyron to the curb and, before she could change her mind, Julian was helping her into the passenger seat. As he rounded the back of the car to the driver's side, he contemplated the evening ahead, excited to find out exactly why Elyse Harper had wanted to meet him. Something told him he was in for a wild ride.

Elyse had seen pictures of Julian Lockett before. She'd watched videos of him on social media. But she had not been prepared for the effect of meeting him in person. Although he wasn't quite six feet, he more than towered over her five-foot-four height. The restaurant had seemed far too small to hold a man like him.

Julian was sex personified dressed in a jet-black suit covering his lean muscled frame. The black shirt beneath the superbly tailored jacket had been teamed with a sleek black tie. Add his smooth, toffee-colored skin, short, neatly cropped curly fade, bushy eyebrows, deep-set light brown eyes rimmed with dark brown lashes, and a sexy five-o'clock shadow on a square jaw… Julian Lockett was one helluva of a lethal combination. Clearly at ease with his place in the world, he exuded wealth, charm and style.

All Elyse could do when she looked at his honed perfection was stare. Though she wasn't around the opposite sex much other than work, she could tell *attraction* lurked in those sexy eyes of his. He was interested in her. That was good. She could use it to her advantage and get close, but she had to play her cards right.

She'd done her homework. He was spoiled and used to getting his way. How could he not be when he was handsome *and* charming? He liked the thrill of the chase and, once he obtained what he'd wanted, he quickly grew bored. Elyse mustn't let that happen. To keep his interest, she would have to be coy and elusive. She'd already given him the upper hand by revealing she'd sought him out, but she'd had to. She saw no way around not telling him that she'd given his date the boot. But she also wasn't about to fall into his bed, either.

Was she prepared to go that far?

No.

Her plan was to get close to Julian and find out any family secrets she could. That, combined with her ammunition about how Josiah swindled her father would ruin Josiah's reputation and take him down a peg. It might not get her father's shares back, but it would certainly hit Josiah where it hurt: in his pocketbook. And Elyse had been using her mother's maiden name for years to conceal her identity so she doubted the Locketts would put two and two together. For now, she was happy where she sat—in the passenger seat of his Bugatti Veyron. Elyse had always wondered what it would be like to have money at your fingertips. *Now she knew.*

"So where are you taking me?" she asked. Julian said he wasn't into the pomp and circumstance of Bacchanalia, so she was curious as to what did move him.

He hazarded a glance at her. "You'll see." And he returned his eyes to the road.

"Aren't you going to ask me how I found about your date tonight?"

He shrugged. "In due time. Besides I'm just happy you saved me from another dull date with one of my mother's minions."

"Ouch, sounds like you don't have a high opinion of these women your mother is introducing you to."

He gave her a side glance. "In her mind, they're all women my age or younger with the right pedigree. Yet she fails to understand that none of them is my type."

"And who is your type?" Elyse asked, folding her arms across her chest and turning to study his profile. The man was so good-looking in person that she had to remind herself to breathe.

"You."

He didn't look at her when he said the one word. Instead, he merely gave Elyse a wolfish smile, telling her he might upend her well-thought-out plan to get even with his father. She was in public relations and knew exactly the kind of damage a scandal like Josiah swindling her father could do to his reputation because he prided himself on being a good business and family man. Elyse would need more ammo and hoped getting closer to Julian might help her obtain info she could exploit. What she hadn't counted on was how charming Julian was or that he'd make her heart go pitter pat.

Julian liked that he'd given Elyse pause. She seemed very self-contained and self-assured. He wondered what it would be like to scratch below the surface to find out what really made her blood boil. And he could see she hadn't expected his answer. That was good. It gave him the upper hand.

Because Elyse wasn't his usual type, either. She wasn't tall or slender, like many of the women he dated. His last lover had been confident, sophisticated and extremely gifted with her mouth, which she'd blatantly used to her advantage. But Elyse seemed reserved and somewhat shy. *Was that what made her all the more appealing?* He would find out.

After a short drive, he pulled into a nondescript parking lot full of cars on a Friday night and turned off the engine. Before he came around to assist her from his car, he removed his jacket and placed it in the trunk. Manuel's didn't stand on ceremony.

"What is this—" The words died on Elyse's lips when she saw the name of the establishment after he'd helped her out. She turned and glanced at him. "I've heard about this place. It's been getting excellent reviews, but I wouldn't—" Once again, she didn't finish her sentence.

"Think I'd be caught dead in a place like this?" Julian inquired, closing her door. "Well, you'd be wrong. I happen to enjoy good food and a great atmosphere, and Manuel's has it in spades. C'mon." He took her hand in his and led her to the front entrance.

After opening the door for Elyse, he followed her inside. The restaurant was wall-to-wall patrons, but Julian wasn't concerned. He knew the owner. He immediately went up to the hostess and whispered in her ear.

"Julian." Elyse tugged on his arm. "There's no way we're going to get seated. Look at all these people."

"Don't worry." He patted her hand. "I've got this."

Several minutes later, the dark-skinned Jamaican owner, dressed in a chef's coat and wearing a smile, came out to greet him.

"Julian, my man." He gave Julian a one-armed hug. "It's great to see you. Why didn't you tell me you were stopping by?"

Julian shrugged. "Spur of the moment, Manuel. I was hoping, if no one had the chef's table, my beautiful date, Elyse, and I—" he glanced at the beauty by his side "—could have it."

"Elyse, welcome to my humble establishment." Manuel shook her offered hand.

"Manuel, I've heard nothing but great things. I look forward to sampling your food," Elyse responded.

"And as for you—" Manuel gave Julian a smile "—you

know I have a permanent table with your name on it. Come on." He inclined his head for them to follow him.

Julian led Elyse back to the kitchen where Manuel and his small team of one sous-chef and two line cooks stood ready to feed the masses outside. Tucked in a corner was a two-seater table with a reserved sign, which Manuel promptly plucked behind his back. "Enjoy the meal." And with that, he left Julian and Elyse alone.

Once Julian assured Elyse was seated, he took the seat across from her and noticed she was shaking her head. "What?"

"Does everyone always do what you want?"

"Which is?"

"Cater to your every whim."

Julian stared at her for several moments before he erupted into laughter. "So you think I'm entitled?" When she didn't answer, he added, "If I'm so terrible, why were you so eager to meet me?"

He focused his gaze on her beautiful face and watched with amazement as she flushed. A woman who still blushed. Oh, he was going to enjoy this night very much.

How was it possible a grown man could have dimples? Elyse wondered as she watched that incredible mouth of his slash into a devilish grin. Dimples on Julian were simply gorgeous and complemented his being an incorrigible flirt. How had the tables turned? Elyse found herself on the receiving end of questions instead of asking them. She had to turn the tide.

"I wanted to find out if there was more substance to you or if it's always smoke and mirrors. Do you ever show anyone your true self?"

Julian stared at her for several beats, all trace of humor gone. Instead, there was a throb of tension. Or was it desire hanging in the air between them?

"Why do I get the feeling you think very little of me?"

Had she backed herself into a corner with her comment? "Whatever gave you that impression? I sought *you* out."

"And yet, I can't seem to figure you out. One minute I think you're interested in me, but then… I can't put my finger on it."

"But you're intrigued?"

His eyes narrowed. "I am or I wouldn't be here."

"Sorry to disturb you lovebirds," Manuel interrupted their banter, "but I thought you might like some refreshments. I took the liberty of bringing over some Red Stripe along with a Jamaican jerk salmon tostada with grilled peach coconut salsa."

"This looks delicious." Elyse's mouth was watering.

"Cheers!" Julian held up his bottle of beer. Elyse tapped hers against his and took a generous swig. Of all the places she'd expected Julian to take her, it hadn't been this small Jamaican restaurant.

"Bon appétit." Not having had anything to eat since lunch, Elyse wasted no time diving in and reaching for a tostada on the platter. The sweet and spicy flavor bomb was something she wouldn't mind eating again. "That was yummy," she said as she licked her lips.

When she looked over at Julian, she found his gaze fixed on her and an arrow of heat went straight to her core. This evening wasn't going as she'd planned. She'd thought Julian would be a show-off, like some of the rich clients she worked with. Instead, she was finding him to be quite down-to-earth.

Manuel followed the appetizer with a red pea soup made of red kidney beans, salted meats, dumplings and fresh herbs. And while Manuel plied Elyse with good food, including curry goat with rice and peas, followed by jerk seafood stew, Julian kept her entertained, talking about the theater, art and politics. She noticed he steered cleared of sports or football in particular. Elyse would have thought he would eagerly talk about his family's franchise, but instead he was doing the opposite.

"A friend of mine is debuting a new play. Perhaps I could take you to the opening?"

"Maybe. I have a very busy schedule ahead of me," Elyse said. "I'm in public relations."

"Are most of your clients corporate accounts?"

Elyse shook her head. "No, mostly actors, entertainers, athletes. I specialize in fixing things."

"Like on *Scandal*?"

"Sometimes." Elyse bunched her shoulders. "I have a special skill set in figuring out how to help folks out of the messes they make and turn public opinion in their favor."

"I imagine that isn't easy."

She laughed derisively. "You don't know the half of it. Occasionally I want to ask them what the hell they were thinking, but I find their actions were usually based on bad decisions involving either sex or drugs."

"That's a shame. One of those activities could be very pleasurable indeed with the right partner."

Elyse blushed. Julian had a way of throwing in little sexual innuendos and she couldn't stop herself from reacting to them. "Or it could get them into a world of trouble. It's best to act after you've made a well thought-out decision."

"Sometimes life is about emotion," Julian said. "It can't be planned. It's a spontaneous feeling. But wait—don't tell me. You don't believe in being spontaneous?"

"I sought you out after overhearing about your date. It was spur of the moment."

He eyed her suspiciously for several minutes. "You'd like me to believe that's true, but I doubt it. Anyway, it takes us back to why we're here this evening." Julian snapped his fingers. "How exactly did you find out about my blind date?"

"Right place. Right time," Elyse responded. "I was in the ladies' room at a restaurant when Tiffany and her friend came in. They were talking rather loudly about her date with you and that you were taking her to Bacchanalia."

"And *you* chose to act on it?"

Elyse smiled. Julian didn't miss a beat, did he. "Yes, I called your office and asked if you could meet me half an hour earlier than scheduled, though I didn't know the original time of the reservation."

"How did you get that info out of my assistant?" Julian asked.

"I'm in public relations, remember? I know how to work people. I merely acted as if I was changing the time, not who you were meeting. She didn't think anything of it, which thereby allowed me to figure when to come meet you."

"Normally, I'd have to give her grief, but if it wasn't for your resourcefulness, we would have never met. And that would be a shame. I'm enjoying your company a lot better than I suspect I would have Tiffany's."

Elyse grinned. She couldn't help it. Julian knew what to say to stroke her womanly ego. "Thank you." She glanced down at her watch. Hours had elapsed since they'd first met at Bacchanalia.

"Can I convince you to stay for dessert? Manuel's Jamaican rum cake is to die for." His wide mouth curved upward and Elyse found herself unable to look away from his brown-eyed gaze.

"Well..." The dessert did sound decadent. "All right, you convinced me." But if Elyse wasn't careful, she was certain Julian was capable of talking her into a lot more before the night was over.

As Julian drove Elyse back to Bacchanalia an hour later, he wished the night wouldn't end. The date with Elyse had been the best he'd ever had because it hadn't been about wowing a woman with his riches. Instead, he'd been himself, no pretenses, and taken Elyse to a place close to his heart. If he'd been with any other woman, she likely would have scoffed when he'd suggested leaving Bacchanalia. Elyse had gone with the flow. And, consequently, enjoyed the food at Manuel's, if the way she'd licked her lips had been any indication.

There had been times throughout the night when she had stirred a fire in his belly, making Julian want to lean over the table and take those lips. To kiss her. To taste her. To devour her. Every masculine response he had roared into life in her company.

Attraction.

Lust.

Hunger.

Yet he'd sat across from her making conversation and getting to know her. Had Elyse been right? Was he superficial—all about smoke and mirrors? He didn't think so. It wasn't all about sex. They'd talked during the evening and he'd learned they shared the same political affiliation: they were Democrats. And he'd learned her interests, like how when she had downtime she enjoyed yoga and Pilates to relax.

Eventually, he pulled into the now empty parking lot of the Michelin-star restaurant where their evening had begun. It was easy to spot her car because it was the only one remaining. He slid the Bugatti Veyron beside her Toyota Camry, but didn't turn off the engine. He turned to her. "I enjoyed your company tonight. I'm glad you switched times with Tiffany, because I was the beneficiary."

"You always seem to know the right thing to say."

"And you like to call me out on it," Julian responded.

A throb of awareness pulsed between them in the sports car. When he looked at Elyse, desire slammed into him, stretching the atmosphere taut with purpose. *Surely she had to sense the sizzle?* There was no way he could let the night end without breaching the sexual tension to see if she'd melt at his touch.

"Julian." The husky way she said his name was a telltale sign she felt it, too.

He heard her sharp intake of breath seconds before he reached for her. Sweeping his head down, Julian let his lips glide sensuously across hers, and she responded. Her mouth opened to his and their tongues engaged in a dance of mutual seduction. Unable to resist, he reached out to touch the sweet mounds of her breasts. When he molded them with his hands, Elyse released a low moan, and Julian deepened the kiss.

They kissed madly. Wet and hot, without restraint and with such lust, Julian thought he might combust, especially when he felt her nipples pucker underneath his fingertips. He wanted to nibble, lick and suck her nipples into his mouth, but he couldn't have her properly in this car, not the way he wanted. But she was kissing him so hard and hot, he heard the thud of his own heartbeat.

Julian was tempted to continue kissing her, to swallow her gasps and moans, to strip her until she was bare right then and there, but he felt Elyse push against his chest, so he tore his mouth from hers. "What's wrong?"

"We can't."

"Can't we?" He was dazed at how incredible it felt to have Elyse in his arms. "Come home with me tonight. You can follow me in your car."

His words must have been like a douse of cold water because her eyes narrowed. "So we can spend the night together and you can tick me off the list like another one of your women?"

"No." He shook his head. "It's not like that." She mesmerized something desperate and needy inside him.

"I think it is." Elyse had unbuckled her seat belt and was jumping out of the Bugatti before Julian could react.

"Wait a sec!" He rushed out of the car toward her, but Elyse, having seconds on him, had reached her vehicle and was jumping inside it. "Elyse, wait! Please!" he implored.

She rolled down the window. "And here I thought the evening we shared was something special, maybe the start of something new, but you'll never change, Julian. You'll always be afraid of something real with a woman. So I'll see you around."

Elyse rolled up the driver's-side window and sped out of the parking lot, leaving Julian stunned in her wake.

How had the moment turned sour so suddenly? Had he really gotten their signals crossed? The look that had passed between them in his car had been timeless. The lust had been tangible, overwhelming. It was unlike anything he'd ever experienced. He'd thought Elyse had felt the same. That she'd wanted him as much as he'd wanted her. He was certain of it. So why was she running scared?

And worst of all, she hadn't given him a way to contact her.

So what was he going to do about it?

Four

Julian was still flummoxed when Monday arrived. He'd never had anything like Friday night happen before. For the first time in his life, someone had surprised him. In a good way. Usually, when he turned on the charm and flirted with women, they were easy targets and fell prey to his charms, but not Elyse Harper. First, she'd intrigued him by switching places with his real date, leading him to believe she couldn't wait to meet him. Then she'd confounded him by turning down his suggestion at the end of the evening to go back to his place.

When had a woman ever turned him down? There were countless beautiful women willing to share his bed, and he was always happy to oblige. He liked women of all shapes, colors and varieties, but Julian had to admit he appreciated Elyse being more discerning about whom she went to bed with. She demanded respect and refused to accept anything less. *Was that what made Julian want her more?*

Was that why he'd been unable to stop thinking about

the pixie-haired beauty with the mesmerizing brown eyes that seemed to look into his very soul? He wanted to know more about her and he wasn't going to let anything stand in his way.

He was musing over his next step when Giana walked into the VIP lounge for the Atlanta Cougars' executives. Julian was by the coffee bar; the lounge also included a central seating area and a restaurant that overlooked the outdoor practice fields.

"Good morning," Giana said as she made her way to the espresso machine.

"Good morning." Julian took a sip from his Cougars' coffee mug.

"So." Giana leaned against the countertop as she waited for the machine to make her frothy concoction. "How was your blind date?"

"You knew about that?"

"Of course. Everyone in the family is gossiping about how you're letting Mama believe she's actually setting you up with the love of your life."

"Au contraire," Julian replied over the zipping of the espresso machine. "I went into her matchmaking scheme with my eyes wide-open. I never claimed I'd meet my soul mate, but I was willing to give it a try. And because of Mama, I may have actually found a woman I'm willing to at least try a normal relationship with."

"Really?" Giana's arched brow rose. "Do tell."

"Her name's Elyse Harper—and she wasn't Mama's choice. She happened to overhear one of Mama's candidates say she was meeting me, and crafty Elyse switched places with her."

Giana frowned, folding her arms at her chest. "You don't find that the slightest bit suspect? Mama is going to be furious. She had such high hopes for her matchmaking."

"I'm sorry to disappoint Mama, but quite frankly, I didn't mind the swap. It was just a date."

"I don't know." Giana turned away to retrieve her filled mug. She took a quick sip. "Seems contrived to me. But, more important, how did it go?"

"Giana, it was one of the best dates I've had in a long time," Julian responded. "Rather than be my usual charming self, I was able to just be me, you know? And Elyse responded. She talked. I mean really talked, not just about the superficial stuff like our favorite food or movie. At the end of the night, I would have liked nothing better than to take Elyse home, but she turned me down."

"She did what?" Giana put her mug down on the countertop. "Didn't you say she approached you? I mean she's the one who stole the place of your intended date. I would have thought she'd be eager to seal the deal."

"And that, my dear sister, is what made Elyse so appealing. Although she made the first move by switching places, she wasn't willing to compromise herself by moving too fast. It made me respect her."

Giana scoffed. "You just love the chase!" She picked up her coffee mug again and drank generously.

"Oh, I'd love to chase," Julian responded. "The thing is, I've never had to. The women I've been with always make the first move, but the alpha in me appreciates a woman taking it back to old school and making me work for it."

Giana chuckled. "That's why I love you, Julian. You say whatever comes to your mind, regardless of the consequences."

"You should do more of it. Perhaps if you did, Father might listen to you more and take your suggestions."

"Hey…how did this become about me?" Giana inquired. "We were talking about your—" she pointed to his chest "—love life."

"Yeah, well, I'm telling it like it is," Julian said. "And as for Elyse, the sneaky minx didn't even leave me her phone number, but that's not a problem. I'll find out where she is and, when I do, she'll be putty in my hands."

"Good luck, big brother. You're going to need it."

Elyse was proud of herself. She'd made first contact with Julian Lockett, sealing the course of their fate. After meeting him, Elyse was certain *he* was the key to getting closer to the Locketts. The problem, however, was that her planned ruse wasn't going to be as easy as she'd thought to maintain because she actually *liked* Julian.

Social media portrayed him as a playboy, a womanizer, constantly on the prowl, but Julian Lockett was more than that. Yes, he was charming and sexy as sin, but he was also smart and funny—beyond what she'd given him credit for. There was a lot more depth to Julian than he let on. She wondered if he used his charm as a way to keep people at bay, so they couldn't see the real him. Maybe it was a coping mechanism. If it was, she understood it because she'd often done the same.

Growing up hadn't been easy. She'd barely been six years old when she'd seen cancer ravage her mother, stealing her joy and vitality. Elyse had watched the father she'd adored turn into a shadow of his former self. She'd learned at a young age just how cruel children could be. Everyone in their neighborhood, knowing her father drank too much, had called him a drunk or a deadbeat to her face. Some of what they'd said was true; her father couldn't hold his liquor, often stumbling into their tiny one-bedroom apartment and passing out on the floor next to where she slept on the couch. Sometimes he forgot to pay the rent until the landlord banged on the door.

And Elyse? Well, she ignored the bullies. But confront them? Stand up for herself? No. Never. She'd felt too helpless, too alone, too isolated, so she'd run away. Hid out, so no one could find her. It had been easier that way. She'd tried to make herself invisible so no one paid attention to her. It had worked. Eventually the bullies had moved on to someone new and Elyse began figuring a way out.

Being tormented had motivated Elyse to want a better life. Why? Because when you were the daughter of the neighborhood drunk, everyone thought you wouldn't amount to much. So in school, she'd worked hard, put everything into her studies until eventually she'd earned herself a scholarship to a boarding school outside the neighborhood. It had been ideal.

Although she'd been a scholarship kid, she'd made friends with some of the girls and would be invited to visit their homes. When she saw how happy they were with their families, Elyse began to wonder just how much she'd missed out on, had lost, because Josiah had stolen her father's dream.

Maybe it was irrational to blame Josiah for her father's gambling, but he knew how much the Atlanta Cougars meant to him. When Josiah caught wind of Frank's gambling rather than help his best friend, he'd gone for the jugular, allowing Frank to offer his shares of the Cougars as collateral during a poker game. By the end of the night, Josiah had the Atlanta Cougars all to himself. Her father's downfall into drunkenness was a direct result of losing the Cougars to Josiah and her mother to cancer.

Her father was why she was doing this, getting closer to Julian Lockett. Elyse was trying to right the wrongs of the past. Her modus operandi might be wrong, but she had to work with the hand she'd been dealt. And Julian was the key. She would get close to Julian to gain information about the Locketts' secrets. Then in her role as a publicist, she would ruin their reputation by exposing them, causing the Cougars' stock to plummet and since they were family owned and the only stockholders, he'd feel it in his pocketbook. Josiah didn't deserve to live the high life after he left her father, her family with nothing.

She'd purposely not given him her phone number because she'd known that a man like Julian would be thrilled by a challenge. Finding her would prove difficult for him because Elyse had no social media accounts. She'd purposely stayed off social media because she'd wanted anonymity when it came time to take back her father's due. She was certain Julian would use any method at his disposal to find her. And when he did, she would use every technique in her handbook to get closer to him, so she could get even closer to his father.

"I need your help, Nico," Julian said, walking into Nico Shapiro's office in the basement of their corporate headquarters later that morning. Not many people knew about Nico. The Atlanta Cougars kept him on hand for matters needing the utmost discretion.

"Oh yeah, what can I help you with?" The sandy-blond man stood.

"I need you to find someone for me." Julian plopped down in the chair opposite his large glass-topped office desk and faced Nico.

Nico sat back down, his blue gaze focused on Julian. "Let me guess, a female?"

Julian frowned. "Am I that predictable?"

"You have a reputation as a ladies' man," Nico responded. "So who is this paragon of virtue you can't live without?"

Julian ignored the sarcastic comment. "Her name's Elyse Harper. We met Friday night at Bacchanalia and she's fantastic."

"So what's the problem?"

"I don't know where to find her."

"What do you mean?"

Julian sighed. "Other than knowing she's in public relations, is a staunch Democrat and likes yoga and Pilates, I don't know much. I was hoping you might be able to fill in the blanks. Basically, I need to know how to reach her. Her cell phone and a work and home address to start."

"So you don't need a full workup?"

Julian shook his head. "Absolutely not. I'd rather learned about her the old-fashioned way."

Nico leaned his forearms against the glass desktop. "And what if the reason Elyse didn't provide you with her digits was because she wasn't interested in seeing you again? Did you ever think about that?"

Julian got to his feet. "No. I think she wants me to find her, and that's where you come in."

"All right, I'll let you know when I have something." Nico rose and offered his hand.

Julian shook it. "I look forward to it."

Nico took care of anything needing fixing with the Atlanta Cougars, so if anyone could find his elusive woman, it was Nico. And once he did, this time Julian wouldn't let her out of his grasp.

"Julian, what's this I hear about you standing up poor Tiffany Mayes," his mother asked later that day when he stopped in at the family estate in Tuxedo Park. He and Roman had been summoned by their father to discuss one of their linebacker's knee injury. Although he hadn't specialized in orthopedic surgery like the head team doctor, Julian disagreed with his decision to return the linebacker to play in the Cougars' current season, so Josiah wanted to discuss it.

"I'm sorry, Mama, I can't talk," Julian said as she followed him down the foyer toward his father's study.

"Oh no you don't." She stepped in front of his path. At five-five, Angelique was several inches shorter than him, but that didn't stop Julian from feeling her anger as she stared up at him. "You're not going to sweep past me without explaining yourself, not after the trouble I went through setting up that date."

Julian stopped. "It wasn't my fault, Mama. Another woman showed up in Tiffany's stead."

His mother's brow furrowed. "Another woman? That's impossible."

"I'm sorry, but it was possible. And I have to tell you, I rather enjoyed her company and plan on seeing her again."

"But who is she?"

"I don't know, Mama, but I intend to find out." Julian left his mother standing in the hall with a perplexed expression and walked to his father's study.

The door was ajar. Josiah and Roman were already talking, and they stopped when he walked in. Both men were in dark tailored suits with handmade dress shoes. Julian's chest tightened at the image of the perfect father-son duo they made. The only difference was their father had a wide chest and husky build while Roman had an athletic frame.

"There you are, boy, come on in." His father motioned him forward. "What's this I hear about you giving a dissenting opinion from Dr. Walters?"

Julian didn't like the accusatory tone in his father's voice, but he wasn't surprised. Josiah was rarely on his side. If anything, he was always looking for fault with Julian and he usually found it. Nothing he ever did was going to please the old man.

"My opinion is based on facts and the MD behind my name," Julian responded hotly. "I don't believe you have one, do you?"

His father came charging toward him. "You getting mouthy with me, Julian?"

"No, sir." Julian didn't back down and instead stared up at his father, who was nearly six inches taller than him.

Living in the Lockett household, he'd learned at an early age you had to stand up to a bully and that's exactly what his father could be at times. "But I know he isn't ready to come back. We need to keep him on the sidelines and ensure his knee is healed properly."

"Dr. Walters says with the therapy he's been getting, he should be ready to start."

Julian shook his head. "I disagree. If nothing else, keep him as a backup, but he's not ready. Pushing him before that knee is fully healed would be to the team's detriment."

"We need him back now!" his father insisted. "And your job is to look out for the Atlanta Cougars."

"That may be so," Julian responded. "But I'm a doctor first. I pledged an oath to do no harm and I stand behind it. I may not have years of surgical experience, but I'm in the trenches with this team day in and day out while Dr. Walters has his own practice."

"Perhaps he can be more objective because of it," Roman said. When Julian fired him an angry glance, he held up his hands. "I'm only playing devil's advocate here, Julian."

"Whatever." Julian shrugged. "The two of you will decide what you want to do no matter what I say."

"That's not true," Roman objected.

"Yes, it is. You've always been on his side." Julian inclined his head toward their father, who was watching them carefully.

"And you, boy…you're always thinking with your heart," Josiah responded. "You need to think like a leader. One day I'll be gone and it'll be up to you two—" he glanced at Julian and then Roman "—to run the Atlanta Cougars. You have to be ready to make hard decisions."

Julian glared at his father. "Then we'll agree to disagree. I have made my position clear. You can choose to listen to it or not." He looked over at Roman, who, as the Cougars' General Manager, was running the organization, though their father was still on the board and refused to retire to let Roman take over completely.

Roman stared at Julian for several beats before saying, "Julian is right. We should sideline him for the first half of the season and bring him in near the halfway point to help get us to the playoffs."

"Well?" Julian looked over at Josiah. It was two against one, but he could override Roman should he so choose.

"Fine. We'll bench him, but you'd better be right, Julian."

"I am." Because if he wasn't, his father would never let him forget it.

"Hey, Daddy," Elyse said as she entered his one-bedroom apartment carrying several bags of groceries after work on Monday evening. "I brought you a few things."

Frank rose from his perch on the couch and followed her into the small galley kitchen. From the look of it, he was sober. He'd also showered, shaved and put on a fresh T-shirt and jeans, though he was in desperate need of a haircut. "You didn't have to do that, baby girl."

"I know I didn't *have* to, I wanted to," Elyse responded, placing her purse and the bags on the countertop. "You need food."

"I'm your father. I should be taking care of you, not the other way around," he said, leaning against the door frame. She unpacked the groceries and began putting them away.

"I'm well past the age of needing you to look after me," Elyse stated. "I do quite well for myself at the PR agency."

"It makes me proud to see you doing so good given I made your life a living a hell growing up."

"Daddy…"

He held up a hand. "Don't, Elyse. Don't make excuses for me. I was and am a terrible father. It's why you left and went to that fancy boarding school."

Elyse paused in her task. "I did that for me as well as

for you, Daddy. You weren't capable of taking care of me after Mama died, and I wanted something more from my life. I don't blame you. I blame the Locketts. Josiah Lockett in particular. He did this to you."

"Yeah, well I made it easy for him, I suppose," her father said, going to the refrigerator and, to her dismay, pulling out a bottle of beer.

Her stomach churned to see him twist off the cap and chug it. "Daddy, you don't need that stuff."

His bloodshot eyes stared back at her. "Yeah, I do. It takes the edge off, baby girl. It helps me forget all that I lost because I was stupid enough to gamble away my shares of the Atlanta Cougars. They're a good team now, though back when Josiah and I purchased them, they were considered a joke in the league."

"But Josiah knew about your gambling habit, didn't he?" Elyse responded.

"Yeah, he did. I already had some debts with some loan sharks he'd covered, but that's what friends do, right? Anyway, he exploited my weakness for the numbers. You'd think he would have stopped the game, considering we grew up together and were as thick as thieves. Instead he joined and encouraged me to bet my half of the team. But Josiah was always ambitious, greedy." He swigged his beer. "He saw an opportunity when I was down-and-out over seeing your mama wither away one day at a time. Josiah took advantage to swindle me out of the team."

"And he will pay, Daddy. I promise you that. I will make him pay for what he did to you, what he did to our family."

Her father regarded her. "I don't need you to avenge me, girl. You need to let sleeping dogs lie, Elyse. You hear me? No good will come of you sticking your nose where it don't belong."

"But, Daddy—"

He interrupted her. "No!" He left the galley kitchen and

Elyse followed him. She didn't like to see him upset. Who knew what harm he was capable of doing to himself if left to his own devices?

"Daddy, please," Elyse pleaded. She grabbed his arm, trying to pull him toward her. "I'm doing this for you, for us. Josiah Lockett owes you."

"And you think you're going to collect?" Her father snorted and it made his face become ugly. The saying "a drunk mind speaks a sober heart" came to Elyse but she shrugged it off.

"Yes. You'll see." She knew her father wasn't innocent in losing his shares of the Cougars to Josiah in a poker game, but Josiah had been like a brother to Frank. They hadn't just been business partners; they'd been family, and family was supposed to look out for one another. Instead, Josiah's actions had been self-serving. It was time for payback and she was just the person to deliver it.

Five

"You found her," Julian said when Nico walked into his office midmorning on Wednesday, a smug smile on his face. Nico was known for getting information no one else could, though Julian suspected finding Elyse Harper had probably been one of the easiest assignments he'd ever had.

"It was pretty easy." Nico slid a file across Julian's desktop. "Elyse Harper, thirty years old, works at King Public Relations here in Atlanta. Currently single, lives alone in Midtown. There's more in that file about her background, such as her family, where she went to school, ex-lovers and more."

Julian slid the file back to Nico, who, as usual, was wearing all black as if to make sure no one could see him coming. "I don't need all that. Just her phone number and address, please."

"You sure?" Nico quirked a brow as he plucked one sheet of paper from the manila folder and handed it to Julian. "Knowing someone's past can help you predict their future behavior."

"Did you come up with that all by yourself?" Julian asked with a smirk.

"Hey!" Nico pointed his finger at Julian. "Don't shoot the messenger and don't say I didn't warn you."

He left the room, leaving Julian blessedly alone and with the info he needed to end his obsession with Elyse. Since the moment they'd met, he'd been unable to get the petite beauty with the pixie cut and sharp tongue out of his mind. The chemistry between them had been tangible and Julian suspected she'd wanted him as much as he'd wanted her.

Instantly, he reached for his cell and thought about dialing her, but from the little he knew of Elyse, she would probably hang up on him. She hadn't given him her number or taken him up on his offer to come home with him; she'd been playing coy and hard to get.

Julian suspected Elyse *wanted* him to chase after her. And chase he would. He pressed the intercom button on his desk phone for his assistant. "Clear my afternoon schedule. I have an errand to run."

Within five minutes, he was easing his Bugatti Veyron away from the Atlanta Cougars' headquarters and toward downtown. He had a lady to say hello to.

"Elyse, can you come into my office?" Pierre asked.

Her boss's phone request shouldn't have caused her anxiety, but for some reason today was different. Call it her Spidey sense, Elyse just knew something was up. Pierre didn't usually ask to see her unless it was scheduled in advance.

Rising, she glanced at Pierre's office from her cubicle, but the door was closed and she couldn't see inside. She'd been away for an appointment and had only just returned. Had something happened?

Elyse started to move, but thought better of it and quickly dug into her desk's bottom drawer. Pulling out her purse, she glanced in her compact mirror to make sure not a hair of her cut was out of place. She smoothed on a fresh coat of lipstick to plump her lips and looked down at her outfit.

Today, she looked smart and professional in straight linen pants with a one-button jacket. She wore a shell underneath and her favorite snakeskin pumps.

As she walked to Pierre's office, she knew he wouldn't find fault with her appearance. Elyse was unprepared, however, for the occupant sitting with Pierre in the office when she arrived.

Julian.

Both men stood as she approached.

"Elyse, you didn't tell me you were courting Julian Lockett's business."

"Pardon?" She glanced at Pierre and then at Julian, who had a wide grin across that devilishly sexy mouth of his. Why, oh why, hadn't she prepared herself for his counterattack? It was a given he'd find her. He was Julian Lockett, after all, but she hadn't planned on him tracking her down to her place of business.

"Julian was just telling me that the Atlanta Cougars' first round draft pick, Curtis Jackson, is in need of someone to handle his media. He mentioned he met you the other day."

"Yes, I was impressed with Elyse and how well she handled Porscha Childs and Mike Ford." Julian approached and Elyse couldn't help the way her heart picked up in pace at his nearness. Or was it the sandalwood smell of his cologne?

"Elyse is one of my star publicists and she would be an asset to any team."

"We're still considering other candidates, but perhaps I could take Elyse out over lunch to discuss the opportunity."

"Of course," Pierre gushed and Elyse could see her fate was sealed. Julian had outmaneuvered her. "You don't mind, do you, Elyse?" As an afterthought, he'd turned and asked for her consent.

Elyse had no choice but to give Pierre her most brilliant smile while shooting daggers at Julian when Pierre turned his head. "Of course not, just give me a moment to get my purse."

"I'll wait for you by the elevators."

Elyse was fuming as she walked to her desk, but then again, maybe Julian had done her a favor. If she could indeed work for the Atlanta Cougars' team, she would have greater access to information in her quest to bring down the Lockett patriarch. Today's events might work in her favor, after all.

"I presume you're quite happy with yourself?" Elyse asked once they were in Julian's car and on their way to lunch.

He couldn't help but grin wolfishly. "Oh c'mon, don't be mad. You had to know after our date Friday night I was going to look you up."

She turned to face him. "You didn't just *look* me up, Julian, you came to my job and sought me out."

"Yeah, I did," Julian answered bluntly, glancing briefly in her direction. "Because, if I didn't know any better, I'd say you wanted me to chase you. Why else would you leave without giving me your number after we had such a great evening?"

"And you fell for it?" She couldn't resist teasing him.

"So you admit you were leading me on?"

"If you do the same and say you enjoyed my cat-and-mouse game."

"I did and I do. I wonder what other games you have in store."

"Wouldn't you like to know," she purred.

If Julian had his way, he would pull the Bugatti over now, take her face in his hands and taste those tempting lips of hers. Instead, he pulled into the parking lot of an upscale American restaurant.

Julian quickly exited the vehicle and helped Elyse out of the car. He watched as she sashayed past him toward the entrance, admiring the view of her backside as she did.

Once inside and immediately seated in a booth, they were handed menus along with glasses of sparkling water. While Elyse perused the menu, Julian used the opportunity to admire her beauty. From her arched eyebrows to her pert nose to her even, light fawn complexion, there wasn't anything he didn't like. He couldn't help but focus on her lips, plump with blush gloss. She was quietly attractive without trying hard like some women. He liked her. A lot.

"Are you done staring?" Elyse asked, looking up and fixing him with her gaze.

Julian grinned. "Not quite, but did you find something on the menu you like?" The waiter had just approached their table.

"Yes, I'll have the grilled chicken and strawberry salad," Elyse said, handing the waiter the menu.

"I'll have a salad, as well. The salmon with fresh field greens," Julian said.

Once their orders were taken, the waiter left them alone, and Elyse quickly started in on him. "I would think the Atlanta Cougars already have a PR firm in place. Was the job opportunity with the Cougars a ploy to get in the door and meet me? Or do I really have a shot?"

"We do have a firm," Julian answered honestly, "however, Curtis's father is very particular about his image. I think it would be good for him to have someone who could help craft and maintain his public persona."

"Have you discussed this with your brother?" Elyse asked. "Isn't he the General Manager?"

"And I'm just the lowly sports doctor, right?" Julian responded with a frown.

"I'm sorry, I didn't mean it that way." Elyse reached across the table and touched his hand.

A spark of fire ignited at her touch and Julian could feel the ripple pass through his body and straight to his groin. He glanced up to see if she'd felt that shock. When he did, he found a smile tipping her lips upward, and his heart accelerated again.

She started to pull her hand away, but Julian placed his large one over hers. "Don't..."

Elyse raised a brow.

"You feel it, too, the chemistry between us?"

"I..." She started to deny it, but must have thought better because the expression on her face softened. "I can't deny there is something here."

Julian appreciated her honesty. "Then we should explore it."

"I'm not sure mixing business with pleasure is a good thing."

"And it's a not given you'll get the job."

She chuckled and Julian had to admit he liked the sound of it. Elyse was different from other women he encountered. They usually fawned all over him. Elyse was making him work for it and he found that refreshing.

"Touché," she said. "It's not a given. I know this opportunity came about because of our...*affiliation*...but I would hope I'm selected because I'm the most qualified candidate not because of what may or may not happen between us."

"Oh, it will happen," Julian replied with an easy smile and a confident stare.

"Are you always this arrogant?" Elyse asked. "Or is it just with me?"

"When I want something, I'm not afraid of going after it."

And he wanted Elyse.

So he intended to have her.

Elyse was unnerved by Julian's sexy swagger. She'd thought her experiences with Lotharios in her work as a publicist would have prepared her for a man like Julian, but they hadn't. Was it because, for the first time, she *was* attracted to one of them?

For the most part, she was a woman who kept herself at a distance from others because she'd been focused on her education and on stepping up the ladder from poverty. Consequently, she'd suffered on a personal level in forming serious relationships with men.

Elyse had been timid and shy. When she'd arrived at boarding school, all the girls had been well beyond her in terms of maturity. In college and beyond, she'd finally ventured out to date and all of those men had been forgettable, including the two lovers she'd had. None of them sparked her attraction until now.

She was here with Julian Lockett, a man she both needed to get justice for her father and a man she feared for bringing out wayward emotions she'd never felt before. The way Julian smiled, leaning back in his chair to regard her as if he didn't have a care in the world, was disarming. Maybe it came from the fact that in essence Julian Lockett probably never had to worry about where his next meal came from or whether he would have to pick up his father from the local bar.

Elyse had to remind herself why she was there. She mustn't take her eye off the prize, despite Julian's charms.

All she had to do was to string him along until she got enough info to bring down his father.

Easy, right?

"Elyse, are you okay?" Julian asked, breaking into her thoughts.

"Hmm?"

"Seems I lost you there for a minute."

"I'm sorry, it must be the effect you're having on me," she said with a broad grin, attempting to flirt.

Julian shook his head. "No, I don't think so. You were deep in thought about something that was troubling you."

"After one date you think you know me?"

"No, but I'd like to, Elyse. You don't have to keep me at a distance."

Was that was she was doing? If so, a man like Julian would quickly become bored if she didn't keep him engaged.

"I'm sorry." She gave a hesitant smile. "I wasn't aware I was doing that. I appreciate you went through such an effort to find me. It's very flattering."

"Is that all?"

"What more do you want?"

Julian was prevented from answering because the waiter arrived with their salads. Once he'd gone, Julian finally responded. "I'd like to get to know you better and for you not to fight me."

"Oh c'mon, what fun would that be?" she said coyly. She reminded herself she had a role to play. Getting closer to Julian meant access to the Locketts.

"Oh, something tells me we're going to have a lot of fun together."

And they did.

They spent the remainder of the lunch talking about Julian's work as one of the team doctors. And, without revealing names, Elyse shared some of the hilarious stories from her job. Before she knew it, lunch was over and Julian was driving her back to the office.

"I enjoyed lunch, thank you," Elyse said, hazarding a glance in Julian's direction once the car stopped outside her office building. Whenever she did so, she felt a tingle deep in the pit of her stomach and it made her uneasy. He was undeniably gorgeous and sexy, so he probably had the same effect on every woman he encountered. Somehow, she needed to keep her guard up but not push Julian away.

"So did I. I'm hoping we can do it again," Julian replied. "Say Friday night? I could pick you up after work?"

"I don't know…" Elyse swiftly reached for the door, but Julian was faster. When he came around and opened her door, Elyse made to go past him, but Julian stopped her by circling his arm around her neck. "Elyse…" He leaned his forehead against hers. He wanted her and suspected she wanted him, too. "Say yes."

She gave his ego a boost when she looked up at him, stroked his jaw and said, "Yes. You can pick me up on Friday."

Julian grinned and seconds later, he crushed her against his chest and his mouth fastened on hers. Her arms wound around his neck and she opened her lips to the pressure of his searching tongue. He tasted and teased her with his tongue, tracing the line of her mouth before plunging inside and taking up every available space and crevice in a slow and intense exploration so erotically charged Elyse thought she might pass out.

Julian left no doubt as to what he wanted and what he was going to have. Elyse was on fire for him. It was as if a dam had broken. She shifted restlessly against him, every part of her treacherous body pleading for his touch. But just then, he broke the kiss and lifted his head.

"Don't treat me like a stranger, Elyse. Not when we are so much more." Julian swept his fingers across her aching lips and then left her with those words as he sauntered back to the driver's side and the Bugatti Veyron roared to life, leaving Elyse standing on the street.

Why was it that the one man she needed to keep at arm's length, was the only man she'd ever wanted to get this close to?

Six

"It's good to see you, Shantel." Julian leaned past her belly to give his best friend a kiss on the cheek as he came into her foyer after work. The Spelman alum's pregnancy had seemingly blossomed overnight. "Jesus, how far along are you?"

Shantel swatted him on the arm. "Thanks a lot, Julian. Don't you know its bad manners to ask a woman that?"

Julian shrugged. "You're not just *any* woman. You're my best friend and if I can't be real with you, who can I be real with?"

"You have a point." She smiled and led him through the paneled living room and into the kitchen of the new house she and Roman had purchased a few months ago. "Can I get you something to drink?"

"I would love a beer if you have one," Julian replied. He followed Shantel over to the stainless-steel refrigerator and watched her pull out a bottle. She handed it to him and he screwed off the top, taking a generous pull.

"So what brings you by?" Shantel asked, leaning against the massive quartz island in the chef's kitchen.

"I can't just come by and visit?" Julian quipped with a frown.

"Of course you can."

But they both knew that since she'd married Roman, Julian had tempered his visits. His brother was possessive and Julian didn't want to cause friction for his favorite girl. "Good, because I need your advice about a woman I met last week."

"Oh, this sounds interesting." Shantel rubbed her hands together with glee. "I do always love a tale about one of Julian's girls."

"This woman is different," Julian responded. "She's not one of my 'girls.'" He used his hands to make air quotes.

"Really?" Shantel's brow rose. "My feet hurt, so let's have a seat on the sofa." She motioned him to the living room.

Julian sank down beside Shantel onto a plush cream sofa with tons of colorful cushions. "So when am I becoming an uncle?" he inquired.

"Oh no you don't," Shantel said. "Don't go changing the subject. You came over to talk about you, not me. But to answer your question—in a couple of months."

"I can't wait." Time certainly flew, Julian thought. It seemed like just yesterday he was trying to convince Shantel to come hang out at Jazz Tastings, a local jazz joint favored by the locals. And now, she was married and about to be a mother.

"So tell me, what woman has you so twisted you've come to me for advice?" Shantel asked.

"Her name is Elyse Harper," Julian said, leaning back and turning to face her. "I met her on Friday when she switched places with one of my mother's arranged blind dates."

"Switched places? What do you mean?"

Julian explained how Elyse had maneuvered to replace the blind date his mother had chosen for him.

"Sounds like she went through quite a lot of trouble to meet you," Shantel said. "So what's the problem?"

Shantel was right. Elyse had set up their meeting, so why was she acting coy now? "I don't know, you would think *I* had propositioned her."

"Hmm...she's playing hard to get. I would tread carefully with this one, Julian. Sounds like she's playing games. I don't like the fact that her actions say one thing, but her words say another."

"Yeah. I have to admit, for the first time, a woman's got me baffled."

"But interested?"

Julian looked at Shantel. She was right. Although Elyse was playing some sort of head game, he was far from bored, which was what usually happened with the women he encountered. Instead, he was curious to find out more about what mysteries lay beneath the surface.

"Yes, I'm intrigued and excited," Julian said. "So much so, I created a potential PR opportunity for her with the Atlanta Cougars."

"What on earth possessed you to make a dumb move like that?"

"I needed a way in and I figured dangling a carrot like doing PR work for Curtis Jackson might do the trick. Anyway, I'm thinking I'll switch tactics. Elyse is very guarded. It's as if she doesn't want me to get too close."

"Women are like onions, Julian. Sometimes you have to peel back the layers."

Julian chuckled. "I know you're a psychologist and all, but you're laying it on a little thick. I think I need to do something to shake her out of her comfort zone."

"Sounds intriguing. What do you have in mind?"

"You'll see." Julian was thinking something grandiose and so over the top, Elyse would have no choice but to finally let her guard down and let him in.

"You want to gallivant off to Saint Lucia when the season is about to get underway?" Giana looked at Julian as if he'd fallen off his rocker when he stopped by her office late Friday morning. He'd been thinking about it since their lunch on Wednesday and knew the next move he needed to make with Elyse.

"What's wrong with taking a little time off? It's not like there aren't other team doctors to take care of the athletes."

"But you've been trying to prove yourself the last couple of years," Giana replied. "To Daddy. Dr. Walters. Even Roman. Are you sure you want to do this?"

"I thought you agreed with me that I needed to do something drastic to get Elyse's attention?"

"I understand this woman has your nose wide open, Julian," Giana said, "but at the end of the day, the Atlanta Cougars always come first."

"Maybe in your world," Julian replied, "but never in mine. Don't you get tired of spending all your time trying to live your life according to our father's wishes?"

Julian knew he sure was. Everything he'd ever done his entire life had been to please his father, but the last few years Julian had decided to hell with it. Thus his reputation as a ladies' man. In college and medical school, Julian had always been a flirt. It wasn't until his residency that he'd finally come into his own. And when he had, he'd realized that nothing he ever did would live up to the old man's expectations. He wasn't Roman and he would always fall short of the brass ring. So why keep trying and beating himself up about it when the result would always be the same?

"That's not fair, Julian. You know how hard it is being a woman in this business, let alone in this family."

"But you've always been Daddy's girl. You can do no wrong in his eyes."

"And consequently never do right. We're in the same boat, Julian. Don't you see that? It's why I'm trying so hard to get a deal with Wynn Starks. Daddy thinks I can never land the multimillionaire sports drink giant because I'm not one of the boys. But if I do, maybe, just maybe, he'll start to see my business chops and give me a bigger role than just fiddling with advertising and marketing. What he calls 'woman's work.'"

"I want that for you, too, baby girl, but it doesn't mean I have to live by your standards. I've given everything for this company and all I'm doing is taking some time off. Hell, every year Xavier goes off to mope because his dreams of being a quarterback went up in flames. Why can't I take some time off?"

Giana rolled her eyes. "You know Xavier was devastated by his injury. He'd played football his whole life."

"I never said he wasn't. He, too, has been living for Daddy. But I'm doing this for me."

"You're doing this to seduce Elyse. That's all. At least admit exactly what this is about."

Was that all he wanted? Julian didn't think so. For the first time in his life, he wanted to get to know a woman, to find out what made her tick. He wasn't looking for the easiest way into her pants, though he wanted that, too. "And if this was any other woman, you'd be right, Giana. I would admit it was the thrill of the chase and once that was gone, I'd be on to the next. But there's something about Elyse..." His voice trailed off. When he looked up, he saw his sister's dark brown eyes staring into his.

"Wow! So, she's special?"

"Yes. It's what I've been telling you for the last half hour and you're just now getting it?" he asked, humor in his voice.

"Yeah, well I can be a bit slow on the uptake at times," Giana said with a smile. "So what do you need from me?"

"Cover for me. I'm going to use the family jet to take her to Saint Lucia."

Her eyes grew large. "You're really going all out."

"Go big or go home."

After he left Giana's office, Julian put his plan into motion. Now all he had to do was to pick up his lady and head to the tropical paradise. He just hoped Elyse wouldn't give him too much flack. He didn't want to go all caveman and throw her over his shoulder to take her with him.

Elyse tried to temporarily put Julian Lockett out of her mind until later that afternoon when they were due to meet, but as much as she attempted to push him to the far recesses, the more he kept showing up in her daydreams. He exuded an animal magnetism few women could ignore, including herself. Today she even found herself staring off into space wondering what it would be like if she were to see Julian again.

"Earth to Elyse," Andrea teased her.

Elyse blinked several times and found Andrea standing beside her cubicle. "I'm sorry, what were you saying?"

"What's got you so out of sorts?" Andrea inquired. "Or should I say who? Is it Julian Lockett? You never did tell me how your lunch date went the other day."

Elyse hadn't because she was trying not to dwell on him too much. She tried to act as if she didn't know what was keeping her up nights, but deep down she knew. She was attracted to Julian, and her rebellious body betrayed her every time she came within a few feet of him. "It was fine, nothing special." Elyse lied through her teeth.

"Oh, it was nothing, was it?" Andrea grinned from ear to ear as if she was in on a joke Elyse didn't know the punch line to.

"What's so funny?"

Andrea shrugged. "Oh, I'm sure it was nothing because why else would Julian Lockett be walking toward us right this moment?"

Swiveling around in her chair, she learned Andrea was on the money because the handsome Lothario was walking with confidence toward her. She'd forgotten she agreed to meet with him after work.

Julian was a man supremely comfortable in his own skin. Every female eye in the open-plan office was staring at him, but he seemed oblivious to the attention, as if accustomed to receiving it on a regular basis.

Julian knew *exactly* the effect he had on women. The dark stubble accentuating his strong jaw and his sinfully perfectly mouth were swoonworthy and, as much as Elyse wanted to dismiss him and glance away, her eyes couldn't resist drinking him in.

He was casually dressed today in dark trousers and navy blue shirt, but he was just as devastating as when he wore a suit.

"Hello, Elyse," Julian said when he arrived at her cubicle. He turned to Andrea. "And you are?"

"Andrea Stevens," she said, offering her hand, which Julian shook while giving Elyse a wink at the same time.

"Pleasure to meet you. Would you mind if I stole your friend away for a private word?"

"Of course not." Andrea beamed a smile at Julian before quickly scuttling off.

Elyse glanced down at her watch. "I didn't realize it was so late."

"Do you need more time?" He smiled warmly at her.

"No, I was just finishing up, give me a moment." Elyse shut down her computer and reached inside her drawer for her purse.

He motioned for her to precede him and as she did

caught several coworkers watching them. "I could have met you outside."

"I needed to come in," Julian said as they walked down the hall side by side. He didn't explain why until they were at the elevator bank.

"That's very cryptic. Is this about Curtis? Because if so, I'm eager to meet him. He's something of an enigma in this town where everyone wants to be seen. He plays it close to the vest, which has the media wondering if he has some of sort of secret to hide."

"That's because there are no skeletons in his closet. Mr. Jackson has kept a close eye on his son. But that's not why I came. I was discussing with Pierre the possibility of you meeting Curtis while he's taking a short break between preseason and the start of our new season's games. He said you should be able to get away for a while."

"That was awfully heavy-handed. Don't you think you should have spoken with me first?"

"You're right, I'm sorry."

The elevator dinged and they both stepped aside to allow some of her coworkers to pass before entering the car. When they did, it was just the two of them, and Elyse's stomach trembled with anticipation. She covered her unease by filling the silence with chatter.

"That's a first. Do you ever look before you leap?"

Julian grinned. "I go with my gut and I'm hoping in this instance it hasn't led me wrong."

"That depends on what you have in store. Where are we going?"

"It's a surprise."

The elevator chimed and the doors opened to the lobby. Julian guided Elyse by the small of her back toward a limousine waiting by the curb. Was this how the other half lived, she wondered, with limos at their disposal?

Elyse climbed inside and was immediately struck with

the sleek, modern interior. She sank into the lush leather seats and sat as rigid as she could, especially when Julian slid in beside her, filling the small space with his magnetic presence.

Mustering her courage, Elyse swallowed and turned to him. "So, are you going to tell me what this is about now?"

Julian ignored her by reaching for the ice bucket she hadn't noticed in the center console and producing a bottle of Dom Pérignon. He uncorked it with ease and poured each of them a flute before handing her one.

"Cheers." He lifted his glass and she did the same, eyeing him warily as she took a sip.

"Limo, champagne, what's next, Julian?"

"Wouldn't you like to know?"

"I would, actually," Elyse said, looking him square in the eye.

"Once I mentioned you meeting a big fish like Curtis, Pierre was only too happy to agree to give you some time off to meet with him."

Her eyes narrowed. "Time off? Why do I have a feeling I won't be meeting Curtis just yet?"

"You will," Julian affirmed. "But first, I thought we could spend some time getting to know each other. Maybe take a little vacation."

"I can't just take a vacation," Elyse responded curtly. "I have a job to do and obligations." Who would look after her father if she was off gallivanting *with* Julian? This was disrupting all her plans to get revenge on his father. "I know that might be hard to understand for someone like you who was born with a silver spoon in your mouth."

"Ouch, I'm wounded by how little you think of me," Julian replied, touching his chest. "So tell me, Elyse, what made you decide to take my date's place and meet me if it wasn't for us to get to know each other better?"

Bam. Score one for Julian.

He was calling her out on the mixed signals she was giving him. She hadn't really thought her actions through when she'd decided to take the place of his original date. In the beginning, she'd only seen him as a means to an end, but now Elyse was finding she rather liked Julian, which complicated getting justice for her father. But if she didn't go with him now, she might not have another chance of getting this close to a Lockett.

"Well?" Julian had settled himself against the back seat, his arm casually across the top, and was watching her expectantly.

"I... I..." Elyse began, but words didn't come. She would have to switch tactics quickly if she didn't want to lose her chance to get closer to the Locketts. If she agreed and went on this getaway with Julian, who knew what sort of secrets might spill out when he was relaxed? Of course, she would have to let down her guard as well, which meant letting Julian get closer and exploring the attraction between them. But Elyse felt like she could trust him, based on the short time they'd spent together and the research she'd done, which hadn't revealed any skeletons in Julian's closet other than him being a ladies' man.

She was willing to risk her heart if it meant getting the dirt on Josiah Lockett. "I'm sorry if I've confused you, it wasn't my intention."

"Well, let me be clear about my intentions," Julian said. "I want you and I'd like you to give us the next week to explore the attraction between us without any artifice. No games. Just be straight up with me and I'll do the same. Can you do that?"

Elyse felt outmatched and outsmarted, and all she could do was give in. "Yes. Yes, I can, but first I'm going to need to pack."

Seven

Julian watched Elyse's eyes gleam with satisfaction when the limo stopped on the tarmac in front of a jet emblazoned with the Atlanta Cougars' logo. The jet was one of his father's prized possessions, and Julian was about to take it off his hands for several hours. He would send the jet back in case it was needed; it was scheduled to return within the week to scoop them back up.

While his chauffeur dealt with their luggage, Julian helped Elyse up the ramp steps into the lush interior with its two large reclining chairs and larger sofa. He noticed Elyse eye the chairs, but she instead went for the sofa. He did the same. Sitting beside her, he caught a whiff of the tantalizingly fruity scent of her perfume. She smelled of lilacs and peaches.

The scent aroused him. But Julian reminded himself that bedding Elyse wasn't the sole reason for his grandiose gesture. He wanted to get to know her without any distractions and without her running away. Now that he'd found her, he had no intention of letting her slip through his fingers.

"So where are we going?" Elyse asked after the pilot had come to give them the standard flight instructions and then returned to the flight cabin.

"Saint Lucia," Julian replied. "It will take about five hours to get there, and I promise, when we do, you'll like it. A decade ago, I visited the island. The people were so warm and friendly, I've been going back ever since."

"Then I look forward to seeing it through your eyes," Elyse responded, looking through the window as the jet taxied down the runway.

Julian cast Elyse a lingering glance. He was thankful she had agreed to his over-the-top fantasy vacation because he was ready to explore the attraction between them. She looked stunning with her chic haircut and just a dab of eyeliner and mascara. She was wearing a sleek designer dress that hugged her curvy bottom.

Julian spent the remainder of the flight regaling Elyse with tales of his youthful follies on the Caribbean island, which included an attempt at surfing that had been an epic failure. And he would tell the story again and again if each time it produced the delicious sound of Elyse's laughter. She was relaxed and carefree, which was exactly what he wanted.

Once the jet landed, a convertible was waiting for them at the private hangar. After their luggage was loaded, Julian hopped in and drove them through the beautiful shoreline hills to a luxury one-story villa he had procured for the week. When they parked, Julian hurried to help Elyse out of the car.

The front door opened and the chef/housekeeper he'd arranged to prepare the villa and keep it well stocked was there to greet them. "Welcome to Saint Lucia. Can I help you with your luggage?"

"Don't worry, I'll get it later," Julian replied with a grin. Ignoring the older woman's shocked expression, he asked, "Are those the keys?" He nodded at the key ring in her hand.

"Oh yes," she said, handing them to Julian. "And I've stocked the refrigerator as you requested."

"Excellent. We'll see you tomorrow, then." Julian dismissed her and immediately grabbed Elyse's hand and ushered her inside. "C'mon, let me show you the place."

"Wait!" She tugged her arm away. "I'd like to get changed first."

A devilish grin spread across his lips. "Clothing is optional."

"Like hell it is."

"I have it covered." He walked forward, leaving Elyse no choice but to follow.

Her shocked gasp was enough to make him stop and turn around. And suddenly he could see the world through her eyes where the sliding-glass doors had been opened to the amazing sunset beyond the infinity swimming pool.

"Julian!" Elyse said, walking onto the terrace and taking in the ocean view. "This place is beautiful!"

In Julian's mind, nothing was more beautiful than Elyse and, once given the chance, he'd show her exactly how much he appreciated that beauty.

Elyse was completed overwhelmed by the grandeur of the expansive views of the Caribbean and bay framed by the hills surrounding the home. Inside the villa, the open-concept kitchen and dining area could easily seat an entire family. The spacious living room was equipped with a large TV and sumptuous furnishings that were much more expensively elegant than anything in her tiny apartment.

Julian toured her around the villa, which boasted four bedrooms with en suite bathrooms and private balconies, but the most exquisite room was the master bedroom. She blushed when she saw the king-size bed with its cozy bedding and imagined her and Julian tangled in the sheets and plush pillows as he made love to her. And she wanted to, but she was also conflicted. If she went to bed with Julian and explored this mutual attraction, it would be sleeping with the enemy. Yet, Julian didn't feel like one. It was disconcerting, so she rushed off to the bathroom, which featured a stand-alone bathtub beside a full glass wall with a view of the ocean.

"What do you think?" Julian asked as she stood flabbergasted at the separate walk-in rainfall shower. "Do you think you could get used to this for a week?"

Elyse tried not to be gauche. "I think so."

He inclined his head. "Follow me."

He led her to double doors inside the bathroom and opened them with a flourish to reveal an array of colorful clothes, from stylish dresses, to pants, tops and swimwear. Elyse walked over to the rack and glanced down at several of the tags. They were all her size.

"I guessed your size. Was I right?"

"This wasn't necessary." And it wasn't, since she'd had the forethought to go back to her place to pack. But was she surprised? Given his reputation with the ladies, of course, he knew the shape of a woman's body. Elyse told herself not to be jealous about any of those women because they weren't here with him now. She was. He'd whisked her off to a Caribbean island to woo and seduce her.

Would she let him? *How far would she go to get close to Julian and gain access to his father and the Atlanta Cougars?*

Later that evening, after a long, hot shower, Elyse donned one of the light sundresses in the closet chock-full of clothes and joined Julian out on deck where a table for two had been set up. The night was warm but not humid, and Elyse had to admit the villa and the view was breathtaking.

"You're looking lovely," Julian commented when she gave a slight twirl upon her arrival.

"So are you." Elyse didn't know where the comment came from, but she couldn't help it. He was dressed in linen trousers and a white shirt with the first few buttons casually undone. He looked and smelled divine. He must have showered in one of the other rooms because he hadn't used the master bath.

"Thank you. Would you like an aperitif before dinner?"

"I'd love one."

"There's wine and some mixers for a cocktail."

"Since we're in the islands, I'll have a rum and Coke."

"Coming right up."

While Julian went back inside to make the drinks, Elyse remained on the terrace, trying to figure out her own mind. In the shower, she'd accepted the position she now found herself in. She'd wanted to find an in with the Locketts and thought Julian, the weak link, was her ticket into their inner circle. So she'd thrown herself at him. And now Julian wasn't only intrigued by her, he had gone to great lengths to secure time alone with her.

Elyse honestly didn't know what to do next. She had never met anyone like Julian. This impromptu trip had showed her she was in way over her head. Yet she couldn't blame Julian. He'd been honest with her. *He wanted her.* And that was a heady feeling, knowing a man like Julian, who could have any woman he wanted, wanted her. Did he expect her to go bed with him tonight? And what would happen after? She wasn't Julian's usual type. She wasn't superrich or an actress or model. So why her? If he seduced her, he'd see through her bravado and quickly learn that she didn't have much experience in the bedroom.

She was debating her quandary when Julian returned with their drinks.

"For you, my lady."

He handed her the tumbler and she noticed he'd opted for a bottle of beer. He didn't strike her as the beer type, but then again, she hardly knew him. Perhaps it was time she changed that. She had to stop making this solely about what Julian wanted, but about what she wanted, too. "Thank you, but do you always travel like this?"

"Like what?"

"Like this?" Elyse swept her hand around. "I mean most people usually stay at a hotel not a private luxury villa."

"Elyse, I can't help that I grew up with money and can afford a place like this," Julian responded. "So, if you're waiting for me to apologize, you'll be waiting a long time. I enjoy life and what I've been given, but that doesn't mean I haven't used that same money for good and to help others."

"You have?"

"Don't sound so shocked. The Lockett Foundation has a done a lot for the community, and my mother was an instrumental part of establishing the charitable foundation. We are also a huge donor to the Salvation Army. But that's not all. We support the community through the Boys & Girls Clubs of America. Then there's the Breast Cancer and Autism Speaks organizations that we contribute to. And we have youth camps for players and their parents. Did you know we invite our players to participate in a nationwide volunteer effort?"

"What's it called?"

"The Cougars' Huddle. Our players give back to the community by volunteering. But it's not just the team. I donate to all the charities and volunteer when my schedule permits at several medical clinics in underprivileged communities. I want to make sure everyone has access to medical care."

"That's incredible." Though she wasn't surprised Angelique Lockett was the spearhead, she had her doubts that Josiah Lockett was capable of helping others.

"Anyway, enough about me, are you hungry? There's quite a spread in the warmer."

"I'm starved."

"Follow me."

Elyse was surprised to find Julian to be quite adept in the kitchen. In no time at all, he put together their salad and dinner plates, which they took outside to eat.

Julian was great company, as always, or perhaps it was the bottle of wine they'd killed along with their meal. In any event, Elyse found herself relaxing so much, she didn't notice when the atmosphere between them changed from lighthearted to electric. The charge between them was arcing uncontrollably.

Elyse glanced up from her wineglass to find Julian devouring her with his eyes. She whet her lips with her tongue and his look told her time had run out. She felt sensitized. Exposed. Raw. And terrified that he might see the real truth hidden beneath her cool exterior.

Julian rose from his chair, but didn't come for her immediately, as she'd expected. Instead he went to the settee and picked up a remote, and soon the entire terrace was flooded with soft music.

Romantic music.

Elyse's heart began thundering loud in her chest. Could he hear the beat? He moved toward her and offered his hand. Elyse slid her hand in his and that chemistry she'd been feeling all night heightened a notch. It didn't help when Julian banded his strong arms around her, bringing her bosom and pelvis into direct contact with his.

She glanced up at him. Handsome didn't come close to describing his beautiful features. He was sexy as all get-out and her body responded. She imagined his hands wrapped around her, skimming over her naked curves.

Swallowing hard, Elyse raised her eyes to Julian's chest and could see a vee of brown skin and a sprinkling of dark hair. He smelled of spice and soap mixed with an indescribable male scent that spoke to everything female in her. She didn't resist when he raised her chin. She watched the slow descent of his mouth toward her own and waited for the kiss she knew would wreck her.

No woman had ever gazed at Julian with everything in her eyes. He felt that warmth flow through him, filling him, melting away any jadedness he may have had from other women he'd been with. He lowered his head, letting his lips sensuously glide across hers. She needed to let him in. When he felt her mouth move against his, telling him she wanted the kiss as much as he did, only then did the kiss become hungrier, hotter, and harder in the span of a heartbeat.

His hands spanned her waist, drawing her to him, and Elyse rose to meet him. He allowed her to feel every hard inch of him. And he was *hard.* For her. Only for her. Her soft curves pressed against him made Julian feel as if he'd been in a desert searching for water and had found the long sought after oasis.

Elyse was lush and sweet, and so responsive, he lost his head completely as he swept his hands over her body. When he felt no bra beneath the sundress she wore, he closed his hand over one of the sweet mounds of her small breasts. Her nipple hardened, making his own body quicken with lust. He hauled her closer still, deepening the kiss. She moaned against his lips and he pulled her closer until they were hip to hip.

Julian lost all finesse and skill. He wasn't thinking about seduction anymore. He just wanted more—more of her, more of her softness, all of her heat. He wanted everything. And that thought terrified him. He wasn't used to being this out of control for anyone. And hadn't he told himself that Elyse was different? She wasn't just another one of his one-night stands even though he wanted to brand her as his in the most basic way imaginable. He had to treat her with care, not have her up against the wall as he wanted to do.

Slowly, he lifted his head and Elyse looked up at him with passion-glazed eyes. He didn't understand why he was pulling back, any more than she did, but he had to.

Taking a deep breath, Julian took several steps away from Elyse until his back hit the wall and kept him upright. He had to get control of himself.

"Did I do something wrong?" she asked, touching her lips, which were swollen from *his* kisses.

He shook his head, unable to talk. His groin was throbbing, his self-restraint stretched to the breaking point as he refrained from taking Elyse to bed. And take her he could have, despite her keeping him at arm's length. It was clear that she wanted him with equal measure. It was only here, away from everyone, that she'd allowed herself to show it.

"Then what?"

When Julian didn't immediately answer, Elyse ran off the terrace. He heard the slamming of a door, telling him he'd ruined what could have been one hell of an amazing night. On the other hand, if he'd taken Elyse to bed, wouldn't he have lived up to all the worst stereotypical notions she had of him. For her, he wanted to be a better man and, by God, he would be!

Eight

Elyse drifted awake alone not knowing where she was. Sheer drapes allowed sunlight to filter in through the windows. Bolting upright, she looked around the enormous bedroom and remembered she was in one of the guest suites of Julian's villa. She'd come here to Saint Lucia yesterday with Julian after he'd whisked her away from Atlanta. She also remembered the romantic candlelit dinner and the subsequent kiss.

Julian was so perfect. So delicious. So incredibly tempting. A temptation she'd blatantly given herself wholeheartedly to last night only to have him push her away. She couldn't believe she'd let herself get so carried away in the moment. She'd nearly gone to bed with the man. Was she so susceptible to Julian because she'd never felt this way about another man?

Tossing off the covers, Elyse rushed to the bathroom to clear her mind. She emerged a half hour later, after having washed every inch of her body and putting on denim shorts and a cold-shoulder tank. Starving, she went in search of food. She found what she was looking for, or rather *who*, in the kitchen.

Julian was looking sinfully gorgeous in a T-shirt and ripped jeans that showed off his well-built physique. He was the picture of vitality and masculine energy. He was cooking what appeared to be the makings of an omelet. There was a carafe of orange juice on the countertop and coffee had been brewed, which told Elyse he'd been up for a while.

She didn't speak. Instead she made herself at home and found a mug. Once she'd poured herself a cup of coffee and drank liberally, she headed over to where he stood.

"How long have you been up?"

Julian shrugged. "I dunno. It was too beautiful a morning to sleep in and I'm excited to show you Saint Lucia."

So he wasn't upset that she'd run off to bed like some spoiled schoolgirl who hadn't gotten her own way? If he was, Julian didn't act like it. Instead, he slid two perfect omelets onto plates and then skated behind her to the toaster where he plopped in two pieces of bread.

"Thank you for making breakfast. I'm starved," she said as she took a seat in the breakfast nook. The toast popped up and Julian added a slice to each of the plates before bringing hers over.

"For you, madam."

"I wouldn't think you'd know how to cook," Elyse said, tucking into her omelet with gusto.

Julian smiled. "Haven't I told you not to underestimate me, Elyse? You shouldn't judge a book by its cover." He put his plate on the table and sat across from her.

She was beginning to realize how right he was. All her preconceived notions about Julian were just that. He wasn't who she'd thought he was. He was better. "This is delicious," she commented on the spinach and mushroom omelet. "Who taught you how to cook?"

"No one really. I just loved being around my mom and with her being from New Orleans, the kitchen was one of her favorite places. Often I found myself there when my father, Roman and Xavier were outside playing football."

She put down her fork and knife. "So I take it you've never been inclined toward sports?"

Julian shook his head. "Nah, that was always Rome's and Xavier's thing, not mine. I much preferred the arts. Activities my father claimed weren't manly enough. Even though my grades were stellar and I could easily have skipped a grade, he kept pushing me to join sports teams. I hated every minute of them, which is why I always got my butt kicked. But Josiah kept pushing, no matter if I got a broken nose or a dislocated shoulder. It was all part of the game and I had to man up."

Even as he said the words, Elyse could see that, even now, the past still affected Julian because his brow was deeply furrowed. It filled her with unease. Hadn't she heard similar stories about the man from her own father? Josiah was a bully and if he could push people around to get his own way, even his own son, she shouldn't be surprised.

"What happened? How did you stop him?"

"I didn't," Julian said and continued eating his omelet.

She was quiet, waiting for him to continue, and he finally did.

"My father didn't believe that a son he'd sired didn't have an athletic bone in his body. So he put me in lacrosse and soccer next."

"How did you fare in those?"

"I was terrible at lacrosse and a joke at a soccer. I had two left feet, but ask me to go out dancing and I'll show you some moves."

Elyse grinned as she pushed her now empty plate aside. "I can't wait for you to take me out dancing, but I suppose your father didn't like that very much."

"Not at all, and I was glad because finally he left me alone to be *me*. An academic with a penchant for cooking and a love of art, music and Broadway shows."

"A Renaissance man."

Julian bowed. "I suppose I am."

"And your relationship with your father now?"

Julian shrugged, grabbed both their plates and rose. "We're fine."

Elyse stood and followed him. "Fine isn't an answer."

Julian put the plates in the sink and turned to face her. "Why does it matter? We all have drama in our family. Let's take you for example. You've told me nothing about your father or your mother for that matter. So don't push."

He spun around, turned on the taps and began rinsing the dishes and placing them in the dishwasher.

He was right.

She hadn't shared her family history and Elyse wasn't sure she could without revealing too much about her father and their parents' shared past. But she could talk to him about her mother. That much she could give.

"Julian," Elyse said, walking up behind him and touching his arm, "I'm sorry I haven't been open about my family."

He turned to face her, his eyes soft and sympathetic, and Elyse knew she could tell him anything. "I lost my mom when I was very young."

"Elyse, that's terrible. I don't know how you managed at such a young age."

"It was awful." Elyse leaned back against the counter. "She wasn't there to tell me the things a little girl needs to know about the birds and the bees, to help when I got my first period, or to show me how to use makeup. I had to figure that out all on my own."

"What about your father?"

"Losing my mother broke him." Elyse could at least

admit that much. "He never truly recovered from her death and, when I needed guidance, he would tell me to go talk to the school nurse."

"You didn't have a grandma? Aunts? Family? Friends?"

Elyse shook her head. "No one. Can you imagine how lonely it was? I was already an introvert."

"No." He shook his head. "Not you."

"Oh yes." Elyse nodded. "I was terribly shy and it wasn't easy to make friends because, after Mama died, we were always moving around because Daddy was constantly looking for work."

"How did she die, if you don't mind my asking?"

"Breast cancer. She was only thirty-five."

"Jesus!" Julian ran a hand over his curly fade. "So young, and to leave a daughter behind who needed her. And your father?"

"He's alive, but not well," Elyse said. "Throughout the chemo, which back then was quite expensive, he developed a drinking habit, a bad one."

"Which made it difficult for him to find steady work?"

She pointed a finger at him. "You guessed it. I was left to pick up the pieces." She pointed to her chest. "I was a kid myself, helping to keep the two of us afloat."

"What a burden to bear," Julian stated. "Sounds like we both had some struggles, though yours trump mine."

"It isn't about who has the saddest sob story," Elyse said, cupping his cheek. "Because look at who we are now and what we've become despite our past."

Julian smiled and tapped her nose with his index finger. "You, my dear, are absolutely right. So let's leave our pasts right here in this kitchen. And instead, let's go out and have some fun. What do you say?"

"I'm all in."

And she was. Even though Julian had pushed her away

last night and she'd felt rejected, he'd opened up to her today and revealed things she doubted he'd ever told another soul. It felt intimate and Elyse felt closer to Julian than she would have if they'd gone to bed together. Elyse was finding herself becoming smitten with Julian Lockett.

"Are you ready for your first adventure in Saint Lucia?" Julian asked.

"Absolutely. What are you thinking?" Elyse asked.

"How are your riding skills?"

"On what?"

Julian grinned mischievously. "On horses."

"I haven't ridden in years, but let's do it!"

After changing and putting on a bikini underneath her clothes, Elyse joined Julian for an hour trip to a ranch where they were placed on two beautiful horses. A palomino for her and a saddlebred for him. Their guide took them on a tour in the Roseau Valley where they stopped at a local banana plantation to rest and to indulge in the delicious fruit. Elyse had no idea the island had over a hundred different varieties. Eventually, their trip led to one of Saint Lucia's sandy beaches and they took the horses in for a swim in the sea.

"That was fantastic," Elyse said when they returned from their trek and decided to take a dip in the villa's pool. It was so hot, Elyse quickly whipped off her tank and shorts, eager to get in. She'd forgotten the bikini was itty-bitty until she turned and noticed Julian was staring at her openmouthed.

Her mouth suddenly became dry. Nervous over the naked hunger in his eyes, she dived into the pool.

When she came back up for air, she found Julian had joined her. His chest was bare and he wore swim shorts as he headed toward her. She quickly dived underneath the water, swimming in circles around him. She thought she'd been quite good at evading him, but when she came up again, Julian was waiting for her.

"Are you running from me, Elyse?"

She shook her head. "Why would I run?" Other than he'd made a fool out of her last night and she wasn't interested in a repeat.

He pushed back her wet slick hair. "I don't know, why would you?" And then he was kissing her with a savage intensity that took her breath away. She felt her knees weaken, but she needn't worry because Julian kept her upright while he lingered, taking his time to coax a response from her. Every part of her mouth burned with fire and need, so when his hands explored the soft lines of her back, her waist and her hips, Elyse instinctively arched into him. When his palm brushed her breasts, she quivered.

Her eyes flickered open and she saw Julian watching her. She gasped when he pushed the flimsy material of her bikini top aside and his lips brushed her nipples, first one and then the other. "Julian…"

"Yes?" Her chest heaved as he traced and licked the brown peaks, causing them to pebble.

Elyse wanted more. She wanted him to suck them into his mouth, but she didn't want to go down this path and have him reject her again despite the evidence of his arousal brushing against her thigh. Besides, their physical relationship confused her. She'd met Julian with a purpose, which had all but been forgotten with the mounting attraction between them. She needed breathing room.

Slowly, she stepped away from him. "I'm… I'm going to get showered." When Julian stepped toward her, she added, "Alone. I'll see you at dinner."

Once in the shower, Elyse stripped and let the water cool her fevered flesh. She was playing a dangerous game with a man for whom seduction came easily. *Was she fighting a losing battle?*

* * *

Julian was surprised when Elyse pulled away. She'd seemed to like his ministrations, to like his mouth on her. At times she wanted him and at others she ran. Didn't she know they were on a precipice and there was no denying how it was going to end? He and Elyse would become lovers, of that there was no doubt, but he would go slowly.

And so he showered and dressed and, after some recommendations from their housekeeper, who'd come to tidy up the villa, Julian took Elyse out to a restaurant. They sampled several local delicacies that erupted with exotic flavor, washing it all down with a bottle of white wine. The place wasn't upscale or five-star, but then again, he preferred to take the road less traveled. Elyse, for one, was certainly different from the other more sophisticated and worldly women he usually dated. She had a certain innocence and mystery, and Julian was curious to find out more.

And so, as they sat at their small table for two overlooking the Pitons, Julian was enraptured. She was a sexy bombshell in a bold print halter dress with a deep side slit showing off her incredible legs. She had on turquoise heeled sandals that her polished toes peeked out of. Julian was going to have do everything in his power to rein in his attraction and take things slow.

"Julian?"

"Hmm…"

"The waitress is asking if you want dessert."

Dessert.

He eyed Elyse. If he had his choice, *she* would definitely be on the menu, but he settled for the mango mousse while Elyse went with the white chocolate parfait.

"Dinner was incredible," Elyse commented. "That passion-fruit glazed shrimp was to die for."

"I'm glad you enjoyed it. Saint Lucia is a hidden gem not

many people know about, but there's lots to see if you're up for it."

"Like what?"

Julian smirked. She'd taken the bait. "The Sulphur Springs for one."

"What's that?"

"It's the only drive-in volcano in the world."

At her awed shock, Julian continued. "It hasn't erupted in over two hundred years, but the best part of the volcano is the ability to dive into the mud baths. It's known to detoxify the body of impurities and has been known to heal certain ailments."

"Is that so? Well, I'm willing to give it a try."

"Really?"

Julian was surprised. Not many of the women he dated would ever be caught dead in a mud bath, ruining their hair and makeup.

He must have voiced his thoughts aloud because Elyse commented, "Then you've clearly been dating the wrong women."

"You might be right on that score," Julian said, lifting his wineglass to his lips. "You just might be right."

After dessert, they retired to the lounge where they cuddled together on a plush love seat to listen to one of the island's foremost jazz musicians. The mood was light and fun. Julian even convinced Elyse to take to the floor, but it was merely an excuse so he could once again wrap his arms around her as he'd done last night. Except this time, he wouldn't ravage her on the dance floor.

At least, not yet.

He swayed with Elyse in his arms and when she looked up at him, his entire body lit up like a sunrise at dawn. Sexual awareness flooded through him and he pulled her closer, a bit harder than he intended, but Elyse didn't seem to mind. So Julian splayed his hands even wider across her hips just above her behind. There was desire in her eyes when she looked at him and she didn't look away.

He lifted a hand, allowing his fingers to play with her stylish short hair, before tipping her head back and lifting her face to meet his, crushing that deliciously pink mouth under his. And just like dry kindling to a match, he went up in flames. He loved how open and responsive Elyse was to his kiss, how she moved closer, seeking contact as he explored the very depths of her.

The deeper the kiss got, the hungrier Julian became. Elyse ignited his senses like no other woman had. He could feel her breasts become fuller against his chest and he ached to explore every inch of her. He would have to stop this now or once again he'd lose his head. His hands still in her hair as he tugged her back from him. She opened her eyes and it took a second for those dark brown orbs to focus on him.

"We should go."

She looked serious, but nodded.

Julian didn't glance around to see if anyone had noticed their spectacle. Instead, he took her hand and led her off the dance floor.

Elyse was like a drug and when they'd been dancing, he'd found her increasingly hard to ignore. When his mouth had moved over hers, heat and madness had entered his head, his body. *Need.* It was all he could think about with her cleaved so tightly to him. He been about to combust.

The time had come to put them both out of their misery.

Nine

Elyse could hardly breathe as she walked with Julian out of the restaurant. The dark fire of his gaze had worked its way through her and she knew that tonight there was no turning back. She would be daring and go forward with whatever wicked plans Julian had in store for her. She'd tried unsuccessfully to steel herself against Julian's charms but the truth of the matter was that she was helpless when it came to him. The closer they got to the car, the more Elyse felt the deep pulse between her legs.

She was hot and needy.

And only Julian could assuage the ache.

The ride was thankfully short because the aching hunger inside her was growing more and more intense with each passing second. She couldn't stop from imagining him cupping her breasts and gripping her bottom as he pulled her beneath him and made her his, so much so, that several times she shifted in her seat. *Could he sense her discom-*

fort? Elyse was relieved when they both quickly disembarked at the villa, forgoing formalities.

That's how eager they were for one another. The house was dimly lit by the moonlight and Julian matched her quick stride as she made for the master bedroom.

Once there, Julian lit several candles, filling the room with a soft hazel glow. But then Julian stepped out of the shadows and she was able to see his face fully in the candlelight. Raw, unadulterated lust etched his beautiful features. "I want you, Elyse."

He clearly felt the same crashing hunger she did and, for the first time, Elyse wasn't afraid of what came next. She wanted him to touch her. "I want you, too. Make love to me, Julian."

He reached for her, sinking his fingers into her hair and pulling her closer. Then his mouth fastened onto hers, tongue searching. He left no doubt as to what it was he wanted and what he was going to have. He caught her against him and walked her back until he brought them down onto the bed together. They kissed and touched like they were starved. And Elyse *was* starved. She hadn't wanted anyone as badly as she wanted Julian.

"I want to touch you all over." His tone had a sexy rough edge that made her quiver.

"Please..." was the only word she could manage to say, and Julian did what she couldn't verbalize. He skimmed his wicked hands along the length of her body, moving his way down until he wrenched the skirt of her dress up to her waist. Then his fingers sought her out.

He lifted his head and his eyes were glazed with desire. "You're wet for me."

Elyse nodded and shifted restlessly underneath him, rocking her hips up to him. He bent down and kissed her, again and again. Her nipples became tight, begging to be taken into his mouth. As if she voiced her words out loud,

Julian reached behind her and untied the halter of her dress, baring her breasts to his avid gaze.

He broke their kiss to pay homage to her breasts. He teased them first between his thumbs before taking one aching nipple into his mouth. Elyse arched up to meet him. His mouth was both a torture and a treat, and she thrilled to every last sensation that his wicked mouth brought her, but he didn't stop there.

He continued tantalizing her by moving south and kissing her belly. He tasted the tender flesh of her inner thigh and Elyse heard herself moan because she could only *feel.* She was diving full-speed into the ocean with no safety net. Was she ready for *this*?

Julian glanced up at her and she realized she was gripping his shoulders. "I can't wait to taste you," he said in that sexy voice of his. Those were the last words she heard because he was snatching her panties down her legs and licking deep into the center of her need.

Elyse bucked against him as his scalding mouth sucked deep. She thought she would die from pleasure, but instead he made her scream. His clever tongue teased, swirled and stroked that particularly sensitive spot. Julian used his shoulders to stretch her thighs wide and then replaced his mouth with a finger, using it to make her even wetter.

She cried out for deliverance because he was eating her alive and she was letting him. It was too much. She tried to close her legs, but he didn't let her; instead his supple finger seemed to find the very depths of her body. The ache inside her intensified tenfold.

Her breathing became choppy, especially when he used his tongue and fingers together to torment her. It was so *intense.* And when Julian added a second finger to the first and began to stroke deep inside her, all Elyse could do was move. Move to the rhythm of his hand until she was thrusting wildly against him. She arched, pulsed and shook, her head falling backward against the bed. The entire experience was so intoxicating. She'd never met a man like Julian that she'd wanted to be this intimate with and she suspected she never would.

He had ruined her for any other man.

Julian couldn't believe how incredibly responsive Elyse was. She'd come on his hands and mouth. He just knew he wanted more. He lifted the fingers he'd had inside her and slowly licked them clean.

Elyse gasped and turned bright red.

"Look at me," he ordered. Slowly, she opened her eyes and held his gaze while breathing heavily. "I want you desperately, Elyse, and that was just the appetizer. An amuse-bouche, if you will. It will be even better when I'm inside you." He stood and began shrugging out of his clothes.

Although he was eager, he would take his time with Elyse and savor her. Savor this moment and the softness of her bare flesh against his hardness. She had a beautiful body. If he was a sculptor, he would showcase her pert breasts, the curve of her hips and slightly rounded buttocks. But now, he wanted Elyse in his arms. He wanted to taste every part of her. He'd already sampled, but he wanted more.

He touched every part of her he could with his hands and his mouth, leaving no part ignored. Then he flipped her over onto her stomach and did the same thing all over again. When he slipped his fingers between her legs, while sucking on the back of her neck, she shattered and fell apart against the pillows. There was a fire burning between them and Julian doubted it would be extinguished anytime soon.

He gave her a moment to recover while he tore open an aluminum condom packet and put on the protection. Then he was turning Elyse over. Her eyes were glazed with passion. She was ready for him. He stretched her arms over her head and finally settled himself between her thighs. He shuddered because the moment felt right. He hadn't rushed into sex like he did with most women. He'd gotten to know her. Was that what made this *feel* different?

Slowly, ever so slowly, he pressed forward into her wet entrance. Elyse moaned from underneath him as she took him in. She was so tight, but he pushed deep until he was fully seated inside her. Her body gripped him like a glove and Julian retreated for a moment only to surge forward again even harder. She cried out, so he did it again. Then he started a slow, inexorable rhythm as he worked himself inside her, in and out. And so it went. They were heat, breath and sweat all rolled into one.

When Elyse spread her fingers over his shoulders, pressing deep, he hit her with another powerful thrust. Her breath hissed and when he tipped his head back, he saw that she was in the throes of ecstasy.

He shouted her name. Then he bent his head to take her mouth again as he revealed his prowess and mastery in multitasking.

Her legs locked onto the back of his as he thrust inside her. She screamed. Shudders began to quake through her and her body contracted around him, squeezing until Julian felt himself pumping hard and fast in a crazy rhythm. He groaned as his orgasm exploded into fire and fury and then sprawled on top of her, breathing hard.

Elyse ran her hands idly down his back and Julian realized he was crushing her. He quickly rolled onto his side and took several steady breaths. Moments later, he looked over to see that Elyse had already fallen asleep.

Julian grinned. He'd worn her out. He would let her sleep a while but then he intended to have her again and again.

A few hours later, Elyse awoke feeling disoriented but gloriously happy. From what she could tell, it was still dark out, which meant she hadn't been asleep for long. She glanced beside her to find Julian sleeping soundly.

A delicious shiver went through her. Sex with Julian had been *everything.* She could still feel his hands all over her, feel him buried inside her.

He was only the third man she'd ever been with. She wasn't a cold fish. The notion that there was something wrong with her had always plagued her. When in fact, she'd just never met the right man to spark her flame. Julian had. She'd never felt more beautiful, more perfect, than she did when she was in his arms.

And now she wanted his touch, craved it, like an addict craved her next fix.

Julian stirred beside her and his eyes popped open. His hand darted out from beneath the sheets and cupped one side of her face, then his thumb began stroking along her lower lip with slow, measured strokes. "Good morning."

"I'm not sure it's quite morning yet," Elyse said, glancing through the sheers and still seeing moonlight.

He grinned devilishly. "Well, then, that means the night is not over yet."

He pulled her to him and his mouth descended inexorably towards hers. Her body fizzed like a firecracker and then he was kissing her again. She opened her mouth to him and his tongue darted inside, stroking against hers. A low, deep groan sounded in his throat and Elyse was thrilled to know she had a sensual power over Julian just like he had over her.

And so they kissed, lingeringly, taking their time to reacquaint themselves with each other. His lips left hers to move down to just below her ear. She shivered and her nipples tightened. That's how desperate she was to feel his touch. Her willpower had completely deserted her over this man. Need fired through her body. She couldn't ignore the throb pulsing at the apex of her thighs. The heat between them was like a forest fire. She might come to regret her decision later, but for now she would revel in him.

Elyse slid her hands across his back and then forward so she could explore the hard plans and ridges of his muscular, hair-roughened chest. He allowed her to use her hands and mouth to rove over him. She felt the hard length of him against her thigh. Clearly, his desire for her had been renewed and so, somewhat shyly, she reached for a foil packet on the nightstand and protected them both before straddling him.

Julian grinned up at her. "Take what you want, baby."

She'd never been this bold before but something told Elyse she could be with Julian. She felt safe with him, and it was strange, given that she had a hidden agenda in meeting him. But none of that mattered. She lowered herself onto him, inch by delicious inch. When he was seated deep inside her, filling her, her mouth came down and sealed his in an incendiary kiss that set her pulse racing. She loved the playful dance of their tongues meeting and the primal call of her body physically connected with his. She began to move, finding a rhythm all her own. Deeper, harder, faster, longer.

She bucked against him, offering him her breasts as her legs tightened around his waist. Julian accepted and suckled them with his mouth, teeth and tongue until pleasure was streaming through her and she cried out his name as she found her release. "Julian!"

He captured her lips while she came against him, his tongue sliding in and out, mimicking their bodies until, eventually, his own release came and he groaned, shuddering underneath her.

Ten

They dozed, and when they eventually awoke, Julian pulled her to her feet and led her to the large bathroom where they shared an incredibly sensual shower.

"We have to leave the bedroom," Julian stated once he'd turned off the taps and handed her a big fluffy towel and began drying himself. "Otherwise I fear I'll do nothing but make love to you all day."

"Would that be such a bad thing?" As soon as she uttered the words, she blushed.

Julian loved that she could still be shy with him after everything they'd done. "No, but I would like you to see more of the city."

"All right. Let's do it."

After quickly getting dressed, Julian in shorts and a T-shirt and Elyse in a floral sundress, they hopped in the convertible. He took her to a downtown craft market in Castries to buy bags of spices and to shop for souvenirs. They ended up with several bags of goodies to take back home to their families. Julian was surprised, however, that most belonged to him. Elyse's shopping list was small. When he questioned her about it, she clammed up.

"I'm not like you, Julian," Elyse said. "I don't have a big family. I told you there's only me and my dad. I was so busy taking care of him that I missed out on the chance to make my own friends."

"I know."

She rolled her eyes. "For Christ's sake, don't look at me like that. I'm not totally alone. There's my friend Andrea."

Julian nodded. He understood she'd lost her mother, but there was something about the look in her eye that told him there was more. Elyse hadn't told him the full story. He didn't want to push her; he just hoped that in time she would feel comfortable enough to share all her secrets with him.

To help lighten the mood, Julian drove them to one of the rum distilleries on the island. They toured the facility, following each step of the rum-making process from the raw materials of molasses and sugarcane to fermentation and distillation. They learned how rum was aged in the barrel before going to the mixer tanks where a special team of master blenders created a variety of flavors.

His favorite part was the rum tasting and watching Elyse get tipsy. There was a plethora of types from Chairman's Reserve to gold and white rums. He noticed Elyse preferred the rum liqueurs and had a healthy sampling of the coconut and banana flavors as well as the nutty rum cream.

Once they were back in the car, Elyse laid her head back in the passenger seat and sighed. "That was really good, but I need to eat something. Let's get dinner."

They ended up in a tiny fishing village between Soufriere and Castries, enjoying grilled fish, crawfish, along with roasted corn and bakes.

"What are bakes?" Elyse inquired.

Julian laughed. "It's a biscuit. Try it, you might like it."

And she did, along with the rest of the food on offer. Julian liked that Elyse could relax and enjoy the simple things in life.

"What?" Elyse asked.

"Nothing." Julian responded, realizing he was staring as she sucked on a crawfish. "I'm just happy to see you eating, that you still have an appetite after the rum tasting."

Elyse put down the crawfish she'd be eating and licked her fingers. "This food is delicious but I suppose the model stick figures you're used to dating don't eat."

Julian released a loud belly laugh. Elyse had that effect on him. She said exactly what was on her mind. "Yeah, they don't usually eat much, and they're missing out," Julian said, reaching for a crawfish himself.

They ended the evening back at the villa in the Jacuzzi where Julian took her with a fierce hunger that hadn't been assuaged after they made love last night. Every kiss, every touch, every moment, was imprinted on his brain. He usually never stayed with women long, had never envisaged his future with anyone. And yet…with Elyse, every time she looked at him, something tugged deep in his chest. He didn't know what it was. All he did know was that he didn't want it to end.

Julian had been amazing the entire week. He'd showed her everything Saint Lucia had to offer. One day he'd taken her to Marigot Bay and chartered a catamaran. The cruise along the magnificent coast had been thrilling, as had the snorkeling in the blue waters. It hadn't ended there. Another day he'd hired a guide and they'd climbed to the top of Gros Piton. The view had been breathtaking, but getting there had been half the fun.

When she'd tired during the hike, Julian had lifted her onto his back and climbed higher and higher until they'd reached the top. Afterward, he'd taken them to a resort on

Sugar Beach where they enjoyed the remainder of the day at the Rainforest Spa.

"This is incredible," Elyse had stated when they were led into one of the seven tree house treatment rooms. "Where did you find this place?"

Julian had simply shrugged and Elyse, realizing it had been with another woman, remained mum. She'd never been such a place as this. She could never have afforded anything like it on her salary. Maybe she could one day, if she received the restitution her father deserved. But it would require her betraying Julian.

The thought hadn't sat well, so Elyse had pushed the negativity aside and lowered herself into the earthen steam dome known as a temascal. The attendant had led them to a double cabana for an organic coconut oil couples massage that was to die for. Elyse couldn't help but think she could get used to a life like this. That thought had stayed with her long after they'd left the spa and she'd spent another night in Julian's arms.

Their last day was another wonder because Julian finally took her to Sulphur Springs, known for its famous mud baths.

"You don't honestly expect me to get in that," Elyse said after she'd donned her bikini and met Julian at the entrance. She had thought she could do it, but hadn't been so sure once she'd eyed the thick mud pool.

"Trust me, you'll love it," he said.

When she hesitated, he asked, "You do trust me, don't you?"

Could she trust the son of Josiah Lockett? She'd certainly trusted him with her body the entire week.

"Of course." She placed her hand in his and together they descended into the warm gray mud. Julian instantly sank into it, but Elyse was wary to let go. So Julian came toward her with mud packed in his hand and lathered it all over her. He did it again and again, the action so sensual, Elyse wondered why the steam hadn't rolled off her.

As was tradition, they washed themselves under a nearby waterfall and drank from a fresh coconut a man had cut with a machete.

The day had been incredibly fun, even if it was their last on the island.

She must have looked wistful because Julian said, "We can have more times like this."

Elyse doubted it. Not if she continued on her quest to destroy his father. Instead, she smiled and they dressed and got back into the convertible to head for the villa. She wanted to lose herself in Julian, to forget what was waiting for them when they returned to Atlanta.

Julian didn't know what had gotten into Elyse. When they'd arrived at the villa, she'd all but jumped him. Not that he was complaining. He was happy that she'd learned to let go and accept the passion between them, which was as strong as ever.

Later, after making love, they stood underneath the rainfall shower, kissing and soaping each other. Her kisses were driving him wild, especially when Elyse grew confident and knelt before him. He was shocked and glanced down. Her eyes were large and flaming with desire. "Are you sure?"

After that first night, he'd gathered she didn't have much experience in the bedroom, which had surprised him given how beautiful and sexy Elyse was.

"Yes," she murmured. "I want to taste you like you have me."

He groaned when her fingers traced his erection. Then she kissed, touched and teased him with light flicks of her tongue. He ran his hand through her water-slicked hair as she pressed her mouth to him.

"Elyse…"

She gripped him firmly and started bobbing her head, increasing the pace. Julian didn't want to come this way. He wanted to be inside her, but his thighs tautened when she didn't let up, and he could feel his climax approaching. She intended to take him, despite his best efforts to rein himself in. A low groan escaped his throat and his pelvis began pumping, piston-like, his fingers twisting in her hair as he gave in and gave up control to Elyse. He let out a hoarse cry as pleasure racked his body in an extreme explosion.

Afterward, he leaned back against the shower wall, the soothing water helping him to recover as he breathed deeply. He looked at her ruefully as she stood. "That was incredible."

She nodded as if drunk with desire. *Did she know what she'd done to him? The sensual torture she'd put him through?*

She molded her wet body against him as her arms encircled his neck, and Julian felt his desire for her renew.

"Give me a moment." He left the steam of the shower only to return wearing a condom. His hands on her waist, he pulled her closer to him.

"Please." She arched in readiness.

Julian took what she offered, angling her body and then pushing to the hilt in one powerful thrust. Elyse rocked her hips as she rode him, meeting him thrust for thrust. Wrapping her arms more tightly around him, she cried out, as if the spasms rippling through her were too much. Julian buried his face in her neck and a pleasure-soaked groan escaped his lips as she wrung every inch of his release.

They were both silent after such an intense experience. Elyse was limp and weak in his arms, so much so that Julian picked her up and carried her to bed. He placed her between the cool sheets, where she swiftly fell asleep. Julian, however, was wide-awake.

It couldn't last, right?

Usually after a few encounters with one woman, he was done and on to the next, but Elyse was different. He wanted her more than ever. He'd gone to great lengths to get Elyse here, alone with him. *Was he obsessed?* If so, it wasn't healthy. Yet, he couldn't seem to care. He was addicted. To the way she made him laugh. To the way she wasn't afraid to try new things. To the way she way made him feel so *alive.*

Maybe when they got back to the real world, this haze would go away as it did with every other woman. But something told Julian he shouldn't count on it.

True to her word, Giana had ensured the Lockett jet was at the private airstrip to greet Julian when it was time. On the flight back, something changed, and Julian soon found out why when he glanced up from a magazine he'd been reading to find Elyse staring at him.

"So tell me, Julian, was the job offer with Curtis real or was it just a big hoax to get me in bed?"

He frowned and tossed the magazine down. "Why would you ask that?"

"Because you never mentioned it the entire trip," Elyse responded. "And now that I'm no longer under a sexual haze, I can think straight."

Julian lowered his head. He knew she wasn't going to like his answer. "Do you want the truth?"

When he glanced up, her eyes were trained on him. "Please."

He swallowed the lump in his throat and persevered. "I admit the job offer isn't imminent, but Curtis does need a publicist. He doesn't have one on payroll."

Elyse's eyes narrowed. "So it was a ruse? Am I just another one of your conquests?"

Julian started to unbuckle his seat belt, but she was

faster, quickly removing hers. She stood and held up a hand. "Don't… I just need some space."

Elyse left the main cabin and rushed towards the back of the plane, which housed a bedroom and bathroom, leaving Julian alone. She didn't return until the captain announced they must return to their seats because they were about to land.

She hardly hazarded Julian a glance and could he blame her? He'd been so eager to get to know Elyse, he'd invented the opportunity with Curtis and now she refused to look at him. Julian didn't know if he could fix this, but he would have to try.

When they landed, she was silent on the drive to her apartment and Julian felt the closer they got, the more distance there was between them.

Had the days and nights of the past week just disappeared with her flick of a switch? But perhaps Elyse was right to put some distance between them. He sure as hell was baffled by the connection they'd found and how he behaved completely out of character. He would follow her lead.

The limousine stopped in front of her apartment complex and Elyse finally turned to face him. "I…" she started and then stopped.

"It's okay, Elyse," Julian said. "Call me when you're ready."

She looked relieved that he was letting her off the hook without some big argument. "Yes, I think that's best." Then she hopped out of the limo.

Julian thought about jumping out and walking her to her door, but instead he took the coward's way and let the driver take her suitcase.

As he watched her walk toward the building, Julian knew he was in deep trouble.

Eleven

Elyse closed the door of her apartment behind her and dropped the designer luggage to the floor. *What had she done?* As soon as they'd begun driving into the city from the airport, it was like the sexual fog she'd been in with Julian in Saint Lucia had disappeared and Elyse realized she was like every other woman. She'd succumbed to the great Julian Lockett's charm and she had no one to blame but herself.

Her mission had been clear: infiltrate the Locketts. And Julian had been her ticket in. Somewhere along the way, she'd gotten caught in his web and the allure of being with him. It wasn't only his incredible body and the things he could do with it, but hadn't she been enthralled with what wealth could bring? A private villa on a Caribbean island that easily cost thousands a night. A brand-new wardrobe when she arrived. A brand-new Porsche convertible at their disposal for the week. Not to mention the chartered yacht and fancy spa in the treetops. His entire world was glamorous. How could she, a poor girl raised by a drunk, not be caught up?

She'd lost sight of the goal: get revenge by outing Josiah for the scumbag he was. She wanted Josiah to lose everything or at the very least feel half the pain and hurt her father had. Maybe once the whole world knew what Josiah had done, her father might feel vindicated and obtain the help he needed. She desperately wanted him to get treatment so he could get sober before she had no parents.

Elyse ran her fingers through her hair. How was she supposed to bring down Josiah? It certainly wouldn't be through work. The job opportunity with Curtis Jackson never really existed. It was just the carrot Julian dangled over her head to get her exactly where he'd wanted her.

His bed.

She was furious with him, but she also couldn't solely blame him. She'd known exactly what she was doing when she'd gone to bed with him over and over and over again. And it hadn't just been bed. It had been the shower, the sofa, the rug in the living room, the terrace, the Jacuzzi and anywhere else he'd wanted. She'd been completely complicit during each of their encounters.

How could she have known how addictive sex could be? But it wasn't just sex. It was sex with *Julian*. Though sometimes she did wonder if it was making love. There was that one time, their last night in Saint Lucia, with Julian seated deep inside her, that she'd felt a naked intimacy she'd never experienced before. He'd been kissing her deeply, then he'd stopped and grabbed both sides of her face and looked her intently in the eye. They'd rocked together until they'd both shuddered and clutched one another during the throes of release.

It was then she'd known that she was falling for the elusive bachelor, which spelled trouble for her plans to take down his father. Even though he deserved it, how could she hurt the father of the man she'd come to care about? Yet, on the other hand, the need for revenge had fueled her all these years. She needed to set the record straight. Only then would she find peace.

But how would she do it? There was no job with the Locketts and she and Julian were at odds. He was sure to want to move on after the way she'd ignored him on the plane and in the limo. *What was she going to do?*

"Well, if it isn't the prodigal son returned home to roost," Josiah commented as Julian walked into his office on Monday morning.

Julian straightened, stopping in the doorway. He certainly hadn't expected his father to pay him a visit. Josiah rarely came into the office. If and when he did, he and Roman were locked away in meetings for much of the day. What had he done to garner a visit from his father?

Steeling himself, he stepped past his father, who was sprawled on the sofa, and walked to his desk. "To what do I owe the pleasure?"

"Don't be snarky with me, boy," his father replied. "Did you think I wouldn't find out you commandeered the jet to fly off to parts unknown with some trollop?"

Julian seethed as he turned to face him. "She's not a trollop."

"No?" His father raised a brow. "Don't tell me someone has finally turned your head. I didn't think it was possible."

"That's because you don't know me," Julian replied, sitting and turning on his laptop. "You never have."

Josiah rose to his full six-foot-five height and stormed toward him. "I don't appreciate your insolence, Julian. You don't get to talk to me that way, not after I'm the reason you're sitting where you are."

"Is that so?" Julian replied, glancing up at his father. "I don't recall you sitting in all those endless college lectures or medical school labs. Or perhaps you spent three years in a relentless residency letting people boss you around?"

His father's eyes turned stormy. "You're really feeling yourself, aren't you? Some girl's got your nose wide open and suddenly you feel six feet tall? Well, you're not, my boy. You're nothing but the runt of the litter that I had to push to turn into something."

It was just like his father to shoot below the belt. "Get out!" Julian yelled.

His father laughed. "This is *my* company, in case you have forgotten."

"Then fire me," Julian responded. He was tired of the endless mind games. "I had the time to take and I took it. Or did I need to ask for your permission?"

His father was silent for several moments. Julian, having learned long ago not to cower to Josiah, otherwise he'd walk all over him, held his ground.

"I don't know who this woman is, but I like the effect she's had on you. Bring her to dinner," Josiah said. His words were a command, not a request. Then he turned to leave, but stopped in the doorway to add, "And the next time you want to use *my* jet, don't use your little sister to do your dirty work. Be a man and call me directly."

His father left the office and Julian was tempted to throw the glass paperweight he hadn't realized was in his hand at the door, but he couldn't. It had been one of the gifts from his mother when he'd become a doctor. He wouldn't give Josiah the satisfaction of having him destroy something that meant a great deal to him. That didn't mean he wasn't furious. His father could always get under his skin.

"Did I just see Daddy leave?" Giana asked, coming into his office several minutes later. She hadn't bothered standing on ceremony and knocking, but had walked right in.

"What do you think?" Julian was livid. He'd thought he

and Josiah had come to a relatively peaceful coexistence of late. He hated being in his father's crosshairs again.

Giana shrugged, smoothing down the jacket of her white pantsuit. "I'm sorry."

"For what?" Julian inquired.

"About telling Daddy that you used the jet."

"You were the rat?"

"Hey!" She gave him the evil eye. "It's not my fault you decided to go gallivanting off during the start of the season. Anyway, Daddy wanted to use the jet the day you left and I had to tell him it was already in use. He was none too pleased. He pretty much browbeat me until I gave you up."

"Oh please," Julian responded. "You're his baby girl. I doubt he browbeat you. It's me he called the runt of the litter."

"Omigod!" Giana looked horrified.

"Don't be so shocked."

Giana came toward him and Julian tried to move away, but his sister wrapped her arms around him. "I'm sorry, Julian. I'm sorry for not protecting you from his wrath."

"It's okay, sis." Julian patted her back, comforting her. "I'm the big brother. I'm supposed to protect you, not the other way around."

She glanced up at him and Julian saw her blinking back tears. "Don't go soft on me, G. You know you have to be tough if you want to hang with the big dogs."

She pushed against his chest to stand straight in her high heels. "I am tough."

"Sure you are, kid." He tweaked her nose.

"Stop that!" She swatted his hand away. "I hated it when you did that when I was six years old and I hate it now when I'm grown woman. So, what did Daddy say anyway?"

"He wants to meet Elyse."

"Oh lord." Giana glanced upward. "You remember how

well it went when Roman brought Shantel home. Do we really have to do this again?"

Julian laughed. "I sure hope not. But, if I don't bring her, Father will just go sniffing around. Better that I get out ahead of his snooping."

Giana sighed. "All right. I just pray it all goes according to plan."

Julian sure hoped so. If not, they were in for a bumpy ride.

"Where have you been?" Frank asked Elyse when she stopped by after work to check in on him. She wasn't surprised her father was curious. Andrea had asked her the same thing, but Elyse had promised to tell her all the details over dinner tonight. She'd intended to just drop off her dad's groceries and be on her way, but when she'd arrived, she could tell that he'd been drinking.

His hair looked like it hadn't been brushed in days and the pants and shirt he wore were mismatched and wrinkled. A half-empty bottle of whiskey sat on the cocktail table in the living room along with an empty tumbler. She rolled her eyes heavenward and prayed for patience as she put on a pot of coffee.

When she didn't immediately answer, Frank joined her in the kitchen, stopping in her path as she put milk and eggs into the bare refrigerator. *What had he eaten since she'd been gone?*

"Well? Are you going to answer me?" he asked belligerently.

Elyse caught the strong whiff of whiskey on his breath. "I went on vacation, Daddy."

He frowned. "Without telling me?"

She'd turned away, ignoring his question, and continued loading cheese, bread and sundries into the refrigerator and small pantry.

"Elyse Harper."

"What?" She spun around in a huff. "Is it so wrong that I took a spur-of-the-moment vacation and did something just for me?" At his downcast expression, Elyse realized she'd hurt him.

"I'm sorry if I've been a burden to you, but you really don't need to worry about me. I can take care of myself." He quickly left the kitchen and went back to the living room to sit in front of the television and watch the football game.

An Atlanta Cougars' game.

Elyse sighed because she knew this didn't bode well. "Daddy, I'm sorry." She put down the bread in her hands and approached the back of the sofa. She wrapped her arms around his shoulders.

"I know it's been hard on you all these years, Elyse. That you've had to grow up sooner than most girls your age. I'm sorry for that." He patted her arm. "I don't think I knew what to do raising a teenager daughter on my own. That was what your mother was for."

Elyse was surprised to hear her father mention her mother. He rarely did, because remembering her was still as painful for him as it was for her. Elyse walked around and joined him on the sofa. "It's okay, Daddy."

"No, it's not." Frank pushed her away. "Don't make excuses for me being a terrible father. I should have done better by you. But I didn't know how. It was hard enough losing your mother to the cancer, but then the bills started piling up and I lost my share of the Cougars. It was all too much." He lowered his head.

She reached for his large brown hand and clutched it in her own. "I understand."

He glanced up and she saw tears on his dark lashes. "I don't think you do. One moment I had everything. A beautiful family, with a wonderful wife and daughter. A big house. A fancy car. Money in the bank. An interest in a football franchise that was starting to thrive after my investment with my best friend. And then suddenly—" he snapped his fingers "—it was all gone. First by God, or fate, or who knows what. Then by the creditors. And finally, my best friend swindled me. The man I thought I could count on through thick and thin."

"Daddy, I know. You've told me before."

"Yeah, well, you can hear it again," he said more forcefully than she knew he'd intended. "Because Josiah Lockett looks out for no one but himself. He saw me struggling, but rather than lend me a hand, he scammed me out of my rightful share of the Altanta Cougars. And now look at them." He pointed to the television. "They're doing great. Better than me or Josiah could ever have imagined. Probably on their way to the championships with this new phenom, Curtis Jackson. While I—" he pounded his chest with his fist "—sit here alone with nothing."

"You're not alone, Daddy." Her voice cracked when she spoke. "You have me. I haven't left you."

Suddenly, as if he realized she was still there, her father looked at Elyse. "That's right. You've always been my sweet girl." He pulled her into his embrace. And she let him. Because sometimes she just needed her father.

After several moments, they both pulled away, tears in their eyes. Her father glanced at the bottle on the table. "I'm sorry I failed you, Elyse. I tried while you were gone, but I just couldn't."

"It's okay." She patted his thigh. "I've made some coffee. Let's get you some."

And that's where she stayed for the rest of the evening, canceling her dinner plans with Andrea, but promising to meet her in the morning for breakfast. Her phone buzzed several times during the evening. It was Julian. Her heart raced at just the thought of him. The time they'd spent together in Saint Lucia had been nothing short of magical.

She doubted she'd ever experience anything like it ever again, but she had to ignore his calls because her father needed her more. She was already struggling with how in the world she could be with Julian, but still remain loyal to herself and her revenge plans against his father. Something would have to give. She just didn't know what.

Julian was going out of his mind with worry. It was evening and he'd tried Elyse for much of the day and, other than a terse text stating she was swamped at work, he hadn't heard a word from her since the night before when he'd dropped her off from the airport.

Last night, Julian had given her space because…hadn't he needed it, too? What was it about Elyse that made him feel a sense of rightness whenever he was with her? He had kissed many women, too many to recall, but with Elyse, every kiss was special. Unique. Kissing her was his new benchmark for what a kiss should be. And when they made love, it had revealed her body was the perfect match for his.

She had a right to be upset with him. He'd dangled a job opportunity as bait in order to get closer to her and it backfired. But did that mean she would end their relationship altogether?

That's why, when he'd come home last night and tried to focus on other tasks like checking his email or working out, he'd quickly become frustrated. But he'd refused to call last night, refused to show just how weak she made him.

So he'd waited. He'd casually called to see if she was free for lunch today, but she'd been busy. When he'd texted her to see about getting together later, she'd told him she had other plans.

Was he getting the brush-off after he'd done all he could to romance her, to show her how special she was? It looked like it because she'd ignored all his attempts. He'd done this enough times to other women to take the hint. Last week was last week, and now that it was over, it was on to the next thing.

So why did knowing that hurt?

Julian had begun to think of Elyse as *the one*. He had planned to take her to meet the family. But clearly, he'd made a mistake. Now he understood just how the women he'd dated felt when he'd ghosted them. He simply never expected to be on the receiving end. Especially after all that he and Elyse had shared. *Had she been faking it? Had the closeness and intimacy all been a figment of his imagination?*

Later, when she finally made it home to her apartment, Elyse was dog-tired. After ensuring her father drank several cups of black coffee and fixing him dinner, she'd stayed and they'd ended up playing a game of gin rummy at the kitchen table. They hadn't done it in years and it reminded Elyse of better times before he'd started drinking.

She'd driven home in a daze, thinking of her father and his hatred of Josiah Lockett on the one hand, and Julian on the other. She loved how impulsive Julian could be, even if he'd lured her to their spur-of-the-moment vacation with a fake job offer. But most of all, she missed his kiss, his touch, and the sensual pleasure she'd found in his arms. Because he'd branded her. Made her *his*.

It made the position she'd put herself untenable. *How could she get the revenge for her father that he so richly deserved without hurting Julian, the man she'd come to care about, maybe even love?*

After kicking off her heels, Elyse started stripping one article of clothing at a time until there was a trail of clothing from her front door to her master bedroom. She was ready for a hot shower.

But the chime of her doorbell startled her. She glanced down at her watch. It was nearly 10:00 p.m. and she certainly wasn't expecting anyone, not on a work night. Swiftly, she grabbed a silk Kimono and wrapped it around her as she headed for the door. Glancing through the peep-hole, she was shocked to see Julian.

"Elyse, are you in there? Are you okay? I've been worried sick all day when I couldn't reach you," Julian said from the other side.

How did he know? Were they really that entwined after their week together? Elyse knew the answer.

Yes.

She unlatched the door and swung it open.

"Thank God, you're okay," Julian said.

"Of course, I am," Elyse replied. "Why wouldn't I be?"

"I called and I text and you didn't answer and I just thought something bad happened to you."

I fell in love with the enemy, she thought, but instead she said, "I'm fine. Do you want to come in?"

He nodded, but didn't move farther than the entrance.

"So, what do you want Julian?" Her voice was barely more than a hoarse whisper.

"Can you forgive me?" Julian asked. "I know I wasn't forthright before, but I promise you I will get you a meeting with the Jacksons."

Elyse glanced up at him and heart sped up at his proximity. "What do you think?"

Before she could say another word, Julian had her in his arms and was slamming the door shut behind him with his foot. What followed was wild and passionate in a way she'd never envisaged.

Julian's mouth crashed down on hers, parting her lips on impact. His tongue delved deep, tangling with her own. A tide of electrifying hunger rushed through Elyse and she didn't make a sound. All she felt was the softness of her couch against her back because her eyes were on Julian as he furiously rid himself of his clothes before joining her on the sofa.

When Julian loosened the knot on her kimono, he growled at finding her naked underneath, and lowered his mouth to the straining points of her dark brown nipples. He lingered there, toying with them until they both became stiff peaks. Elyse's heart hammered in her chest, but she didn't let him have all the fun. She was impossibly greedy for him and was surprised because it had only been a little more than twenty-four hours since they'd been together.

She ran her fingertips over his erect shaft and registered the shudder that crossed his distinctive features when she did so. Up and down her hands and fingers went, reveling in the sensation of his velvet-steel hardness. She continued the rhythm until Julian pushed away from her, but only for a moment. He returned to the sofa with protection in hand and rolled it on. Then he slid over her, eased into her, and Elyse looked up into his taut face to see his dark eyes alight with hunger.

"More," she urged, and Julian gave it to her, slamming into her body. She raked her nails against his smooth back, but right when she was about to soar, he flipped her onto her knees and drove inside her from behind again and again.

Elyse was lost. All she could do was feel. And when Julian slipped his fingers between her legs and stroked her, she shattered and fell apart. Julian was as frantic for her as she'd been him for him, and soon he was groaning his release and collapsing onto her.

In the aftermath, when he dispensed with the protection and they lay snuggled on the couch, Julian apologized. "I'm sorry for attacking you as soon as I walked in the door."

Elyse grinned, but when she glanced up at him, his gaze was intent. "It's okay." She brushed her hand against his cheek. "I wanted you just as desperately."

"You did?" Julian asked. "But today..."

She placed a finger over his lips. "Today, I had a tough day at work with an especially hellish client and then, when I went to visit my father, I found him drunk. I stayed, sobered him up, fixed him a meal and put him to bed. I'm sorry for ignoring you."

Julian smiled ruefully. "I just thought…"

"Julian…" She looked into his light brown eyes and saw doubt lurking in those depths, and that surprised her. He was usually more confident and self-assured. "Our week together meant everything to me, surely you must know that?"

"Yeah, well. We're back to reality and what happens in Saint Lucia, stays in Saint Lucia."

"Not for me. I guess we never really spoke about what happens next, but I'd like to see you again," Elyse said. "Actually, I'd like to be the only woman you're seeing and vice versa. And, I certainly want to be the only woman you're sleeping with."

Her request had nothing to do with revenge and everything to do with Julian and what had transpired on that island. Everything had changed and her revenge plan wasn't so black-and-white. Elyse had no idea how she was going to navigate the murky waters, only that she had to try. She'd even put off Pierre today when he'd inquired about the job offer from Julian. She'd indicated she was a front-runner, but a decision hadn't been made yet. It left her with some time and space to explore this newfound relationship. But how did Julian feel about being with one woman? He was a serial dater with a long list of women. *Was he ready to commit?*

Twelve

Monogamy.

Usually the word sent Julian scurrying in the other direction, but hearing Elyse say she only wanted to spend time with him was music to his ears. Yes, it was scary because his relationships in the past were more transactional. But making love with Elyse was different. He was totally tuned to her in ways he'd never been with other women.

When he'd been back at his condo, he'd literally ached for her. Elyse was the most sexually compatible lover he'd ever had. So much so, he found himself in his car driving over to her apartment when he'd sworn earlier that he was writing her off for ignoring him, which in hindsight was completely selfish. Of course, she had a life and responsibilities that came before him. He couldn't expect her to drop everything.

He'd just been so worried when he couldn't reach her, thinking she'd been in an accident. After everything they'd shared in Saint Lucia, he'd come to care for her.

"Julian?"

He glanced down to see Elyse gazing up at him expectantly and he realized he'd never answered her. "I don't want anyone else, either, Elyse. I want to be with you exclusively."

A smiled beamed across Elyse's beautiful face and it warmed his heart. He tipped her chin and looked into her mascara-framed eyes and kissed her. Her arms slipped around him once again, her lithe body melting against him, and Julian knew he wasn't going home tonight.

"So, are you finally going to tell me what happened between you and the infamous Julian Lockett," Andrea asked Elyse when they met up for breakfast the next morning at a local diner.

"Yes, I'm going to tell you everything," Elyse stated, taking a sip of her coffee. She was going to need plenty of caffeine because she'd gotten very little sleep after spending much of the night making love to Julian.

"Well? I'm waiting," Andrea said, folding her arms across her chest.

"Julian took me by private jet to Saint Lucia."

"By jet? Oh my lord!" Andrea's hand flew to her mouth. "How exciting."

"Spending time with Julian was amazing. He was really adventurous. We chartered yachts, danced in the streets with the locals and had candlelit dinners and treetop spa treatments."

"And the sex? Rumor has it he's a stallion in the bedroom."

Elyse chuckled. "I'm not one to kiss and tell, but suffice it to say, his reputation is well deserved."

Andrea blushed beet red. "I knew all it would take is the right man to get your engines revving."

"Honestly, I'd started believing what men said. That I was an ice queen when it came to the bedroom."

"Does this mean you and Julian are an item?"

"If you mean, have we've agreed to be exclusive, then the answer is a resounding yes!"

"I'm so excited for you, Elyse. I mean Julian Lockett, of all people. Who would have thought he was tamable? So what's next?"

"I'm meeting his family later this week at the Atlanta Cougars' afternoon game and then having dinner at his parents' place afterward." It was unlikely she'd be recognized because she'd been a gangly preteen with acne, braces and long dark hair back when Josiah knew her. Her complexion had since cleared, she had straight teeth and her hair was in a pixie cut.

"Sounds serious."

"I'm looking forward to it." And she was. It was an opportunity to meet Josiah Lockett in person and to see if he truly was the Goliath her father made him out to be. If so, she knew it wouldn't be an easy slingshot. Josiah was well loved and respected in the town, but if she could tarnish his image and find proof of wrongdoing if not by him than a member of his family or team, she could have the ammunition she needed to move forward. Elyse wasn't sure what would happen to her and Julian afterward, and that was the scariest thought of all. She and Julian were in a good place even after the job debacle with Curtis. She'd placed herself in his path to get vengeance, yet all Elyse really wanted was to revel in being Julian's woman. But if she continued down this road, any chance they had would be over. *What choice did she have?* Getting what was due her family might help her father to finally heal, but she was in a no-win situation. If she helped Frank, would she lose Julian, the man she'd fallen for?

The next day, Julian found himself waiting for Elyse outside her office building. After he and Elyse had spent much of the previous night in each other's arms, visions of her had dominated his daydreams and they hadn't all been sexual. Some had been of Elyse. Carefree as they'd lain on the yacht deck catching some rays, or of the joy on her face as they'd danced in the streets with the Saint Lucians, or the open smile that spread across her features every time he walked into the room.

And so, he'd called her to see if she'd be interested in dinner when she got off work and she'd said yes. He wanted to appear casual as he stood leaning against his Bugatti in dark trousers and blue button-down. He'd nixed his blazer and tie, throwing them into the back seat.

She emerged in slacks and a silk blouse. It took every ounce of Julian's self-control not to scoop her up in front of the evening work crowd and take her somewhere private so he could relieve the constant day-long craving he had for her.

"Julian, it's so good to see you." She stood on tippy toes and brushed her lips across his.

"You, too."

"So what did you have in mind for dinner?" Elyse asked. "Because I'm not dressed for much." She glanced down at her attire.

"It's Taco Tuesday. I thought we might go to my favorite taqueria."

"All right." She grinned. "I'm in."

Julian helped her into the passenger seat before walking around and revving up the engine. "How was your day?" he inquired.

"Not bad," Elyse said. "None of my clients shot themselves in the foot by doing something stupid, so I would consider it a good day." She glanced across at him. "And you?"

"A couple of consultations with the players. A rehabilitation session with one of the running backs. All in all, a pretty easy day," Julian replied. "I'm actually considering volunteering some of my time at a local hospital."

"Even with football season in full swing?"

"If the head team doctor, Dr. Walters, can have his own practice, I see no reason why I can't make time to give back to the community."

"I, for one, think it's a great idea."

"You do? You seemed doubtful at first."

"I assumed your family wouldn't be happy about you spreading yourself thin and would want you to devote all your time to the team."

"I'm sure my father thinks that way, but my mom would be on board, considering the hospital I want to volunteer with is in a neighborhood with poor healthcare coverage."

"You shouldn't let anything deter you."

Julian smiled. "I won't."

He pulled into the taqueria and there was already a line outside, but there were a couple of available picnic tables. "Grab one for us," Julian said, "and I'll get the tacos."

"Sure thing."

"Anything particular you like?"

"Surprise me."

Julian ended up ordering an assortment of tacos from tempura fish to brisket to carnitas, along with two ice-cold beers. They were all topped with the taqueria's famous garlic sauce, lettuce, tomato and feta.

"This looks delicious," Elyse said when he set the tray down in front of her on the picnic table. She reached across to grab a beer, plucked the cap off with ease and took a generous swallow.

Julian laughed as she placed it on the table and dug into the box for one of the tacos. He liked that he could be himself, which was sometimes hard to do, even around people he'd known for years.

"Ohmigod!" she moaned. "This is so delicious." He

watched as she licked her lips when some of the garlic sauce dribbled down her chin. He leaned across the table, used his thumb to catch the rest and then sucked it into his mouth.

Her eyes grew large at the blatant sexual move, but she didn't say anything. Instead she continued eating her taco and he joined her in the culinary delight. They finished eating in silence, taking swigs of beer every now and then between bites. He was comfortable with the quiet; it wasn't awkward like silences with some women.

When they were done, Elyse wiped her mouth with a napkin. "I didn't realize how hungry I was, but I guess I shouldn't be surprised. I only had a salad for lunch."

"I'm glad you enjoyed the tacos." Julian removed the trays. When he returned, he nodded in the direction of the road. "Did you save room for dessert?"

"Why?"

He moved aside. There was a smile in her eyes when she saw the ice-cream truck.

"How about it?" He offered her his hand and she rose and grasped it. The electric spark between them was just as powerful as it had been in Saint Lucia. Perhaps more because now they knew each other in and out of bed.

Though after they'd finished their ice cream cones—butter pecan for him and mint chocolate chip for Elyse—that's exactly where they ended up: back in bed.

Julian knew he'd never experienced anything like what he had with Elyse before and it both thrilled and scared the hell out of him. Yet he couldn't, wouldn't, stop seeing her. He had no choice but to introduce her to the family because Elyse wasn't going anywhere. She was a part of his life. At least for now.

"Curtis! How are you feeling?" Julian asked the Cougars wide receiver when he stopped into the physical therapy room on Sunday afternoon to check on the team's new recruit.

"I'm doing good, Doc," Curtis stepped away from the trainer helping him with stretches and gave Julian a fist bump.

"That's good. You know we told your father you were going to be in good hands with the Lockett family. We have to keep our word."

"Aw, Doc, I know you guys look after me. My dad be trippin'. It's always been just me and him since my mom left us, so he's just overprotective."

"As he should be," Julian said. "Hey listen, I have an idea I wanted to run past you."

"Oh yeah? What's that, Doc?"

"I heard you might be in the market soon for a publicist and I know a fantastic candidate. Her name's Elyse Harper. She's done some great work for Porscha Childs."

Curtis grinned. "I love her music. And I'm in need of a good publicist. Can you send me her info and I'll let my dad have a look?"

"Absolutely."

"Great, I'll talk at ya later." Curtis walked back to the trainer and continued his routine before the game.

Julian checked in on several other team members who were on the injured list, talking over the treatments Dr. Walters had prescribed. After ensuring everything was going according to plan, Julian was just leaving the locker room when he ran into Roman.

"Hey, bro. What are you doing down here?" Julian asked. "I'd assumed you and Shantel would be up in the skybox with the big dogs."

"I may be General Manager, but at the end of the day, I'm still a fan and like to hang out with the players."

"I hear you," Julian said. "I was about to head up myself. I sent Elyse a ticket and she's meeting me." He glanced down at his watch. “Actually, she should be here any minute. If you’ll excuse me?”

“Sure thing. I can’t wait to meet the woman who’s got you sprung, bro.”

“Whatever.” Julian rolled his eyes and headed down the corridor to the private entrance for VIP ticket holders and their guests. He found Elyse standing in the lobby, waiting for him.

His heart kicked over in his chest and Julian knew Roman could be right. Elyse may just have stolen his heart.

“Hey, baby girl.”

Elyse only had a moment to study Julian in his faded designer jeans and crisp white shirt. She strove to catch her breath before he swept her off her feet and into his arms.

“Put me down,” she giggled. And he did, but only after he gave her a searing kiss that left her a little dizzy. Once Elyse’s feet were firmly on the ground, Julian led her along the hall, pointing out the locker rooms and the physical therapy and recovery areas, weight rooms and cheerleader workout area.

“This is pretty incredible,” Elyse said. She couldn’t believe she was standing in the back of the house at the Atlanta Cougars’ stadium and that half of all this could have been hers if Josiah hadn’t swindled her father out of his share.

“C’mon, we’d better head up. The game will be starting soon and I want to introduce you to my parents and the rest of the family. Unfortunately, you won’t meet Xavier, he’s on-air talking about the game.”

“No problem. I’ll see him at dinner, right?”

“Yes, he should be wrapped up with his segment by then.”

And so she followed him into the elevator that would lead to the chairman and owner’s lounge where she would finally meet Josiah Lockett.

When they arrived, the floor was humming with attendants and security. Julian led her down the hall, saying hello to several people along the way. She liked that he was friendly and wasn't above speaking to those who worked for his family.

Eventually, they came to the skybox lounge. Security opened the glass doors and Elyse was shocked at the luxury. It had plush beige carpet, upholstered chairs, mahogany-paneled walls holding large television screens, and a huge marble-encased bar with several attendants at the ready to serve the Lockett family and their guests.

But Elyse only had one man on the brain and it wasn't the man standing at her side. Instead, it was the six-foot-five burly man in slacks, a button-down shirt and a sleeveless sweater-vest. Elyse would know Josiah Lockett anywhere even if she hadn't researched the hell out of him.

At his side was a beautiful woman with a peanut butter complexion. She was wearing slacks and a cashmere sweater set. Her hair was set in a classic fifties-style flip, but on Angelique Lockett it didn't look dated, it looked elegant and sophisticated.

"Mom, Dad." Julian ushered Elyse toward them. She felt underdressed in her leather moto jacket, calf-length pencil skirt and high-heeled booties.

Julian's mother came over instantly and swept Elyse into her arms. "So you're the woman whose captured my Julian," she whispered in Elyse's ear, "and foiled all my plans."

Elyse responded. "I'm afraid so."

His mother took both her hands. "I'll forgive you because I've never seen my son look happier." She gave Julian a wink.

Meanwhile, Josiah stayed back behind his wife, regarding Elyse from a distance, and it made her uneasy. She couldn't tell why, but the way he stared at her was quite strange.

"Darling." Angelique walked to her husband. "Please come over and meet Elyse."

Elyse swallowed as the bear of a man moved forward. Josiah towered over her. She was certain he used his stature to intimidate people, but she refused to be one of them.

"Mr. Lockett." She glanced up at him from underneath her lashes. "It's a pleasure to meet you."

"I would say the same, but I'm not sure what your game is here," Josiah stated, glaring at her.

"Pardon?"

"You upstaged my wife, who was hoping to find the great love of Julian's life," he responded with a big belly laugh. He offered Elyse a hand. "Ms. Harper. It's nice to finally meet Julian's girl of the week."

"Josiah, behave," his wife warned.

He shrugged and asked, "Have we met before? You remind me of someone."

Elyse's heart began thudding in her chest. She had met Josiah a few times when she was very young, but her memories were fuzzy. Surely he wouldn't recognize her? It had been over twenty years.

"Please come." Mrs. Lockett ushered Elyse forward. "You have to meet the rest of the family."

Elyse did as she was instructed, yet couldn't help but notice the funny look on Josiah's face as she passed him. She shook it off and walked toward Roman Lockett. Other than Julian, he was the most famous of the Locketts now, having been in several magazines touting his financial prowess. Though Xavier once held that title, but after losing his quarterback status, he'd faded into the background.

Like his father, he was over six feet tall with chocolate skin and dark, deep-set eyes. She didn't want to cross him. Something told Elyse he would make a worthy opponent.

She smiled and held out her hand after his mother introduced them.

"Elyse, I'd like you to meet my wife, Shantel." A beautiful caramel-skinned woman approached her. She was wearing a sweaterdress that showed off her rounded belly. She glowed with a radiance and a smile.

"So nice to finally meet you." Shantel leaned in for a hug. "I've heard nothing but great things about you from Julian."

"Ah, that's right." Elyse pointed to Shantel and Julian at her side. "You two went to school together, right?"

Julian laughed. "Not quite. I was at Morehouse and Shantel was at Spelman, but we have known each other for years."

"Don't forget about us." A statuesque woman sauntered toward Elyse. She was wearing skinny jeans and killer knee-high boots that Elyse just knew had to be designer.

"I'm Giana," the woman said, extending a hand, and Elyse appreciated her firm handshake. "Our baby brother, Xavier, is one of the commentators on the front lines, so you'll have to meet him later."

"I look forward to it."

"Well, stop crowding my lady," Julian said, putting his arm around Elyse's shoulder. "Can I get you something to drink?" He glanced down at her.

"I'd love a white wine," Elyse responded.

"Wine at a beer event?" Josiah scoffed from behind her. Although he'd rejoined the crowd of men he'd been with when she'd arrived, he'd managed to call her out. "Julian, get this girl a beer like the rest of us."

Elyse glanced around and noticed everyone had cozies with beer bottles. When Julian raised an eyebrow, she said, "A Heineken would be great."

"Coming right up." He headed for the bar, leaving Elyse alone with Julian's mother, Giana and Shantel.

"So." Mrs. Lockett, slid her arm through Elyse's. "How are things going with you and Julian?"

Now there was a subject she wouldn't get caught up in. "Everything's great. Better than great." She glanced over at the bar where Julian and Roman were talking.

"Well, you did go through quite a lot of trouble to meet my brother," Giana said. "I mean, ambushing the blind date Mama set up."

"Giana…" There was a warning tone in her mother's voice although she, too, seemed rapt to hear Elyse's response.

Elyse swallowed. "You're right. What can I say? I'd heard a lot about Julian over the years. Who hasn't, living in Atlanta?" Mrs. Lockett's eyes narrowed and Elyse knew she had to tread carefully. "I was curious about the man underneath the façade he shows to the world. And I have to say, I've been pleasantly surprised at how much depth there is to your son, your brother, and your friend." She looked at each of the women in turn.

"Not many women care to see beyond Julian's flashy image and the fancy cars and expensive dinners," Mrs. Lockett said. "I'm glad you're not one of them."

"So tell us a little bit about you," Giana said. "We're all very curious about the woman who's stolen my brother's heart."

"Have I?"

"You're the first woman in a long time Julian has spoken so highly about," his mother said. "And definitely the first he's brought to meet the family."

"Really?" So Julian was talking about her to his family and closest friends? A secret thrill went straight through Elyse that Julian felt as she did. Yet, on the other hand, she couldn't reveal too much about herself for fear she might leak something and reveal the past connection between their families.

"Yes." Giana came over to Elyse. "I've never seen my brother like this before. He's quite enamored with you."

"Is that a bad thing?" Giana seemed very suspicious of her motives.

"Oh of course not." Mrs. Lockett was quick to say. "I'm excited my son feels that way. Perhaps it means he's thinking about settling down and having a family of his own someday."

"Mama, isn't it enough that Roman—" Giana eyed her older brother who was still at the bar with Julian "—is giving you a new grandbaby in a matter of months?" She smiled at Shantel, and Elyse could scc Giana was definitely a fan. She doubted Julian's sister would ever look at her that way because once she realized Elyse's true agenda, she would be persona non grata with the Lockett family.

"Can't I have more than one?" her mother asked, shrugging her shoulders. "Lord knows, it could be years before you decide to give up being a businesswoman to be a wife and mother."

"Who says she has to give it up?" Shantel asked. "I'm living proof that it's possible to have it all, Mama Lockett." She gave her a wink. "I have a thriving psychology practice and at the same time—" she rubbed her large belly "—I'm a wife and soon-to-be mother."

"Your generation has it so much easier than mine. It was a foregone conclusion we would stay home to be wives and mothers. You have more opportunities than we ever did, but I caution you not to leave it too late." She looked at her daughter when she spoke. "Starting a family in your thirties might be ideal for you careers, but your bodies have other ideas. And there—" she stopped herself because Giana was about to interrupt her. "I've said my piece, Giana. You know, I'm old-school."

"I don't know about you ladies—" Elyse glanced at Shantel and Giana "—but I appreciate the motherly advice."

Mrs. Lockett instantly reached for her hand. "I'm sorry, my darling. Julian told me about your mother. I was so sorry to hear of your loss at such a young age."

"Thank you." Elyse offered a half smile.

"Absolutely," his mother said. "We'll move on to happier subjects."

Julian returned with Roman and two beers in hand and brushed a kiss across her forehead. "You all right?" he asked, whispering in her ear as he handed her a bottle of beer.

"Absolutely, I'm not made of glass." She'd endured losing her mother and having a drunk for a father, but she'd done it and made something of herself without giving in to despair. But could she do this? Could she really go after the Locketts to return to her father what should have been his?

Thirteen

Julian reflected on the day as he stood outside on the terrace of the Lockett estate and got a breath of fresh air. He was thrilled with how it had gone. Elyse had blended seamlessly into the Lockett family clan at the stadium and again here at dinner. His mother was enthralled, his siblings were both friendly and gregarious, but his father… He couldn't put his finger on it, but his behavior tonight bothered Julian.

He wasn't outwardly hostile, not like he'd been with Shantel the first time she'd joined Roman for a family dinner and they'd announced their marriage and baby bombshell. But Julian knew his father, and the man was being mysterious. He definitely had something up his sleeve and Julian intended to find out what it was. He wouldn't let Josiah wreck his relationship like he'd nearly done Roman and Shantel's.

As if she'd sensed he was thinking of her, Shantel joined him outside. "Hey—" she shoulder bumped him "—what are you doing out here?"

"Just needed a moment alone from all the ruckus."

"Heck, I'm used to it thanks to the big clan I have in McDonough County," Shantel replied.

She came from a large family with three brothers, their wives and a gaggle of nieces and nephews. Going to one of Shantel's family events was like going to a three-ring circus. Everyone spoke at the same time and you couldn't get a word in edgewise.

"So, what are you up to?" Julian asked.

"I saw you standing out here on my way back from the powder room. You have no idea what pregnancy does to a woman's bladder."

"And I don't want to know," Julian said, laughing as she swatted his arm.

"Seriously, what's going on with you? You seem introspective."

Trust her Spidey sense—or should he say psychologist sense?—to know when something was on his mind. "I'm just thinking about Elyse and me." Julian had always felt like he could talk to Shantel. Over the years, he'd confided in her about prior relationships.

"And?"

"I don't know what's happening to me," Julian said. "Elyse is so beautiful, I can hardly take my eyes off her. And she's spirited and unafraid of sharing her opinion. She's a refreshing change from all the women who've pandered to my every whim."

"That's awesome, but what's the problem?"

"There isn't one," Julian said. "I'm just finding that my feelings for her are more substantive than any woman I've ever been with."

"Then don't fight it," Shantel replied. "Explore those feelings, Julian. Don't close yourself off to what could be your first real love."

Julian frowned. "I didn't say anything about love." That

word wasn't in his vocabulary. Other people like Shantel and Roman and his parents used it, but never him. He only knew familial love.

"You don't want it?"

"What, love?" Julian gave a rueful laugh. "Many people love me."

"Yes, but do they know you?" Shantel asked. "Perhaps it's time you allowed yourself to take a risk and open your heart to love and being loved. You've already admitted that your feelings for Elyse are different. So why deny it could be more?"

"I think you're reading too much into this. And I probably am, too. I'm mistaking good sex for something else."

"Why can't you own your feelings, Julian? What—or shall I say who—has made you so afraid of opening up?" Shantel touched his arm.

Julian snatched his arm away. "Don't shrink me, Shantel. You promised you would never do that."

"And I'm not," she said softly. "I'm just trying to be your friend and get you to see you could have more than you ever thought possible if you just let a little bit of your self-control go."

Julian snorted. "Everyone seems to think I have none."

"That's because they don't know you like I do," she said. "It's a façade to keep everyone at bay."

"Ahem." A loud cough sounded behind them and Julian turned to see Roman standing there. Of course, his brother had come to retrieve his wife, but Shantel would always be *his* best friend.

"Thanks for giving me and my best friend some time to chat." Julian patted Roman on the back and left his brother and his brother's wife on the terrace to talk alone. He went in search of Elyse. *Was Shantel right? Was it possible he could be falling in love with Elyse?*

* * *

The next couple of weeks passed by in a whirlwind for Elyse. When she wasn't at the office working to get her clients out of trouble, she was spending time with Julian. By hitting award-winning restaurants, art shows and charity events, they'd finally made the gossip columns. She and Julian had such an active social life, he'd taken her shopping for a new wardrobe of fashionable evening wear and formal attire.

Initially, Elyse had balked at taking more from Julian given he'd bought her such beautiful vacation wear in Saint Lucia, but he'd been insistent. And a small part of Elyse had secretly enjoyed all the fuss of being treated to the *Pretty Woman* experience. Julian had even splurged on La Perla lingerie, which hadn't lasted long on Elyse. Once he'd taken a look at her, the luxurious lingerie had quickly found residence on the bedroom floor.

Everyone was speculating on how Elyse had snagged Atlanta's illustrious bachelor no other lady could ever seem to hold on to. And when Elyse and Julian weren't painting the town red, they were at his penthouse or her apartment making a homemade dinner, watching a movie or listening to music as they cuddled on the couch. Those were her favorite moments because she got a glimpse of the real Julian. The man he rarely showed the world. The man driven to succeed by working long hours, tempered by a wicked sense of humor. She was falling harder and harder for the reformed playboy with each passing day. And as far as she could tell, there weren't any deep dark secrets for her to exploit, or at least none she'd discovered during pillow talk with Julian. The more she got to know Julian, the more she became unsure that she could use him to get revenge on his father.

Tonight, a Saturday, she and Julian had arranged to meet with Curtis and his father, Tim Jackson, for dinner at Manuel's. Julian told her the older man preferred a more laid-back environment.

Julian introduced her while they waited for a table. "Tim, Curtis, I'd like you to meet Elyse Harper."

"Pleasure to meet you, Ms. Harper," Tim said. "Where have I heard your name before?"

"It's nice meeting you, as well," Elyse said.

"From me, Dad. Remember I told you she's in PR?" Curtis responded.

"Is that right?" Tim raised a brow and looked at Julian. "And are you lobbying for your girlfriend to have the job, Lockett?"

She was surprised when Julian answered honestly. "I was hoping you'd at least consider her."

"But only if you think I'm the right person for the job," Elyse interjected. "Connections can only go so far. I'd hope my background and experience might speak for itself."

"All right, Elyse. Do you mind me calling you by your first name?"

"Not at all."

Over dinner, Elyse filled the Jacksons in on her years in public relations and the successes she'd had with several high-profile clients. Tim listened with an open mind and although he didn't make any promises, Elyse was encouraged she had a fighting chance of winning their business. Julian had made good on his promise to get her an introduction.

By the end of the night, the mood had relaxed from business to personal, and Elyse even had a bellyache from laughing so hard. But when she looked across the table at Julian and he smiled at her, she knew she had to stop fooling herself. She'd fallen in love with Julian Lockett.

Despite all the warnings she'd given herself to keep him at a distance, she'd been unable to stop from loving him. *How could she not love this man she'd given her body to?*

And he'd treated her reverently ever since, as if she truly

meant something special even though Julian Lockett was known to love 'em and leave 'em. But with her vendetta and his history, it was a recipe for disaster. She'd been skating on the edge for weeks, looking for secrets where there were none. Instead, her relationship with Julian had deepened. Revenge was out of the question now. Elyse couldn't do it. She loved him too much to ever hurt Julian in that way. If she did, they'd be over for good.

"What's wrong?" Julian asked on the limo ride home, noting that Elyse was in deep thought. He reached over to grab her hand and squeezed it.

She shook her head. "Nothing."

"Oh lord." He rolled his eyes. "When a woman says that, it means I'm in big trouble."

"You're not," Elyse responded. She reached across the short distance and stroked his cheek. "Not in the slightest." Gripping the back of his neck, she tugged him closer and let her lips find his. The kiss raged as they tasted one another, and Elyse could feel the evidence of his arousal against her thigh.

Elyse pulled away and glanced at the driver in the front seat. "We can't," she whispered.

"I'll roll up the divider."

"Then he'll know." Embarrassed, she pushed Julian's hand aside when he reached for her even though she wanted his touch more than anything. "This has to be continued at my apartment."

"If you insist. But I promise you, you'll pay."

And pay she did, all night long.

"Someone is spending an awful lot of time with Elyse," Giana said when she and Julian decided to take in a game of tennis on one of his rare free Sunday mornings.

"Yeah, I'm sorry about that." Though he wouldn't admit it aloud, even to his baby sister, Julian was having a hard time balancing work, family and his time with Elyse. If he had it his way, he'd be with her every waking moment, which was absurd.

"You don't sound sorry," Giana said, volleying the ball back at him. "In fact, from the corny expression on your face, I'd say you're far from sorry."

"Is it that obvious?" he asked, swinging his racket and sending the ball flying in her direction.

"That you're smitten? Just a little bit."

"I suppose you're right." He'd never really succeeded in a relationship of any kind. Spending time with Elyse had opened up an entirely new world of emotional intimacy, which in the past he'd steadfastly avoided. He was getting to know Elyse on a deeper level and it made Julian realize what he'd been missing out on.

"Elyse is more than just a casual lover, isn't she?" Giana inquired.

Julian nodded.

"You're great at keeping people at a distance. Whenever you get too close, you usually pull up stakes."

"And you think you know me so well?"

"Of course I do. I've had a front-row seat to your exploits with women, but this time is different, and that scares you, doesn't it?"

Julian gave her a crooked smile. "You have no idea." He didn't want to screw this up and ruin a good thing.

"I've never been in love myself, but I believe it exists. Look at Mama and Daddy. If I were you, I'd embrace it because sometimes it only comes once in a lifetime."

Julian had always tried to live his best life and Elyse was destined to be a part of it, so why was he so afraid of that fact?

Because of Julian, Elyse was realizing there was more to life than work, work, work, but it also meant she'd seen very little of her father except the moments she managed to squeeze in when Julian wasn't busy. So she was surprised when she looked up from her cubicle on Monday evening to find her father walking toward her because he rarely came to her office.

"Daddy, what are you doing here?" Elyse asked, rising to greet him with a hug.

"I took a taxi here, why? Can't a father stop in to see his daughter?"

"Yes, of course, please sit down." She motioned to the chair inside her cubicle. "I'm sorry I haven't been by. It's just been a busy couple of weeks."

"Oh, I know you've been busy," Frank said as he sat.

Elyse heard the derision in his tone. "Daddy?"

When he lifted his head to look at her, the scornful expression on his face broke her heart. "You've been busy sleeping with the enemy."

She glanced around her, hoping no one had heard, but most folks had gone home for the evening, save for the janitorial staff. "You don't know the full story, Daddy."

"Oh yeah? And what's that?"

"I'm using Julian to get information," Elyse whispered. "He's just a means to an end." She hated lying to her father, but Julian was the man she loved. He was her lover and her friend, but she could never tell her father how conflicted she was about the situation she was in.

"So have you got anything good?" he asked. "Anything to bring down Josiah? Get back my shares?"

"Not here!" she whispered urgently. "Let me take you home and we can talk in the car." She grabbed her purse and he followed her to the elevator bank.

"I can't believe you would keep something like this from me," he said, folding his arms at his chest while they waited for the elevator.

Elyse didn't respond. She felt terrible for keeping the

truth from him. *Was that why she'd kept her distance, because he might have guessed her true feelings?*

They were quiet on the ride in the elevator to the garage, but once they were inside her car, her father let her have it. "So—" he looked over at Elyse as she started the engine "—are you going to tell me what the hell is going on? Why my daughter is cavorting with my enemy's son? And why in hell I had to read about it on some damn web site instead of my daughter telling me?"

Elyse scrubbed her hand over her face. She wasn't looking forward to this conversation, but it had to be done. She eased the Toyota out of the parking spot and headed for the exit. "It's exactly as I told you," she replied. "I needed a way in with the Locketts. Work wasn't bringing me any closer, so I found a way to meet Julian."

"That's Josiah's oldest?"

Elyse shook her head but kept her eyes on the road. "No, that's Roman. He's married and soon to be a father."

"Really?" Her father dragged his hand across the dark stubble on his jaw. "I remember that boy always following behind Josiah, desperate to be in the thick of things. And he is now."

"Yes. He's General Manager, but Josiah is still on the board. I thought getting close to Julian, who's second oldest, was the next best thing." She shrugged her shoulders as she glanced in her father's direction. "And it worked. We hit it off."

Her father regarded her. "Yeah, that much was obvious from the photos and gossip columns."

"I won't lie to you, Daddy. I like Julian, which has made this difficult. But if there's a will, there's a way. And I won't stop trying to find a crack in the armor."

He looked. "Are you sure, baby girl? Because I told you to back away and you didn't, so I assumed you could handle it, but if you can't... If the pressure is too much..." His voice trailed off.

"It's not." Elyse fervently shook her head. She didn't want to let her father down when everyone else in his life, his so-called friends, had abandoned or taken advantage of him. She had to do better. "I'll make this right."

"If you say so."

When they arrived at his apartment, Frank didn't wait for Elyse to walk him inside. Instead, he hopped out of the vehicle without giving her a hug or a kiss goodbye.

She watched his retreating figure as her father rushed inside the building. The man she'd once looked up to and adored was hurting. Tears welled in her eyes, reminding Elyse of how she'd failed him by letting her feelings—no, her *love*—for Julian blind her to the end goal.

What she and Julian shared wasn't real. She told herself Julian had been romancing her like every other woman he'd ever been with and she'd been caught up in the fantasy of it all. What woman wouldn't want to be swept up by Prince Charming? But it was time to put her foolishness on the shelf and get down to business.

And several days later, fate gave her a push in the right direction when Curtis Jackson, the Atlanta Cougars' most lauded and heralded player, got caught in a scandal.

Elyse couldn't have asked for a better outcome than if she'd created it herself. The Jacksons and Locketts would need a publicist and crisis manager. Someone used to managing a celebrity's public image. Someone skilled enough to handle the job. And since she'd already met with Curtis and his father, the odds looked favorable that that someone was *her*.

Fourteen

"How in the hell did you let something like this happen?" Josiah railed at Roman early Saturday morning. He'd called an emergency family meeting at the estate in Tuxedo Park. Julian had barely been able to brush his teeth and shower when he'd received the summons in no uncertain terms telling him to hightail it over.

He and Roman had arrived within seconds of each other. Julian wore a tracksuit while Roman was dressed in Dockers and a pullover sweater. Giana and Xavier were already waiting in the great room, since Xavier lived in the main house and Giana in Roman's old place on the family grounds. They, too, were dressed casually. Xavier in a graphic T-shirt and jeans, Giana in a silk blouse and slacks. *How was it his sister still managed to look sophisticated at this hour?*

"*I* didn't let anything happen," Roman responded. "I couldn't have predicted Curtis would slip past his security."

"Well, you should have," their father responded. "A young man like him, whose been sheltered by a domineering father, would be anxious to be his own man. You should have expected this."

Roman rolled his eyes and Julian couldn't resist letting out a laugh, which Josiah immediately pounced on. "You think something is funny?" he asked. "Tim Jackson is livid that his son is involved in a scandal. He's concerned about the caliber of people Curtis is hanging out with after *we*—" he pointed to his children in the room "—assured him his son was in good hands. It makes all of us look like a bunch of idiots."

"Include yourself on that," Julian responded, leaning back against the couch. "*I* look after Curtis's health and he's in prime physical condition. This has nothing to do with me."

"It has everything to do with you." His father barked, coming toward him and looking down at him. "You're a member of this family or had you forgotten? Has that pretty girl of yours got you so whipped, you can't think straight?"

"That pretty girl of mine..." Julian shot to his feet because he hated when Josiah towered over him like some sort of superhero. "That pretty girl of mine is a publicist. She's good at what she does, and this crisis is right up her alley. We should hire her."

"I don't need your help with this, Julian," Roman interjected. "The PR team we have on retainer is perfectly capable of handling this mess."

"A mess is exactly what this is," his father responded. "He was detained by the police after being caught in a hotel room with an exotic dancer. It's the height of stupidity."

"It's my understanding," Roman replied, "that Curtis didn't even play a primary role in this. She was there when he arrived at the hotel suite and, when he saw her being mistreated during a fight, he immediately tried to step in. That's when the police were called."

"Then why are the press are acting like he's some sort of sleaze?" Giana inquired.

"Because some aren't interested in the facts. They just want something salacious and Curtis gave it to them," Josiah said.

"I'll take care of it," Roman asserted.

"And Elyse can help," Julian proclaimed. "Look at what she did for that politician Mike Ford or that singer Porscha Childs. Their reputations have been redeemed. Furthermore, she already met with Curtis and Tim and they hit it off."

"Why are you so intent on pushing this woman on us?" his father asked. "I mean, how much do you really know about her and her past?"

"Enough!" Julian responded to his father's raised brow.

"There's something about her that's familiar to me and I just can't put my finger on it," Josiah stated. "She's hiding something."

"Well, why you're thinking about it, why not give her a chance, Rome?" Julian inquired, facing his brother.

"Julian does have a point about Elyse," Giana said, and he could have kissed his sister for standing behind him when their father seemed dead set against *his woman*. "I thought Porscha's career was over after the overdose, but she's rebounded and doing better than ever. She has a brand-new album out. If she's already met with the Jacksons, I see no reason not to give her a chance."

"Fine, I'll hear her out," Roman said, "but I make no promises."

"Thank you." Julian just knew Elyse could help Curtis. All Julian wanted was for his family to see Elyse as an asset because, if their relationship continued the way it was going, she could potentially be one of them in the near future.

"Elyse, can I see you in my office, please?" Pierre asked over the speakerphone in her cubicle.

"Yes, sir. I'll be right there." Elyse left her open work

area and headed to her boss's office. She suspected she knew why she was being summoned.

It was hard not to notice that Curtis Jackson was being vilified in the press for being in the room where an exotic dancer had been assaulted. The Locketts would need someone skilled in damage control and Elyse hoped they were calling her to the rescue.

Pierre rose and met her halfway when she knocked on his door several seconds later. "Elyse, come in."

They sat across from each other at the breakout table he kept in his office for such occasions where he required a more personal touch.

"What can I do for you, sir?"

"Your beau has finally come through and offered you the opportunity to meet with his brother Roman Lockett, General Manager of the Atlanta Cougars, on representing Curtis Jackson during this fiasco."

"Really?" She feigned surprised when she'd known this was coming. "That's wonderful. I would be happy to speak with Mr. Lockett and hopefully bring their business to this firm."

"I don't need to tell you how important a client this is," Pierre went on to say. "It could open doors for us in the sports market."

"Then I will make you proud." She rose and shook his hand. Once she was out of his office, she gave herself a mental high-five and smiled at her coworkers as she made her way back to her cubicle. Curtis's predicament presented her with a slippery slope. She could move forward with her agenda, but at what cost? She would be risking her career if she betrayed the Locketts. Josiah Lockett would want payback and have her fired. Not to mention, she would lose Julian in the process. Yet, the idea niggled at her that she was finally in a position to dole out her revenge. She was confused as to which way to turn.

Andrea was waiting for her. "Well, what did he say?"

"The firm—or rather, *I* have a shot at representing Curtis Jackson during his PR crisis."

"Sounds exciting!" Andrea beamed. "And I suppose your boyfriend had nothing to do with this?"

Elyse laughed and put her thumb and index finger together. "Julian may have a little something to do with it."

"Go knock 'em dead."

That's exactly what Elyse intended to do. Maybe not literately, but figuratively. The Atlanta Cougars had touted Curtis Jackson as their future and, prior to this incident, his reputation had been squeaky-clean thanks to his overbearing father. But this was catastrophic.

Now, Elyse had to figure out how to use the circumstances to her advantage.

"Are you sure about this, Julian?" Roman asked from behind him as they waited for Elyse to arrive in the conference room where she'd meet with Roman about her résumé and skill set.

Julian spun around to face his brother. "Of course, I am."

"Really?" Roman eyed him suspiciously. "You sure you're not using your heart instead of your head?"

"I resent the implication that I don't know my own mind," Julian said. "I'm not some dumb jock led around by male anatomy. This is sound business. Elyse has handled some high-profile clients. Her reputation should speak for itself regardless of the fact we're seeing each other."

"But that's precisely why she's here," Roman stated. "If it weren't at your insistence, I wouldn't even give her a chance. I'm doing this for you."

He gave his brother a thin-lipped smile. "Well, don't do me any favors. If you don't feel like she's the best person for the job, then don't choose her. I never asked you to hire

Elyse, I asked that you speak with her because I'm certain you'll see for yourself how talented she is."

Roman stared at him for several moments, a strange expression on his face.

"What?" Julian asked.

"I've never seen you like this before," Roman said. "You're speaking so passionately about Elyse."

"And that's a problem?"

"Quite the opposite. I'm happy to see you this serious over a woman. Shows me you've put your playboy ways aside."

Julian laughed wryly. "I never said anything about that."

"But you've thought about it?"

How could Roman tell? *Was he wearing his heart on his sleeve?*

"What's on your mind?" Roman asked. "Because a look of abject terror just crossed your face."

"I don't know. You might be right," Julian said. He refused to say more because he would have to come to terms with his feelings for Elyse in his own time and in his own way.

There was a knock at the conference room door and Julian didn't wait for Roman to answer. Instead, he went and opened it himself. His heart thudded in his chest at seeing Elyse on the other side. She looked beautiful and sophisticated in an orange sheath with a matching moto jacket. If he had his preference, he would sweep her into his arms and give her a real kiss. Instead, he said, "Good to see you."

She smiled and nodded as Roman came forward. "Elyse, so glad of you to come in so quickly."

"Of course." She stepped into the room, her portfolio under her arm.

Julian glanced at Elyse and then at Roman. "Well, I guess I'll leave the two of you alone so you can get right to it." He gave her a thumbs-up signal and sent a warning glance at Roman to not to be too hard on his lady, and then closed the door.

Julian wished he could be in the room, but there was no way Roman would allow it. The Atlanta Cougars marketing team had staked its new branding campaign on Curtis and his spotless image. Roman wasn't going to let anything jeopardize that, certainly not Julian's relationship with Elyse.

Julian would have to wait, like every other significant other, about news of her interview. But if anyone could knock 'em dead, he was certain it was Elyse.

"Please sit down." Roman motioned to the seat across the table from where he'd put his legal pad. "Can I get you anything to drink?"

Elyse shook her head. She hadn't had many dealings with Roman other than that first family meeting and a subsequent dinner at his and Shantel's. She'd been delighted to spend more time with Shantel, Julian's oldest friend. She hadn't felt jealous in the slightest even after Julian revealed he'd once thought of Shantel as his backup plan once he gave up his playboy ways. She and Shantel were nothing alike and Julian needed someone with more fire than the beautiful, poised psychologist.

"So, Elyse, tell me something about yourself. Something other than what's on this résumé," Roman began.

Elyse did the best she could without revealing too much about her background that might give her away. Roman was a couple of years older than Julian and might remember her father. "I grew up here in Atlanta. My mother died from cancer when I was young, so I grew up having to look after myself and my father. I suppose that's what drove me to succeed, to make something of myself, so my mother could be proud."

"I hear you," Roman stated. "And you've been with King Public Relations for a few years?"

"Yes, it's been a great stomping ground for me to get my feet wet in the PR business."

"How did you end up with Mike Ford as a client?"

"A fluke, I'm sure you're thinking," Elyse said. "And you would be right. Typically, he would have been handled by a more senior publicist, but they were out with the flu during the crisis. I stepped in and helped change the tide of public opinion."

"Impressive," Roma stated. "And I'm sure you've heard of the predicament Curtis Jackson finds himself in?"

"I do."

"Tell me how you might handle it."

Over the course of the next thirty minutes, Elyse outlined her plan to help counteract the negative press coming at the wide receiver. When she was done, she closed her portfolio containing her notes and waited.

"I see why my brother thinks so highly of you," Roman said. "Not only are we protective of Curtis, but the press is being particularly vicious, so I warn you, it could be quite an undertaking if you're given the opportunity."

"I know I may not have as many clients as people at some of the larger firms, but I promise you, I will give it everything I have and you *will* see results."

"Then you're hired."

"Pardon?" Elyse thought she might get more opposition from the hard-nosed General Manager.

"I go with my gut, Elyse," Roman said. "And I've met with other firms, but you were the first person to think about Curtis and how all this might affect him. That's the kind of person who will fit in around here."

"Excellent." Elyse smiled warmly. "I'm ready to start. Where's the big guy?"

"In my office."

"Let's go."

Elyse found herself being led through the inner sanctum of the Atlanta Cougars' headquarters as she headed to Roman's office. She'd always wondered what her life might have been like if her father hadn't lost his share to Josiah. Would her life have been like this? Surrounded by high ceilings, beautiful moldings, state-of-the-art light installations, sumptuous carpets and luxuriously appointed furniture.

Roman stopped in front of his office and opened the door. Curtis stood, as did the older man at his side, who immediately rushed forward.

"Lockett." The man's eyes narrowed. "Where is the publicist you promised us? This story has been out for hours and I don't trust any of the bozos you've brought in thus far."

"Tim, meet Elyse Harper. She's the fixer."

"Elyse, it's a pleasure to see you again," Tim said, a slight smile across his tight expression. "I was hoping you would be included on the list of candidates."

"Don't you worry. I've got this all under control," Elyse responded.

She would either win public opinion in his son's favor or sink Curtis's future at great risk to her own. How far was she willing to go to exact revenge on Josiah Lockett?

Fifteen

Elyse was exhausted when she arrived at her apartment later that evening. She'd told Curtis and his father, Tim, that the best thing they had going for them was the truth. Curtis had stopped the situation in the hotel suite from getting further out of hand. Now they had to tailor his image and PR to support the narrative. She'd given them a strategy to help save his career.

With her contacts, Elyse could ensure Curtis got in front of this story. She had him scheduled to appear on one of the national morning shows the following day, to tell his side of the story, and the day after that he would been seen on the biggest sports program in the nation. She'd also lined up several representatives of his charitable organizations to talk about the programs he'd been helping to roll out in the community. It would be a marathon, not a sprint, to reverse the tide of public opinion, but they would take it one day at a time.

When she'd gone over the elements with Pierre later

that evening, he'd thought she was spot-on, but little did he know she had thought of another angle. A more devious one that would send the franchise built around Curtis Jackson to its knees. She could represent the exotic dancer and have her sell her story to the major network and newspapers. The slightest intimation from the dancer that Curtis wasn't as squeaky-clean as he appeared, or that the Atlanta Cougars made a habit of throwing these types of parties, would cripple the football franchise.

And if she came forward with her father's story of how Josiah Lockett had swindled him out of his shares, it would be yet another nail in their coffin. Surely, having public outrage against Josiah along with a barrage of bad press might convince the patriarch to do the right thing? Of course, if Elyse went this route, it would surely tank her career because Pierre would fire her. *Was this really the direction she wanted to take? Especially after toiling so hard in the trenches all these years.*

Elyse tossed her notepad on the table along with a file she'd kept on the Locketts and Atlanta Cougars. The research she'd done over the years put her in a position to know their strengths and weaknesses. It was a huge risk, but it could be worth if it helped give her father back everything he'd lost.

On the other hand, if she went down this path, Elyse would lose Julian. He would learn of her connection to Frank Robinson and that she'd targeted the middle son from the start as a way to get closer to the Locketts. He would hate her for trying to bring down his family and hurting those he loved. He would never forgive her.

Elyse was grappling with what to do. Help the only family she had left or be true to the man she loved? She was in a lose-lose situation and she didn't see a way out. But she'd brought this all upon herself by trying to right the wrong done to her father all those years ago. If she'd just left well enough alone, she wouldn't be in the predicament she was in now. Then again, she would never have met Julian and known the happiness she'd found in his arms over the last month.

If she had to do it all over again, would she? The answer was an unflappable yes.

Julian didn't know why his father had asked him to come to his office. They rarely spent time together other than the family dinners and game days, so he'd been surprised to receive a request to visit him.

If he had his wish, he would be heading over to Elyse's and finding bliss in her arms. But he knew she'd had a long day with Roman, Tim and Curtis about the plan of action to salvage the wide receiver's reputation, so he was trying to be patient, but it was hard.

Elyse Harper had come to mean more to him than any woman ever had. Being with her felt right. He was tired of the endless stream of women. She'd destroyed the invisible barrier he'd had around his heart and showed him it was possible to love someone other than his family. His heart wasn't made of stone, even though, at times, growing up in the Lockett household he'd felt he couldn't show emotion because Josiah saw it as weakness.

The door to his father's office was open, so Julian didn't bother knocking. He just walked right in.

"Close the door, son." His father's face was a mask of stone.

Julian steeled himself to his father's tone and walked toward him. "What's going on?"

"Remember when I told you something about your girl was familiar?"

"Yes." Dread filled Julian. Suspecting he wasn't going to like hearing what Josiah had to say next, he decided to sit.

"Well, I was right. She's not who she says she is. I had Nico look into it." His father leaned forward, his large elbows on the glass desktop.

"Oh yeah? Is she a spy or something?" Julian joked.

"You could say that." Josiah looked him square in the eye. "She's Frank Robinson's daughter."

Julian's forehead creased into a frown. "Am I supposed to know who that is?"

His father snorted. "No, I don't suppose you would. You were pretty young when I had dealings with Frank."

"What does all this have to do with me and Elyse?"

"She's here for vengeance."

"Why? What on earth for?" Julian asked. "What did you do to her father?"

"Why do you assume I did something?" his father growled.

"Because I know you," Julian responded, jumping to his feet. "You're a bully. And you take what you want from those who can't stand up to you."

"Is that truly what you think of me?"

"Tell me I'm wrong," Julian responded. "Tell me what happened between you and this Frank Robinson."

"Fine, but it's nothing sordid. It was all aboveboard."

"What was?"

"Frank sold his shares of the Atlanta Cougars to me, twenty-five years ago."

"Why is this the first I'm hearing about it?" Julian inquired. He couldn't recall his father ever mentioning the name. Or that he'd had a partner years ago.

"Because—" Josiah looked away "—Frank and I were once friends. The closest of friends, actually. We were savvy investment bankers who'd made a killing on the market and we wanted to get into the football business. You see, at the time, there weren't any African American football owners in the league. The Atlanta Cougars' franchise was on the market for a steal and we struck while the iron was hot."

"And?"

"The franchise was in shambles. It required a lot of capital in the early days to keep afloat. For me, investment banking has always been akin to gambling, but I knew when to call it quits. Frank, however, did not. And then his wife, Nadine, had been diagnosed with cancer and the cost of the treatments was killing him."

"And you took advantage of him?" Julian finished. *Why am I not surprised?* He knew his father didn't have many scruples, but to take advantage of a friend during a time of need was low even for Josiah.

Josiah shook his head. "No. It wasn't like that. Frank had developed a bad gambling habit. I think he thought he could make some extra cash to help out with the medical bills. And he just got in deeper and deeper. I tried to talk him out of it, but he wouldn't listen, and I couldn't let him put the Cougars at risk. Who knows if his shares would have ended up with some loan shark? I protected the company and I won't apologize for it."

"I see. I've heard enough." Julian turned to leave, but his father stopped him with his words.

"Have you? Because I promise you, there's a reason his daughter is here. Why she sought you out. Why she's so eager to work for the Atlanta Cougars. She wants revenge for her father."

"Or maybe she wants to take back what you stole from him."

"I didn't steal it!"

"Does it really matter?" Julian asked. "Why couldn't you have just left well enough alone? Because you couldn't, could you? You interfered, just like you did in Roman and Shantel's relationship. *Why can't you just let me be happy?* You claim to love us, but I'm beginning to wonder."

"That's not fair. I do love you, Julian, that's why I'm trying to save you from a woman who's using you."

"Because I'm the weakest Lockett heir, right?" Julian had always suspected that was how his father felt about him, but it was clear now.

"No, because you're my son and I'm protecting you."

"I'm a grown man and I can protect myself." Julian stormed out of his office. He had to find Elyse. He needed to find out if everything his father had said was true. *Was he just a means to an end for her?* Had everything they'd shared up to this point been a lie so she could ruin his family? He had to know and he wouldn't leave her apartment until she told him the truth.

Elyse was perusing her notes at home when her cell phone rang a little after 8:00 p.m. Dread filled her when she saw Matt's name on the caller ID. When she picked up, the bartender told her Frank was once again at the bar, drowning his sorrows. She couldn't help but wonder if she was the reason. If it was because he couldn't take her association with the Locketts. Didn't he understand that she was doing all of this *for him*?

She quickly dressed in some leggings and a sweater, grabbed her purse and rushed out the door.

Fifteen minutes later, she swung open the bar's behemoth front door and, indeed, found her father slumped in the corner over the bar.

"How long has he been like this?" she asked Matt.

"Not long. He seemed especially agitated after someone brought up seeing you on Instagram with Julian Lockett at some movie premiere," Matt replied with a frown. "Didn't know you hung out with those high-society types. Thought you were one of us." He turned away and began drying more glasses behind the counter.

She ignored his derisive comment, rushed over to the

edge of the bar, and placed her hand on her father's back. "Daddy?"

He glanced up, but when he saw her, he looked away. "What do you want?"

"I'm here to take you home."

"I'm surprised you have the time," her father said, lifting his head to look at her with anger in his eyes.

"I always have time for you, Daddy. C'mon." She helped him out of his seat and, this time, Matt didn't come from behind the bar like he usually did to help her. He was jealous, so she struggled alone with her father all the way to her car.

He passed out on the short drive to his Old Fourth Ward apartment and she had to rouse him from his slumber. He stumbled in his steps into the apartment, where Elyse put him to bed, removing his shoes and covering him with a blanket.

Leaning against the bedroom door Elyse felt like a failure. She'd gone to great lengths to get close to the Locketts, but she just didn't think she had the heart to betray Julian.

She couldn't do it.

She'd fallen in love with Julian and her heart was full of him. There was no way she could do anything that would hurt his family. The knowledge should have put her at ease, but looking at her father tonight, she doubted it would bring him much comfort. She'd let him down like everyone else.

And she'd failed Julian, too. She would have to tell him the truth about why she'd switched places that first night at dinner. She had to come clean. And pray that one day he might forgive her.

Julian didn't know what to believe as he drove to Elyse's apartment because she wasn't taking his calls. That the woman he cared for, possibly even loved, had set a sinister plan in motion? To do what? Bring down his family? His father?

No.

He shook his head. He wouldn't believe that of Elyse. She was too kind, too caring, too giving. He wouldn't, couldn't, believe she would betray him like that. He had to go to her. Look her in the eye and ask her about her father. Would he know if she lied to him? Julian sure hoped so. They'd been together for a while nonstop.

When he arrived, he noticed her Toyota wasn't in the parking lot. So he used the key she'd so graciously given him one night a couple of weeks ago. She'd given him the spare and told him to use it anytime he wanted. He'd teased her about her being afraid of him looking through her drawers, but she'd said she had nothing to hide and he'd believed her.

Was he that bad a judge of character?

The apartment was empty, but the lights were on. She must have run to the store, Julian thought, closing the door behind him. He could use a drink and he was sure she could after the day she'd had with Curtis. He would have a bottle of wine open and ready.

Julian was walking to the kitchen when he noticed several files sitting on the coffee table. He didn't know what made him look, but when he glanced down, he saw a file labeled "Locketts" and another labeled "Atlanta Cougars." Any other day, Julian might have left them there because Elyse had been hired to work for the Cougars team, so they were probably work-related. But given what his father had insinuated, his curiosity had him opening the top folder.

Inside were dossiers on each and every one of the Lockett family members, including himself. There were several news clippings and printouts of online gossip columns about him and his dating life. *What on earth was she doing with all this?*

Julian glanced at the legal pad and saw her scribbled notes about Curtis, but upon further inspection, he realized there was more. She'd listed a strategy to save the Atlanta Cougars and a strategy to *destroy* them. Julian's stomach sank, his eyes blurring as he read the flowing script that ripped his heart out.

Everything they'd shared had been a lie. A farce. Elyse had used him to get close to his family and gain information. Hadn't her research showed Roman would have been the better subject? As a team doctor, Julian had no power at the company, yet she must have thought she could use him in some way. Why hadn't he seen through her act? He'd opened up to her about his family, about wanting to be of value as a physician, and allowed her to see the real him.

She was a damn good actress because she'd honestly had Julian believing he'd fallen in love. That what they shared was real, lasting. He'd been played.

Anger bloomed inside him, but he would rein it in. He would like to see the seductress's face when he called her out on every one of her lies. Because the time for truth was now.

The door slammed shut and Julian spun around to face Elyse.

"Babe, what are you..." The words died on her tongue when she saw Julian holding her notepad.

"You were going to bury us!" he shouted. "Weren't you?"

"No!" Elyse rushed toward him but Julian sidestepped her and walked to the farthest side of the room. He couldn't stand to be near her because that sweet scent of hers might lure him into her web of deceit again.

"I know what you're holding in your hand is damning, but I wasn't going to use it. I would never betray you."

"Lies, Elyse. It's all lies." Julian tossed the notepad across the room. "My father told me everything. I know you're Frank Robinson's daughter. Yet you've been using the name Elyse Harper."

"Harper is my mother's maiden name."

"You used it as a cover so no one would recognize you, least of all my father because you blame him for ruining yours."

"He did!" Elyse yelled.

"So you admit it?" Julian charged, pointing at her. "Okay—" he tore off the blazer he was wearing "—now we're finally going to get somewhere."

"I don't know what your father told you, Julian—"

Julian interrupted her. "He told me the truth. Something you wouldn't know anything about."

"I know he swindled my father out of his share of the Atlanta Cougars."

"And did your father tell you about his gambling habits?"

"Yes. I know about them, but at the end of the day, Josiah was supposed to be his friend and instead he took what was rightfully my father's."

"Because he would have gambled it all away," Julian said. He couldn't believe he was defending his father, of all people, but in light of what Elyse had done, it was the right thing. "But all of this…this past history between our fathers is beside the point. The point is—you sought *me* out and I want to know why."

"I—"

Julian held up a hand to stop her. "Don't you dare lie to me! I want the truth, Elyse. That's if you know how to give it."

Tears rolled down her beautiful fawn cheeks. It hurt Julian to see them because he cared about her so deeply, but he'd been a blind, besotted fool. No more. He wanted answers.

Elyse wiped away tears with the back of her hand. "I'd done my research. I knew you were the playboy in the family who liked women. I knew I wasn't bad on the eyes and might have a chance with you, but I had no idea how to go about it. It's not like we traveled in the same circles."

"Go on."

"But one day I happened to be in the ladies' room when I overheard Tiffany Mayes talking. I saw that as my window of opportunity to meet you, so I switched places with her."

"You've already told me this. I know the *how. I want to know the why.*"

She lowered her head briefly. When she looked up at him, the guilt in her eyes betrayed her. "Because I thought you were an easy target."

Julian nodded. He'd wanted to know and now he did. He'd been played for a fool.

"But then I got to know you, Julian, and I realized you weren't just the playboy that you presented to the world. There was so much more to you. I began to realize that the revenge I sought wasn't going to be black-and-white."

"But you were prepared to go far, weren't you, Elyse? You let me make love to you over and over and over again. Do you know what that makes you?"

"It makes me a woman in love, Julian."

Curses fell from his mouth as his temper flared. "Please, Elyse, stop acting. Don't demean yourself or me with this farce anymore. You've been caught, found out."

"It's true, Julian. I fell head over heels in love with you in Saint Lucia."

Julian laughed as he shook his head. "My God. You're an incredible actress. I have to give you that." He had to get out of there. Otherwise, she'd have him believing her. That's how much she had him wrapped around her pinky finger. "From the moment we met, it's all been lies. We're over, Elyse. I never want to see you again."

After snatching up his blazer, he started for the door.

Elyse grabbed his arm, holding on to him, but he continued walking. "Please don't leave, Julian. Not like this. I love you. I would never hurt you."

When he reached the door, Julian peeled her fingers from around his forearm. "You didn't, Elyse. Didn't all your research tell you I don't have a heart to hurt?"

Julian left Elyse's apartment a broken man.

Sixteen

Elyse awoke early the next morning, well before dawn, to find herself on the couch where she'd crumbled after Julian had walked out on her. She'd tried to explain the truth to him, but he'd already come to his own conclusion after finding her notes. Why, oh why, had she left the files and her notes out like that? Because she'd gotten the emergency call about her father at the bar. And now her entire life was falling apart.

Because Julian was her life.

Elyse didn't know how it happened, but he'd become her whole world and, less than ten hours later, it felt like the rug had been pulled out from underneath her. She'd tried to call Julian after he'd left, but her calls went straight to his voice mail. She didn't blame him for hating her.

She'd lied to him. Deceived him. She had no one to blame but herself. She'd wanted to do right by her father, but she hadn't been able to. There was no going back. What was done was done. Telling the world about her father's poor decisions and Josiah's ruthlessness would only make Frank look foolish.

But she could do one thing right. She could finish what she'd started and help free Curtis Jackson from the negative spotlight. She was certain the Locketts would fire her, so she would have to do a preemptive strike and get to Tim Jackson first. It was a long shot, to prove to Julian her intentions were pure, but it was all the ammunition she had.

And so she showered and dressed with care in a tailored pantsuit and drove into the heart of downtown. She arrived at 7:00 a.m. and was greeted by a bleary-eyed Tim Jackson, who was surprised to find her on his son's doorstep so early.

"May I have a minute of your time?" Elyse asked. "I know it's early."

"Well, you're here, so you might as well come in."

Thirty minutes later, after she'd filled him in on all the gory details of how and why she'd come into the Lockett circle, Tim stared back at her. "You're a gutsy lady. The Locketts won't be happy that you're here trying to intercept them."

"I'm aware," Elyse said. "But I have to do this because I gave you and your son—" she glanced at Curtis, who'd emerged several minutes ago to sit with them "—my word that I would get him out of this and I can, if you allow me the opportunity."

"And refresh me on how you will do that," Tim said, "because my son has worked his entire life to be where he is."

Elyse outlined her plan to save Curtis's image to his father from the morning TV show appearances to the sports programs to the charitable organizations he was helping roll out in the community. "We can turn the tide, Mr. Jackson."

"I don't doubt you know your job, Elyse, but your family's past with the Locketts is a complicated tale. Why should I trust you?"

"I came here today and told you the truth at great risk to my career because, quite honestly, it's all I have left."

"Maybe," Tim replied. "Julian is like any man. His pride is hurt because you used him, but forgiveness makes strange bedfellows."

"So what do you say?" Elyse asked. "Give me seventy-two hours to turn the tide. I promise you, you won't be disappointed."

"You're on. I liked you from the start, Elyse, and I listen to my instincts. It hasn't led me wrong thus far." Tim Jackson shook Elyse's hand and she breathed a sigh of relief. But it was only one stop on her road to penance and hopefully winning Julian's heart back one day.

"Thanks for putting me up last night, Shantel," Julian said when he strolled into the kitchen in yesterday's attire.

"You're welcome," she said as she poured him a mug of coffee from the carafe.

He'd arrived on her doorstep a hot mess. He'd thought his brother would turn him away because it wasn't like the old days when he could turn up at Shantel's and commiserate his woes, but Roman had been in a giving mood.

Julian and Shantel had stayed up talking for hours. He'd shared with her everything Josiah told him and Elyse's explanation. Julian still couldn't believe he'd fallen for her routine hook, line and sinker.

"Don't be so hard on yourself, Julian," Shantel said. "She had us all fooled, but she could be telling you the truth that she wasn't going to betray you."

"And pigs can fly."

Just then Roman walked in, his phone to his ear. "Thank you, Tim. Thanks for letting me know." He ended the call.

"What's that look for, Rome?" Julian asked at the angry look crossing Roman's dark features.

"That girl of yours has struck again."

Julian tossed back his head. He couldn't take much more. His chest constricted in a tight vise. "Jesus, what now?"

"She went to the Jacksons and pled her case. They've agreed to keep her on as their publicist—against my wishes."

"What?" Julian straightened. "They can't do that."

"They just did!" Roman said, tossing his iPhone on the counter. He strolled over to his wife, still in her robe, and leaned down to give her a kiss.

"Did you tell them she can't be trusted?"

"Apparently, Tim thinks otherwise because she came clean with him about everything including her family's past history with our father."

"She didn't?" Julian was surprised. *That took guts.*

"Yep. And he refuses to back down," Roman said, "despite my misgivings."

"I think it's a good thing," Shantel said, looking at both Lockett men, who were staring at her as if she'd fallen off her rocker. "It's my guess that this is Elyse's attempt to make amends to the family by showing she holds no ill will."

"She could have fooled me," Roman snorted.

"I guess we'll have to wait and see how this plays out," Julian stated. "And if you'll excuse me, I'm going to head to my place to get cleaned up. Roman, I'll see you at the office."

In the car, Julian wondered about Elyse's motivations. Was Shantel right? Was she trying to make amends? *Or was this all another elaborate ploy to sabotage his family by using the Jacksons?*

If it was, he would make sure she never worked in this town again.

"He hates me, Andrea," Elyse cried to her friend when she came over later that evening.

Andrea had brought a bottle of wine along with a pepperoni pizza with her, and Elyse was thankful. She hadn't had an appetite all day and had been holding it together thanks to energy drinks.

"He doesn't hate you though maybe he should. What you thought about doing was terrible, Elyse," Andrea said, sipping her wine on the couch after they'd polished off half the pizza.

"Don't you think I know that?" Elyse huffed. "I thought you were my friend."

"A friend would tell you it's wrong to lie and deceive people for revenge. But by the same token, you realized you couldn't do it so I'm glad about that. And as for Julian, I've seen how he looks at you. He adores you."

"Maybe he did once," Elyse said, tucking her legs underneath her on her sofa, "but he doesn't anymore." She took a long generous sip from her wineglass.

Andrea shook her head. "He's upset and disappointed in you, as he should be, but that doesn't make what you and he shared any less real."

"I was fooling myself thinking I could have a man like Julian," Elyse replied. "Especially when I'd built our relationship on lies and half-truths."

"It's not over," Andrea said. "You never know, he could forgive you and you guys will kiss and make up."

Elyse chuckled at Andrea's rose-colored-glasses view of the world. "I love you, sweetheart, but I don't know if anything can heal the rift between me and Julian."

"I don't know about that. Once he sees everything you've done for Curtis, he'll realize you're meant to be."

Oh how Elyse wished that were true. Wished she could go back in time and tell him the truth about their fathers' past connection. He might have believed her then, if she'd come clean, but too much time had passed. Now he questioned her motives, their lovemaking—hell, everything that had ever happened between them. Their time together had meant everything to Elyse. Julian was the only man she'd ever loved and she was certain he always would be, even if he never forgave her.

"You know I should have fired you," Pierre told Elyse several days later when she was called into his office.

"Why didn't you?" Elyse had been wondering about that. She was certain the Locketts would have wanted her head on silver platter, considering she'd gone over their heads to Tim Jackson.

"Because your client's father intervened," Pierre replied. "He insisted you be allowed to implement the plan you'd outlined to save his son's reputation. And bully for you, it worked."

Her strategy to help Curtis Jackson put a positive spin on his scandal was working. His interview on the morning program and on the national sports talk show had turned the tide. And to help their case, the exotic dancer had come forward to reveal how Curtis was the one who'd saved her from being assaulted.

Everyone was calling Curtis Jackson a hero and the negative whispers had been obliterated. And Curtis's positive press was great for the Atlanta Cougars, too.

"Thank you, Pierre. I know it wasn't easy going against the Locketts."

"This is *my* firm and I run it how *I* see fit," Pierre said. "But you have to know that you were crossing the line."

"Yes, I know that and at the end of the day I didn't betray their family or your business."

"But you thought about it."

Elyse nodded.

"You're a good publicist, Elyse, which is why I didn't fire you, but you're on probation, and if I get one whiff of wrongdoing, you're out!"

"Thank you, Pierre." Elyse exited his office without another word.

She was happy for a career win, but Elyse couldn't say the same for her personal life. If Julian had seen the positive press, he hadn't said a word to her. She'd even sent him flowers. *Could he not see that she was trying to right the wrongs she'd done?*

Elyse didn't know what else to do. She was at the end of her rope. Still, it didn't stop her from loving Julian. If he never forgave her, she would always love him. His charm. His humor. His kindness. She didn't know if she'd be lucky enough to ever meet someone as special as him.

On the way to her desk, the receptionist came up and whispered something in her ear. As she listened to what the woman was saying, her blood ran cold.

Elyse was shell-shocked but she sprang into action, rushing to Andrea's desk to tell her the news. "I have to leave. My father is in the hospital."

"I'll drive you." Andrea was instantly by her side and Elyse rushed for the elevators. She couldn't lose her father, too. She had only one parent left.

"These are beautiful," Angelique told Julian when he presented her with the red roses Elyse had delivered to his office earlier that morning. "Where did you get them?"

"They were delivered."

"From Elyse?" his mother asked as she stirred a pot of gumbo on the stove. If anything would make him feel better, it was a pot of his mama's famous gumbo. She'd been upset to learn of Elyse's duplicity because she'd thought so highly of her and felt they had a relationship that might go the distance.

"Yeah." Julian sat on one of the bar stools and watched her add the meats she'd already prepared. Chicken, shrimp and andouille. He'd come over to the house not just to drop off the flowers and to have a home-cooked meal, but for a change of scenery. It felt as if his and Elyse's best moments were being played like a movie reel over and over again in his head. He couldn't go through a single minute of the day without thinking of her.

"Have you spoken to her yet?"

"Noooo." Julian wasn't sure when or if he'd ever be ready to speak to her. And that hurt. It was like a pain in his chest because he couldn't believe how gullible he'd been to her charms. He didn't trust that he could be sensible when it came to her. He literally *ached* for her. His body seemed to be in a perpetual state of physical torment from missing hers. And then there was the *L* word. The word he couldn't think of and kept trying to put out of his mind.

"And your father?" When Julian had told his mother his father had looked into Elyse's past and had a dossier completed, she'd been livid. He suspected it was the cause of some strain in their marriage because, at today's meeting, his father had glowered at Julian from across the table despite Roman's good news that Elyse's PR efforts had been successful and Curtis's good name was on the mend.

"You know Dad and I will never see eye to eye." He popped one of the cooked shrimp sitting in a bowl on the counter into his mouth. He loved how his mother stayed true to her Creole roots. She could have a team of chefs in the kitchen but a couple of nights a week she preferred to cook. She said it kept her skills in the kitchen sharp.

"You know he meant well." She strained the crab legs cooking in another pot and tossed them and the shrimp into the bubbling gumbo mixture.

"Did he, though?" Julian wasn't so sure. He'd seen the damage his father had caused to Roman and Shantel's relationship when he'd threatened to disown Roman if he didn't get a prenup. Roman had threatened to leave the company until Josiah stepped down as General Manager.

"Why are you two so hard on each other?" his mother asked, turning to face him and placing her spoon on the holder.

"Because I've never been Rome or Xavier," Julian responded. "And I'm never going to be. I've never been athletically inclined and therefore we've never had much in common. I've always been more like you, Mom, and you know it."

She shrugged. "I suppose, of all my children, you're the most like me. But surely you can find some common ground with your father. I don't like dissension in the family."

"For you, I'll try. How about that?"

"Fair enough. And Elyse?"

"What about her?"

"Julian?" His mother wiped her hands on her apron and then came over to cup his cheeks with her hands. "People make mistakes. We're not perfect."

"I know that."

"Then forgive her."

"How can I, Mama, after what she's done?"

"It won't be easy, but you love her, don't you? And you're miserable without her. I can see it in your eyes."

He frowned as he peered into her eyes. "How did you know?"

"I'm your mama, boy. I raised you. I know you better than anyone. And it's because I do that I know you have the capacity to forgive." She softly caressed his cheek. "Think about it."

"I will."

His mother's words lingered with Julian long after he'd left the house. Was she right? Could he forgive Elyse? Did he want to? He'd laid so much on the line with Elyse, allowed her into dark places he'd never let anyone else. He supposed that's why her lies and half-truths had hurt so much, because he did care for her.

No, he was being honest.

He loved Elyse.

Julian didn't know when it happened, but somehow it had snuck up on him, and he didn't know what to do with the emotion. If this is what love felt like, if it made you hurt like hell, then Julian wanted no part of it. He could live his life without love. He'd done it before. So why did the thought now make him feel hollow inside?

"It's alcohol poisoning, Ms. Harper," the doctor told Elyse when she arrived at the hospital emergency room to find out what happened to her father.

"Omigod!" Elyse's hand flew to her mouth.

"Because of your father's binge drinking, he lost consciousness. His blood alcohol level was point one five. He has all the classic symptoms—confusion, abnormal breathing and, of course, severe nausea. We had to pump your father's stomach."

"What do we do now?"

"Wait for his alcohol levels to gradually drop but, Ms. Harper, can I be frank?"

"Yes, of course."

"Your father needs to get into a rehabilitation program. As you know, this isn't his first visit to the hospital."

"It's been so hard to get him to agree."

"To save his life, you must. The next time, he could have a heart attack, go into a coma or, even worse, lose his kidneys."

Andrea squeezed Elyse's shoulder after the doctor left. "It's going to be okay."

"I don't know," Elyse cried, and her head fell into Andrea's lap. "I've tried everything I can to get him into a rehab program, but he never goes."

"Maybe this time will be different."

Elyse nodded. She would have to try because she refused to lose her father to this illness.

Julian called Elyse's office the next day from his office at the arena. He didn't know why. He just knew he had to. He'd stayed up half the night thinking about what his mother had said about forgiveness. Elyse could have buried his family under bad press. She knew how. Instead, she'd helped Curtis, one of their star players, and consequently the Atlanta Cougars had a better reputation than ever before.

"Can I speak to Elyse Harper."

"I'm sorry, she isn't here," the receptionist replied.

After getting nowhere with the receptionist she patched him through to Pierre, who informed him she was in the hospital.

Julian barely heard the name—and heard nothing else—because he was already rushing toward the elevator bank.

Thankfully, the elevator had just arrived and he hopped inside. His mind went to the last few days and all the calls and texts she'd sent him, which he'd ignored because he'd been so angry at her, so hurt. But he would never want anything to happen to her.

Dear God. He hoped everything was okay. It had to be. Elyse was the picture of health. *Why on earth would she be in the hospital?* He called her on her phone, but the call went immediately to her voice mail. Julian's mind raced with the worst things imaginable. She'd been in a car crash or hit her head in her apartment. All sorts of crazy ideas sprang into his mind as he raced to the hospital.

He slid his Bugatti Veyron into a visitor parking space and quickly ran inside to the emergency room. He charged up to the nurses' station and asked for Elyse Harper, but the staffer stated no one was there with that name.

"What do you mean?" he roared. "I know she's here. Her boss told me."

"I'm sorry, sir, but she isn't here," the nurse stated firmly.

Julian ran his fingers through his hair and paced around in a circle. That's when he saw her. Elyse, holding a coffee cup and wearing sweats, was coming down the hall with her friend Andrea.

"Julian?" she said when she came within a few feet of him. Her eyes were red-rimmed, as if she'd been crying all night. "What are you doing here?"

Julian let out a long sigh of relief. "Thank God, you're all right. When I heard you were at the hospital, I nearly lost my mind. I thought..."

"You thought what?" she asked, confusion crossing her beautiful features.

"I'm just going to go," Julian heard Andrea whisper from somewhere off in the distance.

"I thought something had happened to you, and I couldn't bear it." He reached for her, pulling her by the waist and clutching her to him. "I couldn't bear it because I love you so, so much, Elyse." He kissed the top of her head. At first, Elyse didn't return the hug, but within seconds she was gripping him back, holding on to him as if her life depended on it.

When they finally separated, there were tears in Elyse's eyes. "I love you, too, Julian. And I'm sorry for everything. I got so caught up in the past and in right and wrong, revenge and justice, that I lost sight of what was important. But never again." She glanced up at him and he could see the truth in her eyes. "I promise you, if you give me another chance, I will never lie to you again. Your heart is safe with me."

He framed her face with hands. "And you, Elyse, are everything I could ever want. You complete me and challenge me in a way I never imagined. I thought my life plan was perfect, but then I met you and it made me realize what I was missing. This week has been half a life without you."

"Same here. I was just hoping against hope that you would find some way to forgive me. I made a terrible mistake in not telling you the truth."

"I forgive you," Julian said, because he knew she needed to hear him to say the words. "Okay. So let's put the past in the past and be together. You're not alone anymore, Elyse. You can lean on me. I'll help you through all of this."

"I love you more than I can say," Elyse responded.

Julian lowered his mouth to hers and the happiness he hadn't known all week surged through him. He knew that he wanted to spend the rest of his life with this woman. He'd spent most of his adulthood running away from commitment, but no more.

Eventually, they pulled apart, both breathing hard, as if they'd run a marathon.

"Come." He pulled her over to the nearest section of chairs in the waiting room and they sat side by side. Julian held Elyse's small hand in his. "So tell me what's going on," he said. "Why are you here at the hospital?"

"It's my dad. He has alcohol poisoning and was admitted. He's in serious condition, Julian."

"I'm so sorry, baby." Julian pulled her to him again. He couldn't stop holding her, touching her. It had been several long agonizing days that he never wanted to repeat again.

"If he comes out of this—"

"*When* he comes out of this…" Julian corrected.

"When he does, I'm taking him to rehab. I don't care if he's kicking and screaming, but this has to stop. I can't lose another parent. I just can't."

She wept aloud, rocking back and forth, and Julian held her, whispering words of comfort. "You won't. We'll get him into the best program there is."

"We?" She glanced up as if finally hearing him.

"Yes, *we.*" Julian wiped away her tears with the back of his hand. "I'm never going to leave your side again, Elyse Harper Robinson. So you're stuck with me."

"I'm happy to be stuck with you, Julian."

"Good," he said and, without thinking or caring where he was, he got down on one knee. "Will you marry me, Elyse? Will you spend the rest of your life with me?"

Elyse peered down at him and then pressed a soft kiss to his mouth. "Yes, I'll marry you, Julian."

Seventeen

Elyse lifted her fingers to her lips and the magic of his kiss. She couldn't believe Julian was forgiving her. It was more than she could have ever hoped for. And wasn't that why she loved him? He had a big heart, capable of love. She was just happy to be a recipient of his love and that's why his arms felt like home. She did as Julian suggested. She leaned on him, drew strength from him. As her tired eyes closed and she fell asleep, Julian's strong arms tightened around her and she felt safe, loved, cared for.

Julian remained at Elyse's side until her father regained consciousness hours later. And when he did, Elyse was prepared to lay down the law about rehab, but her father beat her to the punch.

"I'm so sorry, baby girl," Frank said when he spoke to her from his hospital bed. "And seeing what I've put you through has made me realize that I need to get help."

"It's time, Daddy." Elyse wiped an errant tear from her

cheek. "I've found a great place and they can take you as soon as you're released."

He nodded. "And you?" He inclined his head at Julian, who hadn't left her side since he'd arrived. "I assume you're the Lockett my daughter has fallen for?"

"My name is Julian Lockett, sir, and I love Elyse." Julian grasped one of her hands at her side. "I've asked her to be my wife. I'm sorry for not getting your blessing beforehand. My proposal was kind of spontaneous."

Her father glanced at Elyse. "Marriage? Isn't this kind of sudden?"

"Maybe," Elyse replied. "But it's kind of like what you said happened with you and Mama. When you know, you just know."

Her father's eyes filled with tears. "My heart was so full of love for your mother. She was m-my wh-whole world." His voice shook.

"I know, Daddy."

"When I lost her..." He paused. "I lost myself and I couldn't recover from the heartache. I used alcohol and gambling as a refuge from the pain, but they only made life worse for me and for you." He glanced in her direction. "Because of it, you had to grow up way too soon and take care of me. I'm sorry for that, you didn't get to be a kid."

"It's okay."

"No, it's not." He shook his head fervently. "I owe you a debt of gratitude and I will spend the rest of my life making it up to you."

"You're my father. You owe me nothing but your love and to get better."

"And the truth. I owe you that."

Elyse's brow furrowed. "What do you mean?"

"I wasn't completely forthcoming when I spoke to you about Josiah. I told you that he swindled me out of my shares of the Atlanta Cougars when, in fact, it was quite the opposite."

"But you said—"

"I embellished the truth," he interrupted. "Josiah tried to get me to quit gambling, but once I'd started, I was addicted to the high. Add the alcohol… Both were an escape from the pain of losing your mother. The more I played, the worse it got, until I'd mortgaged our house to the hilt. Josiah asked me to go to rehab, but I refused. I thought I had it under control, until one day there was nothing but my shares. I sold them to Josiah."

"Did he pay you a fair price?" Julian inquired.

Her father nodded. "Probably more than what they were worth at the time because, back then, the team wasn't what it is now."

"Thank you for telling me, Mr. Robinson," Julian said. "My father can be pretty ruthless, so I wasn't sure what to believe."

"I'm telling you both, so you—" he looked at Elyse "—can let go of any animosity you might have about the past. I don't want you trying to exact a revenge for a wrong that was never committed. The past needs to be left in the past."

"I can't believe you lied to me," Elyse cried, shaking her head in dismay. "After everything we've been through." She'd tried to destroy a family who'd done nothing wrong.

"I'm sorry, baby girl. I didn't know how to tell you the truth. It was bad enough I'd fallen so far down from that pedestal you had me on. I didn't want to disappoint you further."

"The lies hurt me more, Daddy, more than the truth ever could. We have to stop lying to each other and ourselves." Because she wasn't blameless, either, considering that she'd lied to Julian, his family, and even her father about her relationship with Julian. "Do you think we can do that?"

Frank nodded.

"Oh, Daddy." Elyse threw herself in his arms. He caught her and hugged her tight.

"I love you, Elyse. You're the only thing this old man has ever done right in this life. I don't want you to lose out on your happy-ever-after."

Elyse lifted her head to look into her father's dark brown eyes, but it was Julian who spoke. "She won't."

After their heart-to-heart with her father, they left him to rest and Julian took Elyse back to his condo. For the first time in a long time, Elyse felt completely free. Free to be who she was. Free to love Julian.

And in his bedroom that night, she expressed her love and covered his mouth with her kisses that made the ache inside her body rise to fever pitch. It had been nearly a week since they'd been together and she could see the effect it had on Julian. His jaw was stubbly, as if he hadn't shaved in days, but that was just fine with her.

She welcomed the raw feel of him in her arms again and when he surged into her after donning a condom, Elyse's senses spun out of control. She was tossed into a maelstrom of emotions because this time, after declaring their love, they were *making love.*

And as Julian thrust deeply and rhythmically inside her, the pressure built. "I missed you," he blurted. And then he pumped into her until they reached breaking point.

"Yes!" Elyse cried, her nails curling into his rigid muscles as she held him tightly. She'd missed him so much. Julian was right behind her in the throes of their passion and roared as he reached an earth-shattering climax that made her shudder and him quake as ripple after ripple traveled through them.

"I love you," Elyse whispered.

Julian brushed back her short pixie-plastered hair from her face. "And I love you, Elyse."

* * *

"I don't know about this, Julian," Elyse said from Julian's side as they walked up the steps to the family estate in Tuxedo Park the following Sunday. "I doubt very much your family will want to see me after everything's that happened."

"I thought you wanted to apologize."

"I do." But her face was clouded with uneasiness.

"Then we'll do what we came to do. If they can't accept it..." He shrugged.

"Then what? I won't come between you and your family, Julian."

"You leave my family to me," Julian said. And he meant it. Nothing and no one was coming between them ever again. He squeezed Elyse's clammy hand in his and opened the front door. He followed the sound of voices to the great room, where the entire family was gathered.

All conversation stopped when Julian and Elyse entered the room. Elyse tensed by his side and Julian prepared himself to walk away from his family if need be. But it was his mother who came forward first.

"Elyse, so nice of you to join us again," she said, glancing at his father. There was no mistaking the warning look she gave him.

"I'm sorry to stop by uninvited," Elyse said, easing her hand out of Julian's, "but I wanted to apologize to all of you." She looked around the room at the entire Lockett clan. "When I met Julian, I had an ulterior motive. Revenge for a perceived wrong against my father." She moistened her lips.

"Yes, you did." His father's chest puffed out, but his mother put a hand on his arm.

"But then I got to know your son, your brother." She glanced at his siblings. Roman was being stalwart, but Julian suspected that was Shantel's influence. Giana had a wary expression and Xavier was nowhere to be seen. Where was his younger brother these days? He'd taken to disappearing without telling the family. "And I fell hard. It made me realize I could never betray him, despite Julian finding that folder with my plans."

"And what about your father?" Josiah asked, folding his arms as he scrutinized his son's fiancée. "Do you still believe the lies he's told you?"

"Josiah?" his mother quipped.

"It's okay, Mrs. Lockett. It's a fair question," Elyse said. "No, I don't, but I want you to know that it didn't matter. That's why I went to the Jacksons. It was my way to make amends to you, but to answer you, Mr. Lockett, a couple of days ago, my father had an epiphany after alcohol poisoning landed him in the hospital."

His father's expression grew softer. "Is Frank okay?"

Elyse nodded. "Yes. And he finally told me the truth, which is that you tried to help him."

"I did."

"But he spiraled out of control after my mom's death and let gambling and alcohol consume him. He taught me to hate you, Mr. Lockett, but it was lies. All of it. I know it and so does he. He's finally agreed to go to rehab. And maybe I can finally move on with my life." She reached for Julian's hand again. "Our life."

His mother was the first to ask. "Has something happened?"

"Yes," Julian added. "I asked Elyse to marry me and she's accepted. I hope, as my family—" he glanced around the room "—you can be happy for us, because everything from before is water under the bridge. I'm hoping today can be a fresh start for both our families. What do you say, Dad?"

His father stared at him a long moment. "Welcome to the family, Elyse." Julian was shocked when Josiah held out his arms to Elyse and she walked into them. "I'm happy Frank is getting the help he needs."

Julian was thrilled to see the Locketts and Robinsons mending fences, but more important, he was happy to have found the love of his life. Because if Elyse hadn't sought him out, they might never have connected and he would never have known he could feel a love like this.

Epilogue

One month later...

Julian and Elyse rushed down the hall of the hospital holding a big bear, balloons and flowers from the gift shop. As soon as they'd gotten the call that Shantel was in labor, they'd rushed over. When they reached the corridor, Julian saw his brother in the hallway.

"Is everything okay?" Julian asked.

A broad smile crossed Roman's features and Julian breathed a sigh of relief at seeing his pearly whites. "Congratulations, you're an uncle." Roman reached inside the back pocket of his jeans and produced a cigar.

Julian beamed. "I'm an uncle." He glanced at Elyse. "I'm an uncle."

"Yes, you are," Elyse said.

"How's Shantel?" Julian asked his brother.

"Exhausted. Overwhelmed. Excited. All of the above,"

Roman said with a grin. "Would you like to see her and the baby?"

"Absolutely."

"C'mon." Roman led him down the sterile corridor of the maternity ward until he reached Room 310. He swung the door open and inside were their parents and half the Wilsons of McDonough County.

"Give him some room," Roman said, parting the large group until Julian and Elyse could step forward. That's when Julian saw Shantel, her smile wide as she held a beautiful brown-skinned baby swaddled in a blanket.

"Say hello to Ethan Julian Lockett," Shantel said, offering her son to Julian.

"You gave him m-my name." Julian was touched as he accepted the tiny bundle. His heart felt so full of love for his nephew.

"It's a wonderful name. I hope you don't mind, Elyse, but Julian's gotten me through some rough times." Shantel said.

"Absolutely not. And now that've you had the baby, we can share some news of our own." Elyse rubbed her belly. "Julian and I are expecting."

"What?" Angelique rushed over to Elyse and grasped her forearms.

"It's a total surprise, but apparently I'm already a few months along. I guess with all the craziness, I didn't realize it," Elyse said. And they hadn't. With their schedules and the family feud, Elyse had ignored the fact she hadn't had a period. And Julian had been so caught up in their passion, it had escaped his notice. But Julian was thrilled at becoming a father and having Elyse as his wife.

"Omigod!" His mother clutched her chest. "Another rush wedding!"

Julian laughed as he held his nephew in his arms. "I'm afraid so, Mom. Elyse and I—" he pulled his fiancée to him with his free hand and brushed a kiss across her lips "—want to get married as soon as possible at the courthouse and a more formal ceremony once Frank is out of rehab."

"Giana." His mother looked to his sister. "Promise me, you'll give me time to plan a proper wedding when you get married."

"Oh, Mama, I'm not getting married anytime soon."

Julian and Elyse smiled at each other.

Famous last words.

*****

THE FAKE ENGAGEMENT FAVOUR

CHARLENE SANDS

Dedicated to my sweet daughter, Nikki, with all my love.

You deserve all good and wonderful things in life!

Happy Birthday!

One

"Are we really going to do this?" Gianna asked handsome, cocky Gage Tremaine. She sat on a patio chair facing the gorgeously groomed Tremaine estate, hardly believing she'd agreed to being Gage's newfound love. His pretend fiancée, for heaven's sake, until the country music superstar got his life back on track.

"Do you have a boyfriend or someone who'd object to this?"

"Just…uh, no. Not at the moment," she said quietly.

"Then I think we're doing it," he drawled in the Texas twang that his fans adored. "I hate to admit this, but you're the perfect choice. You're out of the public eye and have a very honorable profession. You're smart and upstanding and a good family friend. It makes sense, Gianna."

She was all those things, yet hearing Gage say it made it all seem so…uninspiring.

"But I'm hardly your type." She wasn't. Not by a long

shot. She wasn't stylish or trendy. She wore her hair in a messy bun at the top of her head most times and could barely see a thing without her eyeglasses.

"Are you suggesting you're too darn intelligent for me, Professor Marino?"

Good God. He would go there. At times, she wasn't even sure she liked Gage all that much. He was always teasing her, about her brains, about her looks. She'd grown up around the Tremaines, and she wasn't gonna lie, Gage had been like a thorn in her side. But then he'd smile and tell her he didn't mean it, and she'd forgive him.

"You know I am."

He grinned. "True."

His incredible blue eyes darkened and then a serious expression stole over his face. "I know this is a lot to ask. But I'm in a bind and Regan Fitzgerald, my manager, came up with this little scheme to make nice with the press. I don't like it, either, but I have to restore my image. I've been at this a long time, and I'm no saint, but I'm also not as bad as people make me out to be. My record sales are down some."

"And you need to land that film role in *Sunday in Montana*."

"Bad boys don't get the lead in a family movie."

"I get it. But—but there must be dozens of girls out there who'd like to play house with you, even if it is pretend."

"I wouldn't *trust* anyone but you," he said, his eyes clear, revealing the truth. "If word got out, this could ruin me."

"Really?" He had that much faith in her? Well, he should. She would never betray a Tremaine. They were her second family, going back decades. Her mother and Rose Tremaine, Gage's mom, had been like sisters. Rose had been a godsend when her mama got sick. She'd helped pay the medical bills a young local Fairmont University professor couldn't afford.

Rose had held her hand when her mama passed on, their quiet sobs binding them ever closer.

"Yeah, according to Regan, if it slipped that I hired someone to be my fake fiancée, after all the other scandals I've had this past year, I'd stand to lose my reputation for good."

"You have had quite a few," she said tactfully. Three scandals, to be exact, and each time, Gage had a valid excuse or reason for what transpired. He made headlines, and often the media printed lies about the eligible bachelor with the deep, sexy voice that drove women wild. Even she had to admit that Gage had immense talent. And she wasn't even a fan of country music. "You almost lost your life over the last one."

Gage put his hand up to his neck, carefully touching the wound that was still visible from the barroom brawl where a broken bottle slashed his throat. "Don't remind me. I learned my lesson on that one."

"Don't try to rescue a damsel in distress?"

"Don't butt in when a girl is arguing with her boyfriend. But, in my own defense, what I saw at the bar was a drunken cowboy manhandling a woman against her wishes."

The way Gage told it, once the police arrived, he was bleeding at the throat from a broken bottle, his band members were all banged up and the bar was a total mess. To top it off, the girl had stuck up for her abusive boyfriend instead of siding with Gage. He wound up getting blamed for starting the fight and had paid for all the damages. His photo was splashed across the covers of all the tabloids, taking down his reputation one more notch.

The other two scandals weren't violent yet had dragged his name through the mud. Cheating on his girlfriend—and pushing a news reporter to the ground when asked about it—wasn't a way to win friends and gain influence. Gage claimed his innocence on both, but it didn't matter. The paparazzi ate it all up.

Rose walked outside carrying a tray of Texas sun tea and cookies. Gianna's mind flashed to another time, a happier time. Mom and Rose having their sun tea on this very deck.

A knot formed in her stomach. It was still so new to her, losing her mother. The pain never went away. She couldn't stop thinking about her.

"Have some iced tea, Gianna. Gage, will you pour it?" She set the tray down on a side table.

"Sure, Mom." He rose and looked up from the tray. "There's only two glasses here."

"Yes, I'm going to let you two talk some more. I came out here to tell you, Gianna, that there's no pressure if you refuse Gage's request." Rose put a hand on her arm and squeezed. "I know it's a lot to ask of you, sweetheart."

"Look, when we travel, I promise we'll always get a suite with two rooms. And you'll have plenty of time to do your research," Gage said.

"And it would only be for a month, right?"

"Six or seven weeks," he said. "Long enough for me to make some scheduled appearances and nail down that role."

That would be most of the summer. "What happens after that?"

"Well, we haven't quite figured that out yet. But once summer is over, you'd have to go back to teaching, right?" he asked.

She nodded.

"And hopefully, our story would fade into the background if there are no more rumors or scandals. We could have a quiet breakup sometime in the future."

"The future? As in how long?"

Gage shrugged. "Not sure. Does it matter?"

Rose shot her son a hard look. "Of course it matters. Gianna can't put her life on hold indefinitely."

His assumption that she had no life, or *love life*, outside of teaching rattled her. She dated once in a while. Okay, but only when her friend Brooke set her up on blind dates. She did have a keen affection for Timothy Bellamy, a history professor at the university. But so far, all they'd had were a few coffee dates. No sparks yet, but she was mourning her mother and focused on her career—she wasn't exactly in the market for sparks.

"Sorry, right." He scrubbed at his stubbled jaw.

Rose looked her in the eye and smiled sweetly. "Remember, if you decide you can't do this, everyone will understand. You're always going to be a part of this family."

"Thanks, Rose. That means a lot."

Rose kissed her cheek and left the patio.

She turned to Gage. "Your mom always makes me feel so welcome."

"She loves you, Gianna."

"She misses Mom almost as much as I do."

"Yeah, your mother was pretty awesome."

"She was a fan of yours, too, even before your fame." Though, for the life of her, Gianna couldn't understand why. She released a deep sigh. "I still can't believe she's gone."

Gage nodded. He was quiet for a while, staring out to the landscape before him. He wasn't always cocky and smug. Sometimes he was nice, and she couldn't imagine turning down his request. She owed the Tremaine family her loyalty, and this would be one way to repay their kindness. Her heart hurt every day, and maybe helping Gage would take her mind off her grief for a little bit.

"I'm a terrible liar," she blurted. "I'm in a committed relationship with the truth."

Gage blinked, his head jerking back, and he took a few moments to process her blunt declaration. "Most of what we say will be the truth. We're childhood friends, and we became reacquainted this summer. And we realized our feelings for each other…"

"After you were injured in that brawl?"

"That works. You're not such a bad liar after all."

"I'm a problem solver, Gage. Not a liar. We need to puzzle this out before the public sees us together."

"So, then, you're sure?"

She nodded, totally unsure, but she wasn't going to refuse to help a Tremaine. Even if it meant going against all her well-honed instincts. "When do we get engaged?"

Gage grinned, his teeth flashing in a bright smile. He was good-looking to a fault, and talented, a golden boy who somehow had to pretend to be in love with her.

It would put his acting chops to the test. He could probably pull it off.

But could she?

"You know the last person who lived in this guesthouse ended up falling in love with my brother Cade," Gage's sister, Lily, told Gianna.

Gianna flopped onto the sofa next to Lily, grabbed a pillow and tucked it under her arms. Over the years she'd stayed on the property many times, sometimes at the main house, sometimes here in this cottage guesthouse. She enjoyed the privacy afforded her here, where she could pull her thoughts together without interference. "I've met Harper. She's perfectly suited for Cade. And vice versa."

"I know. I'm happy I had a hand in getting them together. Though not purposely. But it all worked out. Who knows what will happen between you and Gage?" Lily grinned at her, and Gianna's mouth dropped open.

"Lily, whatever you're thinking, don't. Nothing like that's going to happen between me and Gage. He's…he's… not my type."

"You have a type?"

"No. Yes. I suppose I do. Someone who's into fine art, history and philosophy."

"Ah, so you mean, not someone who sings for his supper and has women dropping at his feet?"

Gianna rolled her eyes. "I'm not impressed by those things."

Lily didn't appear convinced. "I'm just saying, Gage can be charming. He may just surprise you."

"I'm fully prepared to deal with Gage. When the time comes." She could go head to head with him in mental battles all day long. It was the other part of the deal that worried her. She'd always been true to herself and honest in her feelings. So this pretense didn't come naturally to her. Like she'd told Gage, she was committed to telling the truth. And she'd meant it.

"That time may be coming sooner than you think. We have one week before the family's big Fourth of July celebration. That's where Gage plans to announce your engagement."

This was all becoming very real. In a week's time, their little charade would begin, and a part of her welcomed the distraction. It would keep her grief at bay, but a larger part of her felt uncertain and wary. Gianna rose from the sofa and walked over to the beveled glass window, catching her reflection through the pane. She saw a grieving woman with pale olive skin, plain clothes and thick-rimmed glasses. Her shoulders drooped, and she turned to Lily. "Do you think anyone's going to believe that Gage and I are in love?"

"Gage will convince them."

But Gianna needed more than that. She needed to feel confident that she could pull this off. "Lily? I think I need your help."

"With?"

"You're an interior designer and quite talented at what you do. But have you ever worked with exteriors?"

"Yes, sometimes. I've reworked and renovated outdoor patios and verandas and such. In fact, I just finished revamping a pool and lounge exterior for the Goldens' estate down the road."

"I meant, human exteriors?"

Lily caught her meaning and gave her a look. "You want a makeover?"

"No, I don't *want* a makeover, but I think I need one. It's not going to be easy pretending, especially since I don't fit into Gage's world. At all. But if I looked the part, it might make it easier for me."

Lily gave her an assessing once-over. Gianna removed her eyeglasses and immediately began to squint.

"Have you ever tried contacts?"

"Yes, but they irritate my eyes."

"Actually, your face is well suited for glasses. You don't need contacts. And honestly, you're quite lovely, Gianna. You just need to highlight your best features. Just a little. And maybe have a wardrobe renovation." Lily smiled.

"So, you'll do it?"

"Of course. It's not going to be a drastic change, but you'd be surprised what a little makeup and a new hairstyle can do for a woman. Here, let me show you what I mean with your wardrobe."

She followed Lily to the foyer mirror.

"Some things need to be tweaked," Lily said. "Like this boxy white blouse you're wearing. It's long and gives you no shape at all. But watch this," Lily said, rolling up the sleeves above her elbows and unbuttoning the bottom three buttons of the blouse. Next, she took the tails of the blouse, pulled them taut and tied a knot right at her waistline. "There. Take a look at the difference. From baggy to stylish, with just a little ingenuity."

Gianna studied herself in the mirror. She still had a long way to go, but in just under a minute, Lily had really made a big difference.

"Tomorrow we'll go to the salon, give that thick hair of yours some pretty highlights and a fresh cut. And then we'll go shopping."

"Thanks, Lily."

"You're welcome. But you know, Gage doesn't expect you to do all this."

"I'm not doing it for him, Lil. I kinda need to do this for myself."

"I get it. You're such a good friend, Gianna." Lily squeezed her tight, and the affection brought warmth to her heart.

If she was going to play the part, it only made sense to go all in.

Gianna never did anything halfway.

Gage stood at the guesthouse door, ready to knock. He wasn't ready for this date, a trip to the town ice cream shop. He'd thought he'd have at least a few more days before the charade would begin. In his opinion it wasn't necessary, but his manager, Regan, had other ideas. *You need to be seen in public a few times before you actually get engaged. It'll make it look more realistic.*

He didn't agree, but Regan knew how to get him out of a bind—she was an expert at it—and he'd finally learned to listen to her.

So now, here he was trapped into going on a first date with Gianna. He should be glad he'd convinced her while on the phone. She was doing him a big favor. But she didn't like this idea any more than he did, so he wouldn't feel guilty about it. Neither of them wanted to do this. And in typical Gianna form, she'd overanalyzed the situation, making her arguments why they shouldn't be going out until the big engagement announcement. It would have less impact on the press. It was too soon. Neither of them was ready.

Gianna wasn't wrong about any of these things, but Regan had a point. It had to look like their relationship was evolving naturally.

He knocked on the door, trying to adjust his frown into some semblance of a smile. He waited almost a minute, then knocked again.

Finally, the door opened and Gianna appeared.

At least he thought it was Gianna. Well, damn. It was her, all right. For a second, his throat closed up. What the hell? Her hair was cut to just past her shoulders, glossed to a deep chestnut brown and parted on the side. Thin-rimmed glasses kept hair from falling onto her cheeks and amplified her gorgeous light green eyes through the lenses. She wore a halter-top denim dress that exposed a hint of eye-popping cleavage. Gianna had cleavage? She'd always worn super-baggy clothes that hid her female shape.

There was a blush to her complexion, and he wasn't sure if it was due to his immediate reaction to her. The slight rosy color blended with her smooth olive skin. He scanned her up and down, catching the strappy sandals encasing her feet, her toenails painted a pale pink.

"You're staring," she said.

He was. He couldn't take his eyes off her, and that wasn't good. He didn't like the jolts of electricity shooting through his system. He didn't like the attraction that immediately caused his breath to catch. Gianna was... stunning.

He hadn't signed up for this. He hadn't reacted this way to a woman in years; the instant magnetism shifted his perspective into something he didn't recognize. Gianna was forbidden fruit, and he'd have to remember that. She was like family, a girl he'd known for years and the daughter of his mother's best friend. To top it off, she was in mourning and very vulnerable right now.

"What did you do to yourself?" It was his knee-jerk response to her hot appearance. Emphasis on *jerk*. It pissed him off that she'd made this transformation, giving him a bit of a shock and throwing him off balance.

Her chin went up. "Nothing," she said sharply.

"Brainiac, you've done something."

"Brickhead, I thought you were taking me for ice cream?"

His mouth twitched, but he held back a smile. Using their childhood nicknames for each other oddly put him at ease. When they were kids, he'd played with her unless there'd been something better to do. Admittedly, he'd sorta tormented her, but Gianna never cowered. She'd held her ground and dished out equal justice. He'd always admired that about her. She didn't back down. Nope, she was too quick, too clever to let him get the best of her. "I am. Ready to go?"

Taking her to the best ice cream shop in Juliet, Triple

Scoop, was the only way he could coax her into going out tonight. If memory served, she could devour a Triple Decker without batting an eyelash.

She nodded. “Let’s get this over with.”

He couldn’t agree more, but somehow hearing her say it stung.

In the driveway, he opened the passenger side door for her and caught a glimpse of her tanned legs as she flounced into the seat. She caught him looking, and he pretended not to notice. He climbed in, started the engine of his midnight-blue Aston Martin and sped off.

Halfway to town, Gage glanced over at Gianna. “I’m not complaining, but why’d you do it?”

She turned her face away to stare out the window. “Seems like you are complaining.”

“Are you gonna answer my question?”

She pushed air out of her lungs. The sigh was dramatic and real. “It only makes sense, Gage. I weighed the options and came to the conclusion that if we’re to have people believe we’re together, I need to look the part. Lily gave me some help.”

“Lily did a good job.”

“Is that a backhanded compliment?”

His lips twitched again. She’d made it clear—she hadn’t dressed to impress, or at least to impress *him*. It was a calculated move on her part to ensure their little scheme worked. Gianna wasn’t the type to fish for compliments, but he owed her this one. “You look very pretty, Gianna.”

It was the understatement of the year.

“Thank you,” she replied.

Once in town, he parked the car two blocks from the ice cream shop, and Gianna glanced at him curiously. “Why are we parking here?”

“A little walk will do us good.”

"Let me guess, Regan's idea? So more people will see us together?"

He didn't give her the satisfaction of an answer, because she was right and he hated to admit it. "Usually the townsfolk don't pester me too much, but, just a warning, that all might change when I'm spotted with you on my arm."

He got out of the car, opened the car door for her and offered his hand.

She slipped her hand in his, and the delicate softness of her skin pummeled through him as he helped her step out. He closed the door and set the car alarm. It beeped and off they went, strolling down the street hand in hand.

A bright sunset was making its descent, the summer air heavy and thick. Beads of sweat circled his neck and made his jeans stick to his legs. Gianna seemed unaffected by the heat. She walked along the street, her chin up, her cool demeanor unmarred. A few women came out of a lingerie store and stopped to gape. Quickly, they took out their phones and snapped pictures of Gage and Gianna. One lady approached and asked for a selfie.

"Sure, let's get Gianna in on this, too," he told her.

The woman didn't hesitate. "Okay."

She snapped a picture of the three of them and then thanked them, giving Gianna a puzzled look. Her wheels must've been turning as she wondered who his date was. Soon, hopefully, everyone would know. Gage took Gianna's hand again and ventured on.

He was stopped two more times by fans who wanted photos before they entered the crowded ice cream shop.

"No doubt those photos will be all over the internet in less than an hour," Gianna whispered. "I guess Regan knows what she's talking about."

"Yep, she usually does."

She'd been his manager for going on nine years now.

She hadn't steered him wrong on any of the decisions they'd made. Any trouble he'd been involved in wasn't a result of bad managing. He'd gotten into that trouble all on his own, but lucky for him, Regan knew how to prevent his image from tanking. He just had to keep his nose clean for the next six weeks or so and he could move on with his life.

Gianna sat across the round café table from Gage, bringing her tongue across the top layer of her Triple Decker, feeling self-conscious as at least a dozen pairs of eyes darted glances her way. Gage had already signed four autographs for giddy girls who deemed themselves lucky to have had an ice cream craving at the same time he did. They lingered, watching his every move, and not until he'd finally given them a wave and a "See ya" did they dash back to their own table, cell phones in hand, typing as fast as their thumbs would allow.

"Geesh, is it always like this?" Gianna asked.

"This is nothing," Gage said. "Sometimes I have to run for my life."

"You're joking, right?"

He shook his handsome head, his eyes twinkling. "The forty-year-olds are worse than these kids. They want a piece of me I'm not willin' to give."

"Like what?" She took another lick of her cone. The Triple Decker consisted of three scoops of your favorite flavors along with toppings for each layer. She was demolishing rocky road with raspberry topping at the moment, with a scoop of French vanilla topped with chocolate sprinkles and a scoop of mocha fudge, swimming in nuts, just waiting for her. Ice cream was the guiltiest of guilty pleasures and her weak spot.

"They try to rip off my clothes. And touch places they have no business touching."

"Really, they do that?" She was appalled. Even though celebrities expected to be adored by their fans, and wanted to be, there were limits. No one had a right to abuse those boundaries.

"Concerts are the worst. The venues provide security teams, but every once in a while someone gets by them. It's why I need a bodyguard sometimes."

"So where is he now?"

"He gets time off when I'm home in Juliet. Like I said, the townsfolk aren't out for my blood. They let me live my life, pretty much."

"Glad to hear that."

"That's all gonna change on the Fourth. Regan's got all the local news reporters coming. That's when things will heat up." His gaze slid down to her mouth as she licked her cone. "You're sure enjoying that."

The look in his eyes made her edgy. "My favorite."

"I remember."

"You're a party poop for not getting the Triple."

Unfazed, he licked at his all-chocolate cone, one scoop. No toppings. "Sometimes more is not better."

She wound her tongue around the last of her rocky road. "Oh, but when it's better, it's way better."

"Hold on a sec," he said, reaching into his pocket. "Let's get a picture of this. Our first date."

"Probably smart to document it."

"Yeah," he said, nodding. "That's what I was going for."

His head came close to hers, enough so that she could smell his scent—something expensive, oozing with masculinity. "Smile," he told her.

She did, and he snapped the photo.

"That's perfect," he said, glancing at the picture, grinning like a fool.

"Let me see it."

He handed her the phone. She glimpsed her image and gasped. "You!"

In the photo, Gianna was smiling, but her mouth was smudged all over with raspberry sauce. She looked like a ten-year-old kid, and right now, she felt like one, too. She grabbed a napkin, wiped her mouth, then crumpled it up and tossed it at him. "You never change."

He caught the napkin on a chuckle. "That's what you get for calling me, of all people, a party poop."

"So you're saying *I* started it?"

"If the shoe fits, Cinderella."

She felt like Cinderella, playing dress-up with the handsome prince. But unlike Cinderella, she'd be happy when the ball ended, so she could go back to being her own pumpkin self again.

She deleted the picture, then caught a few photos of him with his band. Some were taken while he was onstage, lights beaming down, his hat shadowing his face and beads of sweat dripping down. She imagined his fans standing up, singing along with him, knowing the words to all his songs.

This was what he was trying to hang on to. This was what he was trying to protect. He wasn't just a newbie country singer with a few hits. He was a brand all his own and carried the weight of countless behind-the-scenes crew members on his shoulders, as well as many other vendors and producers and musicians.

She gave him back his phone, sobered now. "It's not about the money, is it, Gage? That's not why we're doing this."

He didn't pretend not to know what she was talking about. "It never was."

He was rich in his own right. His family was one of the wealthiest in all of Texas. But she couldn't imagine Gage working in an office, going over ledgers and spreadsheets. Gage had a freer spirit than that. He was talented and loved what he did for a living. He wanted to be the one to decide when his career ended, not the other way around. In a sense, he was fighting for that right. To decide his own future. And as silly as having a fake fiancée seemed, she understood why he was invested in this ruse.

"I know," she said.

"Gianna, sometimes you get me better than anyone else."

"Is that why you always picked on me?"

He shrugged, thinking on it. "You were the one person I couldn't fool. Sorta pissed me off, if I'm being honest."

He infuriated her at times, but she never let him see it. "Now we're grown-ups and we can forget playing those silly gotcha games. We have a goal in mind and we should stick to it, Gage."

"Where's the fun in that?"

"Nothing about this is fun for me."

His smile waned, and the joy in his expression disappeared.

She wouldn't rub it in too much, but she was doing him a big favor. And she wanted it to go smoothly, without any bumps in the road. Putting up with the insufferable Gage Tremaine for the summer wasn't her idea of a good time.

They finished their cones, and Gage offered his hand when it was time to leave. He held on firmly and then kissed her cheek, a subtle little peck, but one that told all the roving eyes in the ice cream shop that she was his and vice versa.

And that peck came as a complete surprise. Her face tingled where his lips had touched her skin. That subtle touch and the way he'd looked at her when she'd opened the guesthouse door worried her. Because she'd felt something spark and sizzle inside her. For a moment.

Gianna held a secret close to her heart, one that ensured she wouldn't fall for Gage. It was something she'd never told another soul. Something that made her avoid men like Gage Tremaine. All she would ever have with Gage was a fake engagement. Period.

There was no doubt Gage was an appealing man. But she didn't want to notice. She didn't want to be charmed. She supposed that at some point Gage would actually have to kiss her in front of an audience.

And she dreaded it.

Two

Gianna stood facing Juliet Jewelry on Main Street, Gage by her side. It'd been two days since their date at the ice cream shop, and social media had been all abuzz with news of their romance. Now they were making a pit stop at the jewelry store before their dinner date. "I still don't think we need to do this," she said, feeling grossly uncomfortable. She didn't know why Gage insisted on buying her a ring. "I can wear my mother's ring, Gage. It's a pretty engagement band."

Gage shook his head. "We've been over this already. I need to buy you a ring to make things look official. If this were real, you'd have a rock on your left hand that everyone would notice."

He looked at her hand. "Besides, you've worn that ring on your right hand since your mama passed," he said softly. "It wouldn't be right to use it that way."

She sensed he was being considerate so she couldn't fault him. He was adamant about getting her a ring, and this was one argument she wasn't going to win. "Okay, fine. But I don't want anything flashy."

"I wouldn't think you'd do flashy. Whatever size and shape you want is what you'll have, Gianna." Gage took her hand. "Ready to do this?"

She nodded. "Yes. Let's go pick out a ring."

Gage had made special arrangements with the shop owner for a private appointment, and they were greeted immediately by a man named Jeffrey Danes as they entered the store. Marble floors and rich stone walls spoke of class and wealth. The shop wasn't large, but the three long cases set in a horseshoe shape were cleaned to a brilliant shine and displayed all manner of jewels. Overhead, a spectacular sparkling chandelier hung in the center of the room.

"Jeffrey, I'd like to introduce you to my girlfriend, Professor Gianna Marino."

The man took her hand without giving it a shake. "Pleasure to meet you. I hope we can find the perfect ring for you. And congratulations on your upcoming engagement."

Heat rushed up her neck. She hated lying. "Thank you very much."

"We haven't announced our engagement yet," Gage said. "And we'd appreciate your discretion until we make the announcement."

"Always," Jeffrey assured them. "I've been doing business with your family for years. You can trust me. Now, let me show you our best-quality rings." He gestured to the case at the back of the shop. Already, Gianna's hackles were raised. She didn't want to wear an expensive ring. She didn't want Gage to spend a fortune for a ring she was only going to return to him. It wasn't necessary. None of this was.

"Have a seat, please."

They both sat on plush chairs as the man pulled out a

black velvet drawer and set it on top of the jewel case, giving Gage a big smile. Gianna nearly choked seeing the size of the diamonds.

"You can have any one you want, sweetheart," Gage said, dead serious.

"Do any of these lovely rings interest you?" Jeffrey asked. "They are of the finest quality and, as you can see, very unique in style."

Was Gage crazy? Or was he putting on a good show? No way was she going to pick out a ring that cost more than his sports car. She shook that notion off and pretended interest in the six rings shown to her, taking a bit of time, trying to play the part, but then shook her head. "They are a bit ornate for my taste. Do you have something simpler? And smaller?"

Gage's mouth twitched. He was amused by her discomfort.

Jeffrey blinked, hiding his true emotions. He wasn't going to make a killing on a ring today. "Of course. I have an entire array of rings to show you. Or, if you prefer, you can pick out a setting and we can find you the perfect diamond."

"Oh, no. That's not necessary. I'm sure I can find one I like." Gianna rose from her seat and wandered the shop, only to stop at a case up at the front of the store. "May I see these?" she asked, pointing to group of solitaire rings.

Jeffrey rushed right over. "Oh, those aren't—"

Gage was right behind him. "Aren't what?"

"They're, uh, fine and all. We only carry the best, but are you sure?" He looked at Gianna.

"I'd like to see the marquise, please." She pointed to a ring any woman wouldn't mind wearing—if they weren't getting engaged to a superstar. She didn't want to give Jeffrey a stroke, but she wasn't going to pick anything worth over a few thousand dollars.

"It's a solitaire, platinum band, but I'm afraid it's only one carat." He slid the door open and took out the ring. "Here you go," he said, setting the ring down on a square of black velvet, trying not to appear annoyed. Jeffrey probably hadn't run into too many women who were given carte blanche and then opted for such a small, plain ring. "Try it on if you'd like."

"Is that the one you like the most, Gianna?" Gage asked.

She put the ring on her left ring finger. "It's simple and just the right size for me. Yes, I'd love this one."

Gage looked at Jeffrey. "I think the lady has found her ring."

"Yes, yes. Good choice," he told Gianna as he tried to show some enthusiasm.

"Gianna, why don't you look around a bit while I settle up with Jeffrey?" Gage kissed her cheek for good measure, and she sucked in a breath at the sensation of his lips on her skin yet again. She walked out of the store, needing to clear her head. She'd just picked out a ring for her fake engagement—just one lie of many more to come.

So it hadn't been a fluke the other day. Gianna had dressed for their second date in a fitted cream lace dress that highlighted her tiny waist and dipped into delicious cleavage at the neckline. Her meadow-green eyes dazzled from behind her glasses, and the overhead lights in the Rhinestone Room reflected on her hair. Again, she looked amazing. His soon-to-be fiancée. She'd given poor Jeffrey at the jewelry store a migraine for sure by picking out the least expensive ring in his shop. Practical, analytical and ever-cautious Gianna didn't want to stick him with a hefty price tag. Little did she know that the ring was hers. He wouldn't take it back under any circumstances. It was a small price to pay for her help.

As the maître d' led them to a table at the back of the restaurant, heads turned, but this time it was Gianna who captured the attention. Not him. Not only did she look pretty, but she was now a bit of a curiosity. Compounding the social media buzz, local papers and online news outlets had already picked up on Gage Tremaine's latest love interest, and while they didn't know who she was, the photos at the ice cream shop spoke volumes.

Once seated, Gage ordered red wine as soft music played throughout the restaurant. Cellphones popped out of hiding from the other patrons, and they seemed to snap endless photos of the two of them. Gage had learned not to engage with his audience, not to look them in the eye. He'd learned to keep his focus on his dinner dates and enjoy himself, despite having his every move scrutinized. He'd always chosen a back table for that very reason. It made it harder for people to be discreet with their observations and photo trigger fingers. Though it went against his motives, he wanted to have a few private moments with Gianna.

"Have you been here before?" he asked Gianna.

"Yes, several times."

"With a date?" he blurted. Damn, he hadn't intended to sound incredulous.

"Would that surprise you?"

"No. But, uh, never mind." The Rhinestone Room was exclusive, and it wasn't a place you took a woman unless you were serious about her. Not only was the food excellent and the service impeccable, but it made a statement. It said, *you're special*. And it had been Regan's idea to bring Gianna here to send the right message.

"If you must know, I was honored with an award here just last year."

He lifted his brows. He wasn't surprised, but rather, impressed. "What was it for?"

"I received the Fairmont Faculty Award for Excellence in Teaching. We had a special dinner here."

"Congratulations. I bet your mom was proud."

Gage shouldn't have brought up her mother, but it was too late. Fortunately, Gianna didn't seem to mind the memory.

She smiled. "She was."

The wine arrived, and after two glasses were poured, Gage lifted his glass. "Let's toast to your mother, Gianna."

"Let's." She picked up her glass and touched his with a soft clink. "To my mom and to yours," she said. "The best women I've ever known."

"Me, too," he said. After they sipped, Gage put down his glass. "You said you were here several times."

"My best friend, Brooke, set me up on a blind date, and he took me here. We dated for a short time, and then he brought me here to break it off."

"Wow. That's cold."

"Not really. He was a nice guy, and he knew I liked this place. It just didn't work out between us. We didn't mesh. He was into sports and cars. His big dream was to go to a baseball game in every ballpark in America."

"A real dud, huh." As a boy, Gage had that very same dream. He'd pitched on his high school varsity team, but then he got the music bug and it had become his passion. He found he could play guitar pretty well, and the deep pitch of his voice worked well with the songs he chose to sing. But he still loved baseball, watched it on TV and played it whenever he could get his bandmates on the field.

"So, no sports or cars." She wasn't much into fashion or the latest trends. Gage got the feeling his sister, Lily, was totally responsible for her wardrobe choices, too. "What do you like, Gianna, besides books?"

"I like teaching."

"A given."

"I like ice cream."

"Three scoops, got that. What else?"

"I'm on the board of the Learning and Literacy Foundation at the university. It's a charity to help promote reading. It's a passion of mine. There's a lot of children out there really struggling to read. The university does its fair share of fund-raising."

"Great cause. But do you do anything for fun? Just for the hell of it?"

"I used to travel. Until my mom got sick. That all stopped, but I imagine I'll do it again at some point."

"We're going to do some traveling together. I've got a trip planned to Nashville after the Fourth. And then on to Los Angeles."

"And it's imperative that I go with you?" she asked, looking at him over the rim of her wineglass.

"It's necessary, Gianna."

He had to be blunt. None of this would work if she didn't take these trips with him. It's what she'd signed up for, but if she put up too much of a fuss, he'd have to make some allowances. "There's some great history in Nashville. It's not all about music. I promise to make it bearable."

"After the Fourth, I'll be deep in research for the Family Studies seminar I'm giving at the university at the end of the month. It's a study of major theories regarding family development and delves into the biological, psychological and historical factors that influence family patterns and behavior."

"In English, please?"

Her mouth formed an adorable pout. "Never mind. Just know that while we're on the road, I'll be working in the separate bedroom you promised me, when I'm not with you."

"Fair enough. And speaking of the Fourth, will you agree to be my temporary fiancée, Gianna?" He dipped into his pocket, covering his hand completely over the ring box.

She smiled a beautiful smile. "You have a way with words, Gage."

"I want you to have the ring tonight, but you don't have to wear it until the Fourth. I thought it would be less awkward for you than having me get down on one knee in front of everyone at the party. This way, it's an announcement instead of the actual proposal. And if anyone asks, you can tell them I proposed to you tonight and gave you the ring over dinner at the Rhinestone Room. It wouldn't be a lie. You can keep your committed relationship with the truth." He smiled.

She smiled, too. "I appreciate that and it makes sense."

"Thank you again for doing this." He closed his hand over the ring box and placed it into her palm. Her fingers curled around it, keeping it out of view, and she immediately tucked it into her purse.

"Oh, and there's just one more thing." He reached into his other pocket and came up with a gold velvet drawstring jewelry bag. "This goes with the ring." He slid the bag across the table. "For you, Gianna."

Surprise lit in her eyes. "What's this?"

"Open it."

She stared at him a second and then picked up the bag, looking a bit wary. She undid the drawstring and pulled out the necklace. "It's beautiful," she whispered in awe.

A dozen small diamonds forming a vee dropped down to a single strand that held one delicate marquise diamond. Jeffrey had called it a drop necklace.

She ran the necklace over her palm, the delicate strand caressing her fingers. Her expression changed instantly, and her awe dissolved. "I can't accept this, Gage."

"It'll look perfect on you, Gianna. And yes, you can accept it."

"I'll just have to return it to you when I return the diamond ring."

"All sales are final. Otherwise Jeffrey would have a heart attack."

Gianna's eyes widened. "Are you saying you can't return it?"

"I'm saying…yes. It's unreturnable. Don't you like it?"

"I…love it. But it's too much."

"Let me be the judge of that."

"How did you do this, anyway? When?"

"Let's just say, Jeffrey showed it to me after you walked out of the store. He and I both agreed it would look great on you."

She snapped her fingers. "And just like that, you bought it."

"Yeah."

Gage hadn't been totally unselfish in buying that necklace. He wanted Gianna to have it because of the unorthodox favor she was doing for him. But it was also a way to keep her invested in this scheme. One good turn deserved another. He was asking a lot of her, and he needed to keep her onboard. He wasn't buying her loyalty, but rather showing her how much her sacrifice meant to him. At least, he hoped she viewed it that way.

He couldn't afford for anything to go wrong.

His livelihood depended upon it.

It depended on her.

Gianna wasn't thrilled with Gage's gift, but she kept her irritation to a simmer. They were out in public, and she didn't want to blow her cover. She had given her word to be in this charade until the very end. But she hadn't asked for jewelry—she hadn't asked for anything in return for her favor. Okay, it made sense that he'd give her a ring. She needed to show up at the party wearing it when they made their engagement announcement, but the necklace? That was a different story.

She was more than mildly insulted that Gage thought he had to buy her off with diamonds. She'd like to think otherwise of him, but there was no other logical explanation for him going to such extremes. She ventured to guess the necklace was far more expensive than the ring she'd picked out. Why did he do it? Did he have so little faith in her?

Before she could stop him, he rose from his chair and took the necklace from her hand.

"Allow me," he said.

Baffled, she simply sat there at the table while Gage came around to rest his hand on her shoulder. Gently, he brushed her hair to one side, the backs of his fingers caressing her throat ever so softly. She drew breath into her lungs at his touch, and tingles of awareness flitted through her belly. While his hands worked the clasp, she sat stiffly, perplexed at her reaction to him, to his unnerving presence behind her. She couldn't let him see how he affected her. When he was through and the necklace was fastened, he arranged her hair back in place, his fingers grazing her skin once again. She squeezed her eyes closed briefly, holding her breath.

He sat down, eyeing the drop necklace that landed in the hollow between her breasts. His baby blues lingered long enough to heat her body and make her squirm a bit, not from annoyance this time but from something much more dangerous.

"Gianna, it's perfect on you."

He sounded sincere. No matter what his motives, she couldn't deny the necklace was a beauty. "Thank you."

All during dinner, Gage's eyes dipped down to her breasts. Was he only admiring the gift he'd given her? She surely hoped so. There was no room in her heart for anything else. She was filled with grief, still mourning the passing of her dear mother. Besides, the notion of anything happening between her and Gage in real life was ridiculous. Even if his touch brought flutters. She hadn't been intimate with a man for quite some time, so of course the first bit of contact again would give her butterflies.

Gage poured her a second glass of wine and they spent time talking about him, his concerts, what to expect when they were on the road. Gianna's head began to swim, but she continued to drink, only because Gage was a master storyteller and she actually enjoyed hearing about his antics with his siblings and bandmates. The more she drank, the funnier his stories became, but then suddenly, Gage stopped talking.

"What's wrong?" she asked, swaying a bit. Suddenly, it was hard to focus her eyes. "Tell me m-more."

"Geesh, Gianna, you're a lightweight," Gage said, staring at her. "What'd you have, two and a half glasses of wine?"

"Something like th-that. I'm not much of a drinker."

"I can see that," he muttered. "I'd better get you home."

"I don't want to go h-home." She sounded like a child, but she didn't care.

"Exactly why I need to get you home."

Next, she was being lifted out of her seat and ushered through the restaurant. She smiled at people as she passed by, Gage hurrying her along. He held her tight, his strength kind of a turn-on, and then she was in his car and being buckled in. The air around her was heavy with masculine musk. "Mmm. I l-like the way you smell."

"I'll remember that."

After that, everything was a blur. Houses passed her by. She couldn't stop giggling, even when her eyes were closed. And then, again, Gage had her in his arms. First, they were outside and now they were inside. And she was on a bed, a soft, cozy bed, and her eyes slowly opened.

"Gage?"

"Get some sleep. I'll check on you in the morning."

Her hair was brushed aside, and she felt his lips on her forehead.

She lifted her arms, grabbing for him. "Don't g-go."

He broke away from her, setting her arms down gently. "Got to, Brainiac."

She giggled and then closed her eyes again.

And drifted off.

Morning broke through the windows in Gianna's bedroom, the sunlight penetrating the gaps in the shutters. Her lids were like lead, too heavy to open right now. The light was too bright. She needed the dark. All she wanted to do was sleep off her pounding headache.

She let out a long, low groan of pain, but that wasn't the only reason the grotesque noise rumbled up from her chest. What she could remember of last night gave her hives. She'd made a blubbering fool out of herself at dinner. Gage had had to hold her tight, his arm propping her up as they left the restaurant, and Lord only knew what on earth she'd said to him on the drive home. Or worse yet, what she'd said to him as he'd tucked her into bed.

"Oh, man," she muttered. She was supposed to be the stable, responsible one of the pair and not act like a drunken roadie. She prayed no one snapped a picture of her, or worse yet, took video as she left the Rhinestone Room with Gage. This was not the image she wanted to portray. As all sorts of humiliating scenarios played out in her mind, she dug herself deeper down into the covers.

Gage's voice rang out on her cell phone. A song about a brokenhearted woman. She didn't know the tune, but Gage had assured her it was one of his biggest hits, and it would be only natural to have his ringtone on her cell phone. He had even done the honors of changing it for her yesterday.

Still prone on her bed, she rummaged through her purse on the nightstand and came up with her phone. Another groan escaped her throat as Brooke's face popped up. Gianna debated answering the call or not, but knowing her best friend, she'd probably call her back every five minutes until she answered.

"Hello," she whispered, the shallow sound of her voice making her cringe.

"Do I have to be the last one to know?" Brooke said.

Her mind was cloudy enough without having to guess anything. "To know what?"

"That you're dating Gage Tremaine."

Gianna sat upright on the bed, forgetting about the ache in her head. She hadn't yet figured out how to explain this to her best friend, or if she even should. "Why do you think that?"

"Is it true, Gia?"

"Well, uh…tell me why you think that?"

"You were seen with him at Triple Scoop. And last night, you had dinner with him at the Rhinestone Room, for heaven's sake. It's been all over social media."

It's exactly what Gage's manager wanted. The social media buzz meant their little plan was working. But Brooke was a true-blue friend, and she hated lying to her. Gianna didn't know if she could, especially since their engagement announcement would make big news tomorrow.

"I can explain all that." But could she? Could she explain away her phony relationship with Gage? Her mind wasn't clear enough to make that decision now.

"I'm listening."

"I can't really talk right now. Someone took a sledgehammer to my head," she whispered. "I drank too much last night. I can barely focus on anything. Can I call you later?"

Brooke hesitated. "Are you…okay, Gianna?"

Brooke knew she'd been having trouble accepting her mother's passing. And her friend had been regularly checking in on her, making sure she was managing. "Because if you need me, I'll come right over."

"Thank you. You're the best, but I'll be fine."

"But Gage, Gia? That worries me. He's so…not your type. I know he's hot, and has those killer blue eyes, but honestly, I hope your explanation doesn't include romance with that guy."

It didn't. At least she could admit that. Gianna would never fall for a guy like Gage. And her reasons were justified, the secret she held wouldn't allow it. "We'll talk. I'll get myself together and call you later. I promise."

"Okay, we'll talk later," Brooke said, sounding a bit more relieved. "Take care of yourself."

"I will." Gianna ended the call and silenced the ringer. She wanted no more interruptions. She laid her head onto the pillow and tried to relax. Not five minutes later, there was a knock on her door.

"Go away," she muttered. She ducked her head under the covers, needing peace and not an unwanted visitor. But it could be Rose. And Gianna didn't want to ignore her if she was the one the knocking.

She got up very slowly and sat a second, gathering her wits, allowing her head to adjust to the upright position.

It was idiotic that two glasses of wine could do this to her. *Never again*, she vowed and rose, gently donning a well-worn chenille bathrobe.

The knocking grew louder, and then she heard Gage's voice from behind the door. "Gianna, it's Gage."

She bit her lip. She didn't want to see him. She didn't want *him* to see her in this state, either. "Gage, what are you doing here?" she asked, just behind the door.

"Helping. Let me in."

"I don't need your help."

"I have the key."

Her shoulders slumped. Of course he had the key. He came prepared. He had been a Boy Scout once, after all.

"That's blackmail."

"It's me helping. Open the door, Gianna."

She put her hand on the knob, pursed her lips and then slowly cracked the door.

Gage came bearing gifts. And not of the diamond variety this time. The coffeepot on the tray smelled good, solid and strong. He'd also brought a bottle of aspirin. She could use both items about now.

She stepped away from the door, and he moved inside, heading for the kitchen. "I'd ask you how you're feeling, but your face says it all."

"Compliments, so early in the morning."

His mouth crooked up, and he eyed the ratty robe she was wearing. He might as well have told her she looked like something the cat dragged in, with that expression. He took her hand, dropped two aspirin in her palm and handed her half a glass of water. "Take them."

She did.

Next, he poured coffee into two cups and set them on the table. His hands came to her shoulders and pointed her toward the kitchen chair. "Sit."

She lowered down slowly and lifted her coffee mug, breathing in the aroma before taking a sip. Hot coffee was just what she needed. She knew enough that coffee didn't really dilute the alcohol, but it sure tasted good going down. Lucky for her, her tummy was fine. It was the gremlins stomping on her head that hurt the most.

Gage sat, too. He took a plate of plain toast off the tray and put it her under her nose. "Can you eat?"

"Should I? I mean, you're the expert on hangovers."

His mouth twisted, but his eyes were soft with pity. She hated that he pitied her.

"Am I? I certainly can handle much more than a thimble of wine."

"I have no doubt."

"Did you sleep all night?"

"Up until some rude person began pounding on my door."

"It's ten o'clock in the morning, Gianna. And you should be thanking me for bringing you remedies. It's obvious you don't know how to help yourself."

"So, I'm not an expert on hangovers."

"'Bout the only thing you don't think you're an expert on."

She bit into her toast and chewed and chewed. It was as dry as straw, and she washed it down with coffee. She was in a foul mood because her head ached, but also because she didn't remember what had happened last night, exactly. And she hated being out of control.

"You're wrong. I'm not an expert on fake engagements, either, so forgive me if I overindulged."

"You're forgiven."

She ground her teeth. Which only made her head ache more.

"Actually, I sorta liked you all loose and giddy." Gage

took a sip of coffee. "Makes me think there's more to you than I originally thought."

"More to me?"

"Yeah, a fun side of you."

"Fun?" What did he mean by that? She couldn't recall the end of the night. And it bugged the stuffing out of her. "What made you think that?"

He grabbed a piece of toast, took a bite and chewed, making her wait. She wasn't sure she wanted to hear his answer. And yet she had to know.

"I carried you into the bedroom and laid you down on the bed."

Oh, man.

"And when I said good-night to you, you asked me not to go."

A chuckle burst out of her chest, as if he'd said the sky was green. Actually, that notion was more conceivable. "No way. I'd never say that to you."

Gage's brows lifted, and an earnest expression crossed his features, as if…as if he wasn't lying. Then his mouth twitched, in the teasing way he had. "You're right, Gianna. You didn't say that."

But last night, she did recall the feel of his breath against her throat, his hands in her hair and the gentle way he'd fastened the diamond necklace from behind. His touch made her nerves rattle. Made her aware of his masculinity. The scent of his cologne had been strong then, and now there was a hint of it still wafting to her nostrils. She remembered her heart pounding when his hands had been on her shoulders. Even now, the scent of him threatened to make her weak.

But it wasn't like Gage to concede so soon, and now she truly wondered. "I kn-know. I wouldn't."

Would she?

But one thing was certain—this was the last time she was going to let loose like that. She wouldn't give Gage the upper hand again.

No matter his striking appeal.

Or how his bluer than blue eyes could melt her.

Three

"Nobody has to know the truth, Cade. Just the family," Gage remarked to his brother on the morning of the Fourth. Later this evening, the real fireworks would begin for him and Gianna.

"I don't like Harper being in on your charade. She's had enough negative press to last a lifetime."

Cade sat down at the kitchen table, a hot cup of coffee steaming right in front of him. It was natural for his brother to feel protective of his fiancée. They'd had a bumpy road finding each other, and Harper had been put through the wringer with bad press. At one point, Harper had been the most hated reality star in the country. But it had all worked out in the end. And if all went well with Regan's little scheme, no one would be the wiser. Once the summer was over, Gage's high-profile engagement would fade into oblivion, his reputation would hopefully be restored, and then a low-key breakup would follow.

"I didn't ask her to cater the event, Cade. She offered to

help. Besides, I don't see how we could avoid telling her the truth. We couldn't lie to her."

"That's right, Cade. I'm glad I know the truth. And I volunteered to help with the food on my own." Harper sat down next to her fiancé and took his hand. "I'm a chef and if I want to do this for your family," she said softly, "I'm *going* to do it. And as far as the charade goes, in a few months, I'll officially be a Tremaine, so I'm all in." She kissed Cade on the cheek. "You don't have to worry about me, sweetheart. I don't feel offended. I feel *included*."

Gage gave his brother a shrug, trying not to appear glib. He liked Harper. She had spunk and was the perfect match for his uptight brother. Cade had never been happier, and it showed.

"All right, I hear both of you. We'll play along until the end." Cade sipped coffee and picked up a biscuit. "But don't you go thinking about catering our wedding day, sweetheart. That day, I want you all to myself."

"I wouldn't dream of it. I really can't wait for that day to come."

"Me, too."

Cade gave his fiancée a solid kiss that lasted long enough for Gage to wonder if he'd ever fall head over heels in love with a woman. He'd never really loved a woman before, not the way his father had loved his mother. Not the way Cade loved Harper. His relationships with women weren't heavy or powerful. Mostly, he didn't have time to devote to making one woman that important to him. His father's words rang in his ears every time he'd think about getting serious—"It's not the woman you can live with, it's the woman you can't live without."

So far, Gage hadn't met a woman he couldn't live without. And he wondered if it was him. Was he incapable of loving that hard, that powerfully?

"Now, both of you need to give me some space. I've got my team coming in to prep for the day." Harper gestured with a sweep of her hands. "Let the chef do her work."

Gage rose and kissed Harper on the cheek. "You fit into this family already, Harp. Thanks for everything you're doing. I'll see you later."

She gave him a big smile. Gage had never thought he'd be envious of Cade, not in the female department for sure, but something jabbed him right smack in the heart every time Cade's eyes lit as soon as Harper walked into the room.

Cade had the real thing.

While Gage was only pretending.

Gage walked past the parlor and spied his mother sitting in her chair reading the newspaper. He did an immediate about-face, but he wasn't quick enough.

"Gage, a word, please," she said, catching him ducking out.

"Ah, sure, Mom." He gave her a big smile, one that probably hadn't fooled her since his teenage days. "What can I do for you?"

"Have a seat."

He sat down on the sofa in the giant living room. It was the centerpiece of the entire house, a room with tall beveled-glass windows, polished wood flooring, a floor-to-ceiling stone fireplace and various sitting areas throughout the space. His mother liked to call the decor "rustic elegance." And the Texas estate suited her style: character and charm with country flair. Gage had always loved this room. It reminded him of his father and the hard work he'd put in to be able to build this house for his family. But at this exact moment, he felt more like a schoolboy being summoned into the principal's office.

"It's a big day today," Rose said, a master of the obvious. "How are you holding up?"

"Me? I'm fine."

Her brows arched, her way of expressing skepticism. "You are? No worries or concerns about your announcement tonight?"

"No, ma'am. I'll be doing just fine."

"So you're sure about this?"

"Yeah, I am," he assured her. His mother had never been keen on the fake engagement idea, yet she'd given him her support, and he wanted to ease her trepidation.

"I hope you are. Because this isn't a small favor you're asking of Gianna. She's been through so much already, caring for Tonette, only to lose her this year. And now she's being thrust into this little charade. She's a good sport, as you know. You certainly badgered her enough over the years, and she always came out fighting."

"She points that out every chance she gets," he said. "The badgering, I mean. I was pretty rough on her, because she always had to be right. And it bugged me because she actually was right most of the time. She really is a brain. But as you said, Gianna is no wilting flower. She gives as much as she takes."

"I love that about her, Gage. In fact, I love her, period. She's like a second daughter to me. This year has been especially tough." The edges of his mother's eyes crinkled as tears welled up. His mom reached for his hand. "I'm trusting you, Gage. To be good to Gianna. I wouldn't want to see her hurt again, by any means. I know she's intelligent, but she's also very vulnerable right now. I need your promise now that you'll be mindful of that. You'll be careful with her. Don't lead her down a path—"

"Mom, you have nothing to worry about." Gage figured his mother would be protective of Gianna. They had a strong bond, but her worries weren't justified. Gianna might look pretty in a dress and a new hairstyle, but he knew his place. She was helping him out of a jam, and that's all there was to it. Nothing more. "I'll be careful, and if it'll make you sleep better at night, I can tell you, Gianna and I are complete opposites. We don't jell, and she'd be the first one to tell you that. So put your worries to rest. At the very least, Gianna will be too distracted to be sad over her mama's death. And at the very best, she'll be able to travel some. She hasn't been able to do that for quite a few years, and she misses it."

His mother sighed heavily. "That does make me feel better, Gage. I needed your promise on this, son."

"You have it. I'll take good care of Gianna."

"Thank you." She folded up the newspaper and laid it down. "That's what I needed to hear." His mother stood, and Gage rose as well. "Now it's time to check with Lily about the plans for tonight's barbecue. I'm hoping all is under control. I'm getting excited. Our guests will be arriving for the party in less than four hours."

Gage smiled. His mom loved the annual Tremaine Fourth of July party. It was her way of celebrating the holiday with family and friends in their community while honoring the birth of the country. And tonight, he'd make the announcement to the world that he and Gianna were in love and getting married.

Suddenly, reality bit him in the ass. He'd made a lot of promises to a lot of people in the past, but the one he'd just made to his mother was one he had to uphold.

No matter what.

Gage stood behind Gianna's door, wishing he didn't have to do this. Wishing there was some other way. She wasn't going to like it, and that was a gross understatement. What he wanted to do was grab his suitcase and head on back to the main house, but his back was against the wall, and he couldn't turn and run like he wanted to do.

Instead, he braved a knock on her door, holding his breath. Gianna opened it seconds later. "Gage, what are you doing here? You're four hours early."

Not by choice, he wanted to say as his brows rose at her appearance. She wore baggy gray sweats with Fairmont University Tigers printed in bold letters on her shirt. Her hair was in a tight twisty thing at the top of her head, her glasses were nearly on the tip of her nose and a ballpoint pen was tucked behind her ear.

"I know. Something's come up. Am I interrupting?" He looked over her shoulder, finding her computer screen flashing.

"Yes, actually you are. I'm in the middle of my research project for the upcoming seminar."

"You're working?" He found it incredible that Gianna could focus on work today. Didn't most women spend half the day getting ready for an important occasion? And this wasn't just any occasion, but the day they would announce their engagement to the world. A day that would change Gianna's entire life. At least temporarily.

"You can see that I am." Her eyes drew down to his suitcase curiously. "Are you going someplace?" Then she smiled. "I know, you've given up on this whole crazy idea and you're off on some wild vacation."

Didn't that sound like fun? "Not even close."

He leaned against her door frame. "My band surprised me and showed up for the Fourth of July bash. Whenever they're in town, they know they have a place to stay here. Toby, Lionel and Paolo usually stay in the guesthouse."

"So, what's the problem? They'll stay at the main house, right?"

Gage scrubbed his jaw. "Right. Yep. That's where they're staying, but—"

"Wait a minute. You're not planning on moving in here." She began shaking her head adamantly, her eyes as round as silver dollars. "Tell me that's not what your luggage on the doorstep is all about."

"I knew with your quick wit, you'd figure it out."

"No. No. Not gonna happen, Gage. Are you crazy?" She folded her arms across her middle.

"Gianna, we're supposed to be in love and getting married. If I sleep in the house, the guys are gonna know something's up. Don't worry. Stay where you are and I'll take one of the other bedrooms."

She glared at him, but he didn't have time to waste. "Sorry. I can't stand out here arguing with you." Gage grabbed his suitcase and strode past her, entering the house. She remained at the front door, in disbelief.

He turned to her. "It's either this or you move into my bedroom with me at the main house. There's only one bed in my room—granted, it's pretty big," he said, the innuendo clear. Oddly, he visualized Gianna naked in his bed waiting for him, her hair spilling down her shoulders and caressing her soft skin, her eyes filled with yearning.

Get a grip, Gage.

Oh, man, after having that conversation with his mother, he should be struck down by lightning for giving any credence to that notion.

"Not on your life." Right on cue, Gianna set him straight.

"So, I'll take the far bedroom," he said.

Gianna shut the front door, her mouth in a pout. "Fine."

His shoulders slumped. The Gianna he knew never made things easy for him, and if this was how it was going to be from now on, he was in for a mighty long summer.

"Just don't make it a habit of surprising me with this kind of thing," she said.

"You know when we go on the road, we'll be staying in a hotel room together, right?"

"I'm aware," she said, her chin pointed up. "But you promised me a suite with two rooms."

"You'll have that, Gianna."

"Okay, then. I've really got to get back to work."

That was Gianna. Always with her nose in a book or her head in the computer.

That didn't seem to bother him right now. But what did was that her appearance in shapeless clothes and uncombed hair no longer turned him off.

Because he knew what was hidden underneath all those less-than-appealing trappings.

And he wasn't just talking about her sexy-as-sin body. Some might say her brilliant mind was a big turn-on. Not him, of course. But suddenly he was grateful she didn't like him all that much. Suddenly, he was glad she looked upon him with disdain at times.

"Go, Gianna," he told her. "Get back to what you were doing. You won't even know I'm here."

"No more interruptions?"

"None. We'll head over to the house about four o'clock. How's that?"

She sighed. "I'll be ready."

He stared into Gianna's pretty green eyes as they shared a moment of deep acknowledgment. Their little charade was about to begin.

And very soon, they'd be under the spotlight together.

Everything from here on out would be one big, fat lie.

Four

Gianna walked out of her bedroom, fully dressed for the Fourth of July barbecue, and found Gage standing in the front room, gazing out the window. From the back, he looked pretty stellar in black jeans and a matching Western shirt embroidered along the shoulders with a swirling pattern that ran down his sleeves. He wore a Stetson that he usually called his "John B." Sensing she was in the room, he turned to face her, and the full impact of his appeal hit her smack between the eyes.

Masculine, rugged and handsome. She knew why women fawned over him, aside from the deep tones of his voice. He was the picture of pure country male.

He gave her outfit a look, and a smile lifted the corners of his mouth. "Wow," he said, "you look—"

"Patriotic?"

Gage shook his head. "Very pretty, Gianna."

"Thanks. Lily's doing again." Gianna didn't want to

overdress for the occasion. To everyone else in attendance, it was simply an Independence Day celebration, so she'd wanted to keep with the theme instead of going too fancy. Her off-the-shoulder white dress was tiered with lace on its bell sleeves and also at the hem just above her knees. The scoop neck had a drawstring pull that Lily insisted she tie loosely, allowing for a deep dip at the chest. Gianna thought the look too bold, but there was no arguing with Lily. She knew fashion. A wide silver belt decorated with turquoise stones and a choker of the same design completed the outfit, along with a red cowgirl hat and matching leather boots. "I never would've put this together," she said honestly.

"Oh, so you've never been line dancing?" Gage grinned.

Horrified, she blinked. "Is that what I look like?"

"Only ten times better. And just right for the party tonight. The hat's a nice touch."

She touched the brim, sliding her fingers along the edge. "It's not me. I'm not a hat person."

"I'd say you are. Hats make a statement. Takes a confident woman to wear one. And that's you."

She wasn't entirely sure of that, but she could pretend. This whole night was about faking it, so what was one more thing to fake? "Well, you look nice, too."

He shrugged. "Not my Sunday best, but something fittin' for a party."

Or one of his concerts. She'd seen him wear flashy clothes like that onstage.

He glanced at his watch. "It's just about time to go."

She put her head down, regrouping. This was it. Her nerves rattling, her heart pounding, she prayed she could pull off the deception. She'd given her word and she couldn't back out, so she lifted her lids to Gage and nodded. "Let's do this."

Gage studied her a minute, his gaze sharp and steady. Then the dark hue of his eyes softened, and in a true honest moment, he said, "Thank you."

He put out his hand and entwined their fingers. They exited the guesthouse together, strolling up the road to where the backyard grounds were transformed with patriotic balloons, streamers and bunting. There was a dance floor set up, and tables and chairs. Music was piped in, and Gage explained that his band wasn't scheduled to play, but they might put together a few songs later on in the evening. Barbecues and smokers sent a spicy, delectable aroma throughout the property.

Rose was the first to greet them. She gave Gianna a hug and kiss on the cheek and then did the same to Gage. Cade and Harper were busy speaking with a bartender at the backyard bar. Lily was there chatting with Nathan, the Tremaine horse wrangler. Guests were starting to arrive. Gianna recognized a few of them, having been to many of the Tremaines' parties in the past.

Toby, Leo and Paolo walked up. Gianna had met them before, but she couldn't recall who was who. One of them slapped their lead singer on the back, wearing a big smile. "Hey, Gage. You're holding out on us. Who's this pretty lady?"

"This is Gianna Marino. You've met before," Gage said, "at least once or twice backstage."

Gage put his arm around Gianna's waist and drew her close. The move surprised her, and she forced a big smile. Gage held her possessively and their bodies meshing together created goose bumps on her arms. "Gianna, this is Leo. He's our lead guitarist. And Paolo over here, with the rat's nest beard, is the best drummer Nashville has ever produced." He turned toward a young man with long blond hair. "This is Toby. He plays the fiddle."

"Hi, guys," she said. "Nice seeing you again."

Each one appeared puzzled, as if they couldn't place her. Had her appearance changed that much? "Same here," Toby said. "I do remember you now. You're a family friend, right? You came backstage one night with Rose and your mother."

"Yes, that's right. My mother, Tonette, was with us that night."

She felt Gage's muscles tense up. He shifted a bit. "Gianna lost her mother a short time ago," he said, as if warning them to drop the subject.

"Sorry to hear that," Toby said, and the others muttered their condolences as well.

"Gianna is more than a family friend," Gage said, looking at her with adoring eyes. "We're together now."

Gage's band members hid their reactions well. If they'd seen anything about them on social media, they didn't acknowledge it.

"Cool," Leo said, and the others politely agreed. She felt them assessing her, and she wasn't sure if they were buying it. They'd toured with Gage for years, knew him pretty well and knew his taste in women. To her knowledge, Gage had never had a serious relationship. He must hate lying to his band members, but they'd agreed that only those who absolutely had to know the truth would be told. The lie was too much of a burden for their friends to carry.

Gage motioned toward the bar. "You boys ready for a drink? The bartender is making some sort of Independence Day explosion up at the bar."

"As long as they have whiskey straight up, I'm good," Paolo said.

"Well, an explosion sounds pretty dang good to me." Toby grinned. "Think I'll try one."

"You boys go on, and we'll see you in a bit. I'm glad you all made it tonight." He winked. "Gonna be a special night all the way around."

The three took off, and just as Gage was steering her toward Cade and Harper, a female voice called out from behind them. "Gage."

Gage and Gianna turned in unison. "Regan? You made it," he said, puzzled. "I thought you got held up in Nashville."

Gage's manager's face was flushed as she approached, her blond hair falling from the pins that held it up. She wore a gorgeous sapphire-blue dress that hit just above the knees, a stunning ruby necklace draping her throat and white designer slingbacks. "I did—almost didn't make the flight."

Gage released Gianna to give his fortysomething manager a big hug. He seemed genuinely pleased to see her. "Well, I appreciate the effort. Sorry about the trouble you went through."

"It's okay. It's my job…anything for you," she said, her eyes sparkling. She turned to Gianna. "I almost didn't recognize you." She looked Gianna up and down, her mouth in a bit of pout as if she were measuring her up, making sure she was fit to be the country superstar's fiancée. Then, as if she passed inspection, Regan smiled. "Are you all set for this, Gianna?"

"As ready as I'll ever be, I guess."

"Gage and I appreciate you doing this."

There was something in the way she spoke, rather possessively, that Gianna thought odd. But then, the woman had been Gage's manager and mentor for most of his career. If anyone had the right to look out for Gage, it would be her. "I need a private moment with Gage, if you don't mind," his manager told her. "It's business."

Gianna stiffened. The last thing she wanted was to face the crowd alone.

"Can we do it later, Regan?" Gage asked.

"Not really. We need to nail a few things down regarding your schedule. You know how hard I've worked on setting it up." She looked at Gianna. "It's boring stuff, and I promise it'll only take a few minutes. You understand, right?"

Gage was nodding his head, encouraging her, so she took his cue. "Of course."

"Thanks. Maybe you could go talk with Lily," he said, relieved. "This shouldn't take too long."

"Sure. You go on. I'll be fine." Suddenly, she was fully aware where she placed in Gage's pecking order. His career came first, that was a given, but she hadn't expected him to abandon her tonight. They were to portray a unified front. At least while in the public eye.

Luckily, Lily was heading her way, and the two joined up over by the pool area, where red, white and blue candles floated in the water, ready to be lit as soon as the sun went down.

"Wow, you look fantastic, Gianna," Lily said. "That outfit really works for you."

"That's only because you do excellent exterior work. And I love your dress, too." It was an off-the-shoulder cherry-red dress that flounced when she walked and suited Lily's personality perfectly.

"I bet my brother flipped when he saw you. Where is he, anyway?" Lily scanned the grounds for him. "I thought I saw you two together a few minutes ago."

"You did. We were just joining the party, but Regan had some important business to discuss with him."

"Tonight?" Lily sighed. "I swear, that woman never lets up. She shouldn't have dragged him away tonight of all nights."

That's what Gianna thought, too. "But she's helping him repair his reputation, so she has a vested interest in him."

"That, or some other interest, but let's not go there. How about we go grab a drink? You have to try the Explosion. I hear it's amazing."

Gianna didn't question her cryptic comment. Gage's relationship with Regan was none of her business, and she wanted to keep it that way. "How about I have a sip of yours? I need to keep my wits about me tonight."

"Sure." Then Lily linked their arms and led her toward the bar.

Gianna was too much of a lightweight to master a drink blended with several types of liquor. The last time she had too much wine, according to Gage, she'd thrown herself at him. Asked him not to leave her bedside.

But when she called bullshit on him, he'd given in too easily. Which made her wonder about his motives. About her innermost desires.

When all her inhibitions were gone, did she secretly have a thing for her soon-to-be fake fiancé?

As the sun began to set, Gianna found her place at the Tremaine table along with Gage, Rose, Cade, Harper and the band members. Brisket was a given at a Texas barbecue, and Gianna watched Gage eat up heartily. He had a heaping plate filled with beans and coleslaw and hush puppies. Laughter filled the air, everyone having a good time eating and conversing. There were at least eighty people here, maybe more. Harper had told her the guest list topped one hundred, and guests were still strolling in, finding the bar and buffet line easily enough.

Gianna had been to these Tremaine parties before and had always felt a bit left out. She wasn't one for big crowds—unless they were her students in a lecture hall—

or making small talk to people she'd just met. There were politicians here, the mayor of Juliet, as well as CEOs of big oil companies. Ranchers and rodeo riders, people who defined Texas high society, were dressed accordingly in big hats and belt buckles and thousand-dollar leather boots. According to Regan, news reporters were here under direct orders to steer clear of all the guests, use discretion and photograph the party from a distance. She'd promised them an interview with Gage after the celebration was over.

Gianna never felt comfortable at these kinds of shindigs. She wasn't a snob, but rather a misfit, a girl who'd rather have her nose in a book than be the life of the party. A Texan who loved to learn and loved to teach. She must've appeared a little befuddled, her dinner plate barely touched, because Gage covered her hand with his and gave her a smile. It was a heart-melter, one he was practiced at, but it did manage to calm her quivering nerves. He leaned in and spoke into her ear. "I'll make our announcement right after supper," he said.

She nodded and pulled back to gaze into his eyes. He winked, as if this was all some sort of carefree game. Sure, *his* life wasn't going to change. His life would stay the same, while she was tasked with going along for the ride—*his ride.*

Her mama's image popped into her mind. She had been a gentle lady with nothing but love in her heart. Oh, how Gianna missed her. It had been the two of them against the world, it seemed, for the longest time. But Rose had been there, too, always a friend, always with a kind word to ease her mother's burden. Her mama had loved all the Tremaines, and she would have wanted her to help Gage. She'd be proud of the sacrifice Gianna was making to help out a friend. The thought brought comfort and made sense of this whole thing.

Thirty minutes later, dinner was winding down, and the dishes were being cleared. "I'm ready," she told Gage. She gazed down at the engagement ring she'd just put on her finger. She hadn't wanted to wear it, until absolutely necessary. It sorta made the lie she was living a little easier to take.

Gage squeezed her hand, and an electric jolt seized her for a second. She stared at Gage's smiling face and smiled back.

Gage pulled her along, past the dance floor and up onto a little stage they had set up. The party was in full swing.

Harper and Regan made sure everyone had a flute of champagne in their hand as Gage assessed the group, gave the cue to shut down the music and then picked up the microphone. "Hey, everyone. On behalf of my mother, Rose, and all the Tremaines, I want to thank you for celebrating this special night with us."

At the sound of Gage's voice, everyone dropped what they were doing and turned toward the stage to listen. Gianna felt all eyes shift from him to her as guests curiously wondered what she was doing onstage with him.

"It's the birth of our nation. The good ole US of A. Our Independence Day. And that's certainly something great to celebrate."

Cheers went up all the way around.

"But it's also the day I'm happily losing my independence." He turned to Gianna, his blue eyes arrowed straight at her. "Everyone, this beautiful woman beside me is Professor Gianna Marino. We've known each other since forever. And…well, I'm crazy about her. Lucky for me, Gianna feels the same way. I've asked Gianna to marry me, and she said yes, so I'm here to announce that Gianna and I are engaged."

Gasps of surprise filled the yard. Many cheered and

some applauded. Gianna smiled, but she was afraid she came off as too timid. Gage laced a possessive arm around her waist, drawing her extremely close. Then he turned to face her, his eyes heated and darkened to midnight blue. The pounding in her chest escalated. He leaned forward, tilting her head up, alerting her of his intent. She braced herself, her heart hammering, racing so darn fast. He was going to kiss her right here onstage in front of a hundred pairs of eyes.

And at the first touch of his delicious mouth on hers, she stilled. Breath froze in her throat. She couldn't seem to form a rational thought. But Gage had mastered the art of seduction, and the shock ebbed quickly, replaced by a slow, hot burn, rocking her, tossing her off balance. It was crazy how his lips, meshed with hers, could elicit such instant heat. She fell deeply into the kiss, fully absorbing his power, his desire. Sensations swept over her body, unleashing uncanny abandon. She wrapped her arms around his neck, tugging him closer, and he deepened the kiss, claiming her mouth with what seemed like very little effort. A little moan of pleasure escaped her throat, and she could feel Gage smile, his lips curling up as he continued to possess her. His hand around her waist lowered to just above the curve of her buttocks, a place somewhere between decency and too far. It was as if he'd ignited something fiery in her. Everything below her waist burned. Lusty notions she'd never entertained before rushed forth with alarming speed.

Wolf calls and whistles from the guests brought her back to earth. They'd kissed for far too long, and the partygoers were eating it up.

Oh, God.

She popped her eyes open to Gage's handsome face. He stared at her for a long moment, hunger evident in his eyes—and maybe a bit of shock, too. He blinked several times before taking half a step back.

His breathing was as labored as hers. Had he lost himself, too? Had he been as floored as she'd been to discover the red-hot chemistry between them?

"That was…good," he rasped for her ears only. "Wait till you see what comes next."

Did he mean she'd put on a good display or…

He entwined their fingers and turned both of them toward the guests.

News reporters rushed toward the stage, snapping photos and shouting questions. For half a second there, Gianna had forgotten why she was here. She'd forgotten their little ruse. For half a second, she'd felt connected to another person in a way she'd never felt before. A sigh escaped her throat, and she turned away from the crowd to look at Gage again.

He was grinning, holding her close, posing them both for the cameras.

A loud boom made her jump, and all eyes lifted upward. Rockets soared skyward, and red, white and blue fireworks illuminated the hills behind the Tremaine estate. They exploded in succession, splashing the heavens with brilliant color as patriotic music played in the background. It was the perfect ending to their little charade, something no one in attendance would soon forget.

Gage had wanted to make a big scene, and he'd sure gotten one. News of their engagement would be cemented in the headlines now. His fans would be happy. This engagement would impact the country music scene and allow Gage the positive publicity he craved.

She was his stabilizer. The woman behind the man. She had the perfect résumé—a young, stable family friend with a squeaky-clean image and a position at a university.

She was just what the doctor ordered.

Correction—she was just what Gage had ordered.

Oh, Mama, what have I gotten myself into?

After the announcement was made, Gage fielded questions from reporters and posed for a few photos with Gianna right by his side. Most of the questions were regarding his mystery woman, someone who'd come out of the blue to become his fiancée. And while he'd answered those questions as vaguely as possible, being somewhat of an expert at evading the press, he tried to keep his responses as truthful as he could.

He was learning Gianna's body language already. She stiffened every time he was asked a probing question about her. She clearly wasn't comfortable with this line of interrogation.

"Yes, we've known each other since we were children."

"No, we never dated prior to this. I was kind of a thorn in her side, to tell you the truth."

All eyes turned to Gianna. She forced a smile. He was determined to control the dialogue. He wouldn't bring up her mother's recent death. No, he wouldn't use Tonette that way. Or Gianna, for that matter. At all costs, he wanted to keep Gianna's grief out of the public eye. The fact was, she didn't like lying, and neither did he, but this one time it was a must.

"We might've always been a little bit in love, but it took me getting injured for us to realize our true feelings for each other. My time at home lately made me take stock of my future, and I realized Gianna had to be a part of that future. We're in love and we've wasted enough time being apart."

At least part of that was true. And that killer of a kiss would've definitely convinced any skeptics. Wow, where had all that passion come from? He hadn't expected it. Hadn't given a thought about kissing Gianna in front everyone. Yet, once his mouth claimed hers, he'd been struck by something powerful, something overwhelming. The heat, the chemistry, the burn of desire ripped through him. It wasn't all for show. Oh, it'd started out that way, but a second into the kiss, he was captivated and hungry for more.

Another reporter asked a question, bringing him out of his thoughts.

He answered it, and then Gage dismissed the reporters, asking them to respect his privacy and let them get back to the party.

A few more photos were snapped, and then, to his surprise, no one lingered. The news-hungry reporters were probably eager to get their stories in to their editors for the morning edition. Afterward, Gage and Gianna were congratulated by just about every person at the shindig. He held her hand throughout, keeping her close and doing most of the talking.

Paolo, Toby and Leo joined in to shake his hand and give Gianna a big hug.

Paolo put his hand on Gage's shoulder, nodding his head in approval. "It's about time this guy settled down."

"Spoken by the only married one in the band."

"Why should I be the only one to suffer?" Paolo grinned and winked at Gianna. "Joking. I love my family. My wife, Jessica, and I just had a baby. It's a boy." He took out his phone and, instantly, a chubby little guy appeared, showing off a big, toothless smile.

"He's adorable," Gianna said, her eyes going soft. "I bet you miss him."

"I do. Every minute. But since we're not touring right now, I can spend a lot of time with him. He'll be six months old next week."

"What's his name?"

"Paolo Jr. But we're calling him Paulie right now."

"That's so cute."

Paolo turned his attention to his bandmate. "Can't wait for you to have a kid."

"A kid? Me?" Gage hadn't thought about having kids. He'd always been career-minded. Yet, seeing Gianna looking adoringly at little chubby cheeks, he could almost imagine it. Maybe. Nah. What was wrong with him? That kiss had rattled his mind. "I have to walk down the aisle first."

"So, when's the wedding?" Toby asked.

Gage had prepared himself for these kinds of questions, but he wasn't sure Gianna had. He wrapped his arm around her waist and dragged her to his side. "We're thinking on it. Right, sugar?" he asked Gianna.

Gianna's brow shot up. She didn't like the endearment. He figured he'd get an earful from her later.

"We still have so much to decide, honey bun." She sent an adoring smile his way.

Gage did a mental eye roll. His quick-witted fake fiancée could go toe to toe with him. He'd almost forgotten. "We'll be sure to let you all know when we decide."

Regan strolled up, and one by one, the guys found an excuse to walk away. They were not her biggest fans, but she'd been loyal and true to him all these years, so he pretty much let it slide.

"It's done," Regan said quietly.

"It sure is."

"You kinda laid it on pretty thick with that kiss." Regan smiled, darting a glance at Gianna, whose cheeks suddenly appeared rosy red. A difficult feat for an olive-skinned Italian girl.

"There should be no room for doubt now," he said.

Gianna flinched, and he envisioned the wheels in her mind turning. He'd come off as callous when he'd really been stunned by the impact of her kiss. Stunned and amazed and pleasantly surprised.

"Anything for the cause," Gianna responded. She toyed with the frames of her glasses. "Guess I'm a good actress after all."

"Guess you are," Gage shot back, irritated.

"Well, there's no turning back now," Regan said, glancing at the both of them. "You're off to the races."

"No, no turning back," Gage repeated, trying to hide his annoyance. Just who was he annoyed at? Himself for being caught so incredibly off guard and enjoying that kiss far too much, or Gianna for making light of it and pretending she wasn't as astonished as he was? "Well, I guess we should get back. Some people are ready to leave."

Regan nodded. "Yes, and I see the mayor and his wife are about to go. I want to catch them before they do." She stepped away and then turned abruptly. "Oh, and keep it up, you two. You're doing great!"

He gave her a nod and she took off, heading back into the fray.

"She's got your back," Gianna said.

"She's a good manager." He paused. "And friend."

"Yes, I can see that."

"You don't approve?" he asked.

"I didn't say that. She concocted this grand plan for you, after all."

"Gianna, if you're upset about something, just lay it on me now. Before we go back to the party. Is it about the kiss?"

"No. Not at all." Her chin cocked up. She looked pissed, but she also looked hot. In that getup, with her perfectly smooth skin, her sexy dress, her meadow-green eyes. Hell, she even looked great wearing those wire-rimmed glasses. It suited her, and the beauty behind those glasses was unmistakable. "But if there's a next time, keep it to a minimum."

He sighed. "A minimum? You mean, don't make you moan?" he whispered.

She shot him a look that told him exactly what she thought of him.

"There will be more kisses, Gianna. Can't be helped. Now, will you smile and pretend you're happy to be my fiancée?"

A few guests were heading in their general direction. She took note and plastered a big smile on her face. After they walked past, though, her smile faded. "How was that?" She batted her eyes like a 1920s movie star.

"It'll do, for starters."

Gianna put him on edge. She was mind-blowingly sexy and didn't even know it. But she was also a pain in his rear end. And he wasn't sure which of the two disturbed him more.

Gianna sat with Lily and Harper at one of the tables, while Gage picked up his guitar and joined his band onstage, treating the late-night die-hard guests to a song. There were fewer than forty people here now, many, she figured, who had waited around for this very thing. To hear Gage Tremaine sing. And he didn't disappoint. His voice was smooth, untarnished by time or repetition, the depth of his tone rich and sincere. He sang a beautiful ballad, aiming his blue-eyed attention not on the guests who sat mesmerized, but on her, as if there wasn't another soul at the party.

Opera and classical music were her preference, but she didn't doubt Gage's immense talent. And the words of the song, about love and loss and newfound hope, touched her deeply. He delivered the song as if he knew he could reach her with those lyrics, with the raw emotion he'd packed in them. As if he was singing of her grief and a future of promise.

Someone gently patted her hand, and she tore her gaze from Gage to look at his sister. "Are you okay?" Lily whispered.

Lily was astute enough to know this whole charade had been thrust upon her quickly and that she had a dozen puzzling thoughts roaming her mind at any one given moment. "I'm fine. It's a pretty song."

"But the way Gage kissed you—"

"It was just for show," she replied immediately.

Lily gave her head a little shake. "Really?" she asked softly. "Because it looked like both of you were into it, hot and heavy."

"That's what Gage wanted everyone to think," she offered.

"My brother's a good man, Gianna. But just be careful. A girl can get swept away by his charm and all the adulation surrounding him."

"Charm? Gage has charm?" She glanced at him again, his voice captivating the audience, making a liar out of her. "Don't worry. He doesn't affect me that way."

Lily didn't appear convinced, but she didn't argue the point.

After the song ended, Gage sang an upbeat tune, and everyone stood and moved along with the music. It was a fun, impromptu moment, and even she had to admit to enjoying herself.

The jam session went on for twenty more minutes, and as soon as Gage was through and the band members dispersed, the rest of the guests started to leave. Several approached to wish them congratulations one more time on their way out.

Gianna's phone buzzed on the table. She picked it up and found a message from Brooke. "Excuse me," she told the rest of Gage's family. She walked over to a far, quiet corner of the yard and read the text.

Having a good time with my folks. Maine's amazing this time of year. Ben's here with Sadie and the kids. They loved the fireworks. How's your Fourth going? Anything delish to tell me? Gage?

The last time they'd spoken, Gianna had skirted the issue of Gage and what they were doing together at the ice cream shop and the Rhinestone Room. She wished she had the nerve to explain the "lie" in a way that Brooke would understand. Brooke worked at the university, too, as a counselor. They'd become great friends over the years, but they were more than that; they'd been each other's confidantes.

Glad you're having a great time. Miss you. Wish you were here tonight at the Tremaine estate. We need to talk.

What? She posted an upside-down emoji. Don't tell me you've fallen madly in love with Gage and your heart's all aflutter?

It was a tease. A joke. But never had Gianna felt the gravity of lying more than right now. She didn't want to do this to Brooke. She'd battled it over and over in her head until her brains were mush. And now her stomach ached in the worst way.

But she had to think on this logically. Because she was a logical kind of girl, right? If Gage hadn't told his band members the truth, guys he felt closest to, the fair thing for her to do was keep the charade going with Brooke.

She'd come to realize that nothing was really fair when the lie was this huge.

Actually, she typed in. Don't fall over, but Gage and I just got engaged. For real.

Her phone rang ten seconds later, and Gianna didn't have to look to know it was Brooke, ready to interrogate her.

She pushed the button to accept the call. "What? Tell me you're joking." Brooke's voice was elevated an octave. "Are you serious?"

She wished she wasn't. "I am serious. It's not a joke, Brooke. We fell in love and have kept it quiet out of reverence for my mother." She squeezed her eyes shut. She should be struck by lightning using that as an excuse.

Sorry, Mama.

"He is the exact opposite of you, Gia."

"I know. I guess it's true, opposites attract," she said. "We've known each other forever, Brooke."

"Maybe you only think you love him because of all the heartache you've been through lately."

"I don't think that's it, Brooke. I, uh, I really love him."

Her friend became very quiet. "And when were you going to tell me?"

"Tomorrow. Honestly, I'm still getting used to the idea myself. I'm sorry if you're hurt, Brooke. It's been a whirlwind."

"I'm not hurt. I only want you to be happy, Gianna. You've had a rough year, but I'm glad you told me tonight."

"Yes, me, too. Well, I'd better get back. I'll talk to you tomorrow, okay?"

"Okay…and congratulations, my friend. I…wish you all the best."

"Thanks. Love you."

"Same."

Ugh, that conversation had been grueling. Brooke still had reservations—she could tell by her skeptical tone. She knew Gianna too well. Brooke hadn't heard passion in her voice while she spoke of Gage. She hadn't heard excitement. Because there was none, and Gianna hadn't been all that convincing.

She tried not to blame Gage for getting her involved in this. But right now, her emotions were overriding her logic and good sense. You reap what you sow. Gage's occupation put his every move in the spotlight, and that very thing was what had caused all the trouble. Now she was a part of a sham that might make her lose Brooke's friendship if the lie was ever discovered, and she couldn't bear the thought of losing yet another person she loved.

By the time she returned, all the guests had gone. She found Gage by the stage, speaking with Cade and their mom. A crew was working cleanup, and servers were removing the last of the dishes and cutlery. Lily was over by the pool with Nathan, and if Gianna wasn't mistaken, the candles glistening on the water didn't twinkle half as much as Lily's eyes as she flirted coyly with the family's horse wrangler.

Gianna had a vivid imagination, but she wasn't imaging the way Nathan was looking at Lily, either, like she was a treasure of gold. Who could blame him? Lily was wonderful.

Gianna sighed and gathered her wits. She was in this thing now, for better or worse, and couldn't back out. She walked over to everyone. "Hi."

"Hello, dear," Rose said, giving her a little kiss on the cheek. "How are you holding up?"

She felt Gage's eyes on her. "I'm doing well. The party

was really great. Harper, those fresh tarts you made were yummy."

"So was the five-layer American flag cake," Cade said, glancing at his soon-to-be wife. "I'm afraid you're stuck now, sweetheart. You're gonna have to make it every year from now on."

"Happy to."

"Yeah, I had two slices and would've gone in for thirds if given the chance," Gage said.

"Well, I think everyone had a nice time. And Gage, your announcement seemed to go over very well," Rose said.

"It'll be all over the news tomorrow. Trust me, I know," Harper said wryly. She'd been a reality star, who'd been disguised and in hiding when she'd met Cade. He hadn't had a clue who she really was. But love conquered all, and the two were as happy as clams now.

"That was the point of all this, wasn't it? To make news?" Cade glanced at his brother. "Do me a favor, bro, don't invite any paparazzi to our wedding. We've had enough of that for three lifetimes."

"Oh, no. That's not going to happen," Gianna declared immediately. "We wouldn't dream of it. Some things are sacred. Your wedding certainly is."

"Damn," Gage said, as if just realizing reporters might try to crash the wedding. "I'll hire security to make sure of it. Nothing's gonna ruin your big day," he assured the couple.

"Well—" Rose placed her hand over her heart "—I certainly hope not."

"I promise, Mom." Gage kissed her cheek. "And thanks for allowing me to hijack the party tonight."

"I'm only glad my family was all here today." She took Gianna's hand. "My whole family."

Tears burned behind Gianna's eyes. She'd needed to hear that. Rose had always made her feel part of the family, but tonight especially, when she was feeling like such a fraud, Rose's love surrounded her and made her feel a bit better.

"I'm pretty tired. I think it's time I turn in." Rose kissed everyone good-night, and Cade and Harper escorted her into the house. Lily was off somewhere with Nathan, she supposed. Gianna hadn't seen her for quite some time now, which left just her and Gage standing in a yard that just a short time ago had been swarming with guests.

"Well, what do you say? Ready to turn in?" Gage asked.

She was beat. The physical toll didn't even begin to match the mental toll this day had taken on her. "My cheeks hurt from all the smiling I did tonight."

Gage reached for her hand, and she pretended not to notice as she turned and began walking toward the guesthouse. She wished to high heaven Gage wouldn't follow her. That he could find another place to sleep tonight. She needed privacy, but she doubted he'd agree, and quite honestly, she wasn't up for an argument.

Not tonight.

Not after that earth-shattering kiss.

Not on the evening of her fake engagement.

Five

Gianna tossed and turned in her bed. She couldn't sleep, the events of the entire day rehashing in her mind. She was living a lie and had to resign herself to the fact that for the next six weeks, she was at Gage's mercy. She'd been fine with that—*until he'd kissed her.* That kiss, powerful, masterful and filled with dire hunger, worried her no end. She was a red-blooded Italian girl who was passionate about her work, her students, her family. But she'd never experienced that kind of unbridled passion and desire for a man. And least of all Gage Tremaine.

"Until now," she whispered into the night.

She punched her pillow and tossed her head back again, squeezing her eyes shut. But it was no use. She knew in her bones that sleep would elude her right now. She might as well not waste her time wrestling with plaguing notions. She always had a ton of research waiting for her. She rose from bed and padded barefoot toward the kitchen, making doubly sure she was quiet as she passed Gage's bedroom.

Entering the kitchen, she filled an electric kettle with water. The pot heated water in twenty seconds flat, and she poured it into a teacup. Chamomile tea steeped, steam billowing up.

Movement caught her eye from the living room. She peeked out and found Gage sitting on the sofa, focused on a laptop, a whiskey glass in his hand. He was deep in thought and didn't seem to notice her. And then, as if he'd read her thoughts, he swiveled his head and spotted her.

Oh, man.

He rose, abandoning his computer. He took a quick sip of whiskey and sauntered over.

"Can't sleep?" he asked quietly.

She swallowed hard, forcing her gaze to his eyes and not on his bare, ultra-ripped chest. All he wore were faded blue jeans, the waistband dipping inches below his navel. There was a presence about him, an aura of sensual prowess causing her heart to pound.

"No, uh, just thought some tea would help."

He smiled and approached, keeping his eyes trained on her face and not the thigh-length white T-shirt she wore that screamed Fairmont U Tigers, complete with a menacing feline on the front. Her hair was up in a ridiculous bun, tousled from her fight with her pillows.

"Try this," he said, coming close and spilling some whiskey into her teacup.

"Gage, what are you doing?"

"Helping you get back to sleep. So I can get back to what I was doing."

"Am I disturbing you?"

He eyed her appearance, from her painted toenails to her legs, up her thighs, and then spending extra time perusing the tiger covering her breasts. She held her breath, wondering what he was thinking. Finally, his gaze roamed over her face to land on her silly hairdo. Hunger flashed in his eyes, and he sipped whiskey again.

"No."

"I'm glad. What are you doing up at this hour?"

"When I can't sleep, I get up and write."

"Write?"

"Songs. Well, the lyrics to music. Didn't think you'd appreciate me fiddling with my guitar this late at night."

"That was probably wise, though I'm up now anyway."

"Sip your tea. It'll knock you out."

"Because I'm a lightweight?"

"Absolutely." He smiled and finished off his drink. "And because I make you nervous."

She set her teacup down, her hands shaking. "What are you talking about?"

"Nothing. Forget I said anything."

"You do not make me nervous, Gage Tremaine."

"I don't? You liked that kiss as much as I did. Admit it."

She folded her arms across her T-shirt, which brought his gaze to her chest again. "I will not admit anything. Besides, it was all for show."

"Yeah, all for show," he repeated, folding his arms across his chest now, too, taking a stance. "But what if it wasn't?"

"I don't deal in what-ifs, Gage."

"I'm just saying, what if that kiss wasn't a fluke? *What if* it's the best kiss either one of us have ever had? *What if* we try it again, just to be sure?"

"You want to kiss me again? Right here and now. Without an audience?" She backed up a step, picked up her teacup and sipped, needing the fortification. The whiskey burned her throat going down, and her eyes opened wide. "No, thanks."

"Nervous?"

"Gage, you can't be serious? Look at us, the way we're dressed, or rather, undressed." She scanned his body again, the muscles in his arms and bare chest so glorious her insides heated up. He was positively beautiful in the flesh.

"I'm looking. And I like what I see."

"Me? I'm a mess. Don't even go there, Gage."

"You don't even know how tempting you are."

She rubbed her forehead. "This is crazy." Then she glared at him. "Are you trying to make me crazy?"

"No."

She grabbed her teacup and walked past him. "Well, you are. So cut it out. I'm going to bed."

"I don't suppose that's an invitation."

She turned to him, suddenly imagining him in her bed. Imagining more kisses like the one tonight. She imagined touching him in all his hard places, and her hesitation caused his brows to rise with hope.

She was just a convenience to him, a woman who was handy and who would be spending the next month with him. She wasn't a superfan, wasn't interested in him. She didn't even like him that much. "Have another drink, Gage. *What if* we forget this conversation ever happened?"

"Sure, I'm good at pretending."

"I know that about you. That's why I'm going to bed now. Alone."

He grinned. "Don't worry. You don't have to lock your door. That's not my style."

The man was impossible. Impossibly sexy. Impossibly confident. But he was right. He didn't have to force a situation. Gage didn't have to work too hard to get women to fall at his feet.

She just had to make sure she wasn't one of those women.

* * *

For the next few days, Gianna's phone rang more than it had the entire year. Suddenly she was sought after. People she hadn't heard from in a long time began calling. Her high school friends, her old roommates, people who hadn't come to her mother's funeral all of a sudden were leaving her messages of congratulations. She was the woman who'd captured Gage Tremaine's heart, and now she was deemed worthy of their attention.

Her engagement to the country superstar had made headline news, and Gage's phone was also ringing off the hook. He was scheduled for morning shows, late-night talk shows and a few music events.

People were curious about their relationship, about their almost minuscule courtship. How had Gage hidden Gianna in plain sight, they wanted to know. When did he fall in love with her, exactly, was the question of the day. Gianna's professional record had been scrutinized pretty thoroughly. They'd reported on her college days and on how she'd come to work at Fairmont U. They'd written about her various awards and accomplishments. Most of what they wrote was complimentary, as if the press and Gage's music colleagues had put their stamp of approval on their engagement.

Tremaine's Engagement Sets off Fireworks.

Gage and the Professor, a Match Made in Country Heaven?

Professor Gives Tremaine an A Grade.

And just like that, Gianna was thrust into Gage's world. Luckily, Gage had left her alone most of the time, allowing her to do her research. She didn't know where he went during the day, but they'd always meet up at the main house for dinner with his family. And in the evenings, he'd walk her back to the guesthouse and wish her good-night.

She relished the peace and quiet, but all that was about to change this morning. She had packed last night for their trip to Nashville, and they were flying out soon.

She was dressed in new jeans and a pink chiffon blouse with bell sleeves. Another one of Lily's picks. A matching jacket would work well when on the plane, she'd said. With Gage's approval, Lily had taken one of his credit cards one day and gone on a shopping spree, coming back with a dozen new outfits for Gianna's travels.

The toaster popped up her bread nice and crispy, and as she spread butter on it, Gage walked into the kitchen, dressed casually, too, his phone to his ear.

"Yeah, okay, Regan," he said, giving Gianna a quick good-morning smile. "We'll be there on time. Gianna, too. I know, I know. We'll talk later."

She poured them both a cup of coffee and sat down at the table. Gage shut off his phone and took a seat facing her. Why did he always look so good in the morning? His hair had yet to be combed. Even tousled, it looked amazing. And the morning scruff darkening his face was heavier than usual today, making him look even *sexier*, if that were possible.

"Thanks for the coffee," he said, running a hand through his hair. The more unruly, the better, it seemed.

"You're welcome." They'd found a certain rhythm together these past few days. Gage had been on his best behavior around her lately, and that made her wary.

He took a sip and sighed. "This is good."

"Problems?" She'd gotten to know his moods, and this one today wasn't good.

"Why do you ask?"

"There's a face you make when you're irritated about something."

"You know my faces?"

"Mostly your sour ones. Remember what I do for a living, Gage. I study emotions and relationships."

"I'll keep that in mind."

"So what's up? And if it's none of my business, I'm sure you'll tell me."

"Unfortunately, it does involve you. And I want you to keep an open mind."

She didn't like the sound of this. "Why? What now?" she asked.

"Well, uh." He sucked in a deep breath, as if he'd rather have a root canal on both sides of his mouth than tell her. "It seems as if our engagement news is bigger than we expected. Regan booked us on *The Johnny O in the Morning* show. It's the hottest ticket on the air in the South, and well, they want to interview both of us."

"Us? As in you and me?" He couldn't be serious. She wasn't supposed to be the story, he was. She was to be his trophy fiancée, showing up at events, but certainly not being a part of them. She didn't sign up for this. "I'm not doing it, Gage."

"Regan said it's important. We did such a good job of convincing the world we're in love that now the public wants to see us together."

"They've got lots of photos of us, Gage. Isn't that enough?"

"Apparently not. Look, I told Regan not to involve you, but she says it's too good an opportunity to pass up. They want us for tomorrow morning. And if you don't show, it's a deal breaker."

She bit her lip, shaking her head. It was a lot to ask of her. "Gage, I don't want to do this."

"All right, I guess I'll call Regan back and tell her to forget it. I suppose it's not the end of the world."

He was surprisingly gracious about it, which made her feel like a heel.

In her heart, she didn't want to sacrifice what little privacy she had left, but her darn analytical brain told her the whole purpose for this ruse was to enhance and revive Gage's image. "If you cancel the interview, that sorta defeats the purpose of this charade, doesn't it? I'm doing this to help boost your image, not to turn down ideal opportunities."

Hope entered his eyes. "Are you changing your mind?"

"I'm looking at it logically. It makes sense. The sooner you fix your reputation, the sooner this whole thing will be over."

"So?" His brows rose, and hope, again, registered on his face. *Like a little boy getting his wish.*

"So…you're gonna owe me for this."

"Ha! You mean more than I already owe you? I would be more than grateful, Gianna. You'd have me over a barrel. Not too many wo—uh, people can say that."

"Gage, you know how much I hate being the center of attention."

"I do know."

"We're opposites in most every way."

"I know that, too. But if anyone can pull off a convincing interview, it would be you. You're a smart cookie."

Was she? Would a smart cookie get herself into this situation in the first place? "I think that's a compliment."

"It is," he said without hesitation.

Gianna squeezed her eyes shut. She knew she had no choice. Regan was right—this was too good an opportunity to squander. And it would get them to the finish line that much sooner. She sighed and looked deep into his eyes. "I might regret it, but I'll do it. Just. This. One. Time."

Gage immediately grinned. He rose, pulling her up from her chair and wrapping both his arms around her in an enormous hug. Her nose went to his neck, and she breathed in his fresh, soapy scent, felt the power of his ripped chest against her breasts, the warmth of his body pulsing around her. "Thank you." He pressed a kiss to her cheek before releasing her.

They stared at each other, a few moments ticking by. Did that demonstrative hug rattle him as much as it did her? She couldn't tell, but she did know one thing—making Gage happy could very well be infectious.

Gage was first to break the silence. "Well, I'll just go get our luggage. Are you all packed?"

"Pretty much."

"The limo will be here in thirty minutes."

"I'll be ready."

But was she ready to spend time with Gage on the road? Spend her nights with him in a hotel room? Pretend that she was madly in love with him while on television?

She sighed. For a woman who kept things simple, her life was getting more and more complicated.

The chartered plane had amenities galore, from luxurious seats and tables to a couch for relaxing and enough food to feed the Fairmont Tigers football team. Gage didn't think much of it. He was accustomed to traveling this way, but for her, a girl with middle-class values, it all seemed over the top.

"The price of fame," Gage had said when they'd first boarded. He wasn't being sarcastic, either. He explained that he couldn't take commercial airlines anymore. It wasn't worth the scrutiny and the constant attention. Folks in other parts of the country weren't as thoughtful as in his hometown in Juliet County.

The trip lasted a little more than an hour, and when they touched down in Nashville, a certain thrill ran up and down her spine. There was so much history here. The town rivaled New Orleans in terms of history, music and excitement.

Gianna's eyes were wide-open as they traveled the streets, taking in the sights, the incredible landscapes. And when they pulled up to the Gaylord Opryland Resort, she was immediately struck by the grandeur and opulence of this fabulous hotel.

A doorman opened their limo door. "Welcome to the Gaylord," he said. Gage unfolded his body to a standing position and then reached for her hand. "Here we are," he said.

Gianna stepped out of the limo and was immediately struck by a blast of humidity. In the South, one could always count on drippy, cling-to-your-body kind of heat in summer. Gianna was used to it. She once spent three days without air-conditioning in her university classroom when the air reached 90 percent humidity. Nashville was no different, it seemed.

But as they approached the entrance, hand in hand, a blast of cool air welcomed them. She stood by Gage's side in the lobby as he checked in, keeping her gaze focused on him and not the dozen pairs of knowing eyes on the country music star.

Ten minutes later, they were in their hotel suite, Gage keeping to his promise of two-bedroom accommodations. She strolled out to the balcony to view cascading waterfalls in a lush green setting. There were waterways and bridges within the interior perimeter of the hotel, brightened by the sun's rays streaming down from the massive overhead skylight.

Gage joined her on the balcony, handing her a glass of ice-cold water. "It's really magnificent."

"It is," he said, leaning against the wrought iron railing. "I love coming here."

"How many times have you sung at the Opry?" she

asked. She'd never been, but everyone knew that singing at the Grand Ole Opry meant you'd hit your career high mark.

"About five times, I'd say. Never gets old."

"No. I guess not."

"So, now that we're here, what's next?" she asked.

"We relax for a bit. Then I'll take you anywhere you want to go."

She smiled. "Really?"

He nodded. "Remember, I owe you."

"I'd love to see some of the city, but shouldn't we go over what I'm going to say at tomorrow's interview?" Her stomach churned just thinking about it. "I mean, I need to know essentials about you, don't I?"

He shot her a glib smile. "I don't think anyone's going to ask you what my favorite color is. Or what I eat for breakfast. Or how many awards I've won."

She hesitated, blinking rapidly. She didn't know any of those things.

"Six, in case you were wondering."

"Six? I had no idea. I'm glad you told me. Who was your last girlfriend?" she asked. "Just because I don't want to be ignorant of your past."

"I haven't dated much. That incident with Bobette Jones sort of destroyed my trust."

"She was the one who claimed you were cheating on her?"

"We'd broken up quietly just a month before, and no one knew. So, when she found out I had a date, *one* date, with another woman, she went to the press and claimed I cheated on her. It was probably the nicest thing she told them about me that day. Hell, one woman is more than enough for me to figure out, much less trying to maneuver two at the same time. But I got the blame. She painted a picture of me as a cheating jerk, just to get back at me."

"Hell hath no fury like a woman scorned."

"Yeah. None of it was true, but then couple that with the other two unfortunate situations I had, and suddenly I'm viewed as some sort of heartbreaker bad boy."

"What she did to you wasn't fair, Gage. I'm sorry. I never knew the entire story. At least now, if I'm asked about it, I can say something in your defense."

His brows arched, and gratitude filled his eyes. "You'd do that?"

She nodded. She didn't want him to get the wrong idea. "Of course. Any fiancée would do that same."

"You'd stand by your man?" He spoke softly, his blue eyes twinkling. And his smile was real—he wasn't teasing her.

"Yeah, that's why I'm here, isn't it? I legitimize you."

He winced, his twinkle gone now. She'd been blunt, but it wasn't anything they hadn't discussed before. "I suppose so."

Gage turned away, looking out onto the view before him. "We've been spotted," he said, gesturing to a group of news reporters on the ground level, and just like that, his hand covered hers and she was being drawn up against his chest. "Legitimize me right now," he whispered, his gaze sharp and penetrating.

"Do you mean…?"

He nodded. "Yes, I mean kiss me."

But he didn't wait—he bent his head and instantly covered her mouth. She was stunned into silence, just like the last time. And while he was putting on a good show, her stomach flipped over itself from his performance. His arms came around her waist and their hips collided. She fought against the urge to moan, to whimper as he drove his tongue into the recesses of her mouth. The invasion was surprisingly welcome. Gage took her on a masterful journey, giving and taking, and then giving again.

Everything below her waist melted. Gage had the opposite dilemma. He was granite-hard, and it was both exhilarating and a little frightening how quickly he could turn on. How quickly *he could turn her on.*

By the time he ended the kiss, she could barely breathe. Gage wasn't doing much better. His chest pumped up and down as he pulled away.

She grabbed the collar of his shirt and gazed adoringly into his eyes. "Well, we showed them, didn't we?" Maybe too well.

He gazed right back at her, catching his breath. "We… did. You're a quick study."

But was it really necessary to put on such a display? She wasn't sure.

He turned his back on the balcony railing and tugged her into the suite, closing the double doors behind him. To all, it looked as if they were heading to the bedroom.

At least, that's what a real couple would do. But they were far from that. "I think I'll unpack and get some rest."

Gage rubbed the back of his neck, hesitating a moment, as if he was going to say something. Then he just nodded and watched her walk away.

"Do you always lose track of time that way when you're working?" Gage asked, sipping red wine as they sat down to dinner at the hotel's outdoor steak house. The soothing rush of the waterfall and soft music playing in the background gave the restaurant a relaxing ambience.

"Most times I do. I swear I was just checking some stats, and then the next thing I know, I'm knee-deep in research." She pushed her glasses up her nose. "The time flew by." They'd never made it outside the hotel today. "I apologize."

"I thought you were napping all that time. Or, worse yet, that you were running scared after we kissed."

"You were wrong on both counts." Gianna sipped her wine. This time she'd stick to half a glass. She had to be on her toes around Gage. He had wild kissing skills.

"So what were you researching that fascinated you so much?" he asked. He'd changed for dinner and looked nice in a snap-down tan shirt and black jeans. His dark hair, touching his collar, was as long as she'd ever seen it. He epitomized a handsome-as-the-devil country rock star. "Divorce rates."

He nearly choked on his merlot. "Divorce rates," he repeated, coming forward in his seat. "I can see how that can keep you awake all afternoon."

Her mouth twitched. Gage was such a tease.

"Tell me something interesting about divorce rates."

She didn't hesitate. "Well, did you know that over thirty percent of divorces occur when the woman feels the man doesn't take her career seriously?"

"Thirty percent, huh? And what's the other seventy percent caused by?"

"Oh, that's from having men overrate their kissing abilities."

Gianna lifted her glass and smiled at Gage.

He burst out laughing. "You really had me going there for a minute."

"I know. And I also know that you think my research isn't valuable. But I assure you it is."

"I never once said anything of the kind."

"You have selective memory. You've teased me about my work hundreds of times."

Gage shook his head. "Teasing doesn't count. It's just what I do, with you."

She smiled because she knew there were eyes on her. She was coming to realize that no matter where they went, people were going to recognize Gage Tremaine. Especially in Nashville, Tennessee.

"So tell me, if you could go anywhere in the world, where would you want to go?" he asked.

"Why are you asking me that?"

"We should keep the conversation going, since we're being watched." He sipped again, swirling wine in the glass. "And I'm curious about what places fascinate you."

"Europe. Brooke and I had a trip planned a year ago. Specifically to visit Italy and Greece. My heritage. I'm one-quarter Greek, too. We were really looking forward to going. It was one of the things on my bucket list. Only, life interfered when Mama got so sick."

"You'll get there one day, Gianna."

"Maybe." She wasn't thinking that far into the future right now. She had to get through one day at a time now.

"Would you like to take a drive with me after dinner?" he asked.

"Where'd you have in mind?"

His mouth quirked up. "The place where I cut my musical teeth."

She tilted her head, giving it some thought. Gage could be charming when he set out to be. And after that kiss, with all the sizzling-hot stirrings it created, she should refuse. She had the perfect excuse. "I do have more research to do." Allotting her plenty of work time was part of the deal they'd agreed to. Going out with him when not absolutely necessary wasn't.

"It's a place you should see. For the interview. You can say it was the first place I took you to in Nashville. And that wouldn't be a lie."

"No, I guess it wouldn't. Is it fancy? Should I change my clothes?" She was wearing a floral summer dress with spaghetti straps, her hair down around her shoulders.

"No need to change. You might be overdressed for the

honky-tonk I'm taking you to, but you sure do look pretty tonight."

Heat rushed up her neck. "Thank you."

An hour later, Gage held her hand as they walked down Broadway, the street bustling with tourists and musicians, Nashville nightlife in full swing. "This is the place where dreams are made. Or hearts are broken. I know some guys, and ladies alike, who've spent years trying to get their big break here."

"It does remind me of New Orleans. There's so much energy here."

"That's a good way to put it."

"So how did you get your big break?"

They strolled the sidewalk, country twang, laughter and conversation pouring out of the bars as they walked along. Several people recognized Gage and stopped to take a picture of him. It didn't faze him much that he had no privacy, but it wasn't a life Gianna could ever get used to.

"Me? I was in a band in college, and on a dare, we came to Nashville. But there were no gigs for amateurs like us. I mean, we were really raw, but we loved making music. I never expected to make a living at it. My path was always to help my family with the business.

"One day, me and the guys sauntered into Lucky Red's Bar to get a beer, and it turned out, the band they had booked was involved in a car accident. None of them were seriously injured, but they couldn't get to Lucky's in time. I guess you could say what was bad luck for them was my lucky break. I wound up singing two sets that night. We did so well, we got booked for the next month. And then one day Regan Fitzgerald walked into Lucky's scouting new talent, and the rest is history."

"Wow, I find it amazing that your career was left to

chance like that. I mean, up until that point, you had no idea if you were going to make it as a musician."

"It's the nature of the beast, I guess. It's a well-known fact that some of the best talent in the country—singers, guitarists, drummers—are pining away in some local honky-tonk. Or playing a lounge act in Vegas. Like I said, some hearts get broken."

"Tough. I couldn't do it. I couldn't leave my future to chance like that. I always knew what I wanted to do with my life."

"And you made that happen. You worked hard for your success."

"Because I knew it was achievable."

"Where's the challenge in that?" He grinned.

She swatted at his arm. "You're impossible."

Gage grabbed her hand and immediately brought her in, looking deep into her eyes. He had a way of cradling her body as if she was something precious, something he didn't want to let go. He tipped his hat lower on his forehead. "We're being watched."

"I know."

He gestured toward the bar in front of them. Lucky Red's. "Want to go inside?"

"It's why we came."

"Always so logical."

Their hands entwined, he led her into the bar. A band was up on the tiniest stage in the back, with just enough room for three musicians and the lead singer. The place was jam-packed, couples dancing on the floor, servers nearly spilling topped-off beers, the music more country rock than twang and loud enough to bust eardrums.

"Want a drink?" he asked, heading over to the bar.

"Sure, I'll take a beer."

He gave her a look. "Beer?"

"Sure, I like beer." Occasionally, she'd have a beer. And she wanted to look like she fit in. "Make that a light beer. And no jokes about me being a lightweight."

"No jokes," he promised and called over to the bartender. The man turned, recognition registering on his face. "Hey, Gage. Good to see you."

"Hey, Red. Same here."

The two men shook hands over the bar. "It's been quite some time, boy. You back to cause a ruckus?"

Gage grinned. "Never in here, Red. I came to show my fiancée, Gianna, the place. She's never been to Nashville. Thought she'd want to see where it all started. Gianna, honey, this ole guy is Red Muldoon. He's owned this honky-tonk going on forty years."

"That's right. Opened the place on New Year's Eve 1982. Nice to meet you, miss. And congratulations. Won't pretend I don't know about your engagement. Been big news around here, you know."

"Yes, I suppose it has," she replied. "Nice to meet you, too, Mr. Muldoon."

The man's mouth twisted up. "It's Red. Just plain ole Red."

She found the whiskered man endearing and immediately liked him. "Okay, Red. It's a great place you have here."

"I appreciate it." He turned to the other barkeep. "Get these two anything they want. On the house."

"Yes, sir." The starstruck young man behind the bar nodded.

"That's not necessary, Red."

"You know your money's not good here. But I wouldn't kick you in the shin if you wanted to give the crowd a taste of your music."

"Will do," Gage said, tipping his hat. "A little later."

"Whenever you're ready. Tell Ronny what you're having and we'll get it to you pronto."

Their attention was brought to the singer onstage crooning a love song, one so poignant the noisy patrons all simmered down to listen.

"He's good, but he's no Gage Tremaine." Red slapped Gage on the back. "Now, go dance with your lady. I'll get a table cleaned up for you both."

"Sounds good."

Red walked off, and Gage ordered their drinks at the bar, giving the guy a huge tip before turning to her. "Want to legitimize me some more?" he asked.

Before Gianna could open her mouth to refuse, her hand was entwined with his and she was led to the dance floor.

"What are you doing?"

"Dancing with my lady." Gage winked playfully. "The crowd expects it."

Gage dragged her to his chest so quickly, air whooshed out of her lungs. His arms were like anchors around her waist, keeping her close. Her heart began to dance, far sooner than her body moved.

Goodness, they were the focus of attention again. This time, she didn't have to look around. She sensed eyes on both of them. "Do you always do what the crowd wants?" she whispered. A hint of his cologne invaded her nostrils, the scent wildly erotic.

"Actually," he whispered back, "I'm at my very best when there isn't a crowd. When it's just one on one."

Goose bumps rose up her arms. Gage liked to keep her close, but the contact battled with her good senses. She couldn't pull away. Others on the dance floor were watching intently, waiting.

A good defense is a powerful offense, and she was learning quickly that she needed to take the helm. "Conceited, aren't you?"

Her jab didn't even faze him. "Nope. Just solid fact."

His confidence stunned her. She gave her head a shake. "Amazing."

"That's what they tell me."

But his boast didn't really bother her, not in the way it should. He had provoked her curiosity about his prowess, about what it would be like to make love with him. To be the object of his desire and have the full force of his sexual attention aimed at her. For real.

She hadn't had a satisfying sexual experience in...well, maybe never. The few men she'd been with didn't exactly make the earth quake.

And there was no doubt, as much as she hated to admit it to herself, Gage Tremaine was...*delicious*. Sexually speaking.

"Put your head on my shoulder," he whispered as the music played on.

"Why?"

"Because for some reason you're scowling."

Oh!

She pressed her head to his chest. The pounding of his heart reverberated in her ears. She shouldn't be surprised by the tight contact. They'd danced this way before. At the Fourth of July bash, when they'd lied to the world about being in love.

"That's better," he said into her ear. "What's with the sour face?"

"Nothing." Except images flashed in her head of getting bare-butt naked with him. It really freaked her out.

"You hate this, don't you?"

She did. She really did. Lusting for her fake fiancée wasn't in the plan. And wouldn't Gage just have a big laugh over it if he ever found out?

"It's not so bad, Gage," she lied. She couldn't let him guess her wanton thoughts. That, if things were different, she'd jump his bones. "I can live with it. For a little while longer."

At the table, after they guzzled beer—well, Gage did all the guzzling, Gianna merely sipped—Red brought over three decadent desserts. Red had a sweet tooth, and his honky-tonk was known for serving a variety of amazing treats. Gianna sampled chocolate surprise, a mound of chocolate infused with warm raspberry sauce. A person could gain three pounds just by looking at it. Gage tried the apple cobbler deluxe, with almonds, walnuts and cashews on top. And they both indulged in a bite of warm cookie pie, the dessert too rich to have more than one bite.

Gianna leaned way back in her chair and rubbed her tummy. "I'm gonna bust right out of this dress if I take one more bite."

Gage's brows rose. "I'd pay good money to see it."

"Funny, Gage."

His eyes shadowed. A deep sigh escaped his throat. Was he imagining her minus her dress? "Is it?"

Okay, maybe not so funny. Awareness struck like a match whenever he teased her this way. She blamed it on the smoky surroundings, the hum of the crowd, the sultry ballad the singer crooned. She wouldn't fall victim to it, to him. She had to remember why she was doing this. She had to remember another man with charm to spare. Another man, like Gage, who'd broken hearts. "Yes, it's ridiculous."

Not a minute later, Red called attention to Gage from the stage. "Everybody, in case you didn't notice, we've got our own Gage Tremaine in the house. And if you're inclined, I think he'll come up here to sing for us."

Whistles and shouts broke out, and the place erupted in applause. Gage rose from his seat, in the limelight once again. But that wasn't enough for him. *Oh, no.* "Come with me," he said, extending his hand.

"What? No," she blurted out quietly. "They don't want to see me."

"Not true. They want to see us. Together." He winked. "C'mon."

Given little choice, she put her hand in his and followed in his footsteps. The crowd parted, some slapping Gage on the back, others happy to eye him or take cell-phone photos. And once they stepped onstage, he held on tight, keeping one arm around her waist.

He said a few words to the band and turned, facing the crowd from behind the mic. "Thanks for the warm welcome," he said. "I appreciate the support. Truth is, I haven't sung in public since a broken beer bottle flew into my neck and slashed my throat. Yeah, that was unfortunate. Some of you might have heard a little something about that."

Chuckles rang out. Gage could be charming when he had to be.

"But then," he said, turning his blue-eyed gaze on her, "I wouldn't have met up with this pretty lady again. Everyone, I'm proud to have you meet Miss Gianna Marino. My fiancée."

Cheers went up, and Gianna smiled and waved.

"And yes, folks, she is a professor and one smart lady." He winked at her again. "'Cause she's marrying me."

The patrons ate it up. Gage was a good actor. The very best.

He took up the mic and sang to her, a fun song about fishing and baseball. Everyone in the place knew the words and sang to their hearts' content.

The music was contagious, the song so full of joy that she moved along with the crowd, clapping her hands, tapping her feet. The song ended, and a band member handed

Gage a guitar. He grabbed two bar stools and gestured for her to take a seat.

Darn, the entire crowd watched her lumber up onto it. Grace not her strong suit, she managed to finally make herself comfortable on the thing.

Gage strummed a few notes, and the room quieted. He began to sing again, this time a soulful ballad, a love song that caressed the ears, a sweepingly beautiful tune about finding love for the very first time. Gage kept his eyes on her, and she forced herself to keep her gaze steady on him, but as the song went on, moving her, stroking her and touching her in ways she couldn't logically explain, she was captured by his deep, rich tone and his beautiful blue eyes.

It was a rare moment, to be caught up so fully in one man.

When the song ended, Gianna gazed out to the audience. Many starry-eyed women stared at her, envy in their eyes. A battalion of goose bumps rose up her arms. Was Gage getting to her? Was she falling victim to his charisma, his charm?

Gage's mouth lifted, satisfaction written on his face. He cupped her neck, drew her close and pressed a solid kiss to her lips.

Wow. Really, wow. Her heart sped wildly.

Was she a gooey-eyed woman now, too, mesmerized by a compelling voice and deadly good looks? Wasn't that Gage's intent? To convince people they were madly in love? And judging by the applause breaking out, it was working.

"Thank you, folks. But I'm afraid I have to say goodnight now. It's time for me to take my lady home."

Her feminist side should be up in arms. She wasn't anyone's lady, but Gage's tone indicated something far different. He was hers and she was his, in a way that delighted both women and men alike. Gage obviously knew how to enchant the crowd. And confuse the heck out of her.

She was coming to her senses after his *display.* And she wasn't happy.

He led her offstage, both waving, Gage also tipping his hat. They stopped by the bar and found the owner vigorously wiping down the countertop.

"Good night, Red," Gage said. "Nice seeing you again." The men shook hands.

"Same. You're always welcome here. And don't forget me when you're handing out wedding invites."

Gage put his hand to his heart. "You got it."

"Nice meeting you, miss."

"Thanks for your hospitality." He really was a lovable, kind of rough-around-the-edges ole guy.

"As I said, anytime." He gave her a wink.

They stepped outside, and her shoulders dropped down. Tension oozed out of her. She'd been put on display and that wasn't something she enjoyed. Gage reached for her hand, and instead of giving it to him, she fidgeted with the straps of her purse. She needed breathing room from him. All his touching and kissing was confusing her. He'd warned her they'd have to show affection, but there'd been no clear warning she'd actually respond to it—to him. And enjoy it.

She strode quietly down the street, picking up the pace, getting a few steps away from him. *Breathing room.*

He caught up in just a few strides. "Hey, what's wrong?" he asked.

"Nothing," she snapped. "Thanks for introducing me to Red. But the show's over now. And I'm super tired."

"*Cranky* is a better word."

"Okay, so I'm cranky. Sue me."

"Wow." Noisy air pushed out of his chest. "You're not kiddin'."

"No, I'm not kidding. Are you forgetting about the interview tomorrow? I'm going to have to do this all over again."

"Didn't seem like you minded all that very much. You were getting all moony-eyed and sweet on me."

"I was not sweet on you." She wasn't going to go there with him. "Do you like lying to your friend?"

"No, I…uh. Actually, I don't. But it's a white lie. Not meant to hurt anybody."

"A lie is a lie, Gage."

"Well, then." He crossed his arms over his chest and leaned back on his boot heels. "Why don't you quit lying to yourself?"

Her eyes squeezed shut. "I don't lie to myself."

"You like it when I kiss you."

"Geesh, Gage." She would admit no such thing. Even if it was a little bit true. It would serve no purpose to swell his ego that way. "Don't be ridiculous."

"Okay…but just so you know, for me, kissing you is the very best thing that's come out of this charade. And I'm not *lying*."

"TMI, Gage." The frustrated woman in her wanted to cover her ears. "I don't want to hear it."

She hastened her steps, leaving him in the dust, and this time, he didn't try to catch up.

Six

He rode in the back of the limo, Gianna in the seat beside him, on the way to the television station. The morning show started at 8:00 a.m., and they were just about to arrive. As quiet as a mouse, Gianna sat staring at notes on her tablet. He had no doubt she would deliver. She was smart, sharp and didn't give an inch. Maybe she wore her conservative clothes this morning, a beige dress and matching blazer, to remind herself of who she really was, Professor Gianna Marino, and not some smitten fangirl who'd captured his heart. Her dark hair was up, as tight as her expression, and her shoes were sensible heels.

But she couldn't fool him. They had chemistry; whether it was convenient or not, it was there. No sense denying it. She wasn't faking her response to his kisses. Electricity filled the air when they were in the same room, or the same car. Was it her resistance to him that intrigued him most about her? Was it the challenge she posed? Or the fact that she was forbidden fruit?

His mother's warning came to mind.

Gianna's vulnerable. Don't take advantage of her.

His promises had seemed easy to keep at the time.

Now, not so much.

The limo stopped in front of the WKN building, and the driver opened Gianna's door. Her head up, she exited the limo, taking the chauffeur's helpful hand. Gage got out right after her and immediately entwined their fingers, forming a united front. "Are you ready for this?"

"I always study for an exam."

"Good." The lady came prepared. Gage was more the fly-by-the-seat-of-your-pants kind of guy. That's why he sang for a living and she was an intellect.

"It's normal to be nervous," he assured her. Even though her smile was wide, the expression in her pretty green eyes wavered. "Took me quite a few before I got comfortable answering questions on live TV."

"Then I'm *very* normal. And this is the one and only one, Gage."

"I know. I appreciate it."

Half an hour later, he and Gianna sat on a couch facing Johnny O'Flannery on the live stage. Gage kept his arm around Gianna's shoulder, partly for show, but mostly to give her support. Hell, he'd practically forced her into doing this.

"Welcome back," the host said after the commercial break. "And we have a real treat for you this morning. We're joined by country superstar Gage Tremaine and his lovely brand-new fiancée, Professor Gianna Marino. Hi, you two."

"Good to see you, Johnny," Gage said.

"Nice to be here." Gianna smiled at the famous host.

"Well, can I start out by saying you two make a great couple?"

"Thanks." Gage tightened his hold on Gianna, bringing her shoulders closer to him.

"Gianna, congratulations on your engagement. It came as quite a surprise. Where has Gage been hiding you all this time? Is there any news you want to share with our viewers?"

"News?" Gianna said. "I think I can end the speculation right now. We're not ready to start a family just yet. We want to spend time together first as a married couple." Gianna shot him a warm, loving glance. "One day, maybe. Right, sweetheart?"

Gage cleared his throat. He wasn't prepared for that question right out of the gate. But there must've been some speculation that he'd gotten Gianna pregnant and that was the reason for the quick engagement. Little did they know, aside from a few kisses, he hadn't touched Gianna that way. Yet, man oh man, lately, he'd been imagining it. "Yeah, of course we want kids. But we want to enjoy some time alone. Gianna and I have just reconnected. I want her all to myself first for a little bit."

"Gianna, you've known Gage most of your life. Why now, people are asking?" Johnny asked.

She sat up straighter and leaned forward slightly. Her body language skills were top-notch. "Yes, that's right. Our families are close. Gage and I tiptoed around each other for years, but when he was injured recently in an unfortunate brawl, I realized my true feelings for him. I guess you could say it was mutual, and long overdue. And we didn't have to take time to get to know one another like other couples do." Gianna set her warm, sweet gaze on him. "So our love came naturally, growing over the years."

Gianna spoke with such conviction, her words hitting home, and his heart lurched. He almost believed her, and it didn't scare him or make him flinch. Instead, warmth spread through him like golden honey. Gage took her hand and lifted it to his lips. Her skin was so dang soft, her hand delicate in his, and every time he touched her in any way, even under camera lights, his heart bumped into high gear. He placed a kiss on her hand. Oohs and aahs rang out in the studio audience.

"And very long overdue," he added.

"Gianna, would you say opposites attract? A university professor, who, I heard, doesn't even like country music, marrying a bad boy superstar?"

A sweet smile graced Gianna's expression. "Perhaps they do. But Gage is far from a bad person. I stand behind him completely and believe in his innocence. I have faith in him, in us. And I'm gaining a fine appreciation for country music now. Gage's voice, in my opinion, is unequaled. He's got a gift."

"Can't argue with that," Johnny replied. "But his fans might disagree about his back-to-back scandals lately."

"They're smart people. They know the real Gage Tremaine. He's not a cheater. He's a true gentleman. His fans know that."

Lately, he'd had a series of unfortunate incidents. He couldn't figure his string of bad luck. Sometimes, fame and fortune wasn't all it was cracked up to be. But now he was fighting back, Gianna helping him in his quest.

"So tell us a few things about yourself, Professor," Johnny asked. "The entertainment world wants to get to know you better."

"Well, I was raised by a loving single mother, Tonette Marino," she began. "My father…uh, my father's been gone a long while. Life wasn't always easy for the two of us, but I knew I had Mama's support no matter what I tried to accomplish. I was a scholarship student and achieved my professorship three years ago. I teach communication and family relationships, and my pet project is Learning and Literacy, a special foundation for children. We're always looking for volunteers and donations, for those of your viewers who may be interested in lending a helping hand."

"Is that what inspires you?"

"Everything about learning inspires me, but children who struggle to read are at a great disadvantage."

"I have to say I'm impressed by your dedication. But this must be a difficult time for you. Your mother passed away recently."

Gianna put her head down.

"It's still painful for her," Gage interjected, "so we don't talk about it in public." Gianna shouldn't have to speak about her grief. Some things needed to stay private.

"No, it's okay, sweetheart." Gianna focused on the host, her eyes a little watery. "He's always trying to protect me. Let's just say I miss my mother every second of the day."

"Terribly sorry for your loss, Gianna." Johnny's eyes softened.

Hearing her put it that way softened him up, too. Gianna was in pain every damn day. She wasn't a wilting flower about it, though. She'd done a good job of convincing the world they were a match made in heaven. Hell, he'd even interrupted the interviewer to protect her, and while she might've thought that was all for show, it wasn't. He wouldn't allow anyone to hurt her. Not ever. Where in hell did all this protectiveness come from? Usually, he liked to get under her skin, but lately…

Johnny turned to him, breaking into his thoughts, and thank goodness for that. He asked about his plans for the rest of the year. *Marriage* plans. It was easy enough to be noncommittal and hint at a future date next year.

And tour plans, which were up in the air until he knew whether or not he'd win the starring role in *Sunday in Montana*. They were safe enough subjects and ones he didn't mind answering questions about. All the while, Gianna sat beside him, nodding and agreeing and being a pillar of support.

The interview lasted twenty minutes, an eternity on national morning shows. But it ended on a high note, with well wishes for the newly engaged couple and a plug for Gage's latest album.

On their way to the limo, Gage put his arm around her shoulder and whispered, "You did amazing. I couldn't have asked for a better interview. Mission accomplished."

Gianna had been the picture of grace and refinement. She gave the world a clear look at her life, and all that meant good press for him. She'd been a rock, impressing the hell out of him. So the arm around her shoulder wasn't just for show, but she'd never acknowledge that. She didn't want it there, if not for their little charade. It burned him a little to know she wouldn't give him the time of day otherwise.

"I was terrified," she admitted.

"You didn't seem like it. If your nerves were rattled, I couldn't tell. And that meant that viewers were eating it up."

"I'm just glad it's over with now."

They reached the limo, and the chauffeur opened the door. Gianna slipped in first, and then Gage followed, taking his seat and buckling up.

"Oh, boy. I can't wait to get these shoes off. They're too tight."

She pried them off immediately and sighed, massaging her ankles. How any woman could stand wearing those things always baffled him.

"Back to the hotel now, I've got research to do."

"Not just yet," Gage said. "I have a surprise for you."

"My feet hurt. I can't put those torture devices back on."

"No problem. We'll stop along the way and get you some comfortable shoes."

"I don't feel like shoe shopping."

"You're being difficult. It'll only take a minute. We'll get you some comfy tennis shoes. You're really going to like this surprise."

Gianna plopped back against the seat, her head cushioned by soft leather, and closed her eyes. "I don't like surprises," she mumbled, all her vim and vigor taking a break.

"You'll like this one. I guarantee it."

The interview behind her, Gianna's feet were happy now, encased in white tennies. She stood before the Nashville Parthenon in Centennial Park, the sign before her claiming the building to be the world's only exact-size replica of the original Greek Parthenon, dating back to 400 BC. This one was built in 1897 and was beyond a work of art. It was stunning, and something she'd had on her bucket list. Of course, she'd wanted to see the real thing, but this replica simply took her breath away.

Gage let her gape as long as she wanted, his eyes keen on her and not the structure before him, but she didn't care. It was a totally unexpected surprise. She didn't know why Gage went to the trouble. Well, maybe she did. He'd been asking a lot from her lately, and *taking* a lot from her. Like kisses that made her head spin and made her heart pound. The surprise had surprised her in its thoughtfulness. It was something he didn't have to do. And Gage Tremaine wasn't the kind of man who did things he didn't have to do. If he was reveling in that, so be it. He could tell her "I told you so" about her enjoying the surprise. But he didn't, and she appreciated that as well.

"It's the pride of Nashville, historically speaking," Gage said.

"And you knew I'd love to see it."

"We couldn't leave Nashville without you seeing it."

"It blows my mind." She got out her phone and began snapping pictures. "Brooke's gonna love this."

"You'll have to show her the inside, too."

Gage walked toward the entrance, and she followed. He didn't offer his hand. There were only a few visitors at the site, and he didn't press her about their charade. Chills ran up and down her spine as she took in her surroundings—marvels as far as the eye could see. Every time she saw something new and read the accompanying plaque, she became utterly enthralled. The tall columns surrounding her were indescribable. How on earth had the Greeks ever gotten them to their forty-five-foot height? And the sculptures along the walls were amazingly intricate and lifelike. She stared at the details for several minutes.

Gage came over to her. "Come with me," he said, this time taking her hand and tugging her away from the artwork.

They walked into the second room, and her eyes lifted to the towering gilded statue of Athena. It was massive and beautiful. "Heavens," she said.

"Athena, daughter of Zeus. I read somewhere she was Zeus's favorite child."

"She was strong. The protector of the city. Goddess of warfare," Gianna stated, remembering her Greek mythology.

"She was a lot like you, Gianna."

She turned her head from the statue to gaze at him. "Very funny."

"Not trying to be. She was the goddess of wisdom, too."

She blinked. Gage didn't usually come right out and compliment her. Not unless there was something in it for him. "You think I'm wise?"

"No, I think you're a goddess."

Laughter bubbled up and spilled over, echoing in the chamber. She should know better than to take him seriously.

Only Gage wasn't laughing with her. His sober eyes told a different story. One that brought goose bumps back to her arms. One that made her question why it was that she didn't like Gage all that much. He was all Texan, a hunk with deep-blue eyes, a man who looked at a woman and made her believe she was the only one on earth. It shattered her defenses. She didn't like that. Not at all. "Th-thank you for bringing me here, but we should go."

"I know, you have work to do."

"It's the truth. It's already been an exhausting day, and I'm a little behind schedule."

Gage nodded and put his hand to her lower back, ushering her outside. His constant touching for no good reason made her nerves jump. Not because she didn't enjoy it, but because she did. She walked over to another informational sign, pretending interest, and broke away from him. She didn't want her goose bumps to get goose bumps.

Relief registered immediately. He no longer touched her.

So why was she also terribly, terribly disappointed?

Gage tore up the page of lyrics he'd been writing and tossed it in the trash. Hell, he couldn't concentrate. His mind was on total shutdown. He'd made calls to industry friends and caught up on their news, but his heart wasn't really in it. He turned on the TV. Shut it off. Nothing interested him, not the classic Jimmy Stewart Western he'd seen a dozen times on the screen. Not even the script he'd brought along to look over from *Sunday in Montana*. He got up from the bed and paced back and forth in the hotel room, "wearing out the rug," as his mother would say. He was twitchy and restless. And the source of his restlessness came in the form of the woman in the bedroom ten feet away punching keys on her computer.

How could Gianna turn off the world so easily? How could she shut him out and lose herself in her research when all he kept thinking about was how cute she looked in those doggone sneakers today? And how delighted she'd been to see the Parthenon. How good he'd felt bringing that joy to her, seeing her face light up, her eyes sparkle.

Brainiac, it's been five hours.

Of boredom.

Of being idle.

Of wanting to see her.

Needing a distraction, he ordered room service—a little bit of everything. Then he strode into the living room and poured himself a drink of the good stuff, bourbon that took time coursing down his throat, offering a slow, delicious burn all the way to his gut. It was good, damn good, but not enough to satisfy his edginess.

Not enough to quell his desire. He wanted Gianna. And not because she was here, convenient, and he was bored out of his mind. No, those were reasons to want other women. Women who wanted to hook up with a celeb. Women who didn't really know him. But not Gianna. She was different, special. He knew it as much as he knew the sun set in the west. And he knew it was wrong to want her.

Hell, he knew it and still he walked the steps to her bedroom door. He knocked, three sharp raps, and waited. "Gianna?"

"Just…a…sec," she said, distracted. She opened the door,

and there she stood in a plush white robe, her hair slightly wet, glistening. She'd taken a shower and hadn't redressed. Those black-rimmed glasses perched on her nose told him she'd been working. Still.

"I'm starving." What was she wearing under that robe? And why did he find a cushy bathrobe and tangled, wet hair so damn attractive? He knew the answer, of course. Gianna, unassuming and so damn distracted, was the sexiest thing he'd ever seen. "It's after seven."

"Oh, I didn't realize."

"Lost in your work?"

"I only have another hour of—"

"I've ordered us room service. Should be here any minute."

"Thanks." She stared at him, blinking a few times. And he stared right back into those meadow-green eyes, watching her sweet mouth twist a little. How many times had he seen that particular look, as if she was trying to figure him out? Well, if she had a clue, she should tell him, because he didn't know why his feet weren't moving. Why he couldn't pull himself away from her doorway. He couldn't keep his heart from pounding hard, either. Or keep lust out of his eyes. And he didn't give a flying fig if she could read his mind.

She stood at the door, blocking the entrance as if she'd pulled guard duty. "Is there anything else?"

Her gaze lowered to his mouth, her eyes bold and daring. She was no longer distracted by her work. No, something else fascinated her; something else tempted her. They were inches apart, and raw tension pinged between them. He wouldn't make the first move. But he wouldn't back away, either. This was all Gianna. What she wanted. What they'd been tiptoeing around for days now. This chemistry between them. "Gage," she whispered.

"Right here."

"Maybe you shouldn't be." Yet there was no conviction in her voice.

"Tell me to leave."

She pulled air into her lungs and opened her mouth. But the words didn't come. She reached up and put her hand to his cheek, stroked his face, gently, tenderly. A groan rose up this throat. She was playing with fire.

"I c-can't, Gage. I can't tell you to leave."

It was all he needed to hear. He cupped her face and positioned her mouth, their eyes meeting for a second of confirmation. They were doing this. And there was no protest, no refusal. He brought his mouth over hers and tasted her once, twice. A whimper rose from her throat, and then he took charge, pressing his lips to hers urgently, unleashing his pent-up lust on her. Consuming her with his mouth, his tongue.

Gage wanted more. He wanted everything from her, but he had to slow down. He couldn't rush her. He didn't want to overpower her. He wanted her to come along on this ride beside him. He wanted to please her, pleasure her. It wasn't just about relieving his itch. It was more, because this was Gianna.

They kissed until they were breathless. Gage gave a kick to her door, opening it wider, and then he was backing her up, into the room, toward her bed. Her computer was on, papers all in a tidy pile on her desk. That was her, neat and tidy, and Gage wanted to see her let loose, watch her be free. Give her a reason to go wild.

He lowered her down onto the bed. Her hair spilled out around her, her eyes glowing. She untied the belt and he parted the robe, opening the material wide. His breathing stopped. "My God, Gianna. You're perfect."

Her skin was smooth and tan, creamy. Her small, beautifully rounded breasts filled the cups of her lacy white bra, and below she wore barely there matching panties.

He pulled off his shirt and tossed it, Gianna watching him carefully, her eyes wide and gleaming. She reached her arms out for him, and he nearly lost it. He was harder than granite under the zipper of his jeans, but determined to take this slow.

He lowered himself, and her arms came around his neck. He kissed her again and again, and those little noises she made down deep in her throat rocked him to his core. He touched the swell of her breasts, filling his hands, and he kissed her there over and over. Her nipples pebbled hard. Her breaths were coming sharp and quick, and he flattened his palm to her stomach and drew his hand down to touch her folds underneath her panties. A whimper rose from her throat, and he gave her more, sliding his fingers over her sensitized skin. Her hips arched up. Giving him access to do more, give her more. Panting, she squeezed out a plea. "Gage."

"I know, Gia, honey."

Her release came sharp and fast, her cries of pleasure echoing in his ears. He brought his mouth over hers again, and they shared one long, mind-blowing kiss.

A knock at the front door startled them. Ah, damn. Must be room service. "The food," he whispered. He hated that the moment was interrupted. "They'll leave it outside." No way was he getting up to eat now. Everything he wanted was laid out before him on this bed. "Are you okay?"

Gianna smiled, a satisfied lifting of her lips that told the whole story. "I'm very, very good."

He chuckled and pushed the hairs that had fallen onto her cheeks away from her face. "I'm very, very glad."

From the other room, his phone banged out a tune announcing a caller. He ignored it, hating this interruption even more. But the insistent thing wouldn't stop. "For heaven's sake," he said. "I'll get it."

"I'll watch you get it," Gianna said, rolling onto her side, all legs and creamy skin.

He chuckled again. He was impatient for her now, more than he thought possible.

He picked up the phone from the living room sofa. "You can leave it outside," he said, just barely holding on to his patience.

"Gage? Is that you?"

It was his brother. "Cade? What's up? Now's not a good time."

"No, it's not a good time. Mom's been in a car accident."

It was the last thing he expected to hear. "Crap. Is she okay?"

"She's unconscious."

Gage pinched his nose. He didn't want to hear this news. Blood rushed through his system. "What the hell happened? And where is she?"

"I'll explain all that later. Just come. We're at Juliet Memorial."

"Cade? How bad is it?"

"She's banged up, Gage. The doctor is in with her now."

"Okay, okay. I'll be there as soon as I can." He hung up the phone, his eyes slowly closing, and he envisioned his strong, beautiful mother lying in a hospital bed. Injured. Banged up. Frail.

"Gage?"

He turned, and Gianna walked into the room. She took one look at him, and immediately her smile faded. "What is it? What's wrong?" There was panic in her voice. She knew something serious was going on. She closed the lapels of her robe and came to stand beside him. "Gage, you're scaring me."

"Don't mean to."

"Then tell me. Now." More panic.

"It's my mom. She's been in a car accident. She's in the hospital."

"Oh, my God. No. Not Rose." Tears surged to her eyes, filling them with moisture. He had a feeling she was reliving another moment, a frightening one involving her own mother. She'd been so courageous, selflessly caring for her mom until the very end. It had been hard on her, and now this? It might be too much for her to take.

He wrapped her up in his arms, her soft robe pressing against his chest. He kissed her forehead. "Don't cry, Gia."

"I know. I'm sorry. I don't m-mean to make it w-worse. It's just a sh-shock."

"It is. I don't have details, but she's being treated. She hasn't woken up yet."

Gianna gasped. The noisy sound touched every part of him. She was suffering, too. She loved his mother. They both did.

"We have to go. I have to make arrangements."

"I'll get ready," she said softly. Yet she clung to him still, and every protective instinct he possessed didn't want to let her go. She needed comfort. And he wanted to give it to her. It pained him how much.

She broke away all on her own, giving him a brave nod, and strode into her room.

Gage used the speed dial on his phone and called Regan. She'd make the arrangements. She always knew what to do. If anyone could get him home quickly, it was her. And home was exactly where he needed to be.

Seven

"Would you like some coffee, Gianna?" Harper asked. "Cade and I are going to get some."

Gianna shifted in the uncomfortable hospital chair and shook her head. "No, thanks. I'm fine." But she wasn't fine. She'd been scared silly, and the fright had come far too close to home. She and Gage had flown in the dead of night to get to Juliet Memorial, Gage holding her hand the entire time, while she sent up prayers for Rose's recovery. Lily was in with the doctor now, discussing her mother's injuries. Time was creeping by.

Gianna glanced at Gage standing against the wall, speaking quietly to Regan. She'd gotten here before they had and greeted Gage with a big consoling hug. Gianna's heart had pinged then, a totally ridiculous emotion edging its way inside. She had no reason to be jealous. Regan was his manager. She was like a partner to him, too, and he didn't seem to make a move without her blessing. They were close. Gianna understood that, even though, whenever Regan was around, she totally monopolized Gage's time.

Now she had a hand on Gage's arm and they were face-to-face. He nodded his head as whatever she was saying seemed to resonate with him. She was his mentor, a person he relied on, but Gianna suspected Regan's interest in Gage went deeper than that.

But who was she to analyze his relationship with Regan when she couldn't figure out what the heck was happening between her and Gage? She didn't have a clue what had changed between them, except that spending time with him hadn't been horrible. In fact, he'd made their trip memorable. She'd had a good time at Red's, letting loose and dancing, eating decadent desserts and being Gage's sole focus while he sang about love.

The television interview had been difficult, but Gage made up for it with the surprise trip to the Parthenon. And afterward, in the hotel, she hadn't been able to resist him, hadn't been able to send him away. They'd combusted. She'd been unabashedly naked before him, stripped of her cement-hard resolve. And she was glad of it. He'd given her her very first orgasm.

Lily walked over to where the family was waiting. Cade and Harper set down their coffee cups, and Gage moved from the wall to greet her, Regan right by his side. Gianna stood as well, her pulse pounding, her legs wobbly.

"Mom's awake. She has a concussion, but the preliminary tests are showing no further injury. Her left arm is broken, and she has a bruised rib or two. The doctor will be out shortly to explain, but I know you guys were dying to find out. Looks like she's going to be okay."

Relieved sighs filled the room. Tears streaked down Gianna's cheeks. Lily and Harper were also wet puddles of thankful tears. Gage smiled for the first time since they'd learned of the accident. He walked over to her, leaving Regan to stand alone. "Good news, right?"

She nodded. "The very best."

"Are you okay, Gia?"

The pad of his thumb wiped away her tears. His touch also wiped away her worry. His touch made her feel safe. Which was odd, because nothing about Gage was safe. He was stubborn and confident and self-serving at times, and she'd never believed him a safe bet. Especially since they'd practically made love last night. But it wouldn't be fair to fault him for something she'd wanted. That she'd wanted him at all and desperately last night—now *that* was the bigger issue.

She stared into his eyes. "I should be asking you that question."

"I'm all right."

"Me, too. As long as Rose is going to recover, that's all that matters."

"She'll hate every minute of being laid up. You know my mom—she likes to be active."

"We'll entertain her."

Gage smiled, his eyes warm. "We will?"

"I'll do my best. I know she likes to play poker, and I'm pretty good myself."

"You are? I wouldn't have guessed," he said. "Gianna the card sharp."

"It's all about odds and numbers and logical choices."

"Leave it to you to suck the joy outta poker." He flashed a big smile, and she chuckled.

"What? No comeback? You must be exhausted."

"I'm pretty tired." Beat was more like it. It had been a mentally exhausting twenty-four hours.

"How about you go on home? Cade is taking Harper home, and they'll take you back."

"What about you?"

"I'm gonna stay a few more hours. I want to see Mom once they allow visitors. Lily will be here with me. And Regan. She's been working on rescheduling our LA trip."

Gianna had almost forgotten about that. They were supposed to make a few appearances in and around Hollywood this week. It was to beef up his good-guy image to the film studios.

She glanced across the room. Regan had her ear to a phone, speaking rapidly into the receiver, but her eyes were solely on Gage. Eyes didn't lie, Mama had always told her. *Words can deceive, but eyes are the entrance to the soul.*

A question was on her lips about his relationship with Regan, but now was not the time. And she wasn't really sure if she should be asking. Regan was an attractive single woman, if not several years older, and she certainly always had Gage's back, but it was none of Gianna's business. She was his temporary fake fiancée. Period.

It hadn't felt like that last night.

"I think that's a good idea. I'll come check on Rose later."

Gage kissed her cheek and nodded. "I'll tell Cade. Oh, and thanks for being here. Means a lot." He gave her hand a squeeze.

Regan slipped in between them, taking Gage's arm, gently grabbing his attention. "Now that we know your mama is going to be okay, I'd like to speak to you more about LA."

"Sure," he said. "Just let me talk to Cade and then I'm all yours."

Regan's expression brightened as if she'd just won a contest. She turned her way. "Gianna, you should get some rest. This must be hard on you."

"It's very hard," Gianna replied suggestively, focusing her full attention on Gage. "You have no idea."

Regan's triumphant expression faded. Her gaze shifted to Gage and then back to Gianna, weighing the innocent words and finally dismissing the innuendo.

Heavens, sometimes her quick wit needed reining in. That was another thing Mama would warn her about. But Gianna would rarely listen.

Noise from the living room woke Gianna from a restless sleep. Opening her eyes slowly, a glance at the clock on the nightstand confirmed she'd hadn't slept much, maybe a few hours. It was just before noon. She surveyed her surroundings. Every day she woke up in the Tremaine guesthouse, she had to remind herself about her current life situation. Pretending to be Gage's fiancée and living here was her new normal.

It was super weird going over the events of the past few days. From highs to lows. She was grateful that Rose's injuries weren't all that serious. Her prayers had been answered. Thank goodness. She got up and dressed in a pair of jeans and a cotton top, her actions quiet and precise. A glance in the mirror, and a few finger strokes to her hair, said it wasn't going to get much better than this without more effort. She didn't want to make the effort. Gage was back, and she wanted to hear an update on his mother.

She padded barefoot down the hall and into the living room. Gage sat on the sofa, his legs stretched out onto the coffee table, a cup of steaming brew in his hands. He lifted his lids to her, exhaustion written on his face.

"Hi," she said. "Did you just get home?" How strange was it to say those words to him? It was his home—it just wasn't hers. But Gage didn't immediately answer. He was too busy surveying her choice of clothes. His lazy blue gaze leisurely moved up and down her body. He approved, said the glimmer in his eyes. Jeans and a little cotton top earned her high marks—it just didn't make sense. Yet her insides warmed regardless.

"Just a few minutes ago. Did I wake you?"

"No," she fibbed. "I didn't sleep well."

He nodded. "I made coffee."

"Smells good. How's your mom?"

"Have some coffee and I'll tell you." He moved to rise.

She put up her hand. "No, please sit. I'll get it."

Gianna walked into the kitchen, poured herself a mug and came over to sit on the sofa beside him. She put her feet up, too, so there were two sets of toes on the rectangular cocktail table. They sipped coffee quietly and seemed to share an odd sense of peace, being there together. "So?"

"I got to see her. She's pretty banged up. Her face is bruised, and she's going to be sore for quite some time. They set her arm, and well, she's strong. She's not going to let this get the best of her. She was more worried about all of us and how we're doing."

"I get that. She's always been a mama bear. Did she explain how the accident happened?" All she knew was that Rose had lost control of her car and a telephone pole stopped her.

"She was driving home from town. It was dark on the road, and a dog suddenly appeared in her headlights. She swerved to keep from hitting it and ended up wrapped around a telephone pole."

"That's awful, Gage. And scary."

"No, it was actually a blessing. If that pole wasn't there to stop the car, she would've ended up in a ditch ten feet below. She was very lucky."

"Wow. I guess she was." Gianna sucked in a breath. Fate had a way of playing your hand for you. Luckily, this time Rose came out the winner. If one could say anything about getting in an accident was good luck.

"Gage, can I visit her?"

"Maybe later on tonight. She knows you were there, Gianna. She asked about you. But for now, the doctor wants her to rest. The pain meds knocked her out. She was sleeping when I left the hospital."

Tears threatened to spill. Knowing Rose had asked about her grabbed her heart and tugged hard. Rose was a special woman. With shaky hands, she set her mug down and willed herself to be strong. She couldn't fall apart in front of Gage again. He didn't need that.

"Hey," he said softly. He pulled her toward him, his powerful arms wrapping around her shoulders, her head naturally falling to his chest. She curled her feet onto the sofa, Gage her cushion. "Don't cry, Gianna."

"I'm usually not such a wuss."

He chuckled, his chest rising and falling, taking her with him for the ride. "Gia, you never could be. You're just weary. So am I. Close your eyes. Let's try to rest."

"Sounds good," she murmured, her eyes already closed. This time, she wasn't going to question how safe she felt in his arms. She was going to enjoy his comfort and hopefully fall into a blissful slumber, cocooned by his strength.

This wasn't a good idea, yet her needy body said otherwise.

She'd question all the reasons why she shouldn't be doing this, later.

And the list was long.

Afternoon light broke through the shutters in a dim glow, and Gianna woke gazing into a pair of drown-your-heart blue eyes. There wasn't a guy out there with more appealing ones. Beneath her was a rock-solid man, a man who cradled her in his arms—a man whose message below the waist could hardly be ignored.

Her pulse pounded. Her body buzzed.

He brushed hair away from her face and smiled. As if she hadn't just invaded his space, hadn't just slept on top of him for who knows how long. "How long have we been like this?"

"Awhile," he said, stroking her hair.

"You should've woken me," she whispered.

"You needed sleep."

"I'm so sorry." Her hands on his chest, she lifted up. But that only brought her waist down harder on his groin. His arousal couldn't be missed. He was turned on, but so was she. Heavens, she wouldn't lie about it. It would be too hard to pretend otherwise. Only the zippers of their jeans kept them from glory. She should go before this got out of hand. But his look stopped her cold.

He cupped the back of her neck, the longing in his eyes unmistakable. He wanted to kiss her, and, in that moment, there was nothing she wanted more. She leaned in and he pressed his mouth to hers, his powerful kiss shutting off any hesitation she may have had. His touch was all consuming. And oh, thank goodness for that.

"Remember what happened in the hotel room?" he whispered in her ear.

Her first genuine orgasm. How could she forget? She nodded, unable to form the words.

"We're going to finish that, Gia." He kissed her again, and little moans rose up from her throat. The pulsing of his body igniting hers. Red, fierce heat burned in her belly.

She shouldn't do this. Gage wasn't the man for her. He was too much like another man who'd let her down. Another man who'd hurt her. Charming, smug, overly confident. It was a secret she'd held close to her heart for so many years. A secret that burdened her heavily.

But Gage was too tempting, and back in that hotel room, he'd kindled a fire in her. He'd started something that needed finishing. Logic didn't play into this. No, this was about raw, sensual yearnings. This was about sex and satisfaction.

She ran a hand down his strong jaw, caressed the scruff and kissed him there. "Okay," she said softly.

A guttural noise sounded from his throat, a groan touching every edge of her body, and he kissed her back, his tongue staking its claim. There was no turning back. She was going to give herself to Gage, and she was going to take what he offered her in return.

Gage ran his hands through her hair, lifting the tresses, letting them fall loosely about her shoulders. He unbuttoned her blouse, spreading it wide-open. Appreciation gleamed in his eyes, and she'd never felt like more of a woman.

He removed her blouse and bra, and beneath her, his arousal hardened. Quickly, he removed his shirt and tossed it away. He was all muscle and tiny chest hairs and broad shoulders.

"Touch me," he said, taking her wrists and bringing them to his chest. Her hands fanned out, her palms stroking over his torso. Moaning, he closed his eyes to the touch, and she continued to stroke him, to give him pleasure.

Gage cupped her breasts, kissing her there, palming her slowly, gently, until she was nearly out of her mind. He worked magic with his hands, his tongue, and then there was a frenzy to get naked. They needed to see each other fully, to touch and explore, to feel, soft to hard, and to taste everything.

Gage rolled her onto the side of the sofa and unzipped her jeans. He touched her aroused apex with his fingers and then slid the soft denim down her legs. She wiggled the rest of the way out of them, her body humming.

Gianna unzipped his jeans and then slid her hands inside to push them down, this turnaround being fair play. Her hand wound around his thick shaft and his hips arched. She stroked him, tasted him. “Damn,” he gritted out.

And before she was entirely through with all the tasting and exploring, he stopped her, kissed her and then reached into his tossed-aside jeans for a condom. He was an expert at tearing it open quickly and fixing it over his manhood. She didn’t want to know how he’d gotten so adept at it when Gianna had barely any experience at all.

Then she remembered that Gage wasn’t just a family friend, he was a superstar and had beautiful women swarming him all the time. Probably. Most likely. *For sure.*

Gage kissed her again, and all those thoughts leaped out of her mind. He cupped her butt with one hand while playing over her thin, sensitive folds with the other. She was moist there already, but Gage fought for more. Clearly, he wasn’t one to give up, and his stroking went on and on until she couldn’t think, could barely breathe. Shc cried out, her body breaking apart, frenzied, wild. She tossed her head back, and Gage finished his fight. He made her shatter. He made her complete. He gave her another release, this one even more powerful than the first.

Gage waited for Gianna to come down to earth. It was amazing to see her break loose like that, but feeling it was even better. He was so damn ready for her, but his patience would pay off. Gianna wouldn’t disappoint. She had no idea how beautiful she was, how her obvious lack of experience was such a turn-on to him.

She opened her eyes and smiled. “You okay, Brainiac?”

She nodded. “But we’re not through yet.”

He laughed. “Hardly.”

He lifted her and set her over his hips so she straddled him. His hands on her waist, he helped lower her onto his shaft. She touched him once, twice, and he bucked, the sensation so damn good. The next time she moved on him, she took him deeper, and then deeper again. He was fully inside her on the next thrust, the red-hot pleasure bordering on pain.

He focused solely on her. There’d be no closing his eyes. Not this time. Gianna’s olive-skinned body glistened, the sheen of sweat born of sex a heady thing. She moved easily on him now, meeting his thrusts and responding in kind. She tossed her head back, her hair flowing past her shoulders, the rosy tips of her breasts pointing skyward.

Gage couldn’t hold back much longer. Sex with her was the best he’d ever had. She’d turned him on more than any woman he’d ever known. Ironically, he’d gotten a rep for being a bad boy, but he’d never tell that there’d only been six women in his entire life. Gianna being number seven. Lucky number seven.

She moved on him gracefully, meeting him thrust for thrust in a rhythm that was uniquely hers. He let her set the pace and loved how her instincts took over. She wasn’t shy. She gave him what he craved, moving her hips, gyrating to produce the maximum pleasure. His body was on edge. He needed more, and he guided her hips down on him faster, harder. Her eyes closed, she found a faster pace. She gave herself to him without question and moved with his every thrust, his every buck. Then her eyes opened again, wide with surprise and filled with lust. Her mouth dropped open and she whispered, “Gage.”

"Let go," he said, completely awed.

Her eyes squeezed shut then, and she trembled fiercely, the force of her release beautiful to watch.

Gage brought her down, into his arms, and laid her on the sofa. Coming up and over her, he rained kisses onto her sweet face and finally finished what they'd started in Nashville, taking them both home.

Eight

Gage held Gianna's hand as they entered Juliet Memorial together. They walked down the hall and entered the elevator. He kept her close by his side. Was it for the sake of appearances or because he wanted to keep them connected? Even wondering why, she couldn't break away, couldn't puzzle out what she was feeling inside. How could she look at Rose with a straight face without revealing what had happened between them? How does one behave after having earth-shattering sex with a man? She didn't know, because after getting dressed, they'd rushed out of the guesthouse, Gage on the phone with Regan for most of the time.

They reached Rose's hospital room door. "Do you want to go in first?" he asked. "Or do you want to go in together?"

"First," she said, guilt making her cringe inside. She didn't want to deny Gage this time with his mother, but it would be easier to face Rose alone. Plus, now that she was feeling things for Gage, things she didn't want to name, there was something she needed clarification from Rose about—something from her past. Now that her mom was gone, Rose was her only hope in putting some skeletons to rest.

Gage didn't react other than giving her a nod. "Have a good visit," he said and placed a quick kiss to her forehead.

There was a buzz surrounding them, a heat, a current that made her dizzy, made her question everything in her life. What was she doing with this man? "Gage?"

"It's gonna be okay," he said. "Trust me."

But did she? Did she trust Gage Tremaine? Too many questions popped into her mind, too many memories of Gage not being trustworthy. Of him teasing her and picking on her and trying to make her feel inferior. But that was a lifetime ago. That was when they were kids, teens. That wasn't now.

She turned and entered the room. Sterile surroundings, the smell of alcohol and disinfectant, greeted her. Flowers brightened the room, arrangements of sunflowers and daisies and roses—lots of roses.

The woman she'd come here to see gave her a sweet smile. "Gianna."

She strode over to the bed and carefully sat down on the very edge. "How are you, Rose?"

Gianna had never seen Rose looking so frail and wounded. Like a little bird. Tucked into covers, hiding most of her injuries, she sat up straighter and winced. Gianna felt her pain down to her toes. "As you can see, sweet girl, I'm mending. But slowly."

"I'm so sorry you were hurt. You really gave us all a scare."

"And I'm sorry, too, for you. Losing Tonette and now me being in the hospital."

"I'm not the one with a broken arm and bruised ribs.

No need to be sorry. It couldn't be helped. If anything, you saved a dog's life."

"Yes, and I'd probably do it again."

"Well," Gianna said. "I brought you chocolates." She cleared her throat. "Actually, they're from Gage, too. We stopped in town and got you your favorites." She pulled a lavender box with gold lettering out of her purse and set it on the table tray.

"Thank you. That's sweet."

She put out her hand, and Gianna covered it with her own. "How are you and my son holding up?"

Gianna's face flamed. She put her head down. Her relationship with the truth was being tested again and again. "We're fine. Things went well in Nashville. The interview went better than I could've hoped, and that's good because it's the only one I'm *ever* doing." She smiled, grateful to be here speaking to Rose. "You have no idea how worried we were when we got the news about your accident."

"I'm going to be fine, don't you worry." Rose squeezed her hand. "I'm tougher than I look."

Tears welled in her eyes and she was hopeless trying to hide them. "I know. Thank God for that." She couldn't bear to even think about losing Rose, too.

"Gianna? Is there something else troubling you? Is it Gage?"

"No. It's not about Gage." She'd been haunted by a question, a secret and now that her mother was gone, only Rose would know the answer. "It's about my…father."

Rose blinked and stared out the window. "Your father?"

"Yes, my father." *He* was the man who had betrayed her and her mother. The man who kept her from going all in with Gage. "You see, I found these letters, years ago. They were correspondence between my mother and father. Secret letters. Do you know about this, Rose?"

Rose sighed and turned back to face her. "Yes, I know about your mother and father. I'm the only one who knows the truth. And I swore to your mother I wouldn't tell you."

"It's okay, Rose. I already know. I was fifteen when I found and read the letters. My mother never knew. I never told her."

"Why? Why didn't you confront her when you had the chance?"

"Because I knew how much my mother wanted me to believe the fantasy. That they had a loving relationship and we had a perfect family. My mother didn't want to disillusion me. She didn't want me to blame myself for my father leaving us. Abandoning his family."

Rose nodded. "It was important to her that you'd never feel the same pain she'd felt when he ran off with another woman. It was easier to let you believe he had died tragically. As strange as it sounds. Tonette loved you so much, she couldn't hurt you that way."

"I know. That's why I never asked her about it. I never confronted her about the lies she told me. I mean, those letters explained the whole story. He didn't want any part of her, or me."

"She wanted to tell you once you'd grown up, but she was proud of what you'd accomplished in your life and didn't want to upset anything. I don't know, maybe she was scared or worried about telling you."

"Is he still alive?"

"No, he died several years ago. He'd moved to Europe and married a wealthy woman. He'd written to your mom for only one year, and then the letters stopped coming. She was glad of it. Those letters only upset her. Once your mom washed her hands of him, she was a new woman. A stronger woman, like you." Rose gave her hand another gentle squeeze. "I'm sorry about all this."

"I'm fine with it. I made my peace with it years ago. But I do want to know one thing—what was my father like? Can you tell me about him?"

"Uh, yes. I can tell you he was handsome as the devil. Joe Marino was extremely charming and funny when it suited him. He was a man any woman would find hard to resist. But he was also selfish, Gianna. He always wanted what he couldn't have. And once he got it, he discarded it like yesterday's trash. Tonette fell victim to him immediately. Oh, she loved him so, and he broke her heart. I'd say they had three good years of marriage, but then your father got restless. He was an attention seeker and wanted the focus back on himself."

"Wow. I guess I figured all that from the letters, but hearing it now from you makes it all real."

"Your mama always said you were the best thing to come out of the marriage."

Gianna's heart lurched. "I'd have to agree. Thank you, Rose."

"You're welcome, sweetie. And for what it's worth, I think you did the right thing by going along with your mom. She wanted to protect you. It was important to her."

A few taps at the door brought her head around, and Gage appeared at the threshold. "Is all the girl talk done?"

"Come in, Gage," Rose said. "We've had a nice chat."

Rose met her eyes and she nodded. "Yes, we have."

"Anytime you want to talk again, just let me know," Rose told her softly. She appreciated the talk and the truth.

She rose from the bed just as Gage made his way into the room. Gage kissed his mother on the cheek. "Hi, Mom. How's the patient doing?"

"She's busted up some, but anxious to get out of this bed."

Gage took a position right beside Gianna, his arm curling around her back. She moved slightly out of his reach and stood her ground. She couldn't have him touching her. Not in front of Rose. She was too astute, too perceptive.

"One more day and you can come home, Mom."

"I'd better come home. I'm going to dance at Cade's wedding. Arm in a cast or not."

Gianna chuckled. Rose had spunk, and thank goodness she wasn't as badly injured as they'd originally thought. Her bruises would heal—her rib would heal, too. She'd have to deal with a broken arm, but if anyone could manage, it would be Rose.

"And I'll be the first one to whisk you around on the dance floor," Gage said.

Rose smiled and darted curious glances between the two of them. Gianna was afraid she'd ask a question they couldn't answer. That she'd find out they'd given in to desire. It would worry Rose, and that was the last thing she needed right now. "I'll let you two talk. I'll wait for you outside, Gage," she said. She kissed Rose's cheek. "Try to get some rest."

"I will, and you take care, too. Thanks for visiting, sweetheart."

"Of course. I'll see you tomorrow."

"I'll only be a few minutes," Gage announced. She gave him a slight nod and turned away.

She found the restroom and splashed cold water on her face. It didn't help. It didn't clear her mind. She was confused about a lot of things. And she hated being out of control like that. She hated not looking at Gage rationally and seeing the situation for what it was. She was usually more logical, more sensible about things. But after making love with Gage, she'd learned something about herself she hadn't known. She was vulnerable to him, his charm. He'd done things to her body that no man ever had. He'd made her feel womanly and alluring, all things she hadn't thought important. Or necessary. Yet those were wonderful feelings.

But was Gage a man like her father? Gage hadn't had long-lasting relationships with women. From what Lily had told her, he'd never been in love. Was he too self-centered to put someone above himself?

Ten minutes later, Gage entered the waiting room, and their eyes met. "Hi. Mom's resting now."

"That's good," she said, her shoulders stiffening up. Images of Gage naked and gorgeous, touching her, making her cry out, entered her head. When he was in the room, she could hardly think of anything else. "She needs her rest."

"Hopefully, she'll come home tomorrow."

She nodded and stood. "Are you ready to head back? I have work to finish."

Gage laughed under his breath. He rubbed at his chin and then eyed her. "You're dedicated, I'll say that."

"You know I am."

"I also know a lot of things about you I didn't know before."

Gianna wouldn't take the bait. She put her purse strap over her shoulder and walked past him. "Are you coming?" she asked, walking out of the room.

Gage caught up to her in three strides and grabbed her hand. "I go where you go," he teased.

"You've got that backward, don't you?"

"After this afternoon, Gianna, I'm not so sure."

More images flashed of being naked with him. She pulled away from his grip, but he held tight. "The hospital is kinda crowded now. Lots of eyes on us," he whispered in her ear, "and we're a couple, remember?" He tightened his grip on her hand, and goose bumps popped up on her arms. They were back to faking it.

She ground her teeth.

He was impossible.

He was sexy.

He was charming.

It was a combustible combination.

Gage exited the Aston Martin and came around to open the door for her, his Southern manners never taking a back seat to his charm. She'd have preferred to open her own car door, but it wasn't worth the argument. Gage wouldn't agree. They hadn't said much on the way home from the hospital, Gage turning up the radio and singing along with the music. He was carefree and loose, as if his world was going according to plan. She often wished she could let go like that just once. But it wasn't in her DNA. She planned things out, needed to know where she was going at all times. And Gage had disrupted that order in her life.

She entered the house and tossed her purse on the sofa, Gage only steps behind her. She was about to turn his way, but two strong arms wrapped around her waist and pulled her close from behind. The subtle sent of his cologne wafted by, and his warm breath fanned over her throat. "I know you have work to do, but when you're done, I'll be in my room."

She turned in his arms to face him, his eyes deep, dark blue and dangerous. "Gage, we can't—"

He brushed his lips over hers, once, twice, and the familiar taste of him was too hard to resist. The promise of what he offered too hard to refuse. She circled her arms around his neck and kissed him back. His hands roamed over her body, gentle caresses that sent shivers up and down her spine.

Gage stopped kissing her and pulled himself away. "Gianna, just go, do your work," he rasped. "I meant what I said. I'll be waiting. It's your choice."

And then Gage walked out of the room, leaving her trembling, her lips swollen, her body on the brink.

Her legs wobbly, she walked into her room and sat down at her computer. She had a dozen pages of notes to compile into some semblance of order for her workshop. For the first time in a long time, she wasn't thrilled with doing her work. She went through the notes in a kind of trance, trying to focus on their importance, trying to make order out of it all. Usually, she had no trouble deciphering her scribbles. Usually, she found solace in her research, enjoyed putting cohesive and orderly bullet points to paper. "What is wrong with me?" she muttered.

It wasn't rocket science.

Gage had awakened her. He'd shown her how making love should be between a man and woman. Her head was filled with images of him, of them together. Would she ever look at him in the same way?

He wasn't right for her. They were as different as night and day. But she'd learned something from him. Big shock. He'd actually taught her something. That making love and being in love were two different things. He'd taught her that lust wasn't love. It was desire, wanton desire. And it dealt more with the pleasures of the flesh than any real emotion.

Intellectually, she'd known that. Good God, she'd given lectures about human nature and relationships, but what she hadn't known until this moment was that it could pertain to her. That knowing Gage was in his room, waiting for her and willing to give her another night of, well…orgasms, made her lose her focus on work, her concentration shot.

She shut down the computer. No work was to be had today. She debated for half a second about her next move. Then she slid on her boots, tossed on a lightweight jacket and exited her room.

She stopped up short, spotting Gage on his way to the kitchen. He wore faded jeans and an unbuttoned shirt. If there was a female heaven, he was it.

He took one look at her and asked, "Going somewhere?"

"Out."

"Out where?"

"Just out." She'd planned on saddling a horse and riding out. It was a foolish idea. The sun had already set, and she wasn't that experienced a rider. Besides, what did she know about saddling a horse? Nathan was probably off duty by now. It wasn't like her to just…react and not make a solid plan. It was Gage's fault. He made her dizzy. And one thing Gianna was not normally was dizzy.

"Running, Gianna?"

"In boots?" she quipped.

His lips cocked up. "Not the kind of running I meant."

Her shoulders slumped, and a deep sigh pushed out of her mouth. "Gage, I'm not this convenient little toy you can play with."

"You're right. Nothing about you is convenient, Gia," he said softly. He wasn't mocking her. Not this time. "Did you finish your work?"

"No. I can't concentrate." Why did she admit that to him? Sometimes her relationship with the truth got her in trouble.

He sighed and ran a hand through his hair. The strands fell back into place, except for a thick chunk that landed just over his right brow. She had an urge to push it back in place and run her fingers through the rest of his dark locks. Not a safe train of thought.

"I was just getting some ice cream. Want some?" he asked.

"No. Yes. Uh…" She stared at the opening of his shirt, the thin strip of muscle and bronzed skin peeking out. Taunting her. Tempting her.

"It's not a hard question, Gianna. Either you want some or you don't."

She lifted her lids to him. "I want some."

Gage didn't react. He simply took her hand and led her into the kitchen. She took a seat while he opened cabinets, took out two cartons of ice cream from the freezer and scooped up a big dish of chocolate and strawberry, topping the mound with nuts and caramel sauce. He set out one dish, two spoons. "Have at it."

His eyes were on her, so clear, so blue. He picked up his spoon and dug in. As he swallowed, a delicious groan rose up his throat, and suddenly she didn't want ice cream anymore. She wanted to make him groan. She wanted to be that girl who could throw aside her misgivings for once. She wanted to give in to what she was feeling, her rigid rules and vows be damned.

She'd been fighting it, her logical brain battling her vulnerable heart.

She picked up the dish, grabbed his spoon, along with hers, and whispered, "Follow me."

Gage was smart enough not to be shocked—or not to let on if he was. Sometimes he knew her better than she knew herself.

She walked into his room and turned to him. He grabbed the dish out of her hands and set it aside. His arms came around her, drawing her up so close they breathed the same air. Her heart beat crazy fast, and she smiled from the depths of her soul. He smothered her smile with kisses, demanding and potent. Welcome kisses she'd craved. "Gia, sweetheart, I didn't think I could spend another night in this bed without you."

"Same," she said. With that one word, she surrendered herself to him. She was through fighting him.

And she was free at last. Liberated from what she perceived as the right thing. She only had to answer to herself, and she was all in.

Completely in. With Gage Tremaine.

Who would've ever thunk it?

Gage lay lazily beside Gianna now, his naked body close to hers. They'd napped after another burned-into-his-memory bout of sex earlier. They'd totally forgotten about the ice cream, which was now a creamy puddle in the bowl.

Gianna had no idea how she demolished him. Her body, her mind, those funky glasses, all turned him on. But he was greedy. He wanted more. He wanted to take it slow with her. To show her another side of him, the easy side of sex.

He ran his hand along Gianna's leg, starting at the ankle and slowly moving up, past her knee, to the creaminess of her slender thigh. His fingers spreading wide, he needed to touch every inch of her body. Caressing her was instinctive; his hands and mouth knew what she liked and how she liked it.

His fingertips feathered over her apex, and she stirred. She was so damn responsive to him.

"Gage," she murmured, her eyes closed.

"Shh, sweetheart. Just let me touch you."

He fanned over her flat belly and touched the tip of his finger to her navel, circling it once, twice. His palm flat, he moved up her torso and teased the underside of her breasts. Then he flattened one breast gently, enjoying the soft, rounded mound in his hand. Cupping her, he gave her breast one gentle squeeze. He took his time pleasuring her there, pebbling the very tips and tasting them with his tongue.

Gianna stirred again, arching her hips, a little whimper rising from her throat.

Oh, man. Her sexy sounds moved him more than he thought possible. He was solid rock below the waist but determined to see this through.

He slid his hand behind her head and gave her a long, slow, delicious kiss. Then another one, and one more. Slowly, deliberately, lovingly.

He whispered sweet words in her ear, telling her she was beautiful and sexy and how he was going to make love to her slowly.

She moaned her responses.

All the while, Gage held back and waited until the moment was right. Then he covered her body, teasing his manhood over her, and she bucked. It was torture for him, too.

He gave her a little more of himself. And then more again. She moved with him, slowly, patiently. It was heaven and hell at the same time. Holding back, he moved in deep and continued to go slow, to let her absorb the sensations. To feel how good it was between them.

She clutched his shoulders and they moved together, unhurried and deliberate, her pace matching his. But then the moment came and Gianna gritted her teeth, her body sharpening, her release ready. It killed him to keep the pace slow and easy when all he wanted to do was take the ride with her. She shuddered as he continued to stroke her slowly, her climax coming in one long, drawn-out, amazing wave. It was worth the effort. She was sated. Pleasured and awed. It was all expressed on her beautiful face, in her pale green eyes.

Gage took his relief, too, and then wrapped her up in his arms.

"Thank you," she said softly.

"I should be thanking you, Brainiac." He kissed her and again couldn't believe that Gianna Marino was a hidden treasure he had been lucky enough to find.

He just didn't know if he could keep her.

Or if he should.

"I didn't mean to keep you from going to LA with Gage."

Rose had insisted on having afternoon tea outside under the shade of a giant oak tree in the backyard. They sat on comfortable lawn chairs overlooking the Tremaine property. It was good for Rose to be outdoors. She'd been recuperating inside for days and needed the fresh air, so Gianna went along with it. "I know you were planning on doing some traveling with him. And LA is an exciting place," Rose said.

"I suppose it is, but I'll see it another time."

LA might be exciting, but not more than the past week she'd had with Gage. If they weren't out in public or keeping Rose company up in her room, they were holed up in the guesthouse, making love morning and night. They'd been insatiable with each other. Sex with Gage was incredible. And she loved waking up in his arms every morning, but they'd both agreed it would be better for Gianna to stay home this trip. To be with Rose for the next few days. Lily and Harper were knee-deep in wedding plans, the wedding only a month away now, and Cade was working long hours to clear up his schedule for his honeymoon.

"I'm happy to be here with you. I don't think Gage really needed me on this trip. Regan is with him, and it's all supposed to be behind-the-scenes stuff. Meetings with producers and such. I think he's doing one television interview. Thank goodness they don't need me for that."

"Hmm." Rose sipped her tea. "So you and Gage are getting along better now?"

Gianna paused, her heartbeat speeding up. "Uh, yes. We weren't really *not* getting along."

Rose studied her, searching her eyes. "Gianna, I don't mean to pry. You're both adults."

"Rose, it's okay. I can assure you we're sticking to the plan. Everything's okay."

"Good. That's all I need to know."

It wasn't like she was going to fall madly in love with Gage or anything. That would be foolish and illogical. No, they were simply having a fling, something Gianna had never done before. She was determined to keep it simple and easy. Just a few more weeks of this, and they'd go on their separate paths.

Gianna sipped tea and smiled at Rose, yet a pesky little notion flashed into her mind.

Was she lying to Rose? Or, worse yet, was she lying to herself?

She missed Gage like crazy. It wasn't just about their fling. He was becoming important to her. He'd been gone for twenty-four hours already, and she hadn't heard a word from him. It was strange. She hadn't expected him to ignore her.

She was, after all, his fake fiancée.

"How is your work going, Gianna?"

"I'm happy to say I'm almost finished with my workshop. I'll be giving the seminar Friday night at the university. I was honored to be asked to participate in this special summer series Fairmont is offering."

"I know you've been working hard on it."

"It's a passion of mine, so it wasn't that difficult. I enjoy doing it."

Gage had promised to come, which was sweet of him,

but was it out of support for her or to make yet one more public appearance as a couple?

After tea, Gianna spent the rest of the afternoon putting the finishing touches on her seminar. Her three-hour workshop devoted an entire hour to trust in relationships. She had examples and data that proved that trust was one of the key factors in sustaining a good family dynamic.

This one hit close to home due to her family history. Her mother had placed her faith and trust in her father, and he had abandoned them. And her mom had chosen to cover it up. She couldn't fault her mother. But the tiniest part of her wished her mom would've trusted her with the truth.

Her phone buzzed, and she checked the message. The text was from Gage. Her heart raced as she opened the message.

Busy here, going nonstop. Staying an extra day. Be home Saturday. Sorry to miss your seminar. Will make it up to you, Gage.

Her shoulders slumped, and her eyes stung. It wasn't what Gage had said or the rushed way he'd said it that put a knot in her gut. It was what he didn't say. And he wasn't coming to her presentation on Friday evening.

She should be fine with this. Having Gage gone meant less pretending, less deception, and yet dire disappointment washed over her. What had she expected? Roses and chocolates? Claims of love and adoration? No. But at least he could've asked about her well-being. He could've been more considerate. Heck, after all they'd shared, he should've picked up the phone and called her.

The phone in her hand, her fingers itching to respond, her mind filled with snarky comebacks. "Gee, thanks for the split second of your time." Or, "Don't worry about my seminar, I've only worked on it all summer." And her best one: "Brickhead, what on earth is wrong with you?"

She didn't send any one of those texts. Instead, her pride took hold and she simply wrote, See you on Saturday, Gianna.

Her mother used to say, "The heart wants what the heart wants."

Gianna never believed it, though. She was far more rational than that. She never truly believed the heart could take over the mind.

Until now.

She missed her mother.

She missed Gage.

She hit Send on her phone and then flopped onto the sofa.

And burst into tears.

Nine

Gage sat on his LA hotel room bed, staring at his phone. It was late, past ten in Texas. Gianna had probably gone to bed already. He wanted to believe that. Crap. No, he didn't. He itched to punch in the numbers that would bring Gianna's sweet voice to his ears. He itched to speak to her, to tell her how his day went. To ask her how hers went. Hell, he'd texted her when he'd first arrived here a couple of days ago. The message looked like a mindless scribble. But it wasn't. He'd taken a good long time coming up with that message. A message within a message. Damn, his hand trembled trying to come up with the right thing to do. The woman had him reduced to shaking in his boots. He couldn't give her the common courtesy of a "Hi, been thinking of you. Been missing you."

No. Not him. He was running scared. Feeling things for Gianna he shouldn't feel. When he was with her, his willpower evaporated. He couldn't see straight. He couldn't think straight. He craved her body, her sharp wit, her sassy mouth. But now that they were apart, he saw things more clearly. They were apples and oranges. They were oil and water. They were fly-by-the-seat-of-his-pants musician and common sense–intellectual professor.

Sexy professor.

They were *not* two peas in a pod.

He'd made a vow to his mother to tread carefully around the grieving Gianna. To make sure he didn't hurt her. And what had he done? The first chance he got, he'd broken that vow. Shoot, he'd really blown it.

Someone knocked on his door. Whatever they were selling, he didn't want, but the light tapping continued. He rose from his bed and slipped his arms into a shirt. "I'm coming."

He peered through the peephole and then yanked open the door. "Regan?"

"Hi, hope it's not too late for you?" His gaze slid to the champagne bottle and two glass flutes she held in her hand. She wore some sort of stretchy knit dress, her blond locks down around her shoulders.

"Late for what?"

"To celebrate, silly." She slunk past him and entered the room. "Don't worry, no one saw me come in."

Having a woman in his hotel room after hours wouldn't look cool, even if she was his manager and business partner. Regan usually didn't make late-night calls like this.

"What are we celebrating?" he asked.

"Everything." She sat down on his bed and crossed her legs. "Your screen test went really well today. I overheard the producers talking, Gage. You and Leah Marie had great onscreen chemistry. I think you won the part."

"Think?"

"Well, we can't be certain until they make us an offer.

But our little scheme may just have worked. You and Gianna are pretty convincing. The producers like that you're getting married to a professional woman. It's good publicity for the movie."

He supposed it was good news. It's what he'd been hoping to hear. So why did it feel like a rock just dropped in the pit of his stomach?

"Let's drink a toast, Gage. Would you open the bottle for me?"

Regan had worked so hard for him all these years. He wouldn't have a career if it wasn't for her. He couldn't refuse one drink, even though champagne was not, and would never be, his drink of choice. "Sure. I guess one drink won't hurt."

He sat down beside her and took the bottle from her hand. She grabbed his arm. "Gage, I wish you'd smile. You look like you're going to your own execution."

He smiled for her sake. "Sorry. I'm a bit tired. We've had a busy day, is all."

"We have, but I loved every minute of it. Remember, it's black-tie tomorrow night at the charity event."

"I don't really want to go. Any way we can skip it? It's the night of Gianna's seminar, and I promised her I'd be there. I kinda feel like a heel after all she's doing for me."

"The bookworm will understand, Gage. That's really not your thing, now is it?"

The bookworm? His gut tightened. He didn't like hearing her described that way. Even if he'd teased her most of his life, it was a private thing between the two of them. Brickhead and Brainiac, what a team they made. "She's a lot more than that." Hell, his voice had gone to an irritated pitch.

Regan stared at him, her brows gathering, her face going beet red. "Don't tell me you're falling for her? Gage, she doesn't fit into our world."

He put his head down. She wasn't saying anything he didn't already know. He hated hearing it, though. "Regan, lay off, okay? She's just a good friend."

"You need to remember that more than I do." Regan gave his hand a squeeze. "And yes, we have to show up at the party tomorrow night. It's Leah Marie's famous charity event. You know how she is about rescuing cats. She's the star of the movie. We have to make nice."

Make nice? He wanted to make nice with Gianna. The whole time Regan was in his hotel room, on his bed, he was thinking of his fake fiancée and all the things they could be doing to each other right now.

But even more so, he just wanted to hear the soft lull of her voice.

He ushered Regan out of his room twenty minutes later, grateful to have her gone. He had some serious thinking to do about Gianna. He'd been cold to her. That text he'd sent was meant to put her off, but all it had succeeded in doing was wash him with guilt. A good, hard scrubbing of it. He'd thought he was doing the right thing, but now he wasn't sure.

He missed her.

Wanted to talk to her.

Needed to hear her voice.

Man, he had it bad.

Gage's voice crooned in her ear, his specific ringtone waking her up from a sound sleep. She glanced at the clock on her nightstand. It was after eleven. Popping straight up, she nibbled on her lips. Why was Gage calling so late? Had something happened? Through the darkness, she scrounged around for her phone and finally came up with it. She pushed the button. "Hello, Gage?"

"Hi, Gia." His voice was mellow and sweet and…

"Why are you calling so late? Is everything okay?"

"Everything's fine, sweetheart. Sorry if I woke you."

Sweetheart? "It's okay, I guess. I mean, I was sleeping, but now I'm up and so—"

"How are you?"

"Me? I'm doing fine."

"That's good. I have to apologize for not calling sooner. I, uh, I have no excuse, really."

She sat up straighter on the bed. It was intimate speaking to him in total darkness. "So why are you calling now?"

"The truth?" he said ever so softly.

"If you can manage it." She wasn't letting him off so easily.

"I missed you. I needed to hear your voice, Gia."

She squeezed her eyes shut. Did he know what he was doing to her? Did he know that hearing him admit that sent her heart soaring? "Why, Gage? Why call now?"

"Because I've been acting like a jerk," he said, keeping his tone soft, even. "I've been trying to keep a promise I made."

"What promise?"

"Not to hurt you."

"Oh, so you promised your mother you wouldn't hurt me, and you thought pushing me away was the answer?"

"I never meant to push you away. It's just when I got here, I told myself it was for the best that we steer clear of each other unless we were pretending to be engaged. I'd convinced myself of it, and it was only easy for about half a minute. The rest has been a struggle."

"What are you saying?"

"I'm saying I never expected this to happen, this crazy pull I have to you."

"I never expected anything like this, either."

"I miss you like crazy, Gianna. I wish you were here with me right now."

She wasn't exactly sure where this was leading. Did he miss his bed buddy? Or was he speaking straight from the heart? "I miss you, too," she whispered.

"Good," he said, relief in his voice.

"Good?" She chuckled at his logic. "Why good?"

"Gianna, there are things I want to tell you. Things I want to say, but not over the phone. When I see you in person, we'll talk."

The hope and promise in his voice stunned her. His sincere tone meant so very much to her. He'd tried pushing her away and couldn't do it. He missed her. He'd been a jerk to her—he'd admitted it—and she'd forgiven him for that. Tears welled in her eyes.

And then it hit her.

Why her emotions were in shreds, running high and low.

Why she'd been so darn angry with him.

She loved him. She'd fallen in love with her childhood nemesis, the boy who'd teased her mercilessly, the man who'd made her body sing, over and over again.

She loved Gage Tremaine. It slid over her like a beautiful waterfall, cascading over every inch of her body, wetting her mind with endless possibilities. Her and Gage. Gage and her. Her mother had been right.

The heart wants what the heart wants.

"Are you tired?" he asked.

Not anymore. "No."

"And you're in bed?"

"I am."

"What are you wearing, sweetheart?" he drawled, all tall, sexy Texan.

"Wouldn't you like to know?"

"I'm picturing your university shirt, you know the one. Actually, that's not true. I'm picturing it off you, my hands on your soft skin."

"Gage?" Her body reacted, his words turning her on.

"I'm sorry, Gia. But my imagination is kinda going wild."

"I like wild," she whispered.

"I know you do. Wanna do something wild right now?"

With him? "Yes. What do you have in mind?"

"This one time, Brainiac, keep your mind out of this and...*just feel*. Are you with me, Gia?"

Shivers ran down her spine, the anticipation killing her. "I'm with you, Gage." She was with him all the way.

And inside, her heart was brimming with love, making her more vulnerable than ever before.

Gianna stood at the podium in the Fairmont lecture hall and looked out at the students beginning to fill the seats. It was a bigger crowd than she'd expected. She wouldn't fool herself into believing that her Family Studies seminar was the sole attraction to the hall. No, many of the students were here out of curiosity. They wanted to see the woman who'd stolen country superstar and onetime bad boy Gage Tremaine's heart. They wanted to see the woman who had tamed the beast. She laughed silently at that. Just who was taming whom last night during their *phone call* has yet to be determined. But the students were here and hopefully they would learn a thing or two.

Thinking of Gage made her heart ping. He'd called earlier in the afternoon to wish her good luck. To say that he'd wanted to be there for her, but Regan felt the charity event with big-name celebrities was too important a deal to blow off. Gianna had given him a pass on it. Just knowing he cared was enough for her.

Lily and Harper sat in the first row. They gave her a little wave, and she smiled at them. Rose had wanted to come, but sitting in a hard-back university chair for three hours would be difficult for her. Luckily, the three of them banded together and Rose had backed down.

Once the doors were closed and the room was filled to near capacity, Gianna dug deep into her lungs for breath. Her months of hard work and research were about to pay off now. Behind her was a screen that would show her PowerPoint presentation. She spoke into the podium mic.

"Welcome, everyone. I want to thank you all for being here. I know it's summer, and you have many other things going on in your lives, so the fact that you're here today means you're serious about the subject. Today, we'll cover relationships with loved ones, family dynamics and how the ever-changing world challenges and influences the family unit. We'll discuss the importance of understanding, trust and truth using real-life scenarios and examine how lives are often greatly impacted by the three.

"Let me begin by speaking about the power of understanding..."

Gianna continued on, highlighting the most important aspects of her workshop using the PowerPoint graphs behind her. The stats cemented her research and laid the foundation for each of her topics.

Midway through her course, she gave her students a ten-minute break. As she tidied up her notes, her colleague Timothy Bellamy walked over to her to congratulate her on the workshop so far, and on her engagement. She'd noticed him in the audience wearing a three-piece suite, listening intently. His praise meant something to her. She respected his opinion, but suddenly it dawned on her, that what she'd felt for him in the past was miniscule compared to the way she felt about Gage. Brilliant college professor versus sex god country rock star? Maybe that's how others would look at it, but now Gage was so much more to her than that. And wasn't that the biggest surprise of all?

After her brief conversation with Timothy, Lily and Harper walked over to the podium. "You're doing great," Lily said. "And I'm actually learning some things I didn't know."

"That's good," Gianna said, removing her glasses and wiping them with a cloth she kept handy. "So, I'm not boring you?"

"Not at all," Harper said. "The stats you showed are really fascinating. Who knew that, of the three, trust ranked highest in a relationship?"

"I know, that stat rang out to me, too," Lily said.

"But I can see it," Harper said. "When I lost Cade's trust, everything else didn't seem to matter. He was through with me. Luckily, he gave me a second chance. So I get it."

"Ten minutes is almost up," Lily said, glancing at her watch. "What do you say after this we go out for a quick bite to eat?"

"I'd love to, but what about Rose?" Gianna asked.

"Cade's home with her now," Harper said. "They're having dinner together."

"Okay, then. It's a date. And thanks, girls, for coming tonight. It means a lot."

Gianna breezed through the rest of her presentation, the second half of her seminar smooth and flawless, with no technical difficulties. That was always a plus. She spent some time afterward speaking to students. Some had questions, others simply wanted to thank her for the "brilliant workshop." The compliments gave recognition to her hard work.

She met up with Lily and Harper, and the three of them

walked out of the lecture hall together. With the seminar under her belt, she was eager to celebrate with the girls. Maybe have one sole drink of something fruity and delicious. Gage would approve. She could just hear him now, teasing her about it.

Just then, news vans pulled up and men and women with cameras bounded out of them, snapping photos. Gianna had no idea what was happening; they all seemed to be in such a big rush. She glanced at Lily and Harper and they responded with an unknowing shrug. Baffled, they stood there frozen as the paparazzi swarmed her, sticking microphones in her face, shouting questions at her.

"Professor, what do you have to say about your fiancé cheating on you?"

"Did you know about his affair with Leah Marie?" someone shouted.

"Have you seen the photo of them yet?" another one called out.

Curious students walked up to the unfolding scene, and Gianna and her friends were suddenly surrounded by a sizable crowd.

"Didn't you just give a lecture on relationships, Professor?" a female reporter asked.

The questions came in rapid succession, and Gianna had absolutely no clue what they were talking about. Harper, more astute on paparazzi tactics, pulled up a photo from social media on her phone. "Maybe this is what they're talking about, honey."

The sympathy in Harper's voice had her glancing at the photo, still stunned at the onslaught of questions. There were Gage and famous actress and leading lady Leah Marie in a lusty lip lock, two of the beautiful people coming together like a scene on a movie poster, leaving no room for doubt as to what was going on. Photos didn't lie. Not this one, anyway. It was clear what Gage was doing.

Blood left her face, her body shook and she wasn't sure if she trembled only on the inside or if her shaking was visible to everyone. She didn't much care. A knife sliced her heart in two, the pain and shock almost unbearable. Why had Gage called her last night and then again this morning? To make sure she'd play nice? To keep her appeased… *and satisfied.*

Oh, God.

Lily and Harper stood like soldiers beside her, flanking each side, but even their strength couldn't bolster her. She wanted to sink into the ground, never to appear again.

Why had Gage done this to her?

Why couldn't he have waited until their little charade was over?

Why had he humiliated her this way?

"It could be innocent, Gianna," Harper whispered in her ear. "Stand your ground. Don't assume anything until you speak with Gage."

Lily took her hand. "My brother wouldn't do this. There's got to be an explanation."

The image of Gage kissing Leah Marie wrecked her inside. But she had to answer the probing questions being tossed her way. The reporters would never leave her alone otherwise.

Stick to the plan, her intellect told her. *Don't stray. Wait to speak with Gage.* Harper and Lily encouraged her to do just that.

"What do you have to say, Professor?" Another microphone was shoved in her face. She gritted her teeth. Why anyone would choose to go into a profession where your every move was scrutinized like this was beyond her. It only proved how different she and Gage were.

Gianna stood tall. She mustered her courage, even as the knife twisted inside. "I trust my fiancé," she told them. "Gage is a good man. And you're all making too much out of this."

"So, you don't think he's cheating on you?"

"No, I do not. It's obvious he's at a charity event. Trying to do some good."

"Wasn't your seminar tonight about trust?"

"Partly, yes," she answered, keeping a straight face. "I have faith in Gage," she said, her newfound acting chops on full display. "We trust each other."

Lily and Harper grabbed her by the arms and edged her away from the news reporters. They didn't follow. They'd gotten what they wanted from her: her undying loyalty to Gage. A loyalty she no longer believed in. Once in the car, Lily floored it, getting them away from the vultures who'd love to eat her alive.

The first thing in the morning, Gage's phone rang, waking him from a sweet dream about Gianna. When he picked up, Cade and Lily were on the line, giving him a tongue-lashing about something. It took him a minute to clear his head. "Wait, what?"

"There's a picture on the internet of you kissing Leah Marie, Gage," Lily said. She was fuming. It'd been years since he'd heard that tone in his sister's voice. "It looks bad. Real bad, and now it's all over social media. I just sent you the picture. Take a look. Poor Gianna was ambushed outside her lecture hall last night by the paparazzi. It was awful and she's shaken up, but trouper that she was, she defended you and your engagement."

Crap. It was the last thing he wanted to happen to her. "Okay, all right. I have no clue what's going on. I'm coming right home. And listen, nothing happened with Leah Marie. I'm telling you straight."

"Well, don't tell us. Tell Gianna. She's upset. And that's putting it mildly."

"I'll talk to her. I'll explain."

Gage got on the earliest flight he could, and on the way to the airport, his phone rang off the hook. He received dozens of text messages with inquiries about his "affair" with the famous actress and star of *Sunday in Montana*. Granted, the photo had been taken at a precise photo-op moment, where it appeared more fiery a kiss than it actually had been. Hell, the truth was, it had been a quick one-second peck on the mouth that had gotten blown completely out of proportion.

On his flight home, he read everything he could find on the internet about the incident, but what riled him the most was seeing video of Gianna being tormented by the paparazzi outside her lecture hall. Those bastards harassed her into making a comment. And, true to Gianna's nature, she didn't falter. She defended him with such powerful words that tears filled his eyes. She'd been perfect, said all the right things. But it galled him that she was put into that position.

None of this should've happened. It was fake news at its most despicable, a publicity stunt that someone might've engineered, with stories on the internet and social media predicting doom for the newly engaged couple. His biggest concern was for Gianna, but she wasn't answering his calls.

And once he finally got home, he thought better of knocking on the guesthouse door. Instead, he used his key and entered the place. Gianna sat calmly at the kitchen table, drinking coffee.

It was surreal, the calm that surrounded her. While

she looked the picture of serenity, his nerves were jumping jackasses. He couldn't control the trembling inside. He'd given concerts to tens of thousands, and yet this one woman, who refused to look at him, jarred his steely resolve.

He moved closer, breathed in the scent of her, all girly soap and sweet shampoo. Her hair was up in its usual knot; she wore gray sweats and an equally drab tank top, her glasses perched on the bridge of her nose. Yet she was beautiful, a woman who meant something to him.

He took a seat facing her. Finally, she lifted her lids to him. Her sage-green eyes were filled with sorrow. It nearly busted him up inside. "Gianna, none of it is true. You know me. I wouldn't do that to you."

"I don't know if I know you at all, Gage." She said it matter-of-factly. But her eyes betrayed her calm demeanor.

"I don't know who took that picture, but it was completely innocent. Leah is a flirt, and before I knew it, her lips were on mine. But the whole thing lasted no more than a second. I moved away from her, and she teased me about being whipped by my fiancée." He cleared his throat. "Which I am."

Her brows furrowed.

"I mean, she knows I'm…we're engaged."

"But we're not. It's all fake, Gage. I feel like a total fraud."

"Listen, I hated that you had to go through what you did last night." He reached for her hand, and she pulled it away. Okay, so she was pissed. "Those reporters should've never bothered you. It was really nothing."

"Nothing? I was humiliated in front of my students, Gage. In front of the world. I'd worked so hard… Never mind." She sipped her coffee.

"No, I know how hard you've worked these past few

weeks. You've been amazing. You are amazing. And I'm sorry. But honestly, nothing like this is ever going to happen again. I promise."

"You can't promise that, Gage. You're a superstar. You're under a microscope all the time. I said I'd help you and I don't go back on my word, but I'm not going to subject myself to any more humiliation. We're not going to live in this house together anymore."

He laughed, and she turned a sharp eye to him.

"I mean it, Gage. We've been playing house, but that's all ending as of today."

"What do you mean?"

"I mean, I want you to move out. You go back to live in the main house. We only see each other when there's a planned event. I'll bide my time and then we'll break up quietly later in the year."

"No." His heart began to pound hard against his chest. The loss stifled his breathing. She couldn't be serious. "Gianna, you're being unreasonable."

"No, Gage. I'm being logical. It's the only way this is going to work between us."

"I wish you'd stop analyzing everything."

"That's what I do, Gage. That's why you and I don't work. We're complete opposites. We both know how this will end. It's better this way. I'm not going to be your bed buddy anymore."

"My…what?" Was that what she thought? Well, hell. He'd never thought of her that way. Not once.

"You heard me."

"I heard you, but I don't believe it. I, uh, what we had together is something special. I thought you felt the same way. I thought…"

"This is hard for me." Gianna gazed down at the table. "Won't you just go?"

"You're kicking me out of my own house?"

She sucked in a breath and eyed him carefully. "You're right. It is your house. If you don't want to go, then I will. I'll move back to my apartment."

"Hell no. Don't do that. I don't want you to leave."

Gage blinked several times. He couldn't let her go. She needed to be here. He had to see her every day. It dawned on him how important she'd become in his life. But she had him over a barrel. He didn't want what they had to end, but he also didn't want her to leave. She'd put her foot down, and he had to allow her to step all over him. Or else lose her for good.

"I'll go. But before I do, I should thank you for sticking up for me, for us. It probably wasn't easy, but you held your own with those reporters. You kept your part of the deal. And I'm grateful."

"At least there's that. I'm loyal, like a silly little puppy." Gianna rose from the table and walked out of the kitchen, leaving him sitting there alone.

Good God.

He'd never been in love before, but if this was what it felt like, it sucked.

Gage sat on his bed in the main house, his unpacked suitcase beside him.

His mother stood by the threshold studying him. "You've moved back in?"

He hung his head. "That's what it looks like."

"That kiss made the morning news."

"I didn't kiss Leah. She kissed me. And it was over in a second, Mom. Someone snapped a picture to make it look way worse than it was. I didn't think anything of it until Cade and Lily ripped me a new one this morning."

"So Gianna kicked you out?"

He flinched. “That’s one way of putting it.”

“You’re not used to women standing up for themselves.”

“What’s that supposed to mean?”

“I have eyes, son. I see how the two of you look at each other. You care for her. You may even love her.”

Gage ran his hand through his hair. “I don’t know, Mom. I’ve never been in love before.”

His mother walked over and sat down on the edge of his bed. “You know I think Gianna is special. I made you promise not to hurt her. But I don’t think you kept that promise.”

“Things just happened, Mom. I’m no saint, but hurting her is the last thing I want to do. So she asked me to leave, and I did.”

“If you can honestly be happy letting her go, then do it. And both of you will be better for it. But if you have strong feelings for her, do something about it, Gage. Lily tells me there’s a professor at the university who’s interested in her.”

“There is?” Jealousy ripped straight through him. Thinking of Gianna with another man tore him to shreds. He’d never considered she’d have someone waiting for her after this debacle was over. “Apparently, he was at the seminar. Lily saw him talking to her. It’s nothing concrete, and it was just beginning to happen before you stepped in and asked her for the biggest favor of her lifetime.”

“She never said.”

“She wouldn’t. And besides, I think she fell for someone else. Someone worthy of her love.”

“Mom, if you’re scolding me, you’re doing a piss-poor job.”

“I only want my children to be happy.”

“She’s done with me.”

His mom shook her head, giving him her I-know-better smile. "I disagree. You've been selfish with her, Gage, but you can fix it. I think she's waiting for you to make a move, to prove to her that you care."

"I can't toss her over my shoulder and drag her away like a caveman."

"No, but you could be her knight in shining armor for a change. Think of all the times she's rescued you."

He nodded. His mother was right. "How do I do that?"

"You're smart enough to figure it out, Gage. I have faith in you."

He pushed his hands through his hair. He was a mess, missing Gianna so badly it physically hurt. His head ached, and his stomach was in knots.

"I'll be going now," she said, standing. "You have some thinking to do."

Gage stared at her retreat and sighed.

What was it with women walking out on him lately?

Gianna sat down at the dinner table with the Tremaines. It was the first time in two days she'd seen Gage, and she was dead set against allowing her heartache to show in front of the rest of his family. She'd already been humiliated enough, and she needed to be here, to show them she was doing fine. She'd managed to find time to spend with Rose during the day when Gage was out of the house. So far, her plan was working. She'd avoided him until tonight.

It only made sense that she should dine with his family. She wasn't going to let what had happened between them destroy her other relationships. She trusted them; they had her back. She'd trusted Gage, too, but look where that had gotten her.

"I'm excited for the wedding," Lily said. "Just another couple of weeks and it'll be here."

"Me, too," Harper said. "I can't wait, but I'm a little frazzled with all the plans. Luckily for us, Gianna has offered to help out."

"That's lovely, dear," Rose said, giving her an approving nod.

"Lily, are you bringing a plus-one? You haven't said so yet," Harper said.

"Me?" Lily asked. "Uh, well, I'm not sure. I might."

"I'm sure Nathan would love to take you," Rose said. "As friends, of course."

Color rose on Lily's face. "Nathan has a girlfriend."

Cade and Gage exchanged glances. Something was up with Nathan, but both men kept their lips sealed tight.

"That's news to me," Harper said. "The last time I spoke with him, he said he wasn't bringing anyone to the wedding."

"I wouldn't ask him, so there's no point in talking about it," Lily said, ending the subject.

Too bad—the wedding was a safe enough topic of discussion. During the meal, Gianna made a point of not looking Gage's way too often, but whenever she did, she was met with brooding blue eyes, locked on her.

Dinner ended at nine, and Gianna took a leisurely stroll, heading back to the guesthouse. It was one of the cooler summer nights and crickets serenaded her as she walked. Rapid footsteps from behind slapped against the paved road.

"Gianna? Wait up."

"Go away, Gage." She kept on walking. Her emotions were all over the place, and speaking to him would only make it worse.

He caught up to her quickly. "I just want to tell you one thing and then I'll leave you alone."

"For heaven's sake." She stopped and turned. His face

only inches away, a hint of his cologne wafted to her nose, bringing back lurid memories of being down deep under the covers with him, making love to him. The extra stubble on his cheeks and the unruly way his dark hair flipped up in the back was so doggone appealing. Gage was a walking temptation. She needed space between them, not this close contact. She took a step back. "What is it? I know all about the interview tomorrow morning. I'll be there."

She didn't want to go with him, but ever since that photo showed up on social media, he'd been inundated with offers. And because this one news station, and their morning show, *AM Juliet*, had a reputation for being fair to him, Regan had pushed him into going. Gianna was expected to be by his side, of course. "I appreciate that, but that's not it. It's something else."

"What then? Another public appearance?"

He took her hand in his, his eyes searching hers. "I'm giving a concert at the university. I just got word it's a go. All proceeds will go to Learning and Literacy."

Gianna blinked. She couldn't believe her ears. "What on earth?"

"Regan didn't think it was possible on such short notice, but it's happening this weekend. I called in a ton of favors. The band is donating their time. Tickets are set at ten dollars, so all the students and anyone else who wants to attend will be able to. We'll raise a lot of money for the charity."

Her eyes burned, but she refused to cry. She didn't know what to make of this amazing and generous gesture. "Gage, I...don't know what to say. Wh-why are you doing this?"

"I'm doing it for you, Gianna. Because it means something to you. And so many kids will benefit from this. I only wish I'd thought of it sooner."

"It was your idea? Not Regan's?"

"This one is all on me."

Was he doing this for the positive publicity? She could never be sure. But she found sincerity and the yearning to please her in his eyes, on his expression. It really didn't matter why he was doing it. Her favorite charity would benefit, and she loved the idea of that more than anything else he could've done.

"Gianna, I hope you know how much I care about you."

She nodded, not sure what to believe, but she wasn't going to argue the point.

"Thank you for this. I'm totally surprised and *grateful*." She stood on tiptoes and brushed her lips to his cheek.

A low groan emerged from his throat.

She turned quickly and dashed into the house.

Running away from him.

And her emotions, which were, at best, teetering on the edge.

The next day, Gage entwined their hands as soon as they got out of the car and maintained the contact as they walked into the television station. He wore his black John B. with a fancy tan shirt and string tie. He was the picture of a superstar, his demeanor, his presence confident and commanding. He held her close to him the entire time. When it was time for him to go onstage, he gave her a kiss backstage, a sweet brush of the mouth, and walked onto the set of *AM Juliet*.

During the interview, he was brilliant in his handling of the Leah Marie incident, claiming it wasn't anything but a friendly kiss. A full unedited version of a video surfaced days later showing the truth, the kiss barely lasted a second, shutting down rumors of an affair. But Gage also used that time to announce the charity event happening at the university. He made sure television viewers knew how to get tickets and even offered to hold a meet and greet before the show to raise additional funds. He was smooth, working the audience and the host of the interview. While most people would find that assuring and even admirable, she found his charming nature suspect. He could turn it off and on like a light switch. Which Gage was he? Did she even know?

Their worlds were so different, and yet she'd managed to fall in love with him.

Like so many other wide-eyed women.

Women loved him, men identified with him. He was talented, appealing, gorgeous. But he was also stubborn, set in his ways, annoying and…

Gage spoke her name, and her train of thought shut down abruptly. "Gianna's an amazing woman," he told host Bob Lockhart. "I'm a lucky guy. We hope to be married as soon as our schedules allow it."

Those words stole her breath. If only they were true. Gage was so good at lying. He'd never spoken of the future to her. And why should he? They had a deal. They were breaking up, ending this pretense as soon as his reputation recovered.

Maybe then her life would get back to normal, whatever that was.

After the interview, Gianna and Gage shook some hands before they left the television station. Gage opened the car door for her, and she slid inside, glad the pretense was over.

"I'd like to drive by the university," Gage said. "Scope out the pavilion myself. Is that okay with you?"

"Didn't Regan already do that?"

"She did. She met with the event coordinators, but it's been a while since I've been on that campus. I'd like to check it out myself. Besides, who better to show me around than you?"

She couldn't refuse. He was doing a good deed, despite his motives.

"Okay, but I have to get back by two. I'm helping Harper and Cade with some wedding things."

"Two o'clock? That'll give us some time to stop for lunch. I'm starving."

She huffed out a breath. She didn't want to go to lunch with him. But voicing that would only sound petty. She'd already admitted she was free until two o'clock. "Okay."

They picked up sandwiches at a shop just down the street from the television station and brought the food with them to Fairmont U.

This was home to her. This was where she felt safe and familiar. She couldn't imagine teaching anywhere else. She loved the school and her students. Her mood lightened considerably, and after she gave Gage a tour of the campus, including the building where she taught, Gage brought a blanket out from the car. He laid it down under a cottonwood tree in the outdoor pavilion, and they sat there to eat.

Gianna lifted the sub sandwich to her mouth and took a big bite. Still chewing, she said, "This is delicious."

"Guess I'm not the only one here with an appetite. You're demolishing that thing. And not too gracefully, either."

"You're such a jerk." She punched him in the arm.

He chuckled at her sad attempt to cause injury and grabbed her arm, drawing her close. "But I'm your jerk."

She sobered up immediately. "You're not. You can't be. We're too different."

"What does it matter? So we're different," he said softly, his hand caressing her cheek. "We have something good, Gia."

He brought his mouth to hers, and her breathing stopped. Her heart pounded in her chest so hard she wondered if the entire campus could hear it. The kiss filled her with warmth and yearning and everything she'd been trying to forget.

Her ringtone stopped her cold. She broke off the kiss and glanced at her cell phone. It was a text message from Timothy Bellamy. He'd been keeping in touch with her on and off for a few months. He'd managed to make it to her seminar and compliment her on it.

"Who is it?" Gage asked abruptly, his beautiful mouth in a frown.

"It's no one. Just a friend."

She put her phone down, ignoring the text. Her lips still burned from Gage's kiss.

"Who?"

"His name is Professor Timothy Bellamy. He's a colleague of mine, if you must know."

A fierce look entered Gage's eyes. "Are you interested in him?" He spoke through gritted teeth.

"After the way we just kissed, how can you ask me that?"

"I can ask. You sent me packing, in case you don't remember."

"He has nothing to do with…us. We are just a charade. We're not real. We never will be."

"Why, Gianna? Why are you resisting so much?"

He pressed her, and maybe, just maybe, telling him the truth, a truth that had hurt her, would make him understand. "I'm afraid you're like my father," she said quietly.

He blinked a few times. "What does that mean? And be specific."

Gianna spent the next ten minutes explaining to him through tears and stilted speech about her father and the lies her mother had told to protect her and keep her from ever learning the truth. She compared him, maybe unjustly, but she did it just the same, to her philandering father. A man who was full of charm and good looks, a man who seemed to always get his way in life regardless of who got hurt.

Gage listened to her carefully, shaking his head, sympathy in his eyes. "I'm sorry about what you and Tonette went through. I had no idea. But I'm nothing like your father. I'm trying to earn your trust, Gianna."

"To what end? I'm not sure what you want from me, Gage. I'm doing what you asked, helping you get your reputation back. I've lied to a lot of people, and I don't feel good about that. I held my head high and defended you when the Leah Marie photo came out. It was humiliating, but I never let on. That was really hard for me." It hurt to see him with another woman. It hurt to know that their time together would come to an end soon, once he got what he wanted. She hadn't bargained for this. She hadn't expected to fall for him.

"I told you that thing with Leah was innocent," he said. "And I appreciate everything you've done for me. That's why I'm busting my butt to make this concert happen."

"Really? It's not just for the positive publicity?"

His mouth twisted, and that fierce look returned to his eyes. "No, it's not for publicity. It's for you. And you're gonna have to decide whether you believe me or not."

Gage got up and reached for her hand. "Let's go. It's almost two."

Gianna placed her hand in his, but there was no warmth in his touch, no connection. He was cold and angry, and she felt like a heel. She'd told him the truth, and he didn't like it.

She didn't much like it, either.

But her relationship with the truth hadn't changed.

Except now her heart was involved.

And it ached like crazy.

* * *

The sound check was done, his band members making sure everything was working and in order at the pavilion. The outdoor stage was flanked on both sides with partitions, and a crew was setting up a pyrotechnic light show to end the evening. Gage liked to give his audience the full treatment.

Cade stood beside him just offstage, and they both watched Gianna, with a pencil behind her ear and a clipboard in her arms, speak to some of the students. She was in her element here, the joy on her face a testament to her true calling.

Gage sighed, his heart heavy.

"Have you told her yet?" Cade asked.

Gage shook his head. "No."

"Because you know what she's going to say?"

"I'm pretty sure of it, Cade. And I'm not sure I'm ready."

"Hell, man. You're getting everything you want."

He'd gotten the news last night that he'd landed the role in *Sunday in Montana*, and now it was just a matter of formalities. Regan wanted to shout it to the world, take out billboard ads, but he'd made her promise to keep it quiet for a few days.

She was here, walking around, making sure the concert would go as planned, even though she was mad as hell at him. He couldn't blame her—she'd worked hard on his behalf, and when they finally got a win in their column, Gage was making her hold back the news.

"I'm not so sure I'm getting what I want, bro," Gage admitted. He was afraid to tell Gianna he'd landed the role. Afraid she'd want to end things early, and he wasn't ready for that or sure if he'd ever be ready for that. Plus, what if Leah wanted more from him than a little harmless flirtation? Maybe taking the job wasn't the best move after all. "Right now, I'm not sure of much."

"Gianna's got you spinning your wheels?"

"She thinks we're not compatible. We want different things in life."

"So then, you're serious about her? Because if you're not—"

"God, Cade. Do I have to hear it from you, too? Mom's already lectured me like I'm a ten-year-old. I'm not out to hurt Gianna. It's the last thing I want to do."

"Have you told her how you feel?"

Gage ran a hand down his face. "Not in words."

Cade's hand landed on his shoulder. "Buddy, words matter to women. They need reassurances. Hell, we all do. And remember, sometimes it's not what you say but what you don't say that can do real damage."

Gage peered at his brother with newfound respect. How did he get so doggone brilliant? "That's darn good advice."

"I know. Harper taught me well."

Gage laughed.

A few hours later, Gage stood onstage after giving one of his better performances to a crowd of seven thousand fans. He called Gianna up onstage and thanked her for her hard work with the Learning and Literacy Foundation. Taking her hand, he spoke directly to the audience. "We've raised a lot of money tonight, thanks to all of you. And because this is such a special charity, I plan to match the money raised tonight with my own funds."

Gianna gasped, her hands flying up to her mouth, tears welling in her eyes. She mouthed "thank you" and wrapped her arms around his neck. He held on, savoring her warmth, enjoying having her in his arms again.

Immediate applause and cheers broke out. Gage slanted a glance at Regan, who was in the first row. Her face flamed, her eyes piercing his, stone-cold. Usually they discussed everything beforehand, even when he was spending his own money. He didn't make a move without her, but ever since he'd been home this last time, he'd been making more of his own decisions. He smiled Regan's way and shrugged his shoulders. She'd get over it.

He walked Gianna off the stage to stand with the family, front and center. Calls and shouts rang out from the crowd, and he returned to face the audience. His mom, Lily, Cade and Harper were all clamoring for another song, too. He always saved one or two of his biggest hits for the encore.

The crowd quieted as soon as the band started up. He crooned the lyrics to thousands, yet all he could think about was Gianna and her beautiful, stunned surprise when he'd made the donation. Man oh man. He wanted to put that look on her face *for the rest of her life.*

He tripped up on the lyrics, his mind racing a thousand miles an hour, but he made a joke about his "senior moment," and his fans laughed along with him.

A few seconds later, all smiles vanished, and the putrid smell of smoke filled his nostrils.

"Fire!" someone shouted and then more warnings rang out.

He spun around, and flames leaping from backstage surged forward. His band fled the stage, and he jumped off the edge, gathering his family close.

"Let's get out of here," Cade said, ushering Harper, Lily and his mom toward a fire exit.

"Wait!" Gage looked around, panicked, searching the area. "Where's Gia? Mom, where is she?" he shouted over the screams. "She's not here."

"Oh, dear," his mom said. "She said she wanted to speak to you backstage."

Gage sucked in a breath. The stage wasn't fully engulfed yet. "I'm going after her."

"No! Gage!" Regan suddenly appeared, grabbing his arm. "Don't go. You don't love her," Regan shouted with crazy ferocity. "She's not even your real fiancée. Don't risk your life!" Regan broke down, tears forming in her eyes. "Gage, I beg you. Don't go."

"Let go." He yanked his arm free. "I have to find her."

Covering his mouth and nose with a bandanna, he made his way through the smoke and flames. All the while praying for Gianna's safety.

Ten

In her apartment two days later, Gianna balanced her computer screen on her lap and once again viewed the exact moment when her once-stable life had turned to crap. At least a dozen different outlets, including her favorite social media sites, had video of Regan's infamous words revealing to the world that Gianna and country star Gage Tremaine were frauds. The gist was that, as Gianna was giving a lecture on relationships and trust, she was lying and abusing everyone's trust by pretending to be Gage's fiancée. Their hoax had been uncovered. Their lies discovered. Not only had she not saved Gage's reputation, but she'd ruined her own.

"Gianna, would you stop watching those videos," Lily said.

"You're just making yourself feel worse," Brooke added.

Both of her friends were sitting beside her on the sofa, being loyal, being kind, trying to make her forget the scandal she'd helped provoke. "I want to feel worse. I don't want to forget what an idiot I've been. This is a lesson learned times a thousand. I want to keep seeing the fallout, to remind myself that everything was ruined."

"You didn't ruin anything," Lily reprimanded.

"Oh, no? Then why am I sending in my resignation to the university?"

"They didn't ask it of you. You're doing that on your own."

"I have to. I can't face my students. Or the staff. I'm mortified."

"Maybe if you gave it some time," Brooke said. "You love your work, Gianna. It'd be a shame for you to give it all up because of this."

"And why are you trying to make me feel better, Brooke? I've been lying to you for weeks. I hated doing it, not that it makes up for anything."

"I understand why you did it, Gianna. I'm still your friend. Always will be."

Her lips pulled into a frown. Her friends were too good to her.

The sound of Regan's pleading voice rattled through the screen. "You don't love her. She's not even your real fiancée."

"Would you shut that down." Lily reached over and closed the laptop cover. "No more, please. Gage feels terrible about this. He fired Regan. It turns out she was behind some of Gage's scandals. She secretly made trouble so she could fix it and keep a tight rein on him. Keep him beholden to her. She finally admitted she was the one who leaked that photo of Leah Marie and Gage to the press. It's sorta pathetic. She claimed she's been in love with him for years. And it all finally came to a head."

"I know, I read about it," Gianna confessed. "She didn't think Gage would fall for the *mousy bookworm*. Yes, even that's on the internet." Gianna closed her eyes. Her humiliation ran deep, and with each breath she took, her heart ached even more.

"It only proves that not all of it is Gage's fault," Lily said quietly.

"I know that. I promised to do him a favor. It's on me."

"It's not on you," Brooke said, ever her fierce defender. "But, my God, Gianna. He ran into flames to save you. He had no idea how bad the fire was when he ran backstage for you."

"I know. I'll never forget that." She loved him for that. For trying to save her. She would've done the same for him. But it was too late for them. Nothing was right. It was all one big fiasco, and Gianna had given up on the idea of Gage Tremaine.

There was one saving grace—no one had been injured in the fire. While backstage, she'd seen sparks flicker wildly from the pyrotechnic wiring and called 911 immediately. She'd warned everyone behind the scenes to get out, and she'd rushed out, too.

By the time Gage had found her, she was already back with Rose and his family.

She'd never forget the look of relief on his smoke-stained face. It had brought tears to her eyes. He'd grabbed her and hugged her tight, kissing every inch of her face. It was a perfect moment in time, but the before and after would never be perfect, so she'd backed away from Gage.

Letting him go.

Freeing herself, too.

The damage to both their reputations was done.

Their little pretend engagement had gone viral.

Gage tossed back his second shot of whiskey and paced the parlor floor. He was in a mood. Hell, he'd been in a mood for the past week. He'd blown it with Gianna. She wouldn't answer his calls. All he'd gotten from her all week was a text thanking him again for running into the flames to save her. How did she put it? *It was a noble and heroic gesture.*

He didn't feel like a hero. He felt like shit.

She'd left the ranch. Left him.

His chest hurt. While everything else inside him was numb.

"Would you sit down, son? You're making me dizzy."

"Sorry, Mom. I'm not good company. I should go."

"Where? The turmoil you're feeling is only going to follow you."

He nodded. "Things got really messed up, didn't they?" He sat down on a wing chair and faced his mother.

"Things get messy all the time, but usually there's a way to straighten them out."

He shook his head. "Not this time. Lily says Gianna is resigning her position at the university. You know how much she loves that job." He stared into his empty glass, his gut in a knot.

"I do know that."

"Have you spoken to her?"

"Every day. She's struggling, too, Gage."

"It's all my fault. No wonder she won't answer my calls."

"It's not hopeless, son."

"I don't know, Mom. I was a selfish jerk to her. You said so yourself. When I thought Gianna was in danger, nothing was going to stop me from getting to her. I didn't even think twice about it. But now it's maybe too late."

"So you ran into fire for her. And now you're giving up? That doesn't make sense to me. Does she suddenly mean that little to you?"

"Little? How can you say that? I'm not tooting my own horn, but I did risk my life to save her."

"Exactly. You did. So do it again, son. Do it again."

Gage blinked and weighed his mother's words. She was right, of course. She often was. He hadn't exhausted all possibilities yet.

Gianna was worth saving.

Again.

"Here, put this on, Gianna," Lily said, handing her a red baseball cap. "But first put your hair up."

"And take off your glasses, for once," Harper said. "Be a big girl and put in your contacts."

"Geesh. I didn't know you two were so bossy."

"Just do it," Lily said. "You can't hide out in your apartment forever."

"It's only been ten days."

"But who's counting?" Harper asked. "Oh, right, you are. And so are we. You need a girls' night out. And we're going to have fun tonight, even if it kills us."

Gianna rolled her eyes. "Yeah, you'll die of boredom with me." She looked in her bedroom mirror and carefully put in her contacts. She blinked a few dozen times. This was crazy.

"Honey, you are anything but boring."

Ha. They were right. Her escapades with Gage had been the source of entertainment for the mud-slinging gossipmonger crowd lately. And they hadn't let up.

Her friends meant well, but they'd soon find out she wasn't in the mood for partying. She wasn't in the mood for much of anything. For the first time in her life, she had no plan, no sense of direction, and no amount of alcohol consumption was going to change that. "All right, I'll go for an hour. But that's all."

Lily exchanged glances with Harper. "An hour? You are too generous, my friend."

"After the first thirty minutes, you won't want to leave. Trust me. Eddie makes this Texas Tumbler that'll wash all your cares away."

"Okay, but just one. Gage says I'm a liquor lightweight."

Lily smiled. Harper smiled. It was the first time she'd referenced Gage to anyone these past few days.

"One might just be enough," Harper said. "Now, are you ready?"

"I don't know, did you disguise me enough? What's one more scandal anyway, if I'm found out?"

"Hey," Lily said. "We're going to have fun, not take you to a pity party, so knock it off."

Gianna chuckled, nodding. Lil was right. She'd allowed herself a nice long pity party, but it had to end. And tonight was the night. "Okay, I'm ready."

The three of them jumped into Lily's car, and she drove to downtown Juliet, parking in front of Eddie's Bar and Grill. It was in the older section of town, where time had stopped and the shops and establishments paid homage to the past.

Luckily, the place hadn't started jumping yet. It was early, and she was grateful for the lack of customers. They took seats up at the bar, Lily ordering three Texas Tumblers.

The drinks were placed in front of them pretty quickly. Gianna took her first sip, and then another. "This is delicious. What's in it?"

"What isn't in it," Harper said, "is a better question."

Suddenly, Gage's face appeared on the flat-screen television nestled between the liquor shelves behind the bar. He was being interviewed by prime-time national host Lucinda Day.

"I'm leaving," Gianna said, swiveling on the bar stool, ready to get down.

Harper and Lily grabbed her arms, one on each side, stopping her motion.

"Did you set this up?" she asked, feeling their possible betrayal down in her bones.

"I swear I didn't know a thing about it," Lily said earnestly.

"Neither did I," Harper confirmed. "But we're here, and we're not going to run away just because Gage is on TV again."

"Again?"

"Yeah, he's been on a lot of the talk shows this week."

"Why bother?" she asked.

"Maybe we should just listen."

She was trapped. By her friends. By her own curiosity. What on earth did he possibly have to say now?

"Can you turn that up?" Lily asked the bartender.

And then Gage's voice came through loud and clear. "…yeah, my engagement started out as a publicity stunt. But the rest of it is all true. The two of us have been friends for years. Our families were close. And Gianna and I always had…something special."

"Rumor has it, she has a nickname for you," Lucinda said.

He chuckled, his eyes gleaming. "Yeah, she calls me Brickhead." He leaned back in his chair, the picture of confidence. "It's pretty obvious why. She's so intelligent it makes my head spin sometimes."

"What do you call her?"

"Brainiac. Ever since we were kids."

Gianna slumped in her seat. Why, oh why, couldn't Gage let it be?

"The truth is," Gage went on, "I never thought I'd fall for her. We've been family friends for years, but we'd never even liked each other much."

"What changed?" Lucinda asked.

"I got to know her. Really know her. She's amazing. Smart, beautiful, sassy. She was never afraid to tell me no."

"And you liked that?"

"I *loved* that."

Lily squeezed her hand, and Gianna closed her eyes. It hurt to hear him talk about her this way. They were done. D-O-N-E. And there was no getting around it.

"Some say you're only here giving this interview to repair your reputation."

"My reputation will survive. It's Gianna's reputation I'm concerned about. She's worked superhard to get to where she is today. She's dauntless in her pursuit of education. None of this was her doing. It's all on me. I take full responsibility."

"So why come clean now?"

Gage gave her his world-class grin. "Why now? Because I have a newfound relationship with the truth. Gianna taught me that."

Gianna slugged back the rest of her drink.

"Wow," Harper whispered.

"I know, right?" Lily said.

"So what is your truth, Gage Tremaine?" the interviewer asked.

"My truth? That's for Gianna's ears only."

"I think we can guess. We've all seen the footage of you running into flames to save her."

"Yeah, and I'd do it again and again."

"Seems to me, your fans think you're a hero. Maybe you're right. Your reputation will survive all this. We're almost out of time, but there's one more question I need to ask. You're thirty-two years old. And you've never made a commitment to a woman. Have you ever been in love?"

Gage shook his head. "No, never. Not until now."

Not until now? Gianna's heart trembled. "Bartender!"

She needed another drink. She needed sustenance. She needed strength. Of course, her friends would say Gage was telling the truth. But how could she know for sure? How could she ever believe in him again? He'd said he had a newfound relationship with the truth. That line really got to her. "He stands to gain from this interview. By admitting what happened he's getting sympathy and…and…"

"He's telling the truth, Gia. I know my brother," Lily said.

"Cade tells me Gage is crazy about you," Harper added.

The bartender slid another drink her way, and she downed half of it in one huge gulp. "Can we please not talk about Gage anymore? We're supposed to be having fun."

Lily shook her head. "Girl, you might be a brainiac, but, right now, brickhead is a better description of you."

"Fine, fine. Call me whatever you want, just keep the drinks coming."

After his interview with Lucinda Day, which went better than he imagined—and he'd imagined it going pretty badly—he picked up a sandwich at the diner down the street from the television station to eat at home. Usually he'd have dinner with Regan after something like this, but that ship had sailed. Her claims of love didn't persuade him. She'd been sabotaging his relationships and making herself shine in the aftermath, and he'd been too blind to figure it out.

He'd been pretty dense about a few other things, too. And he was doing what he could to remedy them.

His phone rang, and Lily's image appeared on the screen. It was after ten. Usually she didn't call so late. "Hi, sis."

"Gage, thank goodness I got a hold of you."

There was panic in her voice. "Why, what's wrong?"

"God, Gianna's gonna kill me for calling you, but we're at Eddie's in town. We, uh, we took her here for a girls' night out. She didn't want to come, and now she's refusing to leave. She's had quite a bit to drink."

"Crap, Lily. You know she's not a drinker."

"I know that now. We've been trying to get her to leave. But Harper and I can't very well drag her out of here."

"I'm just down the street a ways. I'm coming. Be there in fivc."

Gage floored the engine and pulled up at Eddie's, his heart racing. He had no clue what to expect when he entered the bar. It was smoky and dark, the scents of hot wings and fries permeating the room. He found Gianna sitting at the bar, giggling with no one in particular.

Lily spotted him and ran over to him. "Thank goodness you're here."

"How many has she had?" he asked, keeping his eyes on her from behind.

"Four," Lily squeaked.

"Beers?"

"Texas Tumblers."

"Oh, man, Lily. Are you nuts?"

"I know. We just wanted to cheer her up."

"Why don't you and Harper go on home? I've got this."

"You sure? She's not gonna to be happy to see you?"

"That's too bad. She's gonna see me, and I'm not leaving here without her."

"Okay. Thanks." Lily rose on tiptoes and kissed his cheek. "And, bro, don't waste this opportunity with her. Tell her how you feel."

He scowled. "Right now, she doesn't want to know how I feel."

Lily patted his shoulder. "When did you get to be such a freaking hero all of a sudden?"

"Just go, little sis."

After Harper and Lily left, Gage walked over to the long oak bar and sidled up next to Gianna. He leaned his elbow on the bar and faced her. "Hi."

Gianna stopped with her glass halfway to her mouth. Gage took the glass from her hand and set it down. Her lack of reaction said it all. Well, she did blink a few times.

"Wh-what are you d-doing here?"

"I felt like having a drink."

"Have o-one with H-harper and Lily," she said.

"They left."

"Party p-poops." She giggled her head off. Apparently she thought that was funny.

"You know you're gonna be sick tomorrow."

"But th-there's always r-right now." More giggles.

Gage sensed eyes on them. He'd been recognized, and pretty soon everyone in the place would be whispering behind their backs. "We have to go, Gianna. Don't fight me on this, okay?"

"I d-don't want to go r-right now."

"We're leaving. Now, either you come with me, or I pick you up and carry you out of this place. Your decision. Make it quick."

She surprised him by swiveling around immediately. She put her feet on the ground and stood. But the rest of her swayed off-kilter, and he caught her just before she face-planted. "I d-don't feel so g-good."

"Hang on, sweetheart." He picked her up and carried her out of Eddie's.

"Is th-this kidnapping?" she mumbled.

"It kinda is," he said. "You can have me arrested tomorrow."

Gage maneuvered her into his car and buckled her in. By the time he climbed into his seat and turned on the ignition, she was fast asleep. Man, her head was going to feel like lead in the morning. She'd be lucky not to toss her cookies tonight.

He should take her to her apartment, but instead he steered the car toward the Tremaine estate. She belonged there, and he was going to make her see that, one way or another.

At the guesthouse, he tucked Gianna into bed and slid in beside her. She moaned a little bit, holding her stomach. "It's gonna be okay, Gia," he murmured, trying to ease her discomfort. It wrecked him that she was in pain. He'd certainly been there, done that, so he knew the kind of cramping she was having.

After a time, she slipped into a quiet slumber and Gage removed himself from her bed. He hated leaving her, but this had to be her decision. He set a glass of water and two aspirins on the nightstand for her. She'd know what to do with them. Then he took up a spot on the sofa and hoped for the best when morning came.

Gianna woke up in the guesthouse bedroom, the scent of coffee brewing in the kitchen oddly not rattling her too much. She felt at home here, and she barely remembered what had happened last night, other than Gage showing up at the bar. Things were fuzzy after that. Had he picked her up bodily and carried her out of Eddie's? Had he brought her here and tucked her into bed?

She smiled.

He had.

He was here now, attempting not to make noise in the kitchen.

Her head ached, but it would've ached more if she hadn't taken the pills that had magically shown up on her nightstand. And her stomach ached, too, but only a little. She'd endured most of the cramping in the wee hours of the morning.

She moved slowly, putting on a big old gray sweatshirt, setting her glasses on her nose and twisting her mop of hair at the top of her head.

This was who she was in all her comfortable glory. She had to remind Gage of that.

She made her way to the kitchen. Gage was pouring coffee into two cups. She stood at the edge of the room, eyeing him. He was in the same clothes from last night, looking rumpled and gorgeous.

"Tell me something, Gage," she said, and her heart stopped when he looked up, coffeepot in hand. There was a light shining in his eyes, a blue beam of emotion that struck her instantly.

"Anything."

"Don't you believe in roses and candy? Or sweeping a girl off her feet? And I don't mean picking her up bodily and carrying her out of a bar. What kind of guy goes on national television to profess his love? Why, with you, are cameras always rolling?"

"Good morning to you, too, Gianna. How do you feel?"

"Better than I did last night. I guess I got lucky this time."

"Come and have some coffee. It'll be good for you."

"Answer my question, Gage."

He set the coffeepot down and strode over to her, capturing her gaze. Goodness, she could melt right into those intense blue eyes. "You're not the roses and candy kind of girl, sweetheart."

"I'm not?"

"No, you're way more than that. You're the kind of woman that gets into a man's head until he can't think straight."

"I am?"

"The kind of girl whose brains are ultra sexy."

She gulped. "Ultra?"

He nodded.

"I don't even have a plan for my life now, Gage. I'm lost, I don't know what way to go."

"You're not lost. You haven't lost anything. Not your job. Not your friends. Not anything."

"How can you say that?"

Tenderly, he brushed a stray strand of hair away from her face. The sweet caress streamed all the way down to her toes. "I can say that because I've spoken with the president of Fairmont U. He doesn't want your resignation. He never did."

"And how much did that cost you?" she asked, her mind kicking into high gear.

"Not a penny. They love you. They want you to come back. Gianna, after I explained my part in the charade, the president understood everything."

"You mean, I have my job back?"

Gage's grin wiped out all her doubts. "You never lost it, sweetheart. But I do suggest that you take a leave of absence."

"Why?"

"For one, I declined the role in *Sunday in Montana*."

"You did? But that's why we entered into the charade in the first place. For you to get that role."

"I don't need that gig. I'm a musician, not an actor. I can't believe how relieved I feel about that. I don't want to be away from you for three months."

"No?"

"No, can't do that. I'd miss you too much. Besides, we're going to Europe as soon as we can arrange it. I hear Italy and Greece are beautiful this time of year. And I think we can both use some time away."

"You do, do you?"

"Yeah, I do. Fact is, I pretty much have everything I want. That is, *if I have you*."

"Me?"

"Yeah, you, sweet Gianna."

Gage stared her straight in the eyes and then lowered down on one knee and took her hand. "You're beautiful, Gianna, inside and out. I love you. With my whole heart. I've never been in love before, so it took me a long time to recognize it, but I can't imagine my life without you."

"Gage," she whispered. Was this really happening? Her heart filled with joy.

"I want you by my side, always. I want everything with you. A home, a family. I want us to grow old together. I want to take you on that trip to Europe and go to the opera with you. I want all that, but I have only one condition. You go as my wife. Gianna, will you marry me?"

Tears dripped down her cheeks. "Oh, Gage. I love you, too. And yes, I'll marry you."

Gage stood then, and she fell into his arms. He hugged her tight and brought his mouth to hers. The delicious taste of him filled her senses. The kiss was as perfect as the man she was going to marry.

She put her hand on his stubbly cheek, and her heart swelled. "I was wrong about you, Gage. You're nothing like my father. I'm sorry to have compared you to him. Can you forgive me?"

"I do. I will admit, I gave you reason to doubt me. But never intentionally. I guess I am a brickhead sometimes."

She smiled. "You're a good, good man, Gage Tremaine. And I'm never going to hear the end of it from Lily. She's been in your corner the entire time."

He laughed. "That's good to know, sweetheart." He brought his lips to hers again, this time more urgently.

This time with a promise of what would come later tonight. She could hardly wait.

"You're my fiancée for real this time," Gage said, stroking her cheek gently.

"And I am yours. We're really engaged now."

"I've never been this happy, Gianna."

"Neither have I, my love."

She smiled. Their future was secure now.

With no cameras rolling.

* * * * *

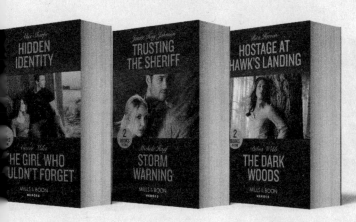